THE PROMISE

THE PROMISE

A NOVEL

BY

ELIEZER NUSSBAUM, M.D.

iUniverse, Inc.
Bloomington

THE PROMISE

iUniverse books may be ordered through booksellers or by contacting:

iUniverse
1663 Liberty Drive
Bloomington, IN 47403
www.iuniverse.com
1-800-Authors (1-800-288-4677)

ISBN: 978-1-4697-9338-2 (sc)
ISBN: 978-1-4697-9339-9 (hc)
ISBN: 978-1-4697-9340-5 (ebk)

Printed in the United States of America

iUniverse rev. date: 06/26/2012

Dedicated to my wife Sara, the rock of our family,
and our 5 great kids:
Shai, Tzvi, Michelle, Rachel, and Ron.

Prologue

Just as despair can come to one only from other human beings, hope, too, can be given to one only by other human beings.

—Elie Wiesel

Nine budding teenage girls, dressed in white cotton blouses and dark skirts, huddled together on the train station platform. They giggled when a group of young German soldiers cast fleeting glances and quick smiles their way. Two Catholic nuns circled their charges like sheep dogs protecting a flock.

Father Dov, a priest from Krakow, noticed the flirting. He smiled, counting it harmless, as natural as the bees buzzing from one blossom to another along the edge of the platform. He and a group of girls from the Catholic Convent of the Blessed Virgin in Katowice awaited the train for Krakow.

A distant train whistled. Father Dov checked his watch: thirty minutes before schedule.

The fieldstones, worn smooth by time and weather, gave the train station an ageless gray look. Early May wildflowers had begun to bloom around the long wooden platform.

The dark metallic hulk of a locomotive labored into view. The train's steam engine huffed and the pistons throbbed. All eyes on the platform turned to the sound.

"Is it our train, Sister?" one of the teenagers asked.

"Perhaps," a nun replied.

The girls crowded into a knot, whispering excitedly. Father Dov had promised a ride on the Vistula River ferry, after a concert in the cathedral in Krakow. They all looked forward to both experiences.

Four years had passed since the start of the war but, thank God, the abomination at this point had not affected the teenage girls' vigor.

A German officer, black boots glistening, hands clasped behind his back and holding a clipboard, marched to the edge of the worn platform and stared at the approaching train.

Father Dov crossed to him. "Is this the train to Krakow?"

The Nazi, a stiff-necked Aryan, around thirty years old, gave him a quick look, but Father Dov did not feel intimidated. The officer glanced at his clipboard and spoke in flawless Polish, "This is a special freight. It is destined for Krakow. It is not a passenger train."

"Thank you." Father Dov turned away. He had learned not to evoke curiosity, and simply glanced at the nuns and shook his head.

A grease-stained brakeman leaned halfway out of the chubby locomotive as it labored into the station. Warm steam billowed from the pistons; dark, soot-filled smoke puffed into the morning sky and mixed with the humid air.

A line of weathered, colorless, slatted wooden freight cars stretched behind the locomotive's tender. Two soldiers stood in the cab with the engineer. The trio looked hot and uncomfortable, glistening with sweat and oil.

The train slowed. Its mechanical brakes shrieked with metal on metal. Several of the girls clamped hands over their ears.

The long freight finally ground to a halt at the base of a water tower, with the locomotive hissing. The brakeman stepped off the train and pulled a cabled, canvas hose to the engine.

The sound of screeching brakes subsided, replaced by a guttural, primal, unnerving noise—the collective mingling cries of human suffering.

Viscous fluids dripped from the boxcars.

Faces of the hundreds jammed inside—young and old, male and female—pressed into the narrow spaces in the slatted sidewalls, more eyes than faces. Eyes red and weary . . . eyes pleading, crying, begging . . .

eyes reflecting horror, fright and anxiety . . . eyes reaching out, linked to the chorus of agonizing sounds.

"Water please! My God, we are dying! Help us! Help us . . . please, water!"

The cries reverberated like raindrops splattering on hard dirt, then mixed, blending to become a single ominous, howling plea.

Father Dov stood paralyzed with shock. He would never get used to such things. His nostrils flared and his fists hung clenched at his side. The horror, the stark reality, stole his breath and numbed his senses. His mouth went dry and his throat constricted.

Stench from the freight cars rolled over the station like an invisible, toxic fog, and Father Dov gasped, "My God."

The girls huddled close, like a frightened school of fish. The waiting soldiers recoiled as the pungent air reached them. A young, ramrod-straight officer tried to give an order, but he choked and spat on the platform.

Near the center of one freight car, and close to the floor, a child's arm reached through the slats, fingers extended, as if trying to grasp freedom. Then quickly, the hand disappeared from sight.

Feeling as if the raw evil might consume him, Father Dov turned from the dreadful scene. "Get the girls away," he shouted, his voice thick with emotion.

The two nuns began pushing their charges toward the open door of the station. The howl of agony continued to hold the teenagers transfixed.

"Go, get inside!" the nuns snapped.

The girls stumbled, bewildered.

Rachel, a sixteen-year-old, stared from the midst of the teenagers. She moved with the others, but then a voice from the train spoke her name: "Rachel! Rachel Gold!"

Rachel stopped and turned. "Gramma," she cried out.

My God, her grandmother. Father Dov hurried to intercept the dazed girl.

An outstretched arm reached toward her. "Rachel . . . help me, please!"

Before Rachel could answer, Father Dov gently touched her shoulder. "Move, child." Then, more desperately, he urged, "Go inside!"

She tripped toward the station.

The priest spread his robe like a mother hen, herding the frightened teens through the door, aware of the young German officer watching. He slammed the doors to the platform behind them.

The girls cowered together, weeping.

Father Dov ignored the shaken, frightened nuns, and spoke directly to Rachel: "Listen to me. What you have seen here today is never to be mentioned . . . never. You are sworn, with God as our witness, to a vow of secrecy."

Rachel stood trembling, holding the hand of the girl beside her, looking deathly ill. A tear traced down her cheek, and she shuddered. She bit her lip until it drew blood.

Father Dov felt powerless to help her. *Where was God? Where was good?*

He prayed no one else had heard her grandmother's voice and linked the poor souls on the train to the innocent child. Only the nuns and Father Dov knew about the Jew hidden in their midst. Rachel Stacowski—her convent school name—hid her identity from others.

Secrets, painful secrets.

Outside, the train whistle blasted as the train started down the tracks.

Rachel closed her eyes and wept.

CHAPTER ONE

THE TIES THAT BIND

Two are better than one . . . for should they fall,
one can lift the other; but woe to him who is alone when
he falls and there is no one to lift him.

Ecclesiastes 4:9-10

Katowice, Poland, 1928

Janusz Dov paced the cluttered living room, waiting for his father. On his way to the window he brushed against a life-size statue of Jesus. Through the grime-caked glass he spotted his uncle Zidov standing on the street corner, holding three fishing poles.

From the only bedroom in the small, messy apartment, Janusz's mother shrieked, "You keep my son away from those Jews, Stanislaw!"

His father's gentle voice murmured, "Do you forget who I am, Theresa?"

Both hurt and impatience came through the sadly calm words. His father had converted from Judaism to Catholicism in order to marry the woman of his dreams.

He picked up a faded black and white wedding portrait from the mantel. Janusz sighed. *What had happened*? He wished his mother had maintained her beauteous joy, and not turned into the reclusive and bitter woman she'd somehow become. Her state of depression and religious fanaticism had taken over their home, edging out all other

1

things. And his father . . . why couldn't that beaming poet from the steel mill find his older self, and smile again?

The bedroom door creaked open and then whispered shut. Janusz set the picture back on its resting place by one of his mother's many religious icons—the only decorations that adorned their humble apartment.

He felt a hand on his shoulder and looked up into his father's careworn face.

Together they quietly moved through the flat.

Janusz held his breath, hoping the slight sound of shutting the front door would not set off his mother again.

Wladislaw Romanov, a member of Janusz's senior high school class, ducked his head out of the apartment door across the hallway. As always, the tall, frail boy with a bad complexion looked straight at Janusz and never even glanced at his father.

Wladislaw's mother shouted from the dingy apartment behind him, "The damned Jews! They are the ones who have robbed us of our lives and made us wallow like pigs. Go down to Prospect Place. Look who owns the stores: Stern, Schwartz, Greenburg, Lieberman. They are the moneychangers. Christ himself cursed them."

Janusz grimaced and slid a glance to his father's stoic expression. Such comments caused an additional burden of pain, for Stanislaw Dov, in his heart, remained a Jew.

Wladislaw withdrew quickly and shut the door.

Janusz's father herded him outside. Uncle Zidov called a greeting from the street corner and tipped his tattered hat. Janusz smiled, feeling the tension drain away at the sight of his uncle's familiar, jovial countenance.

Along with the three roughly-handcrafted fishing poles, Zidov carried a bulging sack of food. Janusz's stomach rumbled at the aroma wafting from the sack. Aunt Tania, his father's older sister, cooked the best meals for miles around. Her legendary bagels brought top dollar at the local bakery and always disappeared first at any social gathering.

Uncle Zidov grinned. "Your aunt prepared too much food for the morning prayer service." He shrugged his wide shoulders. "She may not oppose your father's switch from a Jew to a Catholic, but I believe she's trying to convert you back to Jew through your stomach."

Janusz's father gave a short bark of laughter and clapped his brother-in-law on the back as they fell into step and headed toward the river. "We will catch my sister enough fish to keep her silent and out of my business for a few days."

Janusz chuckled. Nothing could accomplish such a feat. His aunt had taken it upon herself, as the only relation who still acknowledged their family, to make up for the rest of the family members' abandonment.

However, from the time when Janusz, as a toddler, sat on her ample lap, Tania had fed him Jewish stories and repeated a vast variety of teachings she deemed important for his dual-religious education. So, although his father chose to raise Janusz Catholic, Aunt Tania had made sure his Jewish roots remained nourished.

Tania bore a strong family resemblance to her brother Stanislav, Janusz's father. She had a vivacious personality, consistently warm and engaging—a joy to be around.

Uncle Zidov, Tania's husband, although only two years her senior, appeared much older. His easygoing and even temperament made him the perfect companion for Tania.

Once the fishing lines were cast out and set, Uncle Zidov set his pole aside, and his usually open expression turned dark and thoughtful. "Times are worse, Stanislaw. My hands are calloused from hard work. I keep my head down, but my ears still hear the rumors of war and the hatred of Jews as a battle cry." He reached up a great paw of a hand and scratched his temple, slightly dislodging the old hat that covered his balding head.

Janusz settled along the riverbank, slightly away from the older men. He threw out his fishing line and listened intently. Rarely did his easygoing, even-tempered uncle sound so serious.

Zidov's voice held a grim edge as he continued, speaking more softly, "Something is coming. Evil, I say. I will pretend to be Catholic. I am big and strong; I can fit into a Catholic world. I will take a Catholic name, go far into the country, buy land, and become a farmer. This I will do to protect my Tania, your sister."

Janusz muffled a gasp and ducked his head, trying to appear caught up with fishing.

His father remained quiet for a long time. Then he murmured, as if talking to himself, "Jews cannot own land." After another short pause, he said, with a roughened voice, "You will be safe."

Janusz caught his breath, shocked.

His uncle finally picked up his pole and cast out the line. "You should do the same, Stanislaw. This town knows you were a Jew before you fell in love and married. Once a Jew . . ."

Janusz hunched his shoulders. Sometimes his barely educated, handyman uncle seemed wiser than his college graduate, intellectual father.

Every day, Janusz struggled with prejudice from both Catholic and Jewish classmates. Even though he had never practiced Judaism, people still treated him as if his father's religious heritage had left a permanent stain.

Stanislaw shook his head and said confidently, "You worry too much, Zidov. I practice my wife's religion. Nothing will hurt us. Look at my son. He is an altar boy in the Catholic Church. Father Dimitri tells me Janusz has the calling. Besides, I make the owners a lot of money at the steel mill."

Janusz swallowed. He knew his father had an amazing talent for turning pig iron into a hard blend of fine steel, and had recently received a promotion to head metallurgist, but, if his uncle spoke truth, would the mill owners' value of their employee offset whatever evil approached? He shivered in the bright sun. If anything did happen, the Jews and anyone associated with them would most likely suffer the greatest harm.

The two men seemed to fall into brooding contemplations, and Janusz suddenly couldn't sit still anymore. "Father Dimitri asked if I could help prepare for tomorrow's service." He wound up his line and handed the pole to his uncle, pausing long enough to delve into the food sack and grab a couple of bagels.

Father Dimitri had taken Janusz's father into his flock, performed his marriage and, subsequently, baptized Janusz. The priest had always provided safe haven for the young boy torn by his family's turbulent religious heritages.

When neither his father nor his uncle responded, Janusz turned and strode away.

He found the gray-haired priest puttering about the sparse parish garden. Stepping onto church property acted as a soothing balm to Janusz's troubled spirit. He loved the church, in spite of his mother's pushing so hard, because believing in Jesus nurtured his soul. Nowhere did he feel that he fit in more perfectly than in the church.

Father Dimitri's lined face lifted in a vague, welcoming smile. He squinted at Janusz, then waved him toward the rectory. "Come, let me fix us some tea."

———∘∘◦❧◦∘∘———

Because of his father's ancestry, a close-knit fraternity of Jewish boys had accepted Janusz into their midst. He found more in common with the impoverished and alienated youths than with his Catholic peers. They did not cause trouble as some townspeople accused, and they also never took on the more common Jewish demeanor of slumped shoulders and downcast eyes. In their ragtag teenaged numbers they found the courage to stand up straight and face the anti-Semitic Catholic community—a greater crime than stealing a loaf of bread, in some people's opinions.

The leader of the "Jewish gang," Kalman Gold, had become Janusz's best friend, in spite of rebuffs from his mother. Kalman, with good looks, charm and a charismatic personality, thrived in high school, achieving high grades and popularity. His intense blue eyes and athletic build made him an attractive target for the girls. Janusz looked up to him.

Occasionally he would double-date with Kalman, but Janusz's habitual shyness, strict study habits, and demanding mother prevented him from pursuing a serious dating relationship. And lately, he found his interests fell more and more to God.

One afternoon after school, Janusz fell into step with Kalman and listened as his high-energy friend rehashed his newest money scheme. "There are riches in the ground, right within our grasp. Why not go out to the strip mines and see?"

Janusz, along with a few others trailing behind, groaned good-naturedly. He glanced around, catching smirks and gleaming eyes, and winked at them.

For his senior history project, Kalman had studied the whereabouts of the old soft-coal mines along the foothills of the city. Since his first visit to the local library, he'd spoken of little else. As always, his driving ambition and innate business sense worked overtime, looking for a lucrative outlet.

He turned to the other members of the gang. "What if there's more coal there? The miners were from Russia. Dumb as mules. They may have left a fortune behind."

Janusz shoved his hands in his pockets and frowned. He wanted to accompany Kalman on his great adventure, but his mother would be furious if she found out.

The other boys did not relish the idea of becoming coal prospectors, and declined Kalman's invitation to get rich. All but the gentle giant, Zygmunt Pilarski, left them for cleaner, less strenuous pursuits, laughing and jeering.

Zygmunt, affectionately known as the Big Z, stood six-foot-five and weighed over two-hundred-fifty pounds. A tender spirit balanced his impressive size. He secretly loved poetry, although he couldn't read well. Janusz often spent afternoons with him on the riverbank. He would read and Zygmunt would listen. They both enjoyed their time together.

Kalman growled, angry and determined, "I'm getting a shovel and then going to the mines." He glared at Janusz, who'd felt skeptical but remained quiet. "Go home to your mother and your Bible."

"No, no, no, I'll wait here and cheer you on."

Janusz and Zygmunt watched him stomp toward town. They smiled at each other, used to their friend's passionate explosions.

Zygmunt said, "Some day Kalman will be the richest man in Katowice, and we will all work for him."

"Yeah, sure."

Zygmunt changed the subject and murmured, "You know what poetry does?"

Janusz glanced over at his large friend, sensing a snippet of rogue, unvarnished wisdom about to emerge. "What?"

They had stopped on the bridge, and Janusz stared at the river as it flowed, silent and placid. He waited, knowing Zygmunt struggled to find the right words.

Finally, the massive Jewish boy said, "It flattens the hills . . . makes everything level, just and fair. That's what I'm going to be—a fair man, a just man, a poet—with the path of my life."

Janusz studied Zygmunt's serious expression, understanding the meaning beneath the surprisingly beautiful sentiment, feeling slightly awed. "That's noble and brave, for this world is certainly not fair, and justice is almost extinct. One could ask no more of a man."

Zygmunt smiled, displaying a cherubic, innocent expression on his round face. "Thank you."

Wladislaw Romanov came into view as he rounded the curve and sauntered up to where they stood on the stone arch bridge. He called to Janusz, ignoring Zygmunt.

Zygmunt stiffened, but greeted the newcomer with courtesy.

Janusz, fully aware of Wladislaw's rude avoidance of the Jewish Zygmunt, attempted to remain civil, responding, "I am waiting for Kalman to return with a shovel. He and I will prospect for coal and become rich."

Wladislaw scowled. "Don't waste your time with that money-hungry dreamer. Your mother is looking for you."

Zygmunt grumbled, "Don't make trouble for Janusz by telling her about this."

Janusz said quickly, "Wladislaw would never do that. He's my friend."

The entire gang disliked the Catholic, Wladislaw, but the neighbor boy always acted so eager for Janusz's friendship that Janusz ignored their warnings. He preferred to believe the best of people. Some had talked about Wladislaw feeling jealous of Janusz's friendship with the popular Kalman, but Janusz simply shrugged and remained friends with Wladislaw.

Kalman trotted up with a shovel over his shoulder. His blue eyes gleamed, but then he narrowed his gaze on Wladislaw. "So, it is the four of us?"

Wladislaw shook his head and turned away. "I'll not ruin my clothes, getting wet and dirty over a fantasy."

Zygmunt laughed. "Me neither. But I will wait here for you to be the first to listen to your stories when you return."

Kalman grinned, shifted the shovel higher on his shoulder, and waved at the two. He turned to Janusz and lifted a brow. "And what about you?"

Janusz drew in a deep breath before replying, "I'm in."

Together they set out on the six-mile walk through freshly plowed fields, plucking raw potatoes to eat on the way.

Kalman bit into a potato and glanced over at Janusz. "What changed your mind?"

"I couldn't let you have my share of the fortune."

"Ha! See, you *are* a real Jew. I'm glad you came to your senses." Janusz tossed a potato at him.

———∞○—◦◦—

They found the abandoned strip mines easily. The veins of the previously discovered soft coal lay only a few feet beneath the surface. The earth had been pulled away and laid bare in irregular, jagged mounds of broken, lifeless, gray shale, and resembled a disemboweled animal.

Kalman pulled a map from his pocket. He had traced it from a book at the city library, as a part of his history presentation. "We've got to find the last place they dug."

He raced ahead.

Janusz didn't expect to find anything and wished he hadn't come. How could he explain his extreme lateness to his mother?

He opened his mouth, intending to call to Kalman when, suddenly, the earth beneath his feet gave way. He struck his chin on the edge of the pit, slicing his tongue open, and plummeted downward.

Then, managing to grab onto a ledge within the narrow, dark shaft, halting his fall, Janusz screamed, "Kalman!"

The taste of blood filled his mouth. His fingers clawed at the slick, muddy walls but found no handholds. He looked up and saw an oval of daylight about twenty feet above. Grass and weeds rimmed the shaft, camouflaging it. He tried to find a foothold. Earth and rock fell away from the walls where his shoes probed, rattled down the dark shaft, and splashed into water far below.

Janusz's heart raced. "Oh, God, save me."

He lost his grip and fell into the void beneath him.

"Nnnnoooo!"

He plunged deep into icy water. His ears rang and his body ached from the sudden shock of cold. Soaked, his wool jacket and pants hung on him as heavy as lead weights. The frigid, black water stung his senses.

I am going to die.

Janusz kicked and struggled toward the surface, but a spider web of roots tangled around his hands and feet. He jerked, trying to pull free, but one foot remained caught. He twisted and turned, finding it difficult to breathe. Icy water surged up his nose, sending bolts of pain into his sinuses, and when he opened his mouth, freezing brine covered his tongue and throat.

Janusz fought, pulling and twisting. His foot came out of its entangled shoe and he thrashed toward the surface. He burst into the dimness of the shaft, choking and gagging, only to slip beneath the water again. Desperately, he pushed up, knowing he had to clear his throat and conquer the panic if he were to have a chance of surviving. Again he broke the surface, coughing and spitting.

God, the water is so cold.

Janusz took deep breaths, and the choking subsided. He probed for the bottom with his toes, but encountered nothing beneath his feet except icy water.

Calm! Calm! he willed himself as panic threatened.

He searched the wet, slimy, muddy walls of the pit for anything to hold onto, but found nothing that would aid him if he tried to climb out. The reality of his dire situation chilled him more than the freezing water.

Then Kalman's voice came from above. "Janusz!"

Nothing had ever sounded so sweet.

"Janusz!"

"Yes, here. Help me, I am stuck. I will drown."

"Can you climb up?"

"No . . . I am in water! Please, help me!"

"Janusz, I will go for help. Hold on!"

"Don't leave me, Kalman. Please don't leave me!"

"I have to get help. There's nothing here, not even a branch."

Janusz looked up as he treaded water, legs and arms already cramping. About thirty feet above, a small, weed-choked halo of light glowed in the waning afternoon. "Kalman!" he cried again. "Don't leave me."

No response came.

Janusz muttered in the darkness of the watery pit, "Oh, holy Mother of God."

———◦◦◦❧◦◦◦———

Kalman ran for a mile or so before reaching a farm where he hoped to find help. His lungs flamed with exhaustion and strain. With blurred vision and burning eyes, he raced in a sea of sweat toward the lights in the modest farmhouse.

As Kalman neared the gate, a dog barked in the yard. He ignored it and sprinted to the front porch, where he collapsed in a breathless heap.

The dog's barking grew louder. Kalman pushed up to pound on the door. Brittle chips of paint pelted him.

A thin and balding farmer opened the door. Sun and time had weathered his face and a gaping mouth revealed missing teeth. Those that remained looked yellow and crooked.

Kalman struggled for breath and gasped out, "I . . . I need a horse and rope!"

"A horse?" the farmer said in astonishment.

"My friend fell in a pit . . . I have to help him. Please I—"

The farmer cut Kalman short. "You ain't takin' my horse. Who are you?"

"Please, I have to—"

"You're a Jew, aren't you?"

Kalman looked into the barn—a shabby, weathered building—where a big plow horse stomped in its broken-down stall.

"I said you ain't getting my horse."

Kalman had no time to argue. Janusz might already be dead. He turned and bolted for the barn.

"You damned hooligan! I'll have you arrested! I've got a gun!"

Kalman never looked back. He grabbed a coil of rope from inside the open barn door and headed for the horse. The horse eyed Kalman and backed away. Kalman untied the tether that held the animal, yanked on the bit to stop the horse's jittery movements, and swung up onto its bare back.

"Giddap!" he growled, kicking the horse hard in the ribs.

The horse jerked, then galloped toward the road with Kalman bouncing on its back.

The farmer shouted after him, "Goddamned Jew!"

Kalman glanced at the waning light in the western sky. "God, please don't let Janusz die!"

The big plow horse, although responding to the urgency of the situation and obeying the prodding from Kalman's heels in its sides, still went too slowly. Kalman, in addition to fearing Janusz may already be dead, felt uncertain he could find the pit in the fading light.

He kicked the horse again in frustration. "Faster, damn you, faster!"

The big hooves pounded the dirt road as the horse ran on, frothing at the mouth and huffing with strain.

———∘∘∘❧⟨◉⟩❧∘∘∘———

In the blackness of the watery pit, Janusz's faith faced the ultimate test. He had cried out to the blessed Virgin, Jesus Christ, the Holy Father, and every saint he could remember. None seemed to care about his dying in a dark, lonely, water-filled mineshaft. None seemed to care about the promise he had made of a life of sacrifice, were he spared. None seemed to care how empty a life his mother would face without him in it.

He now had severe cramps in his legs and arms. His hands and feet had gone numb from the cold. Dying, he'd learned, would not come easy. Racked with pain, numb, frightened of death, his body struggled to live, but Janusz knew the struggle would soon end.

He recalled one of his duties as an altar boy, snuffing out the candles. They burned for a while, each giving off light, bringing hope to the weary. And then they went dark. Would he soon go dark?

Disappointment filled him. He still had so much to do, so much to see. He prayed not to go dark.

Janusz raised his face to take a final breath before slipping beneath the water.

Just then, a heavy rope hit him squarely in the jaw. "Janusz!" Kalman shouted down the vertical, muddy shaft. "Janusz, grab the rope."

"My hands . . . I can't."

"Janusz, you must try. Damn it, try!"

Janusz thrashed and bobbed, choking and gagging as water filled his mouth. He spun and turned until the rope twisted about him.

"Janusz, have you done it?"

"I think so. I think it's tied. I . . . I don't know," he answered wearily, all strength gone. Fatigue had won over. "I just don't know." His head fell to his chest as he sank beneath the surface.

———∘∘∘❧⟨◉⟩❧∘∘∘———

"Pull!" Kalman slapped the big, sweaty horse on the rump.

The horse, having spent a lifetime pulling a plow, did not hesitate. His big, iron-rimmed hooves bit into the soil and the rope tightened.

Kalman fell to his stomach at the side of the hole and stared down into the darkness as the taut rope buzzed by him. "Please, God, please," he chanted again and again.

Suddenly, Janusz's soaked, limp form sprang from the hole.

"Whoa!" Kalman shouted, and the horse stopped.

Kalman untangled the rope and gathered Janusz into his arms.

Janusz coughed, gasped, and trembled uncontrollably.

Kalman cradled him and brushed matted hair from his forehead. "Thank God, thank God, thank God." He slipped off his coat, wrapped it around his shivering friend, and brushed tears from his cheeks. "I'm sorry I brought you here."

"You know, Kalman," Janusz said through chattering teeth, "in the pit, I looked up from my watery grave and saw the stars through a small halo of light, far above. I asked God to save me. I thought all hope was gone, but then He sent you. God used you, Kalman."

"I am not your Savior . . . just a stupid friend."

"I am alive because of you," Janusz said, holding Kalman's gaze. "I will never forget. I pray, with God as my witness, that He will some day use me to help you."

"He already has." Kalman forced a smile. "He saved my best friend."

CHAPTER TWO

SEEDS OF BETRAYAL

One man wants to live but can't, another man can,
but doesn't want to.

Ethics of the Fathers 4:15

Janusz, exhausted and shaken, with hair and clothing dripping rancid briny water, wrapped his arm around his friend's neck. Kalman half-dragged him to the horse. He eased Janusz up and positioned him on the animal's back. Although Kalman had encased him in his jacket, he shivered.

Zygmunt raced to them as they approached the bridge. "What happened?"

Wladislaw trailed behind, looking worried.

Kalman gasped between heavy breaths, "Janusz fell in a pit." Remorse edged his usual confident tone. "He nearly drowned."

Janusz forced a smile. "Kalman saved my life." He tried to sit higher, but slumped back to maintain his balance. "He and the horse the size of an elephant. God directed them."

Kalman raised one of Janusz's hands. "Here, look under his nails!"

The others crowded around in the faint light. Janusz spread his trembling fingers.

Kalman continued; excitement laced his voice. "See the black under his nails? I tasted it. It's coal!"

"I have sweat under my armpits," Zygmunt mocked. "Would you like to taste it?"

"Go ahead and laugh, you big stump, but I, Kalman Gold, have found my fortune."

Wladislaw sniggered. "Gold finding coal is not exactly a step in the right direction."

Janusz and Zygmunt chuckled at Wladislaw's clever barb.

"Have your laughs," Kalman quipped. "But when you come looking for work, you'll change your tune." He gently helped Janusz down from the horse.

Janusz's legs crumpled, and Zygmunt moved quickly to catch him. He gathered Janusz in his arms like a child. "Where to?"

"The parish," Janusz murmured. "Father Dimitri will help me clean up."

Wladislaw mumbled something about getting home before his mother threw out his dinner and trotted off into the evening gloom.

Zygmunt grunted. "He will make trouble."

Janusz sighed, but said nothing.

Kalman simply shrugged. "I need to return this old horse before the farmer has me arrested." He turned the horse back toward the darkening countryside, muttering something about start-up costs for his coal mine venture.

—∘∘∘🙚🙙∘∘∘—

Janusz stumbled down the long, dim hallway, tripping on the ratty carpet runner. He felt warm and dry, but emotionally overwrought.

Wladislaw stuck his head out the door across from the Dov apartment, looked Janusz up and down and whispered, "Didn't I warn you not to go with Kalman?" A shrill sound came from his mother, somewhere in the grimy dark of the opposing apartment. Wladislaw said in a rush, appearing slightly uneasy, "I could not help it, Janusz, I swear. Your mother saw me come home without you. I had to tell."

Footsteps sounded from behind, and Wladislaw disappeared back into his home.

Janusz groaned, realizing the trouble that awaited him. With a deep breath, he turned the knob and entered the cluttered living room, making as little sound as possible.

His parents, deep into an argument, apparently did not hear or see him come in. His father stood at the edge of the dingy kitchen while his mother paced, fingering her rosary and muttering a chant-like prayer.

She stopped and screeched, "You must put an end to their friendship, Stanislaw. Kalman Gold will be the ruin of our son."

"Janusz is not a child anymore, Theresa," his father said calmly. "He is a young man, and a man must find his own path."

"Keep him away from that Jew, Kalman," Theresa spat at him. "There is no good in that boy."

Stanislaw shook his head. "Is it the boy or the fact he is a Jew that you hate so much, Theresa?"

She glared at him.

Janusz knew that only a little love remained between them.

∙∘∘⋈◈⋈∘∘∙

By the time Kalman plodded up to the rundown farmhouse, darkness shrouded the landscape. He could barely see. When he led the old horse into the rickety barn, he tripped over a bale of hay. Cursing under his breath, he managed to settle the big animal, put some food in the feed bucket, and secure the stall door.

Then, with a deep breath, he strode up to the house and banged on the chipped-paint door. The farmer stomped about inside, and Kalman swallowed hard.

When the door flew open, Kalman said quickly, "I want to thank you, sir, for the use of your horse. He helped me save my friend's life. I promise you, the horse is safely in his stall, fed and watered, and none the worse for wear."

The farmer glared at Kalman for a long moment, then ran a hand through his sparse hair. "Well, I'll be damned. You have a lot of nerve, boy. Don't let me catch you on my property again." With that, he slammed the rotting door in Kalman's face.

Kalman blew out a shaky breath, shoved his hands in his pockets and picked his way down the rough drive. He stopped at the lane and looked back at the dimly flickering light behind a tattered curtain. "When I'm rich, I'll buy that lucky horse from you. Then you'll bless the day we met, and be sorry you treated me like dirt."

With a determined jut to his chin, he turned his steps toward home.

Life proved difficult for Janusz. School became the only refuge from his mother's wrath. One afternoon, soon after the mining pit episode, Janusz confided his misery to Kalman.

His friend patted Janusz's shoulder and gave him a compassionate look. "Her anger will pass."

Janusz shook his head. "It is as if God is punishing me for my doubt while I was in the pit."

Kalman grimaced. "I don't think your mother's anger has anything to do with God." Then he flashed one of his dashing grins. "Nor do I think it likely she'll invite me to your graduation party—even if I agreed to wear a crucifix."

Graduation day arrived. Kalman made valedictorian in their class, and Janusz, close behind, salutatorian. They vowed to stay in touch.

The University in Warsaw had accepted Kalman, and he intended to study coal engineering, still focused on the prospect of making his fortune.

Janusz struggled between yielding to his mother's pressure to enter the priesthood, and the more subtle leading of his father, into the science of metallurgy, which held promise in Poland's growing steel industry.

He sought Father Dimitri's guidance. The priest had become Janusz's spiritual mentor, and a close friend and advisor. Janusz had great respect for him. In his heart, Janusz struggled with the knowledge that, whatever path he chose, one of the two most important men in his life would be disappointed—either his father or his priest.

Kalman received a gold watch for graduating first in his class. He promptly pawned it and, with money in the pocket of his best suit, walked to the farm where he'd "stolen" the horse. To his dismay, he'd learned the gruff old farmer owned the land where the original coal mine existed. He hoped, since the mine had shut down—supposedly depleted—and the property could not be tilled, conditions would work in his favor. If he could convince the farmer to part with the "worthless" land, he would be well on his way to realizing his dreams.

He cleared his throat before knocking.

When the farmer swung open the door and spotted Kalman standing on the dilapidated porch, he growled, "Stealing something else from me, boy?"

Kalman grinned and held up his thin wad of bills. "Today, I want to buy the old coal mine."

The farmer's eyebrows rose as he stared at the money.

Once they agreed on the price, Kalman said, "There is one other thing I want."

The farmer had already extended his hand to receive the cash. "What—what else?"

Kalman glanced toward the broken-down barn. "The horse. The big plow horse. He is to be included."

"Take him," the farmer said, and grabbed the money. "With this I can buy five horses. All better than him. Good luck with your new land." He flashed a yellow-toothed grin and walked away.

Kalman couldn't wait to share the good news with Janusz. He found him with Zygmunt at the bridge, their favorite place to read and chat.

He called down to the two young men lounging at the water's edge, "Hey, come up!"

Zygmunt beat Janusz to the road and gaped at the massive horse grazing on a tuft of grass. "How come you have the farmer's horse, Kalman?"

"He's a symbol of good luck, for the mine."

Janusz puffed up to them, took one look at the old plow horse, and chuckled. "You've bought our old friend, Kalman?"

Zygmunt glanced from one to the other, and a slow grin spread over his wide face.

"I've bought the old mine."

"What?" Janusz chuckled and slapped Kalman on the back. "Zygmunt is right, you *are* a fool."

"I'll prove you wrong."

Kalman handed Zygmunt the reins. "Take him please, and ask your father if you can keep him for me while I'm away at university. Also, I'd appreciate your checking on the property. Make sure there are no fortune hunters trying to steal from me. And, if you have the time, you could do a little prospecting." He slanted a glance to Janusz. "Maybe between the two of you, you could sell a little coal, help me start up business for the Star Coal Mine. You'd get a share of the profits, of course. I'll come home on weekends and holidays to work."

Zygmunt winked at Janusz as he took the horse's lead. "Already he's named the mine and started giving orders." To Kalman, he said, "Of course, Mr. Gold. Would you like me to shine your shoes?"

Kalman laughed and kicked a few rocks in Zygmunt's direction. "Just wait, Big Z, you'll see. Someday I will be a rich man."

Zygmunt snickered and then led the horse down the road toward his parent's small farm.

Janusz shook his head. "Why *Star* Coal Mine?"

Kalman sobered and shoved his hands deep in his pockets. "For you, Janusz."

Janusz swallowed, remembering those awful hours and the promises he'd made to God.

Kalman said, "I want you to be my partner."

Janusz smiled and shook his head. "It's your dream, Kalman. I have to find my own. Plus," he gave his friend a crooked grin, "I could never go near that damnable pit again."

They parted company reluctantly. Kalman would leave in the morning for Warsaw and the university.

Janusz strolled home, slowly, pausing often to look up at the stars. Kalman's heartfelt tribute, by naming the mine for his ordeal, had struck a chord deep inside. Again, through his dear friend, Kalman, God had answered Janusz. The reminder of his promises while battling death swept away all questions. He now knew his destiny. Janusz belonged to God. Although he had no idea what God wanted, and perhaps never would, he *did* know that God had chosen him. He felt humbled and privileged.

Janusz waited two days before asking to talk with Father Dimitri. He wanted to make sure of his decision. They met in the early evening at the parish.

Father Dimitri brewed tea in the humble, candlelit study. "What's on your mind, my young friend?"

"Father, I am convinced it is God's will that I dedicate my life to the church."

"Are you sure it is God's voice you are hearing and not your mother's?"

Janusz smiled. "I respect my mother, but this decision is between me and God. No one else."

The priest nodded. "There are signs of God's hands on your life. I am pleased to hear of your calling, but some choose the priesthood for the wrong reasons. I would not want this to happen to you."

"Father, I'm frightened at the thought of it, for I don't know if I can live a life of sacrifice for others, but I do know I must try."

The priest sipped his tea. "A priest with Jewish heritage. It will be interesting to see where the path leads."

Janusz set his teacup down with a slight rattle, betraying his sudden nervousness. Would the Holy Church in Rome reject him? He said, "Christ was a Jew. And didn't He choose Jews as His disciples?"

Father Dimitri smiled. "Indeed he did. I will petition Rome on your behalf. If they trust my opinion, you will receive a scholarship to the college of theology in Warsaw. In this way, you will stay close to your mother while you complete your education. I believe your father will appreciate your nearness to home, as well. He is a good man, Janusz."

The old priest poured another cup of tea and smiled at Janusz. "Do not worry about your acceptance. God knows your heart. And, with His blessing, it will be done."

Janusz decided to make no announcement to his parents or his friends. This business was between him, Father Dimitri, and God.

His mother hadn't eaten with him or his father for many weeks. She served her family in the dining room and then retreated to the kitchen.

At first, Janusz and his father had found the situation awkward, but soon realized it allowed them time to talk. Work at the steel mill entailed long days and frequent trips. So, now, the evening meals became an important part of their day, and they filled their dinner hour with intimate, shared discussions. Janusz discovered in his father not only a valuable friend, but a confidante as well.

One evening, right after his father returned from a trip to a steel works in Germany, Janusz asked, "Do you think this talk of war is serious?"

"We are casting and stockpiling cannon shells . . . surely not for peace," his father answered grimly.

"But why would they want to use a Polish company?" Janusz pressed. "Poland is not part of this German foolishness."

"Not yet, but they did not send me there to learn of these production methods for idle reasons."

Janusz did not really think war would come. His father's generation seemed haunted by fears of the Great War, now nearly two decades behind them. Hadn't it taught the world that no sane nation wanted such a fruitless and bloody endeavor?

Janusz split his days between checking out the Star Coal Mine and working with the poor at the church.

After completing his chores on the family farm, Zygmunt spent a few hours each week digging up small slabs of coal. Janusz negotiated a fair price for the raw material with a commercial mining operation in town. Together, they hitched up the old plow horse and brought a wagon of coal to sell.

Kalman wrote frequently, and insisted that Janusz pay Zygmunt and himself a small salary, which helped both struggling families to make ends meet.

After a couple of months, Kalman instructed Janusz to have a one-room office built on the site. He'd made enough money to afford to take the next step into the mining business, and he wanted to look a bit more professional. Each long weekend, and every school holiday, Kalman came home to oversee the fledgling operation and go over the accounting with Janusz.

"You must accept my offer of a partnership, Janusz," Kalman said as the two of them stood on the crude steps that led up to the office door. "I insist."

Janusz shook his head and gestured toward the old mine shaft that had changed both of their lives. "I still cannot look at that without a shudder. Besides, my friend, my path leads in another direction."

Kalman put his hands on Janusz's shoulders and smiled. "Perhaps God meant for you to make us a lot of money, Janusz."

Janusz shrugged. "Only time will tell, Kalman."

One day that summer, while Janusz sorted potatoes, Father Dimitri came down the dusty steps into the church's cool, dark food cellar. "Here you are, Janusz."

The season's warm temperatures and high humidity added to the rapid decay of the vegetables. Janusz grimaced, wiping slime onto a gritty apron. "If we don't get rid of the rotten ones, all may be lost."

"Much as it is in life," the aging priest said. "But, I came with good news. I have received a letter from Rome."

Janusz gulped.

"You have been accepted." Father Dimitri smiled. "You will begin college next quarter, in ten days."

Janusz took the priest's hand and kissed it. "Thank you, Father."

"No. Thank God," the priest replied.

That weekend, Kalman arrived at the tiny office situated in the muddy field beside the original shaft Janusz had fallen into. The time had come for Janusz to reveal his calling and to share the good news.

Kalman clapped him on the back and shook his hand. "I am glad, Janusz. The church will make use of that sharp mind of yours. Because you've managed to strike a good deal for the coal Zygmunt brings up, our profits are enough to afford a part-time secretary to take over the books when you leave."

When the time came for Janusz's departure, Kalman introduced him to a friend from college. Aaron Ross, a good-looking young man, studied law at the university.

Aaron stared over the pitiful mining operation and shook his head. "This mud field is your destiny, Kalman? You'll need all the legal help you can get."

Janusz laughed as they shook hands. "Some day Kalman will be the richest man in Katowice, and everyone will work for him. He's told me this many times. But, I must go." He waved to the two university students and trudged through the mud, back to the old apartment building.

His father met him at the door. "I will help you pack. Though I'd hoped you would follow me into metallurgy, I have seen that your heart longs for a different calling. Father Dimitri has done our family a great

21

service. Now you will obtain a proper education, and also follow your heart into the church. He assures me that you will be allowed to come home at the end of each quarter. Your mother and I will live for your return."

CHAPTER THREE

*A friendship founded on business is a good deal better
than a business founded on friendship.*

John D. Rockefeller

Kalman sat in the office at the Dabrowski Steel mill where Stanislaw
Dov worked as an analytical metallurgist. He stood when Janusz's father
entered the room.

"Your hunch was right, Kalman," Stanislaw said, holding up a report.
"The sample you brought in tested as a very high-grade soft coal. If
the sample was taken below a depth of, oh, say, twenty to thirty feet,
it would be a strong indication of a major deposit. Do you know who
owns the land this was found on? I'm sure my boss would be interested
in exploring this as a fuel source for our furnaces."

Kalman grinned. "Yes, sir. I know who owns the land."

Three days later, Kalman signed the papers to form the Star Coal
Mining Company and Aaron set up a meeting with Louis Dabrowski,
owner of the prestigious Dabrowski Steel Mill. If all went well, the steel
magnate would fund Kalman's mining operation.

Aaron, a handsome, square-shouldered, fair-haired man, flashed a
white, even-toothed grin. "Don't worry. I'll take care of your legal affairs."

"Good," Kalman said, "but if you don't make the deal, you don't get
paid. I don't have any money."

"Not so fast." Aaron smiled. "Then I'm your new partner."

Kalman reached out a hand. "Fair enough."

The morning they waited in the luxurious corporate lounge at the well-established and highly prosperous mill, Aaron muttered to Kalman, "I haven't completed college, let alone passed the bar. What am I thinking, trying to hold my own with the seasoned, highly-paid and skilled attorneys representing Dabrowski Steel? My heart is in my throat, and my stomach is in knots."

Kalman paced anxiously. "I'm hoping they'll cooperate, for we have something they need. Coal. Cheap coal."

The needs of both sides resulted in a fair settlement and an agreement on terms. Dabrowski Steel would fund the cost of the Star Coal Mining Company, with an option to buy soft coal at twenty percent below the market rate and share in the gross profits for a period of thirty-six months. If they found no coal in the first eight weeks of mining, title of the property would pass to Dabrowski Steel.

Aaron prepared the contracts, and the cigar-smoking, sixty-eight-year-old Louis Dabrowski stalked in for the signing. His three attorneys and two sons surrounded him. Across the long conference table, Kalman sat with Aaron Ross.

Aaron pushed to his feet and extended a hand to Dabrowski.

The older man made no move to take it. He studied the two young men through his bifocals. "Nobody told me we were doing business with fuckin' kids."

Aaron withdrew his hand and exchanged a quick glance with Kalman. "Kids are like steel, Mister Dabrowski. They can take a lot of punishment, and still last longer than the adults. Now, either we get down to business, or we kids are going to take one of our other offers."

Dabrowski chewed on his cigar. It made circles in his pursed lips. He glared at Aaron, who appeared calm and in control.

Kalman's throat felt tight. *So close, but will it now all slip away?*

Dabrowski finally growled, shooting out a hand. "Give me a goddamned pen."

The Star Coal Mining Company opened its strip-mining operation ten days later. Kalman formally hired his stalwart and trustworthy friend, Zygmunt Pilarski, as the foreman of his new, twenty-man crew. The large plow horse stood tied to a post outside the makeshift shack that served as the site office. Inside, Kalman wore the watch he had pawned.

Every weekend, Kalman took the train from Warsaw and consulted with Stanislav Dov on possible digging sites. Aaron came down as often as possible, lending moral support to Zygmunt's crew as they toiled, often in the mud and rain.

After week seven, when only three days remained before the mine would revert to Dabrowski Steel, shouts from Big Z and the others working in the pit brought Kalman and Aaron on the run, into the pouring rain. The two young businessmen stood out in their suits and ties among the muddy, blackened strip miners standing ankle deep in the slop, but nothing mattered to either as they heard their foreman's news.

Zygmunt raised what looked like a twenty-pound lump of coal above his head. "We found it!" The heavy rain ran down his arms and onto his grimy neck.

Kalman and Aaron joined the others, dancing and jumping in the mud and slop. After fifty-three days of backbreaking work, rain or shine, they had reached the thick vein of soft coal.

· · ·

In Warsaw, Janusz worked as a volunteer in the food kitchen of a neighborhood church when his studies permitted. He took Kalman's letter to read during a lull in serving the poor.

He smiled, certain of God's hand in the matter. God had rewarded Kalman for saving the life of a man who had been "called."

Janusz excused himself from his duties, went into a cool potato cellar, and wept thankful tears.

· · ·

Kalman Gold and Aaron Ross became the talk of Katowice as their fame and fortune grew. Zygmunt and his army of burly diggers brought up coal from the ground like men possessed. There seemed no end to the rich vein.

While Zygmunt provided supervision at the mine, Kalman expanded the market for the tons of newfound soft coal, and soon shipped it as far as Krakow. Aaron Ross followed in Kalman's wake with detailed contracts and agreements. Money followed—more than they had dreamed of—perhaps more than young men should have.

Life was good. It seemed they had it all. Aaron became obsessed with women, flirting and bedding with as many as he could, as if some demon pushed him. Kalman would worry and warn his friend, but thankfully the dalliances never kept Aaron from their blossoming business.

The big yellow plow horse had its own corral and a lean-to for shelter. All the miners, and soon all of Katowice, knew the story of the horse. Zygmunt saw to that. It quickly became a local legend, told in all the beer halls. Hoping to draw on the special luck the horse brought Kalman, miners began to bring carrots and sugar cubes, and the horse's girth swelled.

A new, spacious, five-room frame building replaced the small, weathered shack that had once served as the mining office. The possibility of running a telephone line to the mine office excited the office staff. One room even had a new typewriter. Aaron had bought it in Warsaw.

The shapely young secretary he assigned to the fancy, new machine became the fifth, out of the five-girl staff, he had seduced. "We may have to hire some new girls," he told Kalman the morning after the typewriter arrived.

"You treat sex as if it were candy," Kalman warned. "Someday it will catch up with you."

"Sex is much better than candy," Aaron quipped, "and it doesn't hurt your teeth."

Late that summer, as Kalman sat in his office drinking tea and poring over accounting records, Anne, the senior office clerk, rapped on his open door. "Pardon me, Kalman, but a Wladislaw Romanov is asking to see you."

"Bring him in," Kalman said without hesitation.

Wladislaw, wet and bedraggled, hat in hand, stepped into the doorway a moment later. Wearing a tattered, worn, gray coat, the gaunt-cheeked Wladislaw looked like a desperate man.

Kalman stood and crossed to him to offer a hand. "Good to see you, Wladislaw. How is your mother? I heard the two of you opened your own bakery."

He motioned Wladislaw to a chair and returned to his own.

Wladislaw sat down, clutching his hat in both hands. "My mother's health is not good," he said in a rough voice, "and the bakery has closed."

"I'm sorry to hear that."

"I was wondering," Wladislaw continued, looking at the floor. "Since we were friends in school . . . if you might have some work for me here?"

Kalman nodded, understanding how difficult it must have been for Wladislaw to come to him. "Zygmunt runs the mining crew. I will ask him to find you a spot. I'm afraid that's all we have. It is hard work, but we pay a fair wage."

Wladislaw raised his eyes. "I will take the job."

"Good, then be here tomorrow at 6:00 a.m. Tell Zygmunt we talked."

"Thank you, Kalman."

Kalman studied his old schoolmate. The gloom that had seemed to haunt Wladislaw, even in his youth, now apparently hung heavy on his spirit, much like the gray clouds that choked the summer sky. He swallowed, thanking the fates that Janusz had fallen into that pit and brought back with him Kalman's future. If not for that, Kalman might also have had to beg for work.

Zygmunt stepped into Kalman's office, nodding to Wladislaw as the haggard, downtrodden man left. A frown marred the big foreman's usually cheerful expression. "Wladislaw is not looking well. And I've heard the Romanov's bakery is failing."

Kalman came to stand next to his burly friend and, together, they watched Wladislaw trudge through the rain and mud toward Katowice. "Their business has closed. I promised him a job as one of your workers."

Zygmunt grunted, still frowning at the slump-shouldered figure disappearing into the wet gloom. "His mother's hatred of Jews has passed to him, Kalman. With the failure of the family bakery, and him begging for work from you, he will resent you even more than he did in school, when he competed with you for Janusz's friendship."

Kalman slapped Zygmunt on the back, then returned to the accounting sheets spread over his new, highly-polished desk. "He'll be fine after his first payday and a good meal."

Zygmunt hovered in the doorway and Kalman looked up from his paperwork, waiting.

"Mrs. Romanov has spoon-fed his attitude toward successful Jews since birth. In his gut, hatred burns like a hot coal fire."

Kalman tapped his pencil on the ledger, remembering Janusz's comments about Zygmunt's flashes of unvarnished insight. "Diamonds in the rough," Janusz had called the snippets of wisdom.

After a moment, Zygmunt blew out a heavy breath and gave Kalman a wave. "I will watch him closely." Then he strode out of the office. A few seconds later, the outer door banged shut, and silence reigned.

Kalman stared out the window at the rain, wishing he could see Janusz's stars, then turned his attention back to the day's earnings.

Kalman didn't take success lightly. He arrived at work by seven every morning, and was usually the last to depart.

One Saturday, Aaron Ross surprised him by waiting for him in the mining office, before anyone else had arrived. Aaron—by nature an upbeat optimist—appeared somber. He closed the office door. "I need to talk."

Kalman sat down behind his desk and watched Aaron pace. "What is it?"

"Dina is pregnant."

She was the office accounting clerk. The latest to join the ranks of the Ross girls.

Kalman leaned back in his chair and frowned at his partner. "You do know what causes this, don't you?"

Aaron raked a hand through his hair and grimaced. "I thought she was a smart girl."

"Oh, I see, it's her fault."

"That's not what I meant."

"My uncle once told me," Kalman mused, "the screwing you're after usually matches the screwing you'll get."

Aaron snapped, "I need your help, not your criticism."

"You're a smart man. What are your options?"

Aaron shoved his hands deep into his trouser pockets. "Marry her or flee."

"So, when is the wedding?"

28

Aaron sank into one of the chairs facing the desk, looking defeated—shoulders uncharacteristically slumped, head down. "I knew this is what you would say."

Kalman leaned his elbows on the desk, studying his friend's dismal expression. "It is the right thing to do. To abandon her would brand you a bastard and destroy your career. It's not like she is an old shoe, you know? And besides, she is an attractive girl."

Aaron perked up a little. "And from a respectable, wealthy family."

Kalman nodded. "You don't have to convince me."

"Then I will propose to her today. My child will have no dishonor." Aaron stood, as if to reinforce his decision.

"Good." Kalman sighed with secret relief. Any other choice would have been bad for business.

Respectability and discretion dictated the wedding take place soon. Aaron set the date for within the month. Kalman agreed to serve as the best man and bought a new, dark pinstriped suit for the ceremony.

The family coordinated plans with the Rabbi of Temple Isaac, in Katowice, and sent hundreds of invitations for the wedding and feast. Because of Kalman's and Aaron's prestigious positions, the pending wedding, as well as speculation of its cause, quickly became the talk of the town.

Though Kalman's success brought him favor with women, unlike in his school days, he rarely dated. He felt leery of most women. He wanted to marry for love, not to someone who desired his fortune. He had even considered employing the services of a matchmaker, but hesitated to take that rather permanent step.

Aaron's wedding provided Kalman's answer in the lovely form of Tova Stern, Dina's cousin and bridesmaid. The moment Kalman saw Tova, he fell under her spell. Her presence seemed to light the room. The dark-haired girl with intense, green eyes and creamy complexion moved with a fluid grace and, when introduced to Kalman, spoke softly. The touch of her hand ignited his soul.

However, the feeling did not seem mutual. She acted cool to Kalman's approach and less than impressed by his wealth and position.

Shortly after the wedding feast, she disappeared. Kalman searched everywhere for her.

"She took a night train back to Krakow," the new Mrs. Ross told him. "She's engaged to be married. Her father, a successful jeweler in Krakow, arranged the match."

The news shattered Kalman, but, not one to give up easily, he borrowed the new sedan Aaron had bought for his honeymoon and raced off into the night toward Krakow, leaving the newlyweds to find other means of transportation.

Kalman had no idea what he would say when he got there, but he knew he had to be waiting when Tova Stern stepped off the train. He drove like a man possessed, at breakneck speed, over the rutted, bumpy, dirt roads.

Fate proved kind to Kalman, for he beat the train by ten minutes. He stood tall, putting on his best face, when Tova spotted him on the platform. "What are you doing here?"

Kalman took a deep breath. "I'm here to tell you that I love you. I have often wondered how I would recognize the woman I was to marry. I still don't know how, but I know I have. And you, Tova Stern, are that woman. I'm here to ask you to marry me."

"You've proven one thing, Mr. Gold," Tova answered. "Even successful men make stupid mistakes. I am engaged to marry, and my fiancée would take great exception to your proposal. Goodnight."

She marched away.

It took four months and twenty-three trips to Krakow, as well as four bouquets of roses and three boxes of fine chocolates, before Tova agreed to have dinner with Kalman.

Three months after their first date, Kalman married Tova Stern, shocking her family and former fiancée.

Eleven months and twenty-seven days after their marriage, Tova delivered fraternal twins, a girl and a boy—Rachel and David, revered names in Jewish heritage. Fraternal twins in the small community were rare, and the birth of the twins created an atmosphere of wonder and awe. Hundreds came to visit and stare. The Gold household quickly filled with gifts.

The Rabbi told Kalman, "You are a man God favors."

CHAPTER FOUR

THE SANDS OF TIME

A man is what he is, not what he used to be.

Yiddish Proverb

Janusz graduated from the private theology college six months after Kalman earned his university degree. He celebrated quietly with his married friend, enjoying Kalman's twins. At almost three years old, they ran the Gold household, keeping Tova on her toes.

When he took his leave, he kissed Tova on the cheek and hugged Kalman. "You have been blessed, my friend."

Kalman smiled. "And I owe it all to you, Janusz. I will never forget." He accompanied Janusz to the door.

Janusz waved goodbye and strolled down the well-kept street where Kalman lived in the better part of town. He made his way to the old apartment building Stanislav and Teresa still occupied. On the morrow, he would meet with Father Dimitri, his old friend and mentor.

The old priest hobbled through the gardens of the parish, clucking his tongue at the occasional weed, as he led Janusz into his study. "It has been a while since you visited, my young friend. I hear from the dean of the college that you were a good student. I am proud of you."

The housekeeper brought in a pot of freshly-brewed tea, and Father Dimitri poured two cups. He studied Janusz with a watery stare. "Do you still wish to continue into the priesthood?"

Janusz smiled and nodded. "My calling feels stronger than ever, Father. Is it still possible to enter the seminary under the grant you discussed with me before I left for college?"

Father Dimitri sipped his tea, allowing a long pause before answering. "My dear young man, that grant has been waiting for you all of this time. If you wish it, the train leaves at the end of this month. I have your itinerary, and your tickets will be ready whenever you say."

Janusz, with heartfelt gratitude, felt tears fill his eyes. He could not speak as the old priest walked over to an ancient roll-top desk and pulled out a fat envelope from one of the mail slots. His hands shook as he accepted the paperwork, and he finally managed to utter, "Thank you, Father. All my life's wishes have been granted. God has blessed me."

Father Dimitri bowed his gray head. "God has blessed us all."

That night, over dinner, Janusz shared the news with his father. "It seems you will not be the only member of the Dov family traveling to foreign countries this summer."

His father paused with his fork and knife in the plate of boiled cabbage and lamb and studied Janusz a moment. "You have been accepted for seminary?"

Janusz nodded.

Tears rimmed his father's eyes. "I am proud."

Then he said softly, "Have you told your mother?"

"I wanted to tell you first."

"Thank you, son," Then, to the closed door that led to the kitchen, his father called: "Theresa! Come in! Your son has news!"

But the joy Janusz expected from his mother never came. The days passed and he packed for the trip. His mother sank further into her moody depression and seldom left her room.

On the eve of his quiet departure, as Janusz finished up his work at the church, Father Dimitri sought him out. "You have a visitor in the parish office."

"Who?"

The priest didn't answer. He just smiled and wandered away.

Janusz washed his hands and headed for the office. To his surprise, when he opened the door, Kalman Gold stood by the window, wearing a pinstriped, tailored suit and polished leather shoes. An expensive-looking Derby hat sat on the edge of the old desk.

He offered Janusz a warm smile. "You thought you were going to sneak away without saying goodbye, didn't you?"

Janusz hadn't seen Kalman for almost a month. "You look like a wealthy man."

"Life is good. I'm still your friend, and friends keep each other informed."

Janusz shrugged guiltily. "I'm no good at goodbyes."

Kalman moved to stand in front of Janusz. "Nor am I, but I wanted to see you before you go off to become a man of God. When I see you next, I'll have to bow to you."

"Never, Kalman. I may become a priest, but I'll still be Janusz Dov."

Kalman looked serious. "Things can change people. Time changes people. You will be gone six years."

Janusz took Kalman's hand in his. "Time will change both of us. It already has. I am becoming a priest because you gave me a chance. You saved my life. My debt to you is great."

Kalman pulled his hand from Janusz's, looking uncomfortable. "God gave us life. I owe you because you found the coal. The debt is paid."

"Regardless of debt," Janusz continued, "I am your friend, and I will remain your friend forever."

"Good." Kalman smiled. "Then, when you return, I will buy Father Janusz dinner at the best restaurant in Katowice. We'll invite Zygmunt and make it a grand celebration."

Janusz slapped Kalman's shoulder. "I accept."

An awkward moment of silence fell between them. Their widening paths had now become a fork in the road of their lives. Promises, although sincere, would not be easy to keep.

Kalman retrieved the hat from the worn desk. Fingering the brim, he said, "Well, I have to get out to the mine and check on things."

Janusz nodded.

They hugged, shook hands, and then Kalman stepped out the door.

"Good luck, my friend," Janusz whispered. His eyes watered as he watched Kalman walk jauntily down the parish drive.

Janusz entered the bedroom and kissed his mother on the forehead. Theresa Dov had battled depression for as long as Janusz could remember. She still hadn't spoken in the three days since his return. Though he preferred her silent spells to her angry shrieks, he wished for the thousandth time that she could defeat whatever had taken her down this grim path. Even his father couldn't point to one particular cause.

"Goodbye, Mother. I love you."

An expressionless stare was the only answer.

Janusz's father rode with him in the cab to the rail station. At the curb, he drew Janusz into his arms. "You became a man so fast. The time passed so quickly." He took him by the shoulders and looked in his eyes. "I am a metallurgist. I know when things have the right mix to make them strong and lasting and valuable. Although your heart is soft, son, it is like fine steel. I am certain you will stand the heat in any furnace. Do well. Goodbye." He kissed Janusz and turned away.

Janusz could taste the salt of his father's tears.

Janusz boarded the third coach of the train and sat near a window. He patted the inside breast pocket of his best wool suit. Tucked safely within were a letter of introduction from Father Dimitri and the directions to the seminary in Rome.

The train bumped and began to move. Janusz stared long and hard at Katowice, the city of his birth and youth. That part of his life had ended. Both joy and sorrow filled him. Excitement soon chased away any melancholy of leaving home. Six years until his return.

He wondered how it would change. He wondered how *he* would change.

Janusz transferred trains in Budapest. The size and beauty of the ancient city struck him with awe. Katowice, a gray, colorless town filled with horse-drawn carts and bicycles, could not compare to Budapest, which looked like a crowded, busy international crossroad.

Arabs walked about in flowing robes and wrapped heads. African laborers carried immense loads on their backs, and noisy trucks filled the streets and sidewalks.

Janusz swallowed down a wave of homesickness and felt slightly relieved when the train left for the next stop. He knew, however, that Rome would bring even more differences; after all, the Church had chosen the city as home.

Janusz, stiff and wrinkled from another night of fitful sleep in the hard train seat, awoke to the conductor's call: "Austria."

He eagerly looked out the window to find a mountainous and green countryside. Stone fences lined the farm fields, keeping in fat cattle.

After traveling for hours without seeing a village or town, Janusz decided that few people lived in Austria.

Late in the day, the graying conductor—knowing Janusz's final destination—said in passing, "Welcome to Italy, boy."

Janusz turned to the window. It didn't look any different than Austria, but he took comfort in the familiar, pastoral landscape.

As night fell, Italy disappeared into darkness, broken by an occasional light from a farm or village. Soon, Janusz drifted off. The other passengers slept.

With the first light of dawn, he awoke to find the train laboring along the shores of the Adriatic Sea. He stared in wonder, having never seen such an immense body of water. He stayed glued to the window as the train continued west toward Venice, thrilling at the occasional sail he spotted on the emerald waters.

In late afternoon, Venice rolled into view. Janusz found himself speechless.

Venice, with its Renaissance style of architecture, proved an unfathomable eye feast for a young man from Katowice. History had come to life. He had not dreamed such beauty still survived, and felt numb with delight.

The train station boasted more style and beauty than the museums dedicated to the arts in Poland. He felt he had entered heaven. The two-hour train transfer for Rome came and went much too quickly.

Night came as the mountains of Northern Italy yielded to the flatlands leading to Rome. Janusz had no trouble staying awake, for adrenaline surged through his veins. He spotted the glow of the city from thirty miles away.

"Rome!" he shouted, to the annoyance of the Italian businessman trying to sleep in the seat beside him.

Such light and beauty—it looked awesome. He glimpsed a crumbling, ancient wall as the train labored into the sprawling metropolis. Gas lamps turned night to day. Instead of the sleeping city he'd expected, automobiles, trucks and streetcars clogged the streets. The people dressed in more color than he had ever seen on anyone. And palm trees! He had only read of them.

The rich scents of citrus and perfumed women permeated the train station, intoxicating Janusz. Outside, on the wide, busy and bright streets, the city pulsed with life—vibrant, exciting.

Janusz ignored the directions in the envelope in his pocket, which Father Dimitri had so painstakingly written out for him. He wanted to see, to hear, to feel, to become part of it all. God would certainly choose to live in this place. Janusz looked forward to sharing it with Him.

He went to a crowded sidewalk bar, where all the patrons stood at a high counter, and bought an espresso. It tasted bitter and strong, and he loved it.

Then he walked for over an hour, absorbing the sights and sounds. When the beautiful and colorful women, with make-up and lovely dresses, passed by, he tried not to stare.

An attractive older woman on a busy corner smiled and spoke to him in Italian. She had pouty lips, painted bright red, and she smoked a cigarette. When Janusz shrugged, not understanding, she brazenly reached out and cupped his testicles in her hand. Shocked and horrified, he pulled away and crossed the street, leaving her laughing behind him. He had much to learn, he realized with a shudder.

Janusz perused the streets of Rome, ignoring the time. He rejoiced as the streets began to clear of cars and people with the lateness of the hour, wanting the city to himself. He marveled at the endless succession of splashing, cascading fountains and magnificent statuary crowding every block. The figures looked chalky, and near lifelike, in the blue-white light thrown off by hissing gas lamps. Many he recognized from his studies. In Rome, it seemed history left the textbooks and became a part of life.

Janusz turned a corner and stopped, breathless—the Vatican and St. Peter's Square, bathed in soft, night lighting.

"Thank you, Holy Father," he whispered.

The boy from Katowice, Poland, knew he had come home.

———◦◦◦❁◦◦◦———

One evening, Zygmunt's sobbing wife pounded on the Gold's door. "The police came and took my Ziggy," the humble woman cried. "I didn't know where else to go for help."

An hour later, Kalman arrived at the Katowice jail with Aaron Ross in tow. Zygmunt sat in a small, dimly-lit cell, ripe with the odor of stale urine. He sported a large lump on the side of his head.

Aaron held up a copy of the arrest report. "You are accused of breaking a man's arm and resisting arrest."

Zygmunt nodded. "And I would do it again."

Kalman leaned against the bars and frowned at his old, trusted friend. "These charges are serious."

"And so is what this man did to Pearlman. He was delivering coal to the foundry on Elizabeth Street when Polansky made him pull down his pants and show everyone what a Jewish cock looked like."

Aaron and Kalman exchanged a grim look. A wave of anti-Semitic fervor had not only swept through Katowice, but also all of Poland. Attacks on Jews had, unfortunately, become commonplace and, sometimes, much worse than Zygmunt's altercation.

Kalman shook his head. "You should have told us."

"Telling you would have done nothing. Pearlman is a Jew. The police would have done nothing to Polansky. I did what I had to do."

Kalman patted Zygmunt on the shoulder. "And we will do what we have to do." He called for the guard to let them out and waved to his foreman as he and Aaron left the cell.

Once outside the building, Aaron warned, "He's right, you know. And this isn't going to be easy. He'll be labeled a Jewish sympathizer."

"Do what you must." Kalman rolled his shoulders and straightened his spine. "We take care of our own. Spend what you have to spend. Bribe who you have to bribe, but get him out of that jail."

It took a day for Aaron to find a magistrate with a taste he could afford. Three kegs of German beer and a rack of fresh mutton assured Zygmunt's release on bail.

That evening, Aaron stepped into Kalman's office and closed the door. "Polansky filed a major injury suit against Zygmunt, hoping the growing bias against Jews will favor him. The local press is already declaring Zygmunt guilty."

He paced in front of Kalman's desk, rubbing his handsome face in agitation. "The opposing attorneys are hoping to make it a showcase for all Jewish sympathizers."

"Give it priority," Kalman urged. "Everything else can wait."

Aaron worked on Zygmunt's case day and night for a week. Kalman watched him struggle with the research and paperwork.

One rainy afternoon, as Aaron returned to the mining office from the courthouse, Kalman called him in to his office. "This legal business requires more of you than I thought. Rent an office in town, close to the courthouse, and hire some help." He added sternly, "Remember you have a wife and son to think about, and a case to win. You have no time to dishonor Dina and Stefan, or to let down Zygmunt. They are all depending on you keeping your focus directed and your pants on."

Aaron colored and said angrily, "I love my wife and son. Stefan is my life. They want for nothing, and Dina lives the life of a pampered princess. I swear to you, Kalman, I will not let Zygmunt down."

Kalman nodded. "Good." But his heart felt heavy as he watched his partner stride out of the office.

He sighed and went back to his books.

The week after Aaron set up shop in a second-floor office on Kavinski Street, Kalman stopped by for a midmorning visit to check on the progress of Zygmunt's defense case. Aaron's new secretary, a beautiful nineteen-year-old, greeted him a little breathlessly and ushered him inside.

Kalman groaned silently at her disheveled appearance and the sumptuous amount of cleavage her formfitting dress revealed. He held up a hand as the young woman moved toward the door of the inner office. "I'll show myself in, thank you."

He found Aaron placing files back on the desk, whistling a jaunty tune. "Tuck in your shirt, Aaron," Kalman said sharply.

Aaron jerked around, wide-eyed, then shrugged and adjusted his clothes.

A flame of disappointment burned in Kalman's stomach. "Wipe the lipstick off your face and tell me you are actually working on Zygmunt's defense."

Aaron flushed, then paled, and faced Kalman straight on. Then, suddenly, he bounded around the desk and caught Kalman by the shoulders. All signs of embarrassment disappeared in his victorious demeanor. "I've got him! I've got that bastard Polansky by the balls."

Aaron smiled and gathered his expensive coat from the hanger by the door. "Come on. Let me buy you a cup of coffee. I'll explain."

The day of Zygmunt's trial finally arrived. The courtroom, like the city and Poland itself, was divided into Jews on one side, Poles on the other. Hate filled the room. Anti-Semitism had gained momentum in Germany and now rolled over Europe—especially Poland—like a dark cloud. Many of the wealthier Jews had already fled, or at least sent their families away. Kalman and Aaron had discussed the situation with their wives, but both Tova and Dina had staunchly refused to leave. They both said it would get no worse.

Zygmunt's trial had become a showcase for social ills. The Jewish community rallied around Kalman's burly foreman, believing the outcome would determine the right for Jews to do business, to walk the streets, and to enjoy equal protection under the law.

Aaron had lost his zeal for the case—Kalman guessed this change stemmed from the womanizing attorney feeling compelled to send away his lovely legal assistant—but he still seemed determined, capable and ready. A more perfunctory demeanor replaced Aaron's usual showmanship in the courtroom, and he wasted little time in calling his first witness—the wife of the plaintiff.

A hollow-eyed, frail woman, with bruises on her face and missing teeth, took the stand. The courtroom grew silent as if holding its collective breath.

Aaron approached the witness stand. "Mrs. Polansky, you are the wife of the plaintiff, Leonard Polansky?"

"Yes."

"Tell us how you lost your teeth."

"My husband made me undress in front of another man. When I refused, he beat me."

"Was this the first time he beat you?"

"No, he has done this before. He did the same to our thirteen-year-old daughter and our ten-year-old son."

"Made them undress in front of strange men?"

"Yes, he enjoyed watching them suffer."

"Mrs. Polansky, why didn't you report this to the authorities?"

The woman dabbed a tear from her face. "I was afraid of him. He said he would kill the children and me . . . that the court would do nothing . . . because I am a Jew."

She dared a fleeting look at the graying Judge. "I have come because you said the court would help me."

The courtroom simmered with a near-electric silence.

Aaron addressed the judge, "Your, Honor, I beg the court to recognize how the police have not investigated this matter fully. If we continue with the issue of self-defense on the part of my client, other shocking crimes perpetrated by the plaintiff will come to light. I pray the court will recognize the serious felonies the plaintiff has committed, and that he will be ordered held without bail pending a full investigation. He has brought shame on all Katowice."

The heavily-muscled Leonard Polansky growled and leaped toward Aaron. "You Jew bastard!"

Bailiffs and volunteers from the gallery quickly wrestled the violently angry man to the floor.

The judge's gavel slammed down against the bench. "The case against Zygmunt Pilarski is dismissed, and the plaintiff is ordered held without bail! Summon the chief investigator. I will be in my chambers."

The judge exited the courtroom and pandemonium broke out. A mix of curses and shouts filled the air. Kalman and half a dozen burly miners hurried Aaron and Zygmunt outside.

The court victory proved short and bittersweet. The lot of the Jews in Katowice, as in all Poland, worsened. Bigotry ran out of control.

Then, one evening after the twins' bedtime, Kalman sat in his living room with Tova, enjoying the peace and silence. However, soon, his mood darkened.

Tova looked up from her needlepoint. "What is it, Kalman?"

"We are riding the tiger, Tova. The only thing that protects us from the fate of our Jewish neighbors is our wealth and influence. But even that wears thin now."

Tova rose gracefully from her chair and joined Kalman on the settee. "I fear you are right, my dearest."

Kalman looked deep into her eyes, seeing all that he'd ever wanted in a woman. He captured her hand and brought her fingers to his lips. "The thought of fleeing and leaving behind our heritage, our homeland, and a business I've literally dug from the ground, is unthinkable."

Tova smiled, kissed his temple, and caressed his jaw.

Kalman prayed that he had not gambled with his family's lives. He'd always lived a charmed life. Luck seemed to sit on his shoulder. Each night, he convinced himself that his was a business the war needed, if it came to war.

Kalman focused on the mine and his family. He and Tova both devoted their time and energies to the twins. The innocence of youth diverted them from the harsh reality of the world outside the sanctuary of their home. The children knew nothing of the convulsions the world suffered, and when sharing their laughter and joy, neither did Kalman and Tova.

Kalman dealt with many German customers. He'd become fluent in their language and made sure both children learned to speak and understand the language of the most dominant nation in Europe. He still hoped the storm would pass.

Delegates from the German army and the Luftwaffe frequently visited Kalman's sprawling strip mines. He and Janusz had discovered one of the richest deposits in Europe, which enabled the hungry German blast furnaces to keep producing steel. In essence, German interests protected the business and, in Kalman's success-oriented mind, that's all that mattered.

However, as time went on, and the climate of social tensions and racial hatred escalated, empowered and inflamed by the German government, Kalman's distrust slowly grew.

On a chilly November night, terror that would be forever etched in history swept over Germany—*Kristallnacht*—the night of the broken glass. Frenzied mobs stormed through the streets of major German cities, breaking out the windows of Jewish-owned businesses and homes. They threw store goods into the streets and burned them. Every house occupied by a Jew had its doors and windows smashed. Synagogues were set on fire. News of *Kristallnacht* quickly reached Poland and Katowice.

Less than a week later, the distant sound of breaking glass and raised voices awakened Kalman and Tova in the middle of the night. The crackling sound of wood soon accompanied the noises of the angry mob. With each crash of glass and splinter of timber, shouts resounded in the night air.

Kalman stiffened with fear, understanding that the Polish now imitated the Germans. His heart pounded. A sickening terror filled his stomach. The sounds of hatred and destruction seemed to go on forever. Peering out an upstairs bedroom window, Kalman saw a red glow in the sky . . . then another . . . and another, until the night turned bright with the reflection of fire against the overcast. The wind carried the acrid smell of smoke to his nostrils.

Tova clung to him, terrified. "What is it, Kalman?"

Kalman ordered Tova and the twins to the basement and spent the rest of the night pacing and staring out the window.

At first light, he kissed Tova and the children and left for the mines. "Stay in the house."

Kalman walked to Katowice's wide main street, lined with cafes and shops. His eyes widened in horror as he saw the smashed windows in Jewish-owned stores. Heaps of burning ash lay all over the street—remnants of burned store goods. Smoke clouded the morning air. Kalman shuddered at the sight of broken-down apartment doors.

Worse yet, the synagogue had burned to the ground. Torah scrolls, prayer books, the holy arks and prayer shawls all littered the street.

Kalman pulled his hat down lower, unable to believe his eyes. The devastation seemed surreal: the city of his birth, his home—the home of his father and his grandfather—shattered. He had walked these streets as a child . . . nevermore.

As he passed the homes of his friends, his life crumbled about him with every broken window and smoldering pile of trash. Seeing the ravaged town unnerved him and he shook violently.

How could this happen? Where had the anger come from? What drove the fear? Why the hate? And, where would it lead? His frightened thoughts struck him as deeply as the spectacle that lay all around him.

His mine? His home? Had they escaped the violence because of his business with the Germans?

He held his breath as he topped the slight rise that hid the mine from view . . . untouched.

The day's work had already begun. Kalman rushed to the office. Aaron Ross met him inside, and they hurried into the privacy of Kalman's inner office.

As soon as he shut the door, Kalman asked softly, "Your home and family?"

Aaron nodded and slumped into one of the chairs in front of the desk. "Untouched. And yours?"

Kalman sat down hard, behind his desk. "Frightened, but all right. We have to get them out of Poland."

"You haven't seen the paper?"

"No. Why?"

"All travel is now prohibited."

Kalman surged back to his feet and pounded his fist on the desk. "But the business!"

Aaron responded sarcastically, "Let's pray for a cold winter. Even the Nazis have to stay warm."

"You're right." Kalman sat back down. "I think the worst is probably over."

"Coal has no politic," Aaron said. "That should save us. Hell, it already has." He stood and turned toward the door.

Kalman swallowed hard. "Aaron."

Aaron paused as he reached for the door knob. "Yeah?"

Kalman massaged his chin with thumb and forefinger. "If anything should happen, you know, unexpected, would you look after my family?"

"Nothing's going to happen."

"I hope you're right, but these are difficult times. We make careful plans for business. We should also make plans for our families."

Aaron nodded and crossed to the front of Kalman's desk. "We're partners, right?"

Kalman smiled. "Successful partners."

"Not only in business, but in life." Aaron nodded. "We've known each other longer than we've known our wives. We spend more time with each other than we do with our families. You have my word. As long as I breathe, your children, and your children's children, will be as my own."

Kalman pushed out of his chair and reached a hand across the desk. "And so it will be with me. We are partners in all."

The two men shook hands.

The Nazi war machine invaded Poland in September.

Unfortunately, the forecast was for a mild winter.

———∘oo⟨○⟩oo∘———

Kalman slogged through pouring rain and deep mud, leading the old plow horse. The black night camouflaged his movements and he took care to keep his face down, just in case someone had ventured out into the rainstorm. He couldn't afford to have anyone see him and investigate.

A heavily-padlocked steel box, filled with Kalman's gold and some of Tova's special-occasion and heirloom jewelry, teetered on the sturdy animal's back. They'd kept only enough to sustain them through the onslaught of war, and a calculated bit more, to keep any would-be robbers from suspecting they'd hidden the majority of their wealth elsewhere.

He halted a wary distance from the edge of the pit Janusz had fallen into so many years before. Again, Kalman reflected, this old massive hole would play an important part in his life.

Janusz would shudder with remembered horror, but Kalman grinned, allowing a flush of memory involving his youthful shenanigans to chase away the chill of the dark, wet night.

He carefully attached a thin, strong, steel cable to the box, while he slowly lowered it down into the black depths of the pit. Since he worked without a light, he had to strain to hear the telltale sound of the heavy object striking the surface of the water, at least thirty feet down.

It took another twenty feet of cable to reach the bottom. Panting with exhaustion, his arms aching from the weight of the treasure chest, Kalman urged the plow horse to a nearby rocky outcrop and secured the remaining coil temporarily to its halter. The horse simply stood patiently and shook the rain from his mane.

Then Kalman extracted a shovel from the saddlebag and dug a trench from the old mineshaft to the rocks. The mud and rain made the work miserable and slow, but all of his hard-earned wealth and his family's future were at stake, so he persevered. It took a few hours to painstakingly bury the line of cable and then secure the end to the subterranean part of a boulder that seemed to widen the farther down Kalman dug.

No one would accidentally dislodge such a huge stone. And since the rocky outcropping where the boulder lay sat beyond the coal fields, no one would have any reason to remove it. The Kalman family gold would stay well hidden—safer now than in a bank.

The sides of the boulder served as an anchor for the cable. Once finished with the task of reburying it, Kalman leaned against the long-suffering horse and let the downpour wash some of the mud from his hands and clothes.

In the morning, he would instruct Zygmunt to have some of the men move the latrine to cover the pit. The workers wouldn't complain too much, for they would not have to dig a new hole.

He patted the horse's thickly muscled rump and gathered up the reins, pleased with his scheme. Their current latrine hole had almost reached capacity. *Perfect timing*. Nothing would trigger suspicion, and the gold that would pave his family's future would stay protected until the war ended, when he could safely return to retrieve it.

No one in their right mind would think to delve into the horror of a cesspool.

The German army marched through Warsaw and, by early November, camped on the outskirts of Katowice. The Polish army surrendered. The invasion took less than two months.

CHAPTER FIVE

THE PRODIGAL RETURNS

If I am not for myself, who is for me?
And if I am only for myself, what am I?

Hillel, Ethics of the Fathers 1:14

Janusz spent six years sequestered in seminary, studying the Trinity, the history of the Roman Catholic Church, the history of man, the politics of the church, finance, business administration, and accounting. Though the seminary viewed news from the world as a distraction from serious study and prayer, word of the invasion of Poland reached them.

All accounts reported the incursion as bloodless, a political convenience. It made sense, Janusz concluded, for weaker Poland to become a German state. Perhaps the occupation would bring some stability and equity to a government wracked with corruption and scandal.

The accompanying stories of Jewish persecution seemed beyond belief, and Janusz dismissed most as exaggerated church gossip. The roundup of Jews and the formation of fenced Jewish ghettos and concentration camps seemed totally illogical.

Shortly after his ordination, Janusz received his assignment to the parish in Katowice, under Father Dimitri. Janusz offered praise to God, who answered his prayers.

The travel office in the Vatican prepared his transport to Poland with apparent ease. Perhaps he worried needlessly about the fearful rumors involving his native country.

He arrived at night at the old stone train station in Katowice and stepped down from the rail car wearing his black priest's robe. Several German soldiers stood on the platform but showed no interest in a young clergyman disembarking.

With no one to meet him, Janusz walked the familiar track into the city. Katowice looked somber and gray in the darkness. Many of the businesses had boarded-up windows and doors—the result of change, he supposed. The nearly-vacant streets had few illuminated windows to puncture the darkness.

Had the city changed, or had he? Some of both, he suspected.

Katowice, unlike Rome, had never grown into a thriving cosmopolitan city. Instead, they boasted only a blue-gray, industrial, time-worn community for the working man, with few fountains and no statues of David. Here, simple men and women had lived and worked for centuries with little notice from the outside world.

But Janusz knew God had noticed. He burned with the excitement and conviction that God had not only chosen this place for his birth, but also for his service. Katowice may not have the Roman ambiance, but then, neither did Bethlehem.

In his pocket he carried a leave paper granting him a month's time before reporting to Father Dimitri. Janusz wanted to go everywhere, see everyone, do everything, but he knew what he had to do first. Six years had passed since his father had taken him to the train station for his trip to Rome. He felt eager for the comfort and smell of home, and he quickened his pace.

A German patrol car rumbled by. The occupants gave him barely a fleeting glance.

Janusz sped up as the old apartment building came into view. It looked more rundown than when he'd left, but still, it hadn't really changed.

The same creaking stairs seemed to welcome him home. With a flush of remembered youthful embarrassment, he tread quietly past Wladislaw's door, wondering if Mrs. Romanov still harangued Jews at the top of her shrill voice.

Nostalgia tickled his stomach and pricked his eyes with moisture as he stood before the door to his parents' apartment. Paint had peeled and chipped off, revealing different colors chosen by the landlords over the years. He took a deep breath, then lifted his hand.

Janusz knocked. No response. He tried the knob. Locked. Then, he knocked until his knuckles ached, calling out to his mother and father. Finally, the door inched open. Janusz's father had changed. His eyes were dark and weary, and his uncombed hair had turned snow white.

"Father," Janusz breathed, "it is your son."

His aged parent grabbed him, pulled him inside and wept.

They sat by the light of a single candle in the living room, once filled with religious icons, now bare and gray. Janusz gave his father two oranges he had brought from Rome, then watched while he turned one about in his long fingers. "I've not eaten an orange in three years," he whispered. He set it carefully on the kitchen counter. "Your mother and I will enjoy them."

Janusz followed his father to Theresa's room where she lay silently in bed. Most of her hair had fallen out. She appeared gaunt and frail, and clasped a rosary to her breast.

He kissed a pale cheek. "It is Janusz, Mother." She simply stared at him and fingered her prayer beads.

Stanislav touched Janusz's shoulder and motioned his head toward the door, saying softly, "She hasn't spoken in a few years now."

Janusz covered his mother's hand with his and prayed for her deliverance.

Once back in the uncomfortable living room, Janusz took a deep breath. "Father, my friend Kalman Gold, have you heard from him? I would like to see him."

His father shook his head, and his dark eyes dulled. In the flickering light from the fat candle, he seemed to further age. "I heard he and his family were picked up recently, but I don't know where they were taken. Probably one of the ghettos. A German major now runs the mine."

Janusz exhaled, feeling a sense of impending doom close in upon him. All the rumors he'd discounted as outrageous exaggerations seemed to be true. The terrible reality weighed heavy on his soul. "I must try to find him."

"Jewish sympathizers are not looked on with favor. Some have been shot. It would not be wise for you to go in search of a Jew."

"I'm not searching for a Jew. I'm searching for a friend."

"The Nazis will not quibble over such detail. You are in danger by coming to this house."

Janusz gasped. "But you are Catholic! You haven't been arrested."

The old man nodded. "Remember when you were a child and I helped you put a june bug on a string? I am a bug on a string. The Nazis need me. I am a metallurgist. Someday they will no longer need a metallurgist."

Then his father stood and stretched slowly, showing the strain of the hard work put on his aging frame. "I am just thankful that your aunt and uncle are safely away from here, on their farm out in the country, living as Catholics and not Jews."

He gave Janusz a bear hug and clung to him for a long time, then kissed his temple and trudged off to the other bedroom. Their eyes met for a fraction of a second before he gingerly closed the door behind him.

A sensation of dread and grief struck Janusz at that shared gaze, and he crossed himself.

Sleep did not come easily. Troubling thoughts disturbed Janusz's rest as he lay on the couch in the spartan living room. Why hadn't the church warned him? He couldn't fathom ignorance on their part. Rome had an extensive network of priests, nuns, and loyal Catholics throughout Europe. They had to know. If they knew, why no outcry? Why no protest?

How could Jews be arrested and jailed without trial? How could they lose their homes, their businesses, and their lives without men of God raising a voice in protest? He could come up with no explanation, no reason.

The Church, he believed above all else, was fair. If what his father had told him proved true, then there had to be a reason.

So, not only did he have to search for Kalman and his family, Janusz decided as he reached for sleep; now he had to search for the reason. That reason would reconcile justice and fairness, and also reassure the Jewish blood that surged through his veins. For, although ordained as a priest in the Catholic Church, Janusz was also the son of a Jew. God had made him that, just as God had made him a priest.

Janusz awoke to a kiss on the cheek. Love came through his father's eyes and then he left. It would be easier not saying goodbye. Janusz deeply regretted his presence bringing anxiety to his childhood home.

Intent upon gathering information, and hoping to find some familiar faces, Janusz headed into town. He remembered, fondly, the market at the corners of Witolinska and Grochowska streets in those days before his mother's illness—a smelly, noisy place filled with talk, loud bartering, and endless gossip.

Stalls and canopied carts had lined the streets, overflowing with fresh potatoes and beets, as well as leafy cabbages and big, white onions. In addition to vegetables, seasonal apples, pears and fresh berries were heaped in display baskets within the stands. Beyond the produce sections, farmers had offered chickens, ducks, rabbits and piglets for sale or barter.

Daylight revealed the war-ravished face of Katowice. Though bombs hadn't torn apart the inner city, misery and neglect plagued its silent, gray populace, choking its collective spirit.

I am in a spiritual vacuum, Janusz thought sadly. Had God turned His back on Katowice? The idea unnerved him.

He marched on, trying to ignore the burned-out storefronts, the abandoned shops, the piles of uncollected rubbish, and a German soldier openly urinating in the street.

The marketplace appeared less than a third of its former size. Subdued quiet now replaced the once-bustling atmosphere. Far fewer carts than he remembered lined the streets, and the produce they held looked undersized and sickly.

Janusz noticed something missing—youth. Buyers and sellers were all old—the young men, women and children, gone.

A nagging sense that he could not at first identify plagued him. He stared down the pitiful row of battered stands and broken-down carts, trying to understand what else about the scene bothered his shell-shocked mind. Then it came to him: the hats, the black hats, the yarmulkes, the beards . . . the Jews. The marketplace no longer teemed with them.

Their absence chilled Janusz, as if the birds had suddenly disappeared from the sky—an empty, haunting feeling. Janusz had expected, wanted, craved the familiarity and belonging he'd felt visiting his old stomping grounds, but had found nothing of the sort. The marketplace reflected the spirit of the city: death.

Janusz approached a farmer near a cart of turnips and beets. "I'm looking for a man by the name of Kalman Gold."

"Are you a madman?" the vendor barked. "Get away!"

Another glared at him when he repeated his question, answering, "Do I look like a Jew?"

Then a man wheeling a crate of chickens whispered sadly, "There are no Jews here."

Janusz paused in his meandering search, encouraged by the third, less aggressive response. "Where are they?" But the wizened and bent man simply stared at him with eyes that had beheld decades of hard work and suffering.

"Don't ask," a passerby mumbled.

Janusz's questions brought rebukes, stern warnings or icy stares. Finally, he bought a potato and walked away in despair.

A half block from the marketplace, as he chomped on the potato, an old woman with a kind face, lined with age, touched his arm. She wore a print dress covered with a well-worn, handmade apron, and had pulled her hair into a bun at the back of her head.

"Follow me," she whispered and kept walking.

He obeyed, enacting a casual stroll after her, at a distance, until she turned into the front of a weathered apartment building. A mix of boiling cabbage and fermenting garbage filled the air as Janusz climbed the stairs. One the second floor, the old woman waited at an open door.

Janusz stepped inside. Rags and straw served as a makeshift bed in a far corner of the small and humble room. A big yellow cat looked up at him as the woman closed the door.

She motioned him to a rickety chair. "You are looking for Kalman Gold?"

"Yes. Who are you?"

She murmured, "Sit down and I will tell you what I know."

Janusz sat and watched while she went about making tea at a small sink.

She carried a tray with two cups, placed it on the table, and sat opposite him in an old rocking chair. "My son, Gregory, worked at the coal mine before the Germans took it.

"Now, he works in the fields. My Gregory saw Kalman Gold in a line of men, returning from a labor camp to Ghetto Lodz. He told me he hardly recognized Kalman, for he'd lost weight and looked so much older. But Gregory did remember him."

51

Janusz leaned forward, causing the old chair to creak. "How long ago was this?"

The woman held up a hand, quieting him. "When the line of men paused, Gregory snuck a loaf of bread to Kalman when the guards were not watching. And he was able to find out that Tova, Rachel and David are still alive."

"Why are you telling me this?"

"I used to be the housekeeper for the Golds. They were good to me. I loved their children. They were like my own grandchildren. I was sorry when I heard they had been taken."

"And when was this?" Janusz asked a second time, trying to rein in his impatience.

"Yesterday. Gregory came to see me after working the fields in Lodz. He said the foreman from the mine, a man called Zygmunt, was also in Lodz."

Janusz stood and put a gentle hand on the old woman's thin shoulder. "May God bless your courage for helping me."

He returned to the street, consumed with thoughts of locating his friends. Apparently, the Germans had forcibly taken both Kalman and Zygmunt from their homes and left them in Lodz, now a Jewish ghetto.

The fact that they'd also rounded up Zygmunt truly shocked Janusz. Since Zygmunt and his family had never practiced Judaism, and because of the Pilarskis' big stature, most people did not know their Jewish heritage. Even during the trial, Kalman had written that the court had dubbed Zygmunt a Jewish sympathizer, but not a Jew.

Janusz felt a sickening jolt of dread. *And what of Uncle Zidov and Aunt Tania? Are they safe? Has Zidov's shocking decision to hide in the country as Polish farmers really protected them?* Janusz had received only a few letters from Tania, which had mostly dealt with her concern about whether or not he ate properly.

A grim sense of foreboding and urgency enveloped Janusz. He had to get to Kalman and Zygmunt before anything else could befall them. At least he knew they were still alive and healthy enough to do hard labor for the Nazis. He thanked God for sending Kalman's old housekeeper into his path with her vital message.

Janusz patted the leave papers in his inner jacket pocket. God had brought him home for a deeper purpose, one beyond simply returning to the church and the religious mentor of his childhood. He prayed he would be up to the challenge and turned his steps toward the city of Lodz.

With no other option for transportation, Janusz walked. The trek took him through the city and out across the stone arch bridge. He smiled, remembering the night he and Kalman had crossed the bridge on their way to the then-abandoned coal mines. It seemed half a lifetime ago.

It felt good to leave the dismal city. At least in the countryside, evidence of the German occupation seemed less foreboding. But then he heard the approach of heavy trucks.

Janusz stepped off the road and turned to look. Several big trucks roared past, escorted by a military passenger vehicle carrying an officer and a soldier armed with a machine gun. Guards sat on the rear gates of the canvas-covered vehicles, holding rifles. Behind the guards, in each of the trucks, Janusz spotted the Jews—shaven bald heads and tattered clothes, although many still had beards. Their eyes, still bright and searching, said they were not yet defeated.

Janusz stared as the trucks swept by. Dust billowed around him, turning his black robe gray. Exhaust fumes teased his nostrils. The heat of the engines reached his face. He felt powerless and impotent.

How many men that he'd known while growing up now sat in those trucks? Was Kalman among them?

He raised a hand and waved at the collection of dark eyes looking out from the back of the last truck. None of the shaved occupants acknowledged him, but a uniformed German soldier shifted his rifle and returned the friendly gesture, making Janusz feel naïve and foolish.

When the trucks disappeared around a distant bend, Janusz resumed the dusty journey toward the coal mines, which lay on the route to Lodz. He coughed and sneezed, but did not lessen his pace, driven by determination and fear.

Kalman Gold's strip mining operation finally came into view. If Janusz had not seen the Star Coal Mining sign, he would not have recognized the place.

Tons of dug-up earth lay pushed aside. Large, steam powered diggers and conveyer belts had replaced Kalman's army of workers. A complex of office buildings, equipment sheds and bins dotted the rutted landscape. Work continued, but a German staff car, with flags waving in the slight breeze, sat parked among a tangle of trucks, evidencing the hostile change of management.

The bustling mine filled Janusz with a mix of joy and sadness. He felt immensely proud of Kalman's accomplishment, but bitter and disappointed to see that the Germans had taken it from his best friend.

Janusz walked on, deliberately turning his eyes from the sight, and saw the big plow horse grazing on a tether near an open gate to the mine fields. He stopped in his tracks and stared. A flood of memories washed over him. Tears flooded Janusz's eyes, for he believed God had left the animal as a sign for him.

The horse, as if sensing his gaze, raised its head to look at him. A distinctive white blaze down the center of its face erased the last vestiges of doubt.

"Thank you, Lord." Janusz smiled and walked to the horse.

The big animal had friendly eyes. Janusz patted its neck and untied it, glancing continually at the mine office. With no one in sight, he grabbed a handful of mane and swung up on the horse's back.

"Come on, boy. It's our turn to pull Kalman out of a pit."

Janusz passed through the destroyed and abandoned villages of Chorzow and Sosnowiec. Only skinny, hungry dogs and cats roamed the streets of the ghost towns.

Smoke still curled from razed homes, evidence of deliberately-set fires and exploded bombs. Unburied bodies and partial human skeletons littered the parched ground.

Janusz wept as he murmured prayers for the dead. The horror of the scene so overwhelmed him, he didn't even know what words he spoke, but hoped whatever prayers he uttered brought peace to the souls of the deceased. Nothing in his training had prepared him for such monstrosities. Even Father Dimitri, in his quiet wisdom, could not have guided Janusz through this hellish journey.

As darkness settled, Janusz took refuge in an abandoned building marked by an old sign: *Gornicza Mail Service*. He tied the horse to the rail of a three-step staircase leading to the main entrance.

Heavy footsteps came from behind, and a distinct German accent asked in broken Polish, "Where do you think you're going?"

Janusz turned to find a tall, young lieutenant with blue eyes and blonde hair pulling a medium-sized pistol from its holster.

He pointed the gun at Janusz, hands shaking slightly.

Janusz replied with feigned confidence, "I was telegraphed to serve at the Lodz concentration camp."

The young German re-holstered his sidearm. "Passport and travel permit."

Janusz dug deeply into his black robe to pull out his passport.

The German inspected the documents, then looked up.

Janusz pretended a continued search for a travel permit he didn't have. Sweat formed and ran down the small of his back. His mouth went dry and his pulse pounded in his ears.

The German seemed to lose interest when the glow from his flashlight dimmed on the passport. He pushed it toward Janusz.

"I better not to see you here in the morning, Priest," the lieutenant said, and then disappeared into the darkness.

Relieved, but shaken, Janusz entered the building. He found plenty of room on a hay-padded floor and brought the horse inside with him, for both company and safekeeping.

Sleep again would not come, and he tried to imagine what lay ahead for him. He couldn't fathom life continuing with such fear and hatred.

Where did a priest fit into such a world? Where was the church in the lives of the people? Could one believe in God and live in fear? Somehow he, a man born a Jew, but ordained as a Roman Catholic priest, must make a difference.

Then his thoughts turned to his enslaved friends. Where was Kalman? Had he lost hope? Were Tova and the twins separated from the work parties? How would he find them?

He prayed that Zygmunt kept his slow-to-ignite temper under control. Kalman's big foreman could not afford to stand up for his friends, as he had when he'd landed in jail. The goodhearted Big Z would wind up getting shot for his bravery.

Janusz gave up trying to sleep and opened his eyes. The plow horse's bulky shadow filled the other end of the room. Seeing it and hearing its heavy, steady breath brought Janusz a large measure of comfort. He had the horse God had given him. And since God gave him a horse, it surely meant that Janusz had some places to go.

The sharp crack of a gunshot pierced the night and jarred Janusz out of a light doze. It seemed a distance away, but unmistakable.

Janusz froze. *My God, what has happened to the world?*

He lay awake until dawn's first light, then set out again.

It took Janusz five bone-weary days to reach the outskirts of the city of Lodz.

The horse's sweaty bare back had worn his thighs raw, but he gave thanks for having reliable and familiar transportation. He rode into the center of the city and found a sign identifying the local Gestapo.

Janusz said a silent prayer for courage, tied the horse, and walked into the building, trying not to tremble.

A reception clerk greeted him with bored indifference. Speaking confidently in fluent German, Janusz asked for the colonel in charge of the Lodz ghetto.

The clerk picked up the phone and spoke quickly into the handset. He then directed Janusz to room 118. "Herr Gunther Haas will receive you, Father."

Armed Germans filled the area, but they ignored Janusz as he searched for the office.

Janusz found the correct door and knocked loudly. Goose bumps covered his skin, and he nervously adjusted his robes. Why hadn't he rehearsed what he would say?

A deep German voice barked, "Come in."

Janusz opened the door. A man in his fifties, who, despite baggy uniformed pants on his six-foot frame, couldn't hide his three-hundred-plus pounds, stood staring out the window with his back to the door. His mountainous figure cast an enormous shadow as the sunlight poured through the window into the office.

A humbly-dressed young woman mopped the floor just inside the threshold.

Janusz stepped into the room. She darted a quick glance at him and then went back to her task.

Haas kept his back to Janusz. "What do you want?"

Janusz took a moment to compose himself. Then, in a steady voice, he said, "Herr Colonel, I have come to discuss a mistaken identity. A family of four was taken to the Ghetto Lodz. The Golds. They are not Jewish. They are Pollacks, such as myself. They were loaded on a train in Katowice because their papers were lost. I beg your help. They do not belong here."

The colonel turned around. His cheeks were puffy and red, probably from too much alcohol, his squinty eyes gray and cold.

He pointed a pudgy finger at Janusz, drew in a breath and, in a sarcastic tone, said, "The Golds? You idiot! That does not sound very Polish." An ugly smile creased his face. "I'll give you two hours to leave town. If I find you anywhere in the city after that, you will be hanged. Now, get out!"

Janusz took a step back, shocked that an officer would treat a man of the cloth in such a way. Did the Nazis have no respect for the Church? He could not form words to reply, and just stood there staring at the crude man.

The colonel narrowed his eyes on Janusz, obviously amused by his affect on a young priest. Then the brute looked toward the girl. "You too. You smell like a goat. And have my strudel sent up. With hot tea!" When she didn't move immediately, he shouted, "Get out!"

The girl took the mop and bucket and hurried toward the door. "Yes, Herr Colonel."

Janusz held the door for the girl, then followed her out. Hanging from the end of a rope would help no one. He silently damned himself for not formulating a better plan. Defeat hounded his steps as he walked through the miserable town.

He stopped at a grassy field beside the road, two kilometers outside the oppressive city, to allow the big horse to graze. Propped on an elbow beside the animal, Janusz tried to decide what to do.

The approach of a horse-drawn cart drew him out of his depression. Two men rode on it. Farmers, he concluded—men his age. They posed no threat to him. He would offer a wave as they passed.

They surprised him by stopping.

"Good morning," Janusz said, pushing to his feet.

The smaller of the two pulled a revolver from beneath his coat. "Raise your hands and turn around, Priest." He pointed the gun at Janusz's face.

Janusz sighed and obeyed. *Is there no good remaining in the world?* "I have no money," he said, raising his arms.

"Shut up," the man ordered. "Don't move, or I will kill you."

Janusz stood rigid as someone pulled his arms behind his back and bound them tightly. Then a dusty, heavy sack came down over his head and shoulders.

One of the men took him by the arm. "Move."

"My horse," Janusz pleaded.

"Get the horse," a voice said.

They loaded Janusz onto the cart and covered him with what felt like a tangle of potato sacks. "Don't make a sound, and don't try to get away."

The ride lasted over an hour before bumping to a stop. The men uncovered Janusz and pulled him off the cart, but kept the sack over his head. They lead him down about ten steps to a door which, when opened, released a draft of cool air.

A basement, Janusz guessed.

Voices and movement filled the room.

Someone pushed Janusz down into a chair.

A gruff voice came from right beside him. "You came to Lodz seeking a Polish family in a Jewish ghetto? Who are you, Priest, other than a fool?"

"I am Father Janusz Dov. I can tell you nothing more."

"Can you tell us where you stole your horse?"

"I can only tell you the horse belongs to a friend."

"And that friend would be Kalman Gold?"

Janusz stiffened. His heart raced with fear. Had his foolish rescue attempt put Kalman in even greater danger? "My name is Father Janusz Dov. I cannot tell you more."

"Untie him."

Janusz swallowed hard, certain they planned to shoot him. Someone yanked the potato sack off. Janusz squinted in the dim light of the basement. Five men surrounded him. The face of the biggest of the five finally came into focus.

Janusz cried with joy, "Zygmunt!" He thought his heart would burst in his chest.

His childhood friend grabbed Janusz in a bear hug, slapping him on the back. "I hope we didn't frighten you too much, Janusz! But we have to be careful."

"I have to admit, my heart is beating fast!"

"You're lucky the Germans didn't cut it out. Walking into the Gestapo office and asking for a Jew."

The others laughed.

Janusz clasped Zygmunt's beefy, callused hand. "How did you know?"

"The cleaning girl. She's one of us."

"One of you?"

"The underground," Zygmunt said proudly. "Not all Poles are German puppies."

"Zygmunt, I need help," Janusz pleaded. "Kalman, his wife and children, are in the Lodz ghetto! We've got to get them out."

Zygmunt nodded. "Kalman is a good man. But, if he is here, we must act quickly. When was he arrested?"

"Two, three days ago. I'm not sure. His housekeeper's son saw him in Lodz on a work gang."

"Lodz is crowded with Jews," Zygmunt muttered as he began to pace. "Even the efficient Nazi processing center cannot keep up. Many are being kept in abandoned buildings. Maybe the family is still together. Our informants will tell us."

Janusz frowned at the silent men watching Zygmunt pace. "Informants? How do you get information from the Germans?"

"There are many Polish girls like the one you saw in that pig Haas's office this morning. They have what the Germans want. We get what we want."

Janusz felt ill. "My God."

Zygmunt spoke again, "On the east side of Lodz, near an old synagogue, there's a deserted house. It has green shutters. We'll meet you there tomorrow."

"But the colonel said if I didn't leave Lodz he would hang me."

Zygmunt grabbed Janusz by the shoulders and looked deep into his eyes. "Worse things could happen to you." Then he stepped back and flashed a cagy grin. "Don't worry about the colonel. His memory is about as long as his Aryan dick."

Snickers filled the room.

Janusz, embarrassed, felt his cheeks flush, but he managed, "Shall I take the horse?"

"Leave the horse. It will be taken care of. We have plenty of carrots." Zygmunt patted Janusz on the shoulder.

Once outside again, Janusz patted the horse fondly and said goodbye before heading toward Camp Lodz on foot.

"You'll be there by nightfall," Zygmunt called after him.

Late afternoon and six miles into his trek, Janusz spotted a dusty column of emaciated-looking men approaching from the distance.

Wiser from his journey, he ducked behind a thick stand of brush and watched.

Led by armed Nazi guards and SS officers, they came close to him before turning to enter a wide, gated compound.

A labor camp, Janusz guessed. He crept closer, keeping his head down and using a slight hillock to hide his presence.

A high, wire fence with "DANGER" signs posted every few yards surrounded the camp. Janusz stared at the odd warnings, then realized it was an electric fence.

As he watched the silent procession of shaved heads file inside, an agonized cry came from its midst. "I can't take this . . . I can't take this anymore!"

One of the officers barked an order to halt, and the column stopped. At another sharp command, a frail, stooped man staggered forward, stepping out from the ranks.

The officer shouted, "Put the dogs on the mouthy one."

Even from a distance, Janusz could hear the malice in the man's tone.

Two guards leading four black Dobermans approached the pitiful old man. In a panic, the prisoner bolted toward the fence.

Janusz watched in stunned silence. Every muscle in his body strained wire tight. Automatically, he began to recite the last rites, recognizing the prisoner's approaching doom.

The old man jumped onto the fence as high as he could. The instant flesh touched metal, a cracking, popping sound ripped through the silence, and sparks arced at his feet and hands. His body shook and convulsed as the voltage surged through him.

Sizzling flesh sent vapor curling away on the breeze. His lips parted in a scream, but no sound came. A wisp of smoke emitted from his open mouth as his lungs burned inside him. Finally, he fell in a heap at the base of the fence.

The guards released the Dobermans. The dogs rushed the dead man, snarling and barking. A horrible, gut-wrenching melee of biting, tearing, and ripping followed, as flesh came away from bone.

Janusz choked on the final prayer, completing his duty, and lifted his crucifix to his lips. Then he turned away, feeling pieces of his soul torn from him with each bit of the man's body.

He threw up along the side the road.

CHAPTER SIX

WALKING IN FIRE

Whoever saves one life, it is as if he saved the entire world.

Mishna Sanhedrin 4:5

As Janusz neared the center of the city, he saw armed soldiers everywhere. He hated them. He tried not to, and attempted to cure his hatred with prayer, concentrating on the good, but found nothing good to focus upon. He hated them. Even knowing that his hatred made him no better than they didn't seem to matter. He hated them just the same.

Many of Lodz's buildings lay in a state of destruction from recent air raids, and he saw with regret that a bomb had completely demolished the town's once-beautiful Catholic church, The Resurrection.

Janusz continued on, keeping to the shadows like a thief.

Late in the evening, exhausted and mind-numbed, Janusz finally found the deserted, green-shuttered house in the eastern part of Lodz. He hadn't seen another living human being for nearly an hour. The stench of rotting flesh choked the air. Sporadic gunfire, punctured by screams, sounded in the distance and echoed through the buildings. Huge rats and skinny dogs scurried in and out of hiding—worse than hell itself.

Janusz crept along the lengthening shadows, checking every possible hiding place for enemy soldiers. After several minutes of breathless caution, he hurried into the house and gingerly shut the door on the threatening street.

No signs of recent human habitation showed in the dust and dirt. With a groan, he sat down on the bare floor near a broken window, in what might have once been the family room. Bone-tired and emotionally drained, he quickly fell asleep.

The sound of a car braking to a halt startled Janusz, and he came instantly awake, surprised to find himself curled up on the floor. Daylight filtered in through the broken windows.

His heart hammered in his chest as car doors slammed out front. Then voices and footfalls—the distinct, dull thuds of boots on pavement—sounded right outside. Janusz inched to the edge of the broken window. Careful not to reveal himself, he peered out. What he saw made his heart skip a beat.

A large truck with a canvas canopy displaying a bold, black swastika, along with a Gestapo staff car, sat parked at the curb. Three soldiers in German army uniforms marched toward the front door, talking and joking.

Blood pounded in Janusz's ears. If he ran, he would be shot. If he sat still, he would be shot. Cornered and terrified, not knowing what else to do, Janusz pushed to his feet. "Heavenly Father, deliver me from this evil. I have yet to begin my service to you."

The whispered prayer calmed him, and he straightened his shoulders as he turned to meet his fate. Above all, he was a man of God. He would die with dignity. He braced himself as the door opened and the soldiers stepped inside.

However, rather than shoot him, they simply stood along the walls and stared at him.

An officer, almost as tall and broad as the doorway, crossed over the threshold and turned toward Janusz. Zygmunt smiled beneath the visor of his officer's cap. "Good morning, Herr Janusz. Are you ready to be about the Fuhrer's business?" He gestured to one of the soldiers and the man handed him a uniform.

Janusz gaped at his old friend. Zygmunt wore a fully-decorated Nazi officer's uniform. It took a moment for him to understand, then he surrendered his robe for the uniform of another decorated German officer. He glanced down at his dust-covered clothes and frowned at his grinning friend. "Why make me walk?

"I didn't want to risk you. We had to steal the car. Let's hurry," Zygmunt urged. "The men we borrowed these from may soon be missed."

The staff car, driven by a Polish partisan, carried Zygmunt and Janusz. The truck, carrying four more disguised men, followed close behind as they carefully navigated through the treacherous rubble of the city streets.

Zygmunt turned from the front seat to glance at Janusz, who rode behind him. The big Pollack smiled. "Just like the old days. Remember when we used to play soldier with Kalman?"

"Yes, I remember."

"They will want to see our prisoner transfer papers. We will have to bluff." Zygmunt snapped open the glove box, pulled out a dog-eared manual, and tore out several pages. Then he rifled through the side compartments on the door and extracted an old clipboard.

Once he'd attached the pages from the manual, he turned back to Janusz. "You up to it?"

Janusz felt nauseous with fear, but nodded. "I'm up to it."

As they passed through the outer edges of the city, Zygmunt pointed, and the driver pulled the staff car to the open mouth of a warehouse. A fading sign above the door read "Greenbaum's Furniture Company."

Zygmunt murmured, "This is not a place where decorated officers visit. Our presence should help to unnerve the junior officers in charge."

Tattered and bloodied Jews carried out bodies and stacked the dead onto a furniture truck. A small army of heavily-armed soldiers, many with dogs, surrounded the building. The Germans yelled and cursed the Jews as if engaged in sport.

Janusz clenched his teeth together, forcing himself to remain stoic and silent.

Zygmunt glanced at Janusz and whispered, "They're holding five hundred Jews here. Stay close to me, speak only German . . . and act like an asshole."

Then the reek of the dead and dying reached them. It encompassed them like a toxic, invisible fog.

Squaring his shoulders and lowering the visor of his cap, Zygmunt climbed out of the staff car. Although the papers he carried contained only the instructions on the staff car's maintenance, Zygmunt marched fearlessly into the building.

Janusz followed close behind, hands clasped behind his back in what he hoped emulated a classic military pose.

Zygmunt stopped abruptly, right inside the warehouse doors, and snapped his heels together. Stretching out his arm in the Nazi salute, he barked, "Heil, Hitler!"

Two Nazi guards armed with machine guns, overseeing the removal of the dead, snapped their heels together and returned Zygmunt's salute.

A crush of hundreds of Jews crowding the vast warehouse fell silent and stared.

A young, blond lieutenant marched up to Zygmunt, clearing his throat nervously. He brushed the hair from his forehead, snapped his heels together, and gave a sharp, Nazi salute. "What can I do for you, Herr Captain?"

Zygmunt stared at the mass of prisoners with a convincing look of distaste. "God, they stink." Then he glanced down at the clipboard and ran a finger across the top page. "I am here to pick up a family of four." He returned his attention to the lieutenant and shoved the clipboard under his arm. "The name is Gold. Kalman Gold."

"You have the necessary papers, sir?" the lieutenant asked.

Janusz stepped closer to Zygmunt and whispered in his ear. Zygmunt nodded, keeping his eyes on the waiting lieutenant. "This is taking longer than it should. Do you have a working telephone here?"

The lieutenant paled and his throat worked over a swallow. "No, sir."

Janusz caught Zygmunt's quick, sideways glance, recognizing his cue. He pushed past the flustered lieutenant. His voice boomed out over the silent, shaved heads. "Gold, Kalman Gold!" The name echoed about the warehouse.

All the prisoners stared silently, but no one moved.

Janusz motioned to a nearby soldier. "Come here," he ordered in crisp, flawless German.

"Yes, sir?"

"Go into that cesspool and find me Kalman Gold. Our records show he is here. Either you find me the Jew bastard, and every member of his family, or you're going to take his place in the pit. Do you understand?"

"Yes, sir!" The soldier saluted and then trotted toward the crowd of prisoners, calling out, "Gold family, step forward!"

Zygmunt spat. Then he said to the lieutenant, "Help him. This stench is killing me."

The lieutenant clicked his heels and dipped his head, then strode to a group of soldiers patrolling the outer edges of the warehouse.

Several guards headed toward the prisoners, taking different directions in a crude search grid. They moved through the crowd, pushing, shoving, kicking and calling out, "Gold, Kalman Gold!"

Small children whimpered, and their parents quickly hushed them.

One of the guards motioned toward the midst of the crowd. He pushed inward, knocking men, women, and children aside, and shouted, "You, Gold! Come here, immediately, or I will kill you with my bare hands!"

Fear gnawed at the pit of Janusz's stomach. He held his breath and prayed, *Please, God, please.*

Then he spotted Kalman, but barely recognized his old friend. Kalman's head had been shaved, and he looked gaunt and filthy. Janusz pulled his Nazi uniform cap low over his eyes, fearing recognition and exposure.

Kalman moved hesitantly toward the guard, Tova, his wife, to his right. The children, Rachel and David, cowered behind their parents. Kalman kept his eyes down, never looking at the Nazi closing on him.

Thick silence surrounded the singled-out family as the guard shoved and kicked Kalman toward the entrance. Then the uniformed brute grabbed Tova and yanked her forward, ripping her dress and exposing a breast. Tova cried out as she shielded both breasts with her arms. With her head shaved, Tova looked like a lamb being led to slaughter.

The children still had their hair, looking almost normal, and were crying and holding onto each other as the guard took their parents. A second guard grabbed Rachel and David and dragged them toward Janusz and Zygmunt. The moment the guards released them, the children rushed to their mother, sobbing.

The Golds stood in front of Zygmunt, shaking with fear. Kalman and Tova kept their eyes down. Tova urgently shushed Rachel and David as they clung to her.

Zygmunt drew back a gloved fist and struck Kalman hard in the face. Tova screamed and the children shrieked as Kalman went down hard. Zygmunt drew a Lugar pistol and aimed it at Kalman's head. Tova pushed the twins aside and threw herself on Kalman, shielding her husband with her body.

Janusz stepped up to Zygmunt and grabbed his hand. He spoke in rapid German, "Herr, Captain, Colonel Haas will be unhappy if they die here. He has questions for them."

Zygmunt curled up his lip, nodded, and holstered the pistol. With a glance, he signaled to the other partisans, who had watched from the waiting truck. His men quickly gathered Kalman from the floor and dragged him to the back of the truck, herding the children and Tova behind him.

After they'd secured the Golds and placed them under the false guard, Zygmunt clicked his heels together, shot out his arm, and barked, "Heil, Hitler!"

The lieutenant and several warehouse guards returned the salute.

Zygmunt pivoted and marched toward the staff car, where he said gruffly to the driver, "Get me out of this stench."

The engine revved and the car moved away. Zygmunt gave a cavalier wave in the direction of the building, but stared straight ahead, toward the open road.

Janusz climbed into the back of the stolen German truck as it pulled away. He moved to a bench directly across from the Golds.

Kalman wiped the blood from his swollen lip and huddled with his wife and children. They trembled like frightened rabbits.

"Kalman," Janusz said softly.

Kalman flinched, but didn't lift his eyes.

"Kalman, it is me, Janusz. Zygmunt and I came for you."

Kalman hunched his shoulders, still staring at the floor boards, and didn't answer.

Janusz reached across to lay a hand on his friend's shoulder. "It's all right, Kalman. We are taking you and your family to safety. Neither of us will die in a pit."

Kalman slowly raised his eyes and squinted at Janusz. Many years had gone by since they'd seen each other, but in the dim light in the back of the truck, Janusz watched recognition dawn in his friend's gaze. But then Kalman stared at the Nazi medals on Janusz's chest, and his fearful expression returned. He looked at the other uniformed men, who sat closer to the cab of the truck, and hissed in a shallow breath.

Janusz kept his voice calm and gentle. "They are Zygmunt's men. They are Poles. The uniforms are stolen."

Kalman leaned forward, tears in his eyes. He spoke just barely above a whisper. "Janusz? Is it really you, Janusz?"

"Yes, Kalman, it's really me." Janusz threw his arms around Kalman and sobbed.

"Oh, my God! Janusz . . . Zygmunt . . . thank you! Thank you, God! Thank you! I've never been happier to see anyone in my life!"

Kalman turned to his wife and cried, "Tova, It's Janusz! And Zygmunt! They came to save us!"

Tova grabbed Janusz's hand and kissed it. "Janusz! I can't believe it! Thank you, thank you!" Tears poured down her face.

The children stared with wide eyes from their weeping parents to Janusz, and back. They huddled together, cringing away from Janusz.

Kalman wrapped them in his arms. "It's okay, children. We're safe! This is Janusz, the best friend I've ever had. You were too young to remember him when he left for Rome, but I have told you many stories about him."

Janusz reached out and touched their filthy cheeks. They drew away from his touch in fear. "We are friends, children; we always will be."

The driver called back, "Resume the act! We are coming to Lodz. Janusz, hold your pistol on Kalman."

Janusz quickly drew his gun, grabbed Kalman by the front of his tattered shirt, and shoved the short barrel into Kalman's neck. He whispered, "Forgive me, my friend, but we must pretend a little longer."

He glanced over at Tova, who'd stiffened and clutched the twins, one in each arm. She nodded, wide-eyed and grim, and spoke softly to the children, who'd begun to whimper again.

The truck passed the Lodz reception center, where hundreds of shaved prisoners stood in segregated lines—men in one, women and children in another. Germans with dogs, guns and clubs surrounded them, patrolling. Several of the outer guards shouted to Zygmunt's small convoy, and the driver of Janusz's truck responded in guttural German, as if trading good-natured barbs.

The other Pole, riding shotgun, lifted a hand to the Lodz guards and turned halfway toward the back, speaking in an aside. "Janusz, give them a show."

Janusz waited until the outside guards could see into the truck, then shouted at Kalman in German, "Shut up, you stinking Jew dog! Don't make me waste a bullet on you!"

Tova shrieked and the children wailed. Kalman shuddered and said hoarsely, "Please, do not kill us! I will do anything! Please!"

The Lodz guards jeered and laughed, egging Janusz on. A ripple of movement ran through the prison camp as the shaved heads turned in the direction of the road. Janusz released Kalman and backhanded him across the cheek, knocking him against the side of the truck.

Finally, they rounded a corner and drove out of sight of the reception center. Janusz holstered the pistol and crossed himself, then looked at Kalman with tears in his eyes, unable to speak an apology.

Kalman righted himself on the bench and gave Janusz a crooked smile. "Is this what they taught you in Rome, Father Dov?"

Tova sobbed, hugging the twins tightly. "He is our angel, Kalman, our miracle." She kissed the children and leaned toward Kalman to kiss his dirty cheek. "God has indeed blessed you, my love, for saving the life of a priest—and with a stolen horse."

Aaron Ross stood in the long line of men, waiting for processing. Every once in a while he caught a glimpse of his wife and son clinging to each other among the women and children. A dreadful silence filled the camp, numbing his spirit. Death hung low over the Jews.

He barely registered a commotion at the edges of the camp, by the road, but turned with the others and stared at the Nazi staff car leading a canvas-covered truck. Aaron vaguely noted the massive German officer in the lead car before his attention strayed to the truck. An armed Nazi soldier had a bald prisoner by the neck and held a gun to his head.

A woman shrieked beside the doomed man, and Aaron thought he heard children crying. It took him a moment to recognize Kalman Gold pleading for his life. Horror choked Aaron. The woman and children must be Tova and the twins.

The truck slipped from view, and Aaron held his breath, listening for a gunshot—which would have meant Kalman's death—but heard nothing. He said a prayer for his friend and partner, then turned back with the others in his line.

The Nazis ordered the Jewish women to disrobe—his wife, Dina, among them. More soldiers strode down the line, separating the children from their mothers as they went. Screams shredded the grim silence.

Aaron craned his neck, searching for Dina and Stefan. Through the chaos he managed to spot his family, but armed guards aimed rifles at the men, keeping the male prisoners separated and in line, helplessly watching.

A Polish attendant jerked Stefan from the arms of his naked mother. "Mommy, Mommy!" the boy cried.

Tears ran down Aaron's face. He bit into his lip until it bled as he watched his son disappear into a gray building. Women wailed for their children as the guards herded them into another building.

Aaron inched along with the movement of the line. The Nazis ordered them to undress. Polish men gathered the discarded clothing into old produce wagons pulled by farm horses.

It started to rain. Many tilted up their faces and drank. The line snaked through a door marked "Infirmary."

Finally, Aaron stood naked in front of a man dressed in a white tunic, with a nametag that read "Dr. Mengele." The doctor's gaze swept over Aaron with cold professionalism, then stopped for a long moment on Aaron's genitals. He walked around Aaron as if gauging a horse for sale, before speaking to an assistant holding a clipboard. "A nice specimen for a Jew. Very masculine, virile. Exactly what we need for our virility and castration experiments. Schedule him."

CHAPTER SEVEN

SECRETS AND LIES

*A righteous person knows the oppression of the poor but
an evil person will not comprehend such knowledge.*

Proverbs 29:7

At dusk, the stolen Nazi truck pulled off the road and parked behind the staff car. Janusz watched Kalman and his family sleeping peacefully—no doubt the first real rest they'd had since their capture and internment.

He put a finger to his lips before the others could make a sound. They all understood, and quietly crept outside to stretch and converse.

Zygmunt peered inside, smiled, and helped Janusz down from the truck. Then he pointed toward the dim lights of Katowice. "Many in Katowice know of the Golds and their arrest. They'll find no refuge there."

Janusz sighed and stared at the city of his birth. "What will happen when the Germans realize there has been an escape?"

Zygmunt shook his head and put a big hand on Janusz's shoulder. "The Nazis will hunt them, either until they find them or until the war is over. They are unrelenting, and do not suffer humiliation easily."

Janusz nodded. "We must hide them carefully, and, perhaps, separately. The Nazis will be searching for a family of four."

"Yes, I believe you are right. But you will be the one to tell them, not me." Zygmunt squeezed Janusz's shoulder and strolled into the trees.

A couple of his men followed, leaving Janusz alone with his thoughts. To save Kalman's family, he would have to tear it apart. *God help me.*

He thought perhaps Aunt Tania and Uncle Zidov might take David, and he could ask the Mother Superior at The Blessed Virgin Catholic Convent to take Rachel. He had worked with Mother Regina before going to seminary. She had been strict and firm, but also kind and generous. He hoped to convince the formidable Mother Superior to accept the child into the orphanage.

Then he remembered his schoolmate, Wladislaw, and that he now lived in Rodomsko. Perhaps he would take in Kalman and Tova.

When Zygmunt returned, he mentioned their old friend.

"I never took kindly to him, but Kalman did give him a job at the mines. So, I think he will help. Let's give it a try."

Janusz added, "I have relatives who would be willing to take David, and feel certain I can hide Rachel in the convent."

"Okay, then." Zygmunt called for the others. "Let's go!"

Janusz moved slowly, contemplating the magnitude of what they'd accomplished, and all still to come. He climbed into the truck and smiled at Kalman and Tova, now awake. The twins slept, even when the truck bumped and jerked back onto the road.

As they moved along, Janusz leaned close to the couple. "The Germans will be searching for you the moment they realize they've been duped. Zygmunt believes they will never give up the hunt. We must hide you for a long time."

Janusz let his gaze fall on the beautiful children, curled up together. What he had to say hurt deeply. He looked Kalman in the eye. "They will be searching for a family of four . . . with twin children. We must take the children from you, and also," he paused, "we must separate them."

Kalman closed his eyes. Tova gasped, and quickly covered her mouth with her hand.

Janusz continued, "I feel sure the convent in Katowice will shelter Rachel. I will keep an eye on her, and she will be safe."

When neither parent responded, Janusz asked Kalman, "Do you remember my Aunt Tania and Uncle Zidov, Kalman?"

His friend nodded, and Janusz said softly, "Zidov had the sense to move to the country and become a farmer, posing as a Catholic. He is built like Zygmunt, and has been successful in his pretense. I hope to convince them to take in David. He will be safe, away from the city, on a farm."

Tova sobbed quietly and murmured, "They have never been separated, Kalman. They are closer even than most twins."

Kalman pulled her into his arms while staring at Janusz. "Any twins will generate suspicion, my love, especially twins without a mother and father. I cannot think of anyone more kind than Janusz's aunt and uncle. They will treat our David as if he were their own son."

He sighed, then nodded to Janusz. "A convent is the safest place for my darling Rachel. But, I think, for their sakes, do not tell them of their separation until it is upon them. It will be hard enough at that time. There is no need to panic them now."

Janusz sat back on the bench across from them and fingered his rosary. Once more, his gaze slid to the angelic children. "I intend to hide you with Wladislaw Romanov. Zygmunt tells me you gave him a job when he was in need."

Kalman straightened and his eyes flared with life. "Yes! He will surely remember that kindness. His mother had just lost the family bakery, and they were starving." Then he bent over and grabbed the hem of his pants. "I have a little money sewn in here. It will help him pay for two more mouths to feed. It will lessen the burden."

Janusz smiled, feeling suddenly that things would work out all right.

After another six miles, the two German vehicles swung onto a farm. Everyone climbed out and stretched. The other Poles who'd helped in the rescue said soft "good lucks" and "good nights" as they ambled away and disappeared around one of the buildings.

Zygmunt arranged for a young woman to drive Janusz and the Golds the rest of the way in an old flatbed truck. He nodded at Tova, ruffled David's hair, and gestured for the Golds to climb into the back of the truck.

The big ex-coal-mine foreman hugged Kalman tightly and slapped his back, reminiscent of the old days. "The Germans will be looking for these two vehicles," he said, indicating the canvas-covered truck and staff car. "It's best to make a clean break."

Tova whispered something to Zygmunt before catching Kalman's hand, allowing her husband to pull her up. Janusz and Zygmunt handed over the two children.

The driver immediately set to work. She covered the family with a worn tarp and scattered potatoes on top, making it look as if the produce had fallen out of the baskets.

Janusz stepped behind a nearby tree and changed out of the Nazi uniform with a heartfelt sigh of relief. When he finished dressing, he handed the uniform to Zygmunt as if it were made of hot coals.

He and Zygmunt walked to the front of the truck, where they just stared at each other for a long moment. Pain filled Janusz as he shook Zygmunt's hand and kissed his cheek.

He wondered if he would ever see his large, brave friend again, and murmured, "May God go with you."

Zygmunt smiled. "I don't think God visits many of the places we go."

Janusz shook his head and cupped Zygmunt's cheek. "He is everywhere, my friend."

He climbed in next to the young woman, feeling apprehensive and overwhelmed. She shifted into gear, and the old farm truck groaned forward. As they rounded a bend in the dirt road, he looked back and waved.

Zygmunt lifted a hand in a final farewell.

The long ride to Radomsko followed a network of little-used back roads—at times, as small as cow paths—filled with potholes. Janusz raised his feet as they crossed deep streams, and held his breath as they rounded steep, narrow, rock-strewn passes. He could only imagine how the Golds felt, bumping along, hidden under the heavy potatoes.

They arrived at the Romanov house, just outside Radomsko, well after midnight. The girl stopped the truck a short distance away and turned to Janusz. "I will wait for you here, Father."

Janusz nodded and stepped down from the truck.

A stand of trees masked the house from the road, but through them, Janusz could see a light glowing in a window. He climbed the slightly rickety stairs to the front porch and knocked.

Wladislaw opened the door after three knocks. He held a club in one hand. His cold eyes swept over Janusz, then searched the empty night.

Many years had passed since Janusz had seen Wladislaw, and he barely recognized the short, dumpy man with dark, greasy, gray-streaked hair. "Wladislaw, it's me. Your old friend, Janusz."

Wladislaw jerked and stared at Janusz carefully, then gave him a hesitant smile. "Janusz? What are you doing here? Come in."

They talked in the dim light of a candle in the kitchen. Janusz studied his old friend. Wladislaw had thick, dingy-gray sideburns that only partially hid his pockmarked skin.

After a short catch-up on their lives, Janusz explained the reason for his visit.

Wladislaw said in a raspy voice, "Yes, I remember Kalman. And I have room for them. I have a basement where I can hide them. But I can't afford to take them in. Times are difficult. Rations are sparse."

Janusz nodded. From the looks of things on the small farm, Wladislaw barely scraped by. "Kalman is a wealthy man. He has some money to give you now, and I'm sure at the end of the war he will reward you handsomely."

Wladislaw straightened in his seat and pierced Janusz with a suddenly sharp gaze. "How could a Jew have money?"

"Kalman is a clever man. I'm sure it's tucked safely away."

"Okay then, where is the first payment?"

Janusz dug in his pocket and gave Wladislaw some of his own money. "This will see you through a few weeks. I'll make arrangements to send you more, once I report to my post at the church. Then I'll make sure you receive monthly allotments to cover your costs."

The deal set, Janusz and Wladislaw helped the Golds from beneath the potatoes and took them into the house. The young Polish woman stayed with the truck, urging the two men to hurry.

Janusz sat down with Kalman and Tova in Wladislaw's kitchen. Wladislaw left them alone for their goodbyes and promised to keep his wife from interrupting their privacy.

Each parent held one of the sleeping children. They looked around the sparse and dingy kitchen, but said nothing.

Janusz swallowed and said softly, "It is time. Remember, if the authorities find you, the penalty will be death. I have not told Wladislaw of my plans for your children. I will not risk Rachel and David's safety should you be found, for Wladislaw and his wife would be questioned and also condemned to death."

Tova grimaced and closed her eyes, then lowered her chin to her daughter's small head and wept. Kalman clutched David tighter to his chest.

Tova sniffed and raised her eyes to Janusz. "I know we must, but how do we give up our children?"

Janusz covered her hand and looked into her eyes. "You are not giving them up. You are saving them. You have my word that I will see they are safe. At war's end, I will reunite you. I promise."

Kalman hugged his trembling wife. "He is saving our lives, Tova. We must do as he says."

The anguish of a mother had no tolerance for logic. Tova gritted her teeth and sobbed.

Wladislaw indicated a door to the side of the kitchen and led the way down into a dank-smelling, dusty basement. He handed Janusz a lantern and shuffled back upstairs, grumbling something under his breath.

Janusz looked around the dismal, cluttered space, saddened that his friends would have to call it home. Only a half-boarded-up window would connect them to the outside world while down there. It was a far cry from the fancy mansion Kalman had built for his family during his heyday as a coal magnate. He sighed. As long as they remained safe, the old farm cellar would do. Perhaps with a little cleaning and organization, the area would be more appealing.

They said their goodbyes in the basement. The exhausted children understood little of what their mother told them. "When will I see you again, Mama?" Rachel questioned.

Tova forced a feeble smile through her tears. "Soon, my love, soon."

"Son," Kalman said, kneeling in front of David, "sometimes life is difficult and we have to do what we prefer not to. We have to say goodbye for a while, but I want you to remember, as you grow up, to be a good man. Above all else, always do what is right."

The young boy's lips quivered, but he said bravely, "Yes, Father."

Father and son shook hands and kissed.

Kalman looked to Janusz, who stood waiting. "We'll stay here in the basement." Then he stepped up and hugged Janusz.

"I will treat your children as my own," Janusz promised.

Kalman drew Janusz to a dark corner, away from Tova and the twins. He glanced at the open door across the room and whispered into Janusz's ear, "I have hidden the family's fortune in the pit, where you fell. Then I had my crew make it the new outhouse. A rope is attached to the nearby boulders. My friend, if something befalls me, go back there and get it. Take care of my family. I beg of you, do me this one last favor."

Janusz pulled away, wanting to deny any possibility of Kalman's demise, but then he followed Kalman's gaze to Tova and the children, and nodded. He suddenly chuckled. "You made my pit the outhouse?"

Kalman grinned, tears welling in his eyes.

As Janusz led the twins up the steps, Rachel stared back at her mother. David marched stiffly out the kitchen door and toward the truck, dragging his sister along behind him, mumbling, "I hate this."

Wladislaw and Janusz shifted a heavy sideboard full of mismatched dishes to conceal the basement door. With a silent handshake, Janusz followed the twins outside.

The young Polish woman driving the old truck dropped Janusz and the two children at the train station in Radomsko. She waved a quick goodbye and disappeared into the night.

Janusz forced himself to stay awake, watching the twins sleep on a bench until a train whistle woke them at dawn. They boarded the train for Bendzin, the nearest stop to their next destination—Zidov and Tania's farm.

In addition to civilian passengers, the train—heading west toward Germany—carried Nazi officers and wounded troops returning from the Russian border. The military men showed no interest in a priest with two children in ragged, baggy clothes.

Janusz said another silent prayer of thanks for the twins' unshaven heads. Otherwise, the journey could not have happened.

In the noisy crowd, David and Rachel looked anxiously about. Rachel sobbed quietly.

David tried to comfort his sister. Speaking softly, he said, "Let's make a secret signal to use between us. When you're scared, you give the signal, and I'll give it back. It will make you feel better."

Janusz smiled, watching as they tried several signals. Finally they agreed on one: Two fingers of the right hand—one for Rachel, one for David—would be placed over the heart and tapped twice. One tap for Rachel, and one tap for David. This would be their secret way of saying, "Don't be afraid. I have you in my heart."

For the rest of the long train ride, whenever Rachel felt frightened, she gave David the silent signal. He would immediately give the signal back, and Rachel would instantly calm.

The trio got off the train at Bendzin and walked about three miles to a nearby, small village. Janusz hadn't seen his aunt and uncle for almost seven years. He prayed things hadn't changed as much as they had in Katowice.

They found the farmhouse without any trouble, and Janusz silently thanked God for the untouched countryside. The war had not stretched this far.

When Janusz heard his aunt's contagious laugh through an open side window, a wave of nostalgia washed over him. Memories of her visits during his childhood warmed his heart.

Wearing the oversized, hand-me-down coats Zygmunt's people had given them, Rachel and David stood mutely by as Janusz knocked on the door. They looked apprehensive, clinging to one another.

Rachel heard chairs scraping over a wooden floor and footsteps heading toward the front of the house. The door swung open, revealing the couple, hardly changed a bit since the last time Janusz had seen them.

Aunt Tania stood for a moment, and then clasped her hands over her breast and cried, "Janusz! It has been so long! Why, I hardly recognized you, you are so thin."

Uncle Zidov pulled her aside and ushered the trio into the farmhouse. The moment he shut the door, Aunt Tania grabbed Janusz and hugged him firmly, sniffling a little. The children stood idly by.

Then Zidov clasped Janusz in a strong embrace. He seemed unable to say anything.

Turning her attention to the children, Tania put her hands on her hips and gave a warm laugh. "Since when do priests have children?" She offered them food, still on the breakfast table.

Janusz placed his hands on the twins' shoulders and introduced them. "This is Rachel and David. Their father is my old friend, Kalman Gold. You remember Kalman, don't you, Aunt Tania?"

"Oh yes," she said with enthusiasm. "I remember him. He pulled you from the pit when you nearly drowned."

Janusz nodded, unable to stop an instinctive shudder over the old incident. "Yes, he saved my life years ago, and now I am returning the favor. These are his children. They and their parents have been rescued from the Nazis. Kalman and his wife are hidden in another town. It wasn't safe to keep the children with them. I made a vow to find shelter for the children until the family can be reunited."

He paused, glancing down at David and Rachel. "However, it would be safer if they were separated. The Nazis will be looking for twins."

Rachel stiffened under his hand. She looked at her brother, raised two fingers, and tapped her heart twice. David returned his sister's signal, looking suddenly older than his nine years.

Tania whispered to Janusz, "What does that mean?" He explained it to her in a soft aside.

Janusz patted their shoulders and continued. "I would like you to keep David. He will be safe here, and is well-suited to farm life. Perhaps he will help with some of the more difficult chores, Uncle Zidov."

David snaked his fingers around those of his sister.

Tania studied David for a moment and gave Zidov a questioning look. Zidov stroked his chin and stared at the boy. Then he looked up at Tania and nodded.

Tania's face lit up. "Yes, Janusz. We'll take care of David. We'll do whatever we must to protect him. His father saved your life. We will help to see that his son lives long and well."

Janusz hugged his aunt and pumped Zidov's hand. "Thank you. I knew I could count on you."

Aunt Tania bustled about the cozy kitchen, bringing more food to the table, urging the silent children to eat.

The next morning, as Tania packed food for the remainder of Janusz and Rachel's journey, Janusz knelt to speak with David. "As your father said, David, sometimes life is difficult. I will pray the days pass quickly, and that your time here will be happy. I'll be back to visit you and bring news of your family. Have faith and be brave. I'm going to take Rachel where she will be as safe as you are here. I promise to come for you when all of this is over."

When Janusz urged Rachel to say goodbye to her brother, she simply stood and stared at him blankly.

Janusz touched her shoulder. "Rachel?"

David, too, stood like a wooden soldier, looking at his frozen sister. "Goodbye, Rachel," he said flatly.

Rachel raised her right hand, extended two fingers and tapped her heart twice. David quickly returned the signal.

Rachel turned and walked toward the door.

Two hours later, Rachel and Janusz boarded the train to Katowice. Rachel slept, leaning against Janusz for most of the trip.

Janusz stared out the window. *Oh, God, help me make the right choice to protect the life of this little girl.*

Once the train arrived in Katowice, Janusz—with Rachel in hand—walked to the convent. It had escaped damage by mortars or gunfire, unlike other churches around the country, and he heaved a deep sigh of relief.

He spoke tenderly, "God chooses. This will be your home until the war is over and you can be reunited with your parents and your brother."

While waiting for the nuns to find their Mother Superior, Janusz settled Rachel on a secluded bench in a shady alcove. She remained placid and disturbingly blank, worrying Janusz. The horrors of the concentration camp, the exposure to death and torture, and now the separation of her family had surely overwhelmed her. He stroked her cheek and felt her tremble.

A young nun called for him to meet with the Reverend Mother, and he left Rachel staring out at the late afternoon sky. "I will not be long, my dear Rachel."

She neither moved nor said a word.

Janusz spoke candidly with Mother Regina, explaining all that had transpired. "So, you see, Reverend Mother, Rachel's only hope in escaping the Nazis is to live here, hidden as a Catholic orphan. You must be the only one to know Rachel's history. Tell everyone else the girl's parents died near the Russian border, shortly after the Germans attacked.

"Rachel is one of God's children," Janusz continued. "And, when God looks at her, He does not see a Jew or a Catholic. He sees only an innocent child. He would be pleased if you chose to help her."

Mother Superior smiled. "Did He tell you that, Father?"

Janusz answered without hesitation, "I'm confident He led me here."

The nun dipped her head regally. "I will accept the child, and I will keep Rachel's secret. But Gold is a Jewish name. How shall we call her?"

"Some common Polish name will do. How about Stacowski?"

"Agreed."

Janusz met with Rachel in the shadowy hallway of the convent. He knelt in front of her and held her shoulders as he spoke, looking into her eyes. "As of this moment, you are now Rachel Stacowski. It is very important that you observe all the Catholic teachings.

"You cannot trust anyone by telling them your secret. Only the Reverend Mother knows the truth, and that is the way it must be. Do not let down your guard, Rachel. If anyone discovers you are Jewish, you will be taken back to the ghetto by the Germans. Not only will it cause harm to come to you, but you will bring harm to your family. Do you understand?"

Rachel nodded.

Janusz kissed her on the cheek and stood. "I will not forget you. I promise I will come back for you."

Rachel held his look but did not speak.

Janusz felt his heart breaking as he stared down at her. "Can you tell me goodbye?"

Rachel raised her right hand. This time she extended three fingers, and then tapped them against her heart three times.

Tears welled in Janusz's eyes as he returned the gesture and walked away.

CHAPTER EIGHT

THE GOOD AND THE RIGHTEOUS

*Walk in the way of the good and keep the
paths of the righteous.*

Proverbs 2:20

Janusz had another week remaining in his leave. He'd planned to spend
those days back home, but the war had changed everything. The reality
of his earlier visit still troubled his mind—a deranged, morose mother
and a worried father.

He felt weary down to his soul and looked forward to the solitude
of the church. He hoped to lose himself in his work; the war ensured
no shortage of the needy. He'd heard of Father Dimitri's ordination
to bishop, followed shortly after by his installation to archbishop and
transfer to Krakow.

So Janusz boarded a train to the headquarters of the Archdiocese,
home of St. Joseph's Catholic Church. As he pulled away from the
station, he prayed that somehow life might be better in Krakow.

Immediately upon arrival, he reported to Archbishop Father Dimitri.
Now in his mid-seventies, the old priest had become stooped with age,
and his hair had turned snowy white. He wore thick, wire-rimmed
glasses.

Father Dimitri spoke softly, sounding so unlike the vigorous,
booming voice Janusz remembered. "Come in, come in, my son! Father
Lopez in Rome told me you were on your way. He said you were his

most promising pupil, and that he would miss your many talks. It's good to see you after all of these long years."

Janusz felt a pang of homesickness for his time within the magic world of the Vatican. "Yes, Father Lopez was like a father to me. He helped me find my way through the rigorous tutelage of a neophyte priest. I will miss him as well."

Father Dimitri ushered Janusz into a well-appointed study and asked a dour-looking secretary to make tea. "Have you had a chance to visit your parents?"

"Yes," Janusz answered, but did not elaborate.

"Well, welcome. Come, there is much to do." Father Dimitri settled in his chair and studied Janusz, smiling warmly.

They sipped tea as they talked. The Archbishop paused several times, coughing. As he raised the cup, his hands shook slightly.

After a moment, Father Dimitri said, "My eyesight is not what it once was, and

I find that I can no longer bear the responsibilities of ministering to the parishioners. The other priests help as they have time, but it is not enough. You, Father Dov, will be my right hand. Again, a glimpse of God's plan becomes clear. As my health fails, He has brought you to me."

"I will do all that I can to assist you, dear Father."

Janusz quickly immersed himself in the heavy responsibilities of the diocese. The causalities of war had affected many of the parishioners—families separated, homes destroyed, and fathers killed on the battlefield. Children became orphans every day.

In addition to conducting daily mass at St. Joseph's, he oversaw the food distribution to the poor, officiated at the many funerals, and visited the sick in local hospitals.

His duties also included visiting the dioceses in the nearby cities, and his trips to Katowice included the convent. Rachel's vibrant youth and emerging beauty always renewed his spirit. She had Kalman's good looks and athletic grace. Although only a budding teen, she had the makings of a beautiful woman.

Whenever they saw each other, Rachel would turn away from the curious eyes of the other children and give Janusz her secret, three-fingered signal. If he were free to do so, he returned the gesture; if not, he simply nodded and continued with his work.

When time permitted, Janusz took the evening train to Bendzin and walked to his aunt and uncle's farm. He always carried a few provisions and looked forward to each stolen evening in their company, sharing any news. Once in a while, he brought a token from Rachel for her brother.

David always asked about his hero, Zygmunt, and the underground resistance. Janusz told him what little he knew, wondering when, if ever, he would see his courageous childhood friend, Big Z, again.

Reacquainting himself with David always brought Janusz peace. The boy's rugged stature, just like his twin sister's glowing beauty, reinforced his faith and affirmed his purpose. He caught the dawn train back to Katowice and resumed his duties, with no one but the Mother Superior aware of his "errand."

On one of his return trips, he came upon an awkwardly stooped man in beggar's clothing. Janusz put a hand on the pitiful brute's shoulder and whispered a blessing, but as he turned to continue his hike back up to the parish, the man grabbed his hand.

From beneath the ragged hood of a filthy cloak, a familiar, husky voice said, "Father Dov, I thank you for your kind prayer on my behalf. I've had need of them."

Janusz gasped, recognizing Zygmunt's unforgettable tone. He swallowed quickly as his friend shushed him. After a moment collecting his thoughts and regaining his caution, he said, "God has truly given me a great gift, seeing you again, Zygmunt. I have kept you in my prayers these long months."

They walked into a park and found a private corner, away from the prying eyes of the patrolling Germans. Once settled upon a bench, Zygmunt whispered, "I have followed you, my friend, and I can guess who you visit. Perhaps, in three weeks, you may find time to take a day's journey and visit the others in need of your comfort?"

Janusz drew in a deep breath. Each time he visited the twins, his heart ached to go to Kalman and Tova, to bring news of the children and how they thrived—to reassure, and be reassured. "Yes, I will arrange to be available."

Zygmunt rose slowly, creating a hump in his back beneath the rags of his clothes. "On your next return from the farm, I will meet you again." With that, he limped off, leaving Janusz to stare after him, dumbstruck.

When he entered the convent to conclude his business, he called for Rachel to be brought to the Reverend Mother's private office.

Janusz watched as Rachel tiptoed inside. "Come in, my child. I have news for your ears alone."

She stared wide-eyed and straightened her shoulders. "Father," she whispered. "How nice to see you."

Janusz drew her to a chair in front of the desk and positioned his chair to face her. "I will be going to visit your parents in a few weeks' time, Rachel. Perhaps you have a message you'd like me to give to them? And, have you something for David?"

"Oh, I think I would like to make something," she said excitedly.

At her eagerness, he held up a hand. "Remember, it must not contain any ties to you or this place. Think long and hard. When I come again, I will take it with me. God willing, I will bring something back for you. Okay, now, compose yourself, and go about your day."

She grabbed his hand, kissed it, ran to the door, and stopped. He watched her take several deep breaths before slowly turning the knob and exiting the chambers without a backward glance.

Janusz sighed, leaned back in his chair, and prayed for them all.

Three weeks later, Janusz stared at David, who'd been thrilled to receive a pressed flower from his sister, via Janusz's Bible. Tania and Zidov excused themselves early, leaving the two alone. Janusz put a hand on the boy's shoulder and said softly, "It is possible I will see your parents soon, my son. Zygmunt is making arrangements. Your sister has decided that a lock of her hair would be a nice token for them. It cannot be traced, and is priceless and unique."

He waited by the hearth, enjoying its warmth, while the boy jumped to his feet and paced about the homey living room.

After a short while, David returned to his seat and leaned toward Janusz. His eyes gleamed. "I will also give you a lock of my hair to give to my parents. But can you remember a message?"

Janusz smiled, recognizing Kalman's sly attitude and intelligence in the boy's eager face. "I can."

David puffed out his chest and whispered, "Tell my father I am learning to become the man he wanted me to become. The lessons are hard, as he said they would be, but I will not disappoint him."

Janusz nodded, fighting back tears, and gravely accepted a hastily cut swatch of hair. He watched David walk to the small bedroom off the hallway, then sat and stared at the smoldering embers of the fire.

Uncle Zidow gave him a piglet to take to Wladislaw. Later, while on his hike back to Katowice, lugging the animal in his satchel, a rough gang of men grabbed him and dragged him into an alley. Janusz struggled, afraid the brigands might steal the pig meant for Kalman and Tova's keep, but before he could cry out for help, he spotted a produce truck at the other end of the alley. Zygmunt grinned from the driver's seat and waved.

Janusz wilted with relief. "Holy Mother of God!"

His kidnappers released him and someone clapped him on the back. Janusz took a deep breath and climbed up beside Zygmunt. The other men clambered into the back of the truck to sit among the vegetables.

"Before we get going, Father, it would be best if you changed into working clothes. Speak only German, for all Poles are now subject to arrest followed by deportation either to Germany to work as slaves, or to join the Jews in the concentration camps." He handed Janusz a worn farming outfit and pointed at the large satchel. "What do you carry with you?"

"I bring gifts to Wladislaw, to help ease the pain of feeding extra mouths." He clutched, then nudged the satchel gently. A snort came from deep inside. "A piglet from Zidov. Perhaps it will fetch a good price, or maybe Wladislaw will feed it and slaughter it for food."

Zygmunt laughed and clapped Janusz hard on the back. "Not many men would deliver a pig, Janusz, but this is why God loves you so dearly."

Janusz shrugged good-naturedly and stared out the dirty windshield. He held his breath each time they passed an armed checkpoint, relaxing only after they passed through without incident. Finally, they came to Wladislaw's rundown farmhouse.

Just past the gate, Zygmunt stopped the truck and turned to Janusz. "The men will throw down a couple of bags of flour and a jar of lard to add to your piglet. Remember, you will have only a half hour before we return. Be ready and waiting."

The truck jerked forward before Janusz had completely closed his door. Through the cloud of dust, he saw two sacks of flour and a gallon jar of lard sitting by the side of the road. He smiled, but left the additional gifts where they lay and trudged up to the house.

Wladislaw answered the door on the first knock. His eyes widened on Janusz for a moment, then he quickly ushered him inside. "Welcome, Janusz!"

Janusz hugged his old friend, noting that Wladislaw had gained a bit more weight since the last time they'd met. The money he'd given Wladislaw must have helped with the household more than Janusz had first dared to hope. "You are looking well, Wladislaw. Where is your wife? We have not yet met."

"Oh, she is in the village, buying cabbage for tonight's soup." Wladislaw waved him to a chair and stared at the bulging satchel that had started to move.

Janusz chuckled and untied the drawstrings. "I have brought a gift from one of the parish farms. A piglet." He brought out the squealing baby pig and handed it to Wladislaw. "On the road outside, you will find other things to help you survive. I suggest you collect them before someone comes along and takes them for their own."

As Wladislaw hurried toward the door with the squirming piglet in his arms, Janusz said softly, "While you are about your business, I would like to visit the others here."

Wladislaw shrugged and nodded toward the hidden cellar door. "I will tend to matters outside." With that, he left the house.

Janusz took a deep breath, knocked on the door, opened it, and cautiously walked down the worn stairs. "Kalman, Tova, it is I, Janusz."

From the dimness of the basement he heard a gasp and a sob. Then, suddenly, Kalman wrapped him in a strong embrace. Janusz could not help the instinctive breath he took, or the sharp hiss of disgust for Kalman's rank odor. He covered his reaction quickly and kissed his friend on both cheeks, then broke free to do the same with Tova. She also smelled as if she hadn't bathed in some time.

By the filtered light of a boarded-up window, he opened a small flour sack and extracted the treasures he'd brought for them. "The nuns have taken to making what they call gray soap, from tallow and ashes. It is better than nothing."

Kalman accepted the soap. "I shall ask Wladislaw if we can bring in a couple of buckets of water when the night is moonless. It is good to see you, my friend. We are going mad here, in the dark. Only late at night, or in the early hours of the morning, does Wladislaw allow the 'Jews in the basement' to come upstairs. Then we drink water, eat dry bread—or leftovers, if Wladislaw's unpleasant and overweight wife has made enough to share—and empty the bucket we use as a toilet. The curtains of the kitchen are always closed, and Wladislaw won't allow us in any of the other rooms."

Tova clutched Janusz's jacket and whispered, "Our babies, our children—are they well?"

Janusz felt instantly guilty for not immediately assuring them of the twins' well-being. "Yes, Tova, they are safe and in good health. They have sent gifts—tokens for you to remember them by." He reached into the sack and pulled out a swatch of material folded over the locks of hair. "It was Rachel's idea to give you a lock of hair. The Germans cannot trace the gift, but you will be able to hold it and look at it without fear. David followed suit."

Tova snatched the material and held it to her breast, then she brought it to her face and inhaled deeply. When she looked up, the faint light glistened on her tears. "Thank you, Father." To Kalman, she said urgently, "Smell it, my love. It holds the scent of our children."

Kalman placed his face in the material as she held it for him. He pulled her into his arms and wept softly. Together, with trembling fingers, they unfolded the cloth and stared at the two tied locks of hair.

Janusz moved to a far corner, allowing them a moment of privacy. He wiped tears from his cheeks and said a silent prayer of thanks for the miracle of giving to this deserving couple.

Kalman came to him and embraced him again. "Thank you." His voice sounded choked and hoarse.

Janusz returned the hug, unable to speak at all. Then he straightened and cleared his throat. "David gave me a message for you, Kalman." He recited the boy's words and then bent to extract the last item from his sack. "And I have something special for you. Do you remember our days as children?"

Tova drifted closer, still clutching the cloth with the locks of hair to her breast.

Kalman nodded. "What is it?"

Janusz chuckled and held out a bag of Tania's fragrant bagels.

Tova gasped, inhaling the aroma of fresh baking. Kalman smiled. "I remember such people. You will be sure to send our eternal gratitude and love to them."

A soft rap on the cellar door reminded Janusz of the time. "I must leave now, my friends, but be brave and have faith. God will see you through this test."

"Wait, Father," Tova said breathlessly. She tore two strips from the hem of her dress, tied them into two separate, intricate knots, and handed them to Janusz. "To our children. This was their favorite of my dresses."

Kalman embraced Janusz. "Tell them both that we are proud of them. We keep them in our hearts at all times and, therefore, are never really separated."

Janusz nodded, overcome with grief, and climbed the old stairs. After helping Wladislaw replace the cabinet that hid the door, he whispered, "Wladislaw, why do you not allow them to bathe? Why the darkness?"

Wladislaw hunched his shoulders and averted his eyes. "The Nazis stop by often, searching for anything unusual. I fear risking anything out of the ordinary—anything that would cause suspicions. Better they are alive and dirty than dead and clean, and I will not sacrifice my safety or my wife's—not for anyone."

Janusz put his hands on Wladislaw's shoulders and stared into his eyes. "I am disappointed, but I understand. I will visit again, when I can."

Inside, Janusz felt uneasy about the situation.

A busy, agony-filled summer finally yielded to winter. Janusz compassionately ministered to the sick and dying, broke bread with the poor, and preached hope to a hopeless, war-weary congregation. All the while, his heart clouded with doubt. *Where is God?*

He continued his rounds of the diocese and the secret visits to Rachel and David. And, every month, he sent a tiny stipend to Wladislaw to help buy food and supplies for Kalman and Tova.

The Germans set up government in Krakow and left most of the city intact; however, they arrested the Poles and Jews in the rest of the country. The Nazis either executed the Poles or sent them to Germany as forced labor to keep the massive war machine running. From what whispers Janusz had heard, all of the Jews sent to concentration camps were either used as slave labor or put to death.

It seemed Hitler wanted to eliminate Poland and its native people almost as desperately as he wished to rid the world of Jews. Janusz feared the worst, but could not bring himself to believe the terrible stories circulating about what was occurring in the concentration camps.

The Polish underground resistance (or the Home Army, as they called themselves) continued to strike against the occupying forces at every opportunity. Janusz prayed for Zygmunt's safety. The days of sitting on the bank of the river and reading poetry seemed so far away.

Janusz managed one more visit to Wladislaw before winter arrived, bringing an old horse cart of supplies, buried beneath a pile of potatoes. With his flawless German, Janusz managed to negotiate through the checkpoints.

He brought Wladislaw flour, lard, tea and sugar—precious and rare commodities. To Kalman and Tova, he delivered more small tokens from the twins—straw dolls from David and pressed flowers from Rachel—priceless.

Deep that winter, the Snow From Hell fell on Krakow.

Janusz walked from the parish office into the bitter cold morning to find that a mantle of fresh snow had fallen during the night. Earlier snowfalls had masked the ravaged buildings and turned the otherwise gray city a virginal white, but this snowfall held sandy, gray-blue ash. Janusz touched it and rubbed the gritty substance between his fingers.

"What is this?" he called to a passing police officer on horseback.

"Jews," the officer answered flatly. "From the Nazi ovens."

Holy Mother of God. Janusz quickly brushed his fingers on his robe. He stumbled along the street, horrified by each step, for the dreadful gray snow had fallen thick, covering all surfaces.

Janusz met with Archbishop Dimitri in the parish office. Despite his concern over the older man's frailty, Janusz had to vent his mortification. "Father . . . men, women, and children are dying! Thrown into furnaces to be burned like trash!"

Father Dimitri gave a wheezing sigh and looked at Janusz from deeply sunken eyes. "We are priests of the church. Because we are not policemen or politicians, unfortunately, our hands are tied. If you are troubled by this, remember it in prayer."

Then the archbishop murmured, "The battles we fight are not of flesh and bone. In the army of God there are no bayonets or tanks. We arm ourselves not with rifles, but with faith and trust, because the focus of our business is not with what man is doing, but what God would have us do."

Janusz knew he was right, but left the office discouraged and heartsick. He felt torn between his vows to God and the church, and the outrage that haunted him over the evil ignored by all but those targeted—the Jews. He walked outside into the cold of the night, welcoming the fresh, biting air.

His relief soon dissolved amid the new, fine, gray, falling ash.

Spring came, followed by summer, as Katowice and all of Poland learned to live under occupation. Janusz avoided the Nazis. He knew none personally and hoped he never would.

An obedient servant, Janusz had done as the archbishop directed. He had prayed for guidance and wisdom, but felt unsure about receiving either. Through it all, though, he did learn tolerance.

He longed for the opportunity to pour his heart out to Kalman. As teens, they often confided in one another, but now, God had become his only confidant.

It helped to focus on service, working twelve to fifteen hours a day. Fatigued sleep often brought dreams that took him back to his youth and its welcome innocence. However, at dawn, innocence would disappear and the cycle would start over again.

He thought of the thousands of captives who, no doubt, found escape only within their minds. At least there, the Nazi army could not invade.

Or could they? Hadn't they already invaded *his* mind? He felt the scars—memories that would never fade.

God damn them, he often prayed, with no guilt, feeling only righteous anger.

One day, months later, while Janusz visited a farm—buying beets for the food program—a breathless boy ran up. "Father Janusz, Sister Margaret sent me. She said to come quick. It is the archbishop."

Janusz rushed to St. Mary's Hospital in Krakow. Before going to Father Dimitri's private room, he spoke with the attending physician. The prognosis left no room for hope; the cancer was incurable.

When Janusz entered the room, he found Father Dimitri propped up in bed with many pillows. The archbishop looked pale and jaundiced—eyes and skin yellow. His breathing sounded shallow and difficult.

Father Dimitri spoke softly. "Thank you for coming so quickly. Please give me my Last Rites."

Janusz pulled a chair to the side of the bed, took the old man's hand in his, and leaned toward him. "Dear Heavenly Father . . ."

At the conclusion of the sacrament, Father Dimitri whispered, "Janusz, I received approval from Rome. You will be in charge, until a new bishop arrives. You will now be responsible for the diocese in Krakow. I'm counting on you to collaborate with Archbishop Oppenheimer."

Janusz sat speechless.

The archbishop went into a coughing spasm, and Janusz mopped blood from the old man's chin. Janusz slipped an arm under his back and raised him up so he could breathe more easily.

When the coughing spasm subsided, Father Dimitri signaled the hovering nurse to leave the room.

As soon as she left, he spoke softly to Janusz. "I must confess, the guilt of so many innocent deaths weighs heavily upon me. I am in disagreement with the Holy Chair Pius XII." He paused to catch his breath. "Many of our people encouraged the Nazis to retaliate against the Jews, and others collaborated in sending Jews to the gas chambers. My heart is heavy with the fact that I have done nothing to stop the atrocity."

Janusz opened his mouth to speak, but Dimitri raised a finger to his lips.

"We could have sheltered many of the Jews, and saved lives. It is our responsibility, according to the Old Testament, to protect our fellow man."

He paused again, wheezing slightly.

"I, myself, did very little to help the Jews. But you, Janusz—you grew up in both Jewish and Christian cultures, and see both sides. Perhaps you can help right what we have wronged."

The archbishop struggled to swallow, but couldn't seem to complete the action. Janusz quickly offered him a sip of water.

The old priest managed a few sips between shallow breaths.

"I will not die with this on my conscience. I was a coward and ignored offering a hand to those in distress. Pray with me, Janusz, that God will forgive my indifference."

Janusz took out his rosary and held it against his lips.

Dimitri folded his hands together as tears seeped from the corners of his eyes and ran into his gray hair. He then closed his eyes and prayed, "Dear God, please forgive me, your humble servant. I am a sinner. Forgive me of my sins. Forgive me for failing my fellow man. Into your loving hands, I place my soul. In the name of your son, Jesus Christ, I pray. Thank you for hearing my prayer."

Janusz bowed his head in reverence.

Dimitri patted Janusz's hand. "Thank you for coming and praying with me."

Janusz pressed his lips to Dimitri's hand and kissed it gently.

The archbishop struggled to continue, "Janusz, my son, you are one of God's best. You have a heart for the oppressed. Always remember these words: 'If I am not for myself, who is for me? And if I am only for myself, what am I? And if not now, when?'"

Dimitri began to gasp. His mottled skin turned blue. He sighed as the air left his lungs, and then he stopped breathing.

Janusz kissed the old man's hand a second time and laid it in the center of his chest. "Goodbye, my old friend," he whispered, as a tear traced down his cheek.

CHAPTER NINE

THE HUNTED

He also saw a skull floating upon the water.
Said he to it: Because you drowned others, you were
drowned; and those who drowned you,
will themselves be drowned.

Ethics of the Fathers 2:6

Three summers came and went with little change. One late, warm evening, while Janusz strolled beside Tania's herb garden with Zidov, David Gold tended sheep in the near pasture. This brought to Janusz's mind the Old Testament David. He smiled, thankful that Kalman's son had escaped the dangers during his young life, unlike his biblical namesake. The little boy had turned into a strapping teenager, strong and robust.

Janusz and Zidov paused to watch as David picked up a rock and tossed it at a tree.

Zidov chuckled. "David is bored with the simple life of a farmer. He is fast growing into a young man, hungry for adventure. He has spoken of joining the resistance."

Janusz turned solemn as the sun began to set. "He is but a child, with little understanding of such things. Also, I hear rumors, Uncle, that the Germans are still searching for escapees. Even the loss of one prisoner humiliates them. All other territories and cities are constantly under siege. We must impress upon David that the war still rages. Only the remote quietness here protects him."

Zidov sighed and draped a heavy arm across Janusz's shoulders. "Yes, this I understand. Tania and I often remind him, but the memories of the young are short, and teenagers are quick to turn their minds to fantasies rather than reality."

Janusz felt pleased that his uncle had taken to his young ward. David had become the son Zidov and Tania had never had.

Tania stepped out onto the porch and called them to supper, curtailing their conversation.

Throughout the meal, David questioned Janusz about the Home Army and his father's old mining foreman, Zygmunt, but Janusz refrained from telling stories about Big Z and his band of rebels. Rather, he asked the boy for another token to give to Kalman and Tova, saying, "German hunters have moved farther south, searching for escaped prisoners. Pray that your family stays safely hidden from the Nazis."

David scowled and fell quiet. He finished his supper and brought Janusz a straw soldier he'd adorned with several locks of hair. Then, without another word, he disappeared into his bedroom, shutting the door a little harder than necessary.

Tania heaved a great sigh, shook her head, and cleared the plates from the table.

Janusz picked up his traveling satchel, hugged his aunt and uncle goodbye, and headed toward the train station. On the way, he sent up a silent prayer for David's youthful restlessness to learn patience before harm could find him.

———∞∞✦❈✦∞∞———

A few weeks after Janusz's visit, David idly tended Zidov's sheep on a distant corner of the farm that bordered a dirt roadway. When the sun touched the trees in the west, he planned to move the flock back to a corral near the barn and farmhouse, but a glance told him that wouldn't happen for at least an hour.

In the meantime, he daydreamed of being a soldier—an officer, like those he had seen in Lodz—sharp-dressed military men, never afraid, and never hidden on farms in the middle of nowhere. No one would dare threaten their families.

The ground trembled beneath him, and he scrambled to his feet. Then an ominous, roaring, metallic growl startled him. He shaded his eyes and spotted a massive, gray-blue German Panzer tank. As it approached, it left a swirl of dust churning and spinning in its noisy wake.

David stood frozen. His heart raced with excitement. When the big war machine ground to a halt on the other side of the wooden fence, he thought he might die from the thrill of seeing such a thing up close.

The deafening noise made David quickly glance over his shoulder to check on the flock. However, the sheep simply ignored the intrusion and the sound. He swallowed, grateful that he would avoid embarrassment by having to chase after frightened sheep in front of the soldiers. He knew he should head home, but he wanted to see the tank up close.

The hatch atop the tank clanged open, and a handsome, blond-haired German officer emerged. He wore a pair of smudged goggles.

David's knees trembled, and he staggered backward

The man pulled off the goggles and flashed a disarming, white, even-toothed smile. "Hello, boy. Can you tell us where the road to Majestic is? My driver got us lost."

David's throat felt tight and his mouth dry. Unsure he could speak, he raised an arm and pointed down the road.

"That way? Thanks. Okay if we park here for a little break?"

David nodded. Again, he stayed, knowing full well that he should leave the area.

The German saluted him and looked down into the big tank. "Okay, gang, break time."

Three other soldiers climbed out and waved to David. He watched, awestruck, as they jumped down, straightened their uniforms, and strolled across the road.

The crewmen lounged under the shade of a nearby tree and ate apples. These were the men he was supposed to fear, yet he found himself struggling with a burning desire deep inside to be one of them.

The blond officer motioned David to walk with him around the big machine. It emitted heat and smelled of diesel fuel and oil—intoxicating.

"Want a look inside?"

Why not? Zidov and Tania would be none the wiser. He knew better than to fraternize with the enemy, but when would he ever get another chance like this? He blurted out, "Yes, sir!"

Heart pounding, he climbed up, looked through the cannon's gun sight, sat in the driver's seat, and peered out the machine-gun port.

The officer patted his shoulder and hooked a thumb up to indicate the end of the tour. "You want to taste what we eat when we're out on a mission?"

David nodded and eagerly accepted a sealed packet of food. They sat on the edge of the tank, feet dangling, and chewed on dried beef.

The officer gazed over the fields. "You know, in Germany I grew up on a farm like this."

David watched his every move and admired the pistol strapped on his belt. He did not fear this man.

"We even had a flock of sheep. Want to know a secret?"

David nodded, enthralled.

The officer leaned closer. "The man who owned the farm was a Jew. Not all Jews are bad. How about you, boy? What are you?"

David stilled and his stomach shuddered sickly around the bit of food he'd so gleefully shared a moment before. He managed to answer, "Catholic."

"Pollack, huh? Well, you look more German than Pollack." The officer playfully mussed David's blond hair. Then he patted David's shoulder with another smile. "You know any Jews living around here? Personally, I have nothing against them, but someone blew up a bridge over near Rossmoor. Figure it was Jews. War does crazy things to people."

He lowered his voice to a conspiratorial whisper. "You haven't heard of anybody hiding Jews, have you?"

David swallowed hard. He felt cold all over, as if caught in an ice storm. "No, sir."

"How long have you been living here on the farm?"

David looked away, pretending to check on the sheep. He felt the officer staring at him. He had been warned not to talk to strangers, and now he would pay the price. The sharp-eyed officer would find out his secret and shoot him. Then the Germans eating apples across the way would march over to the farmhouse and hang Zidov and Tania . . . all because of his stupidity.

Then he heard Zidov call sharply, "David!"

He watched with gut-wrenching terror as his foster father marched toward them along the other side of the fence. He wanted to shout at his temporary guardian to run, but he couldn't move or make a sound.

Zidov waved to the officer, then beckoned to David. "Come on, boy. Time to get the sheep in."

David, flushed with guilt and shuddering relief, jumped down off the tank and climbed through the fence. He hurried to stand next to Zidov, still trembling with dread.

The German pointed to David and said to Zidov, "Nice boy."

Zidov nodded and curled a big, callused hand around David's neck. "Thank you. You want to come up to the house? My wife has some berry pie."

The officer seemed to consider for a moment. David held his breath, praying that the Germans wouldn't accept the invitation.

After a moment, the officer jumped down, brushed his hands on his pants, and said, "Maybe next time." He gestured at the big tank. "We have to get Uncle Adolph's car back to the compound."

Zidov waved and nudged David toward the sheep. "Have a good day."

When the tank rumbled down the dirt road, he grabbed David by the collar. "You little fool!" His face had turned red, and David could feel his big hands shaking. "You could have got us all killed!"

Seeing the fear in Zidov's eyes, David swallowed hard.

"Those were Nazi SS! They are looking for Jews. They use their tank on foolish young men like yourself. You were like a fat fish on their hook. You must never go near them again. Do you understand?"

David, for his disobedience, went to bed with no supper and would have to hide in the cellar for two days. He accepted his punishment without protest. He knew Zidov was right. The handsome German's questions had proved that. Embarrassed by his stupidity, he smarted with guilt under the combined wrath of Zidov and Tania.

Lying in bed with an empty stomach, recalling the excitement of the tank and the handsome, clever lieutenant robbed him of sleep. Enemies perhaps, yet still gallant, courageous men. He dreamed of becoming Zygmunt's right-hand man and imagined rescuing his mother, father, and sister.

Janusz huddled in the dark alley, trying not to gag on the odor rising from a pile of rotting garbage. He spoke with Zygmunt, who'd lost a lot of weight, "Can we not meet in the park, as before?"

Zygmunt grimaced. "Father Dov, this is sweet compared to the stench of the death camps. You are lucky not to travel within range of them."

Janusz shuddered. "I give thanks for my blessings every day, my friend. Why have you kidnapped me this time?"

Zygmunt paced across the alley, glancing both ways. "Have you heard of Captain Nevan Shotzberger?"

Janusz shook his head.

"Captain Shotzberger is a member of the SS's Special Problem Unit. He is heading the search for Kalman Gold and his family."

Janusz gasped. "Just the Gold family? No one else? After so long?"

Zygmunt slouched against the wall of the alley, fitting his tall, muscular form into the shelter of a deep shadow. "The Nazis take escape seriously. The fact that Kalman Gold's entire family escaped placed them into a nationwide quest for vengeance."

Hooves clopping along the street outside silenced Zygmunt. Janusz tensed and tried to fade into the shadowy alley. He held his breath and fingered his rosary. An eternity of moments dragged by before the evening fell silent once more, and Janusz breathed in the putrid air.

Zygmunt leaned slightly into the dim light cast by the new moon and said softly, "Shotzberger is known in certain circles as The Ferret, for his relentless determination in finding hidden Jews. He's been set on Kalman's trail, and has found many others along the way—twenty-two men, women and children—and shot them all. This count does not include those who hid the Jews, who were also executed."

Janusz crossed himself and kissed his crucifix, reciting a silent prayer for the souls of the victims.

Zygmunt cleared his throat and continued, "His brutality is meant to send a message to Jewish sympathizers. We have a spy within the Gestapo, and we have learned that The Ferret, having run out of leads for Kalman and Tova, is now convinced the key to finding all the Golds is to find one of the children."

Janusz whispered, "Holy Mother of God!" He bowed his head and closed his eyes.

"The Ferret has begun searching the orphanages."

A sharp pain struck Janusz in the chest. *Rachel!* Memory, like a strike of lightning, replayed the horrible scene at the train station, just a few months before. Janusz had taken the girls from the convent to the cathedral in Krakow to attend a concert. They'd arrived at the station ahead of schedule, and had witnessed one of the prison trains pass through in all of its horror. Rachel's grandmother had called to her, and Rachel had reacted before Janusz could herd the girls inside the building, away from the stench of terror and death.

Had one of the guards heard her?

Zygmunt continued, "He is right now on his way to the Blessed Virgin Convent, here in Katowice. You will come with me, Father Dov. I will take you back to Krakow, where no one can connect you with this convent."

Janusz balked, horrified by the thought of Rachel facing the evil Ferret on her own. What if one of the other girls recalled the incident? An innocent word to the wrong person..." I cannot ignore her, Zygmunt! I must go to her."

But Zygmunt proved too powerful to resist, and Janusz found himself dragged to the other end of the alley and shoved into the back of a waiting farm truck. His large friend held him down as he tried to struggle. "The person in question will look to you for protection, Father, and in so doing, will give herself away. I have not worked all these years to allow this to happen. Say a prayer for her continued safety, and calm yourself."

---∘∘∘⟨⟡⟩∘∘∘---

Rachel Gold assembled in the large backyard of the convent with the other children, keeping slightly behind some of the bigger boys. Mother Superior stood next to a slight, dark-haired man in civilian dress, and three uniformed German soldiers faced the children.

The man stepped forward and said in halting Polish, "I am Captain Shotzberger."

He wore a long, shiny, black leather coat that nearly touched the ground as he walked. His dark eyes seemed to bounce from one child to another, never still. He nodded to the men who'd accompanied him. "Separate the boys from the girls."

Rachel shrank inside. She frantically searched for Mother Regina for reassurance, but saw only the other grim-faced nuns huddling together in small, frightened groups.

Once the boys stood on one side of the yard and the girls on the other, the captain said in a nasal tone, "We have reason to believe you have a child here under false pretenses. We would not want such circumstances to jeopardize your orphanage, so we must find this imposter."

Some of the children cried in fear, others stared in silence. Rachel was among the silent. The sight of uniforms with swastika armbands had triggered a rush of terrifying images.

She remembered the morning a German truck had stopped in front of her house. She could still see the soldiers smashing down the door and, later, her beautiful mother screaming as one of the soldiers shaved her head bald while the others looked on and laughed. She cringed, recalling the embarrassment of having to relieve herself in the midst of a crush of strangers in the Lodz ghetto, and the pain of unbearable hunger in the holding camp.

Rachel still suffered from nightmares of the shocking sight of an old man who had died on the floor during one of the cold nights—his lifeless stare now forever burned into her memory. And, on one occasion, a soldier had urinated in front of her. When he'd noticed her looking at him, he had masturbated and called to her, "Come here, little girl. Have a taste."

Now the evil men had returned, and she knew why. They were looking for her. Somehow her secret had failed. Somehow she had been betrayed.

Then she remembered the train . . . and the stench of the human freight . . . and the cry of her grandmother. Afterward, none of the girls had said anything to her; none had looked at her differently. She'd believed that amidst the horror, none had actually heard her grandmother call her name, or seen her respond, before Father Dov had herded all of the girls into the station.

Rachel's eyes welled with tears, and she trembled with fear. She ached deep inside for the warmth of her mother's bosom or the protection of her father's strong arms. Her hand wanted to lift and tap three fingers against her chest in the childhood signal of reassurance to Father Dov. Instead, she clenched her fists and kept still.

Captain Shotzberger paced back and forth in front of the assembly, arms clasped behind his back. "Listen to me, children. There is a traitor—a Judas—among you. One who has put you all at risk. One who will bring you all to harm. One who has lied. I have been sent here by the highest authority to find this impostor."

He paused in front of Rachel, and his gaze drifted over the ranks of boys and girls. He stood so close to her, she could smell the scent of his leather coat.

Rachel quickly averted her eyes. When she dared to raise them, she looked directly into the captain's, and stiffened.

Captain Shotzberger smiled at her, though his eyes did not convey kindness or warmth. "I don't want harm to come to any of you."

He then resumed his pacing. "But I have my orders. I must find this impostor."

Rachel held her breath and stared at the statue of the Virgin Mary, directly in front of her.

The cold, nasal voice droned on, "Someone here knows the truth. The Bible teaches, 'The truth shall set you free.' Someone must speak up with this truth, for the sake of all."

A fifteen-year-old boy called from the back row, "I know a secret."

Rachel's heart raced. She recognized Alex Jankowski's voice. He had often teased Rachel about her Jewish nose, and she had rebuffed him by calling him a dumb stump. When he had persisted, she'd made fun of his adolescent acne. After that, Alex had avoided her. Now, he would have his revenge.

Her lungs burned for oxygen. She stood frozen with fear and prayed she wouldn't wet her pants.

The captain walked through the ranks to where Alex stood. He smiled at the boy. "Yes, and what is the secret you know?"

Rachel braced for the worst.

Alex pointed at a fourteen-year-old in an adjacent line. "Him! Joshua Dneprovsky."

Rachel gasped, guilty for feeling relieved.

Alex blushed and continued a little less confidently, "I . . . I've seen him . . . down *there*. He is a Jew."

Captain Shotzberger pushed through the ranks to the trembling, singled-out boy. He grabbed the youth and dragged him to the front of the assembly. The boy did not resist, although he shuddered with gasping breaths.

The captain barked, "Pull down your pants!"

The trembling boy pled, "Please, sir?"

The long-coated German struck him hard across the face, and Joshua stumbled backward under the force of the blow.

Cries and whimpers of fear rippled through the children. Mother Regina started toward the captain and the boy, but one of the soldiers blocked her way, lifting a rifle as if to use it against her. The nuns huddling along the outer edges of the assembly shrieked, but didn't make any moves.

"Silence!" Captain Shotzberger ordered. Then he turned back to the boy before him. "Now! Drop your pants."

Joshua's nose bled as he awkwardly regained his balance. He wiped the blood away with the sleeve of his shirt, then pushed his trousers to his ankles.

"Your shorts, too!"

The boy sobbed and slowly, reluctantly obeyed.

Captain Shotzberger stepped back as the boy's shorts fell away to reveal a circumcised penis. "Jew! What is your name?"

"Joshua. I am a Pole. Only my mother was a Jew."

The officer snapped, "If your mother is a Jew, you're a Jew."

The boy sobbed, "My father was a judge in the high court of Katowice."

The German looked to the Mother Superior, who stood with her hands folded in prayer at the side of the assembly. "Is this true, or could his name be Gold?"

The mention of her real name sent a bolt of electric fear shrugging through Rachel.

Mother Regina answered without hesitation, "His name is Joshua Dneprovsky. I knew his father well. His mother died when he was only eight years old. Please!"

"He was born a Jew." The captain drew his pistol and fired.

Joshua's head snapped backward. Blood jetted out of his ears, and a flap of hair sprang from the back of his head, accompanied by a puff of red mist.

As he fell lifelessly to the ground, his head smacked hard against the cobblestone surface of the courtyard. He landed with his dead eyes wide open and seemed to stare directly at Rachel.

Rachel clasped a hand over her mouth as it filled with vomit, and quickly turned away. The girls around her screamed and wailed, clutching each other. A few threw up or fainted. Someone grabbed

Rachel and sobbed against her shoulder. She automatically put her arm around the girl as tears streamed down her cheeks.

The captain jammed the pistol back into his black leather coat. "This will be the fate of every Jew pig that tries to escape by hiding among you." He made a sharp hand motion to the three soldiers positioned around the convent's back yard. "Let this be a lesson to you all."

With that, the Germans marched down the external hallway and exited through the outer gate that led to the street.

Rachel's legs gave out, and she slammed down onto her knees, releasing the other girl who'd clutched her. Though she knew the courtyard reeled with the noise of shock and horror, Rachel heard only the pounding of her heart. She curled up on the ground and hugged herself in numbed disbelief.

CHAPTER TEN

LOST SOULS

From the depths I called you, O Lord, hear my voice,
may Your ears be attentive to the sound of my pleas.

Psalms 130:1-2

Kalman and Tova Gold didn't have much, other than each other, in the damp, mildew-infested dirt basement of Wladislaw Romanov's home. The only difference between day and night came from the occasional shaft of sunlight that sliced through the boarded-up window.

For the few minutes when the sun struck the gaps in the planks just right, Tova would stand in the narrow band of light and let it bathe her face. Kalman studied Tova's profile as she stood illuminated. Lines had begun to form at the corners of her eyes, and gray now streaked her once raven-black hair, which had grown back long and thick.

He whispered from the shadows, "You are a beautiful woman, Tova. Every time I look at you, I fall in love again."

Tova smiled and glanced in his direction. "Do you recall the night you followed me to Krakow?"

Kalman chuckled, remembering the passion and impertinence of his youth. "Of course. I stole Aaron's honeymoon car to do it."

She turned back to the window and positioned herself so the last pinprick of light struck her face. "I knew then, I loved you."

"So, all my flowers and all my trips weren't necessary?"

The sun slipped beyond the narrow space between the boards, and Tova heaved a deep sigh. "Do you suppose we'll ever see flowers again?"

Kalman sat on a wooden crate, their only piece of furniture, and shrugged in the gloom. "One can hope." He scratched at his beard, which had grown long and wild, like his hair.

Tova murmured, still facing the window, "I would like to pick flowers with Rachel. She loved the flowers in our backyard." She had a faraway look in her eyes. "Remember the night we lay in the grass with the kids until it was dark, and then we counted stars? You picked one for Rachel and David. How excited they were."

Kalman smiled. "The stars are still there."

"I pray Rachel and David are, too."

"We have Janusz's word. He'll keep his promise. Were it not for him . . ." Kalman didn't finish.

"Do you suppose it will ever end? It's been over four years."

"It must, for the children's sakes. I've lived more life than most men dare dream of. A successful business, good friends, a beautiful wife, and two perfect children."

Tova crossed to him and sat on a pile of rags at his feet. "I have no regrets, Kalman Gold," she said, and kissed his hand.

Something scraped on the floor above their heads. They fell silent. The familiar footfalls of Wladislaw's heavy-set, mean-spirited wife, Maria, sounded on the kitchen floorboards.

A clamor of pots announced the preparation of the evening meal, but they would wait several hours before partaking of any meager leftovers offered.

Later, after finishing the cold potato soup the Romanovs had left in their bowls, Tova peered out the kitchen windows and inhaled the fresh night air.

Wladislaw came into the room and cried, "Get away from the window! You'll be seen, and we'll all be killed."

Kalman had come to realize that Wladislaw had not agreed to hide them out of the goodness in his heart, but rather for Janusz's payments. Wladislaw received money every month and, on occasion, scarce, black market supplies. Wladislaw had taken all the money sewn into Kalman's cuffs long ago, but the greedy man's money had gone quickly, much of it spent on his incessant thirst for vodka.

He took Tova's hand and led her to the stairs. "Come, Tova. He's right."

As they pulled the hutch away that covered the door to the basement, Wladislaw said, "Kalman, stay. We must talk."

Tova hesitated at the top of the cellar stairs.

Kalman touched her arm to reassure her. "Go. I'll be down in a moment."

Tova descended into the darkness, glancing furtively back at Wladislaw.

Wladislaw motioned for Kalman to join him at the kitchen table. Kalman watched Wladislaw fidget and then pick at the dirt beneath a thumbnail.

Wladislaw spoke softly, avoiding Kalman's gaze. "Before the war, a neighbor and I used to hide black market vodka in my cellar. He paid me a share of his profits. Today he came to me. Since the war is almost over and the Germans are losing—"

"Almost over!" Kalman dared to hope. "The Germans are losing?"

Wladislaw met Kalman's stare and nodded. "Yes, it is true. Many say it will end within days."

Kalman trembled with excitement.

Wladislaw dropped his eyes back to the table and drew patterns on the scratched, wooden surface with a greasy finger. "As a result, many Germans are trying to find money. My neighbor has bought a stolen shipment of German beer from an officer. You see, he wants to hide the beer in my basement, like he once did with vodka. I told him I could not do that, and he asked, 'Why? Have you got something hidden there?'"

Wladislaw licked his dry lips. "The Germans are still paying a reward for hidden Jews. I am afraid he is going to report his suspicions, since I refused him. I have no choice but to move you, but I don't have any resources. I am a poor man who has only tried to help."

Kalman's brief excitement now surrendered to fear. His heart pounded in his ears. "There must be some place you could find, if the war may end in days?"

Wladislaw nodded, still staring down at the table. "There are places, but all take money, and I have none. Janusz has not visited for almost six months. We are on the verge of starvation."

"I've been in your cellar for years. Everyone I know . . ." Kalman's voice trailed away. "Most are dead, I suppose."

"But you were a wealthy man, Kalman. You must have made some provision?"

Kalman studied Wladislaw's puffy, narrowed eyes. His stomach cramped into knots. If Wladislaw were telling the truth, they could be in danger. He would risk anything to protect Tova. Finally he murmured, "Yes, I hid some things."

Wladislaw's small eyes suddenly gleamed. "What things? Where? I'll get them for you. Then we can move you to safety. But we must hurry."

Kalman nodded reluctantly. He did not want to surrender the secret. The hidden fortune would sustain his reunited family after the war—his hope for a new beginning, the seeds for a new generation. Could he risk putting his family's financial future into the hands of a man who was little more than a drunk?

He had limited options. Kalman had to give something to satisfy Wladislaw, or risk the greedy man's desperate nature. Wladislaw could turn Tova and him over to the Germans for the reward, just to purchase a few cases of vodka. Perhaps he could call on an old friend to oversee the recovery of the Gold family fortune.

Drawing in a breath, Kalman said quietly, "There is an old shack at the Star Coal Mining Company, where you once worked. It stands over the pit that Janusz fell into many years ago."

Wladislaw grimaced. "We used that as a cesspool."

"Exactly." Kalman smiled grimly. "Not many Germans would be willing to go near the flies and stench."

"But the shed was falling down. The roof was gone. Everything would rot."

"What is my name, Wladislaw?"

"Kalman."

"My last name?"

Wladislaw beamed as the answer came to him. "Gold! You hid gold in the shack?"

Kalman said softly, "Gold does not rot. It is in a metal box, buried beneath the wooden floor. Find Janusz. He will tell you the secret of retrieving it. Bring me the box, and I will pay you handsomely."

Kalman studied Wladislaw's enthusiastic expression, noting the unmistakable gleam of greed in his old schoolmate's eyes. Could Janusz control the man once he saw the treasure and held it in his hands?

Wladislaw clapped Kalman on the back as he opened the basement door and wished him a jovial good night.

Kalman carefully made his way downstairs in the pitch black. Tova called his name. He shuffled to her and drew her into his arms.

At her whispered question, he spoke directly into her ear, "Wladislaw says the war is almost over, and his neighbor wishes to hide black market liquor here, in the basement."

Tova gasped and clutched Kalman's tattered coat. "What will we do?"

Kalman guided her to a seat on the floor and held her tight. "I have told him where I hid our fortune, for he needs money to move us into a safer hiding place. Janusz has not given him enough to accomplish such a thing."

Tova made a disgusted sound. "Most of the money Janusz has given him, he has spent on foul women and drink. I smell it on him when he comes in late, after dinner is over."

Kalman nodded. "I told him that he must speak to Janusz to learn the secret of retrieving the gold. I pray that Janusz will find some way to protect our money while still protecting us."

He sighed, trying not to give in to despair. "We owe much to our dear friend."

Tova wept, burying her face against Kalman's throat. In a muffled voice, she said, "If Wladislaw does not go to Janusz, then he will dig in human filth and drown."

Kalman shuddered at the venom in her tone, but nodded in agreement. Wladislaw would pay dearly if he meant to steal from them. When Kalman had buried the strongbox under a latrine, he'd planned just such a punishment for any potential thieves, though, at the time, he'd been thinking of Germans, not an old childhood friend.

Wladislaw left early the next morning. His wife refused to speak to the Golds, and ate all of the food in the house, letting them go hungry.

Kalman and Tova took turns at the boarded-up window, each voicing their hopes that they would spot Janusz walking toward the old farmhouse with Wladislaw. They kept up a constant vigil from dawn to dusk, until it was too dark to see.

On the third evening, late at night, a loud banging and scraping startled them awake.

"Kalman," Wladislaw shouted as he yanked open the door to the basement. "Kalman, come up here!"

Tova grasped Kalman's arm. Together they stared up toward the faint light coming from above.

Kalman patted her hands and kissed her cheek, then climbed up to meet Wladislaw at the top of the stairs. He recoiled at the heavy stench radiating from Wladislaw. When his eyes adjusted to the brightness of the kitchen lamps, he realized dried slime from the pit caked Wladislaw from head to toe.

So, Wladislaw had gone after the hidden cache without Janusz. All the warnings Zygmunt had whispered to Kalman throughout the years rushed back into his memory.

A small, suitcase-sized, steel strong box sat on the nearby table. Kalman felt as if the old plow horse had kicked him in the stomach. Dents and scratches evidenced the pounding and prying Wladislaw had inflicted on it, but the box had remained unopened, refusing to yield its treasure.

Wladislaw gestured toward the table. "I can't get it open."

Kalman crossed to the steel box and ran a hand over its sides and corners. "You found it." He stroked his matted beard. "It held."

"Can you open it?" Wladislaw pressed.

Kalman sighed in surrender. He bent down and pulled off a worn leather shoe. It slipped from his foot easily, since it no longer had laces. He plucked at the loose insole, shook it, and a small key fell into his hand.

Wladislaw gaped at him. "You hid that all these years?"

"Not always in my shoe. In Lodz, Tova and I took turns swallowing it."

Kalman pushed the small, polished key into the lock on the face of the metal box. He twisted, and then opened the lid to reveal hundreds of sparkling coins. On one side, each had the Swiss Miss braided hair and a garland of flowers in front of the Alps. On the reverse, an image of the Swiss shield stood out over a background of an oak branch tied with a ribbon.

Kalman lifted a handful of the untarnished gold coins. "Swiss Helvetias, worth 20 francs a piece. I collected them for three years in anticipation of problems with the aggressive Germans. Wars will come and wars will go. Empires will rise and fall. Gold will outlast them all."

Wladislaw stared slack-jawed at the fortune in gold. "I have never seen such wealth. It could buy anything!"

Kalman tossed one of the gold coins to Wladislaw, who snatched it out of the air with crusty hands and dirt-tipped fingernails, then clutched it to his chest. "That should buy us a safe place until the war ends. When it does, I will see you are rewarded for what you've done."

"Kalman," Wladislaw said, inching closer to the table to peer into the box. "How much money is that?"

Kalman looked at the beautifully minted coins and dipped his fingers into them. "Wages for five hundred men. Maybe enough to buy fifteen farms. Certainly enough to start a new business—enough to bring a family hope."

"This makes you a wealthy man, doesn't it?"

"Yes, but not a fortunate one. Without freedom, and without my family, it has no value." Kalman flipped the lid of the box shut. "How long before you can make arrangements, Wladislaw?"

"I've already spoken to my cousin. He has a small grain mill near Landowska canal." As Wladislaw spoke, he polished the gold coin on the sleeve of his sweater. "You will like it there. He's already hiding Jews. A family from Katowice, I think. Maybe you will know them. We will leave at nightfall. Gather your things."

Kalman and Tova trembled with excitement in anticipation of the move. Since Wladislaw had not attempted to take the strongbox from them, they had relaxed the worst of their fears. The news that the war may soon end brought dreams of reuniting with Rachel and David.

He watched as Tova took two of the straw dolls David had sent to them through Janusz and secreted a single gold coin in each. Kalman helped her tie a couple of thin strips of her dress and his shirt around the dolls, and then they placed them on the windowsill in front of the gap in the board.

She whispered, "Now if Janusz brings our children here at the end of the war, they will find these and know that we are waiting for them, hoping to begin our new lives."

Kalman hugged her tightly as they watched the last ray of sun fade from the dolls. "The coins will help pay their way to us. Janusz will know what to do." He sighed, suspecting that his dear friend would have to use the coins to bribe Wladislaw into divulging their new hiding place.

They were waiting with their humble bundles of clothing when Wladislaw's knock finally came at the top of the stairs.

Wladislaw helped them onto a horse-drawn cart that waited outside. He hid Kalman's strongbox under the driver's bench and sat down above it, taking the reins in hand. "It'll be safer there," he whispered.

On the slow, bumpy ride, Kalman sat with Tova in the back of the cart. The moonlit, star-strewn sky was spellbinding. Sounds of the summer night filled the crisp, cool air, as sweet as the most beautiful music ever composed.

Tova snuggled close to Kalman and raised her eyes to the sky. Suddenly, she pointed.

"Look, my love! There's David's star, and there is Rachel's. Soon we will all look at them together once more."

Kalman slipped an arm around her and stared at the magnificent sky.

After an hour's ride, Wladislaw stopped the cart in the night shadow of trees that lined the bank of a canal, and climbed down. "We will let the horse drink."

Kalman and Tova strolled along the bank of the canal, hand in hand, while Wladislaw busied himself with checking the horse's bridle and hooves as it drank.

"Maybe we should leave Poland," Tova suggested when they paused to stare out into the darkness beyond the glimmering, placid water.

"I have family in New York," Kalman said. "A cousin."

A metal click sounded behind them. Kalman and Tova turned. Wladislaw stood a few feet from them, holding a German nine-millimeter pistol aimed at their faces.

"My God," Tova breathed, gripping her husband's arm.

Kalman stepped in front of his wife. "If it's the gold you want, Wladislaw, take it."

Wladislaw motioned at Kalman with the tip of the gun. "Where is the key?" His voice sounded ripe with fear and desperation.

"In my pocket." Kalman extracted the key and tossed it to Wladislaw. "Let us go, old friend," he whispered hoarsely. "You have enough to carry you through the rest of your life."

The gun exploded, loud and sharp in the quiet night. A jagged muzzle flash cut the darkness. Kalman grabbed his neck and fell backward into the dark water of the canal. Tova screamed his name.

A second bright flash filled Kalman's dimming vision with dancing, colored lights. Tova staggered and sank to her knees, holding her stomach. Wladislaw fired again, and Tova fell forward onto her face. She did not move.

Kalman floated downstream, staring up at David's and Rachel's stars.

—∘∘∘◄◘►∘∘∘—

Wladislaw bought vodka and fresh mutton in a nearby village before heading home. A clerk in the butcher shop told him, "There is a rumor the Russians will be in town within two to three days."

Wladislaw emptied the last of a bottle and slurred at the clerk, "My father was a big Russian, you know? Real sonavabitch! Hope the fuckin' Americans get here first." He paid the shocked man with a solid gold Swiss coin.

In no hurry to get home to his unattractive wife, Wladislaw stopped at two beer halls along the way. The locals had only recently dared to brew their own again. Sick of the German lager, they relished imbibing the weak, warm beer laced with vodka. Polish beer transformed Wladislaw into a bright and clever man.

By late afternoon, with the sun far in the west, the cart finally bumped to a halt in front of the farmhouse. The horse, as he had many times, had brought his burden home.

Mrs. Romanov shook her husband awake and dragged him toward the house.

Wladislaw pushed her clumsily away. "The box, the box!"

"What box? The box belonged to the Jews, you drunken idiot. You took them to your cousin's mill."

"Get the box, you stupid cow. It's under the front seat. If you had a brain in your head, you would remember my cousin died two years ago."

Marie gaped at Wladislaw for a moment, then ran toward the patiently waiting horse, still attached to the broken-down cart.

Wladislaw took the heavy box from her and staggered into the kitchen. He set it on the table with a bang and made an awkward flourish of opening the lid, then held up a handful of gleaming coins. "Now, cook the mutton, and tomorrow I will buy you your very own cow."

112

The Romanovs ate the greasy mutton, drank vodka from the bottle, and dreamed of the good life they felt assuredly would come.

Marie wiped her mouth on her apron. "Wladislaw, what will we do? There is no one to eat the scraps!" She tossed a bone onto the floor.

Wladislaw scratched at his crotch under the table, disappointed he'd passed out and missed the whorehouse. The old horse had brought him straight home, out of long habit. He sighed and stared across the table at his wife. Kalman's gold could have bought him pleasures of which he had only dreamed. The idea of sharing a bed with unwashed Marie had no appeal.

But then he smiled and nodded toward the bone on the floor. "Tomorrow I will buy a dog. They make less of a mess than Jews."

Marie laughed uproariously, much the worse for vodka.

Pounding sounded at the front door, and they both froze momentarily.

Wladislaw hurriedly gathered the gold coins to hide them as Marie went to the door. As he pushed the last bottle of vodka from the case into the curtained cupboard, Marie led three uniformed German soldiers and a short-statured man wearing a full-length, black leather coat into the kitchen.

The man in civilian clothes clicked his heels together and said in a nasal tone, "Captain Nevan Shotzberger of the SS."

Wladislaw's legs quaked. He whispered in horror, "The Ferret!"

The sharp-eyed man sneered. "Tidying up, Wladislaw?"

Wladislaw said with a nervous stammer, "We . . . we just finished our supper."

The Ferret sat down at the table and extracted a gold coin from his breast pocket. The precious metal caught the meager light and seemed to glow with damning accusation. "A supper bought with gold. A gold Swiss coin. A coin illegal to possess under the terms of the truce. A gold coin much like the ones purchased by an escaped Jew by the name of Kalman Gold. Perhaps you had this coin because you are hiding Kalman Gold, his wife, and his children?"

Wladislaw mopped his forehead with a soiled handkerchief. "I swear they are not here."

The Ferret held up the coin, twisting it to reflect the lamplight like a diamond. "Perhaps you would explain to me where you got this coin?"

Wladislaw froze with fear.

113

When he failed to answer, Marie gushed, "Tell them. Tell them what you've done!"

Wladislaw hissed between clenched teeth, "Shut up!"

The Ferret looked to Marie. "You seem to be a reasonable woman. Perhaps you could tell us?"

"He shot them," Marie said proudly. "He found them on the road near the canal. He knew they were wanted, and he shot them."

The Ferret nodded with a thoughtful expression. "A very civic-minded and loyal act, but I am afraid it cannot protect you from the fact you stole the property of a felon wanted by the state. Property that belonged to the Third Reich. Property you used to buy meat and vodka."

The Ferret stood and glared at Wladislaw. "Now, where are the Golds, and where are the rest of the Swiss coins?"

Wladislaw spread out his hands in a beseeching manner. "There was only one coin."

The Ferret reached beneath his coat, pulled out a pistol, casually raised it, and shot Marie in the left eye. Blood spattered the wall behind her. She fell hard and her legs kicked several times as blood pumped from her eye socket. Then she went still.

Wladislaw lost control of his bladder. He could hardly breathe.

The Ferret looked to him, aiming the pistol at his head. "As you can see, I am authorized by the highest authority to do what I must. Now, where is the gold?"

Wladislaw didn't hesitate. He pulled aside the curtain covering the cupboard and lifted out the strong box.

The Ferret smiled—a cold, dead expression.

The soldiers bound Wladislaw's hands behind his back and marched him out front. When they loaded him onto the horse cart, he thought his life would be spared, but they brought the cart—still attached to the old workhorse—to a nearby tree, and set up a makeshift gallows.

Wladislaw's knees trembled when one of the soldiers slipped the noose around his neck.

The Ferret stood for a moment, studying him. "We want your body to hang here in front of your house for all to see what happens to those who steal from the Reich."

Then he held up the Swiss coin. "You know what kind of gold this is, Wladislaw Romanov?" He paused for a moment, but Wladislaw didn't answer. "It is fool's gold!"

Captain Shotzberger swung a hand and slapped the flank of the horse.

——∞◦◦❧◐❧◦◦∞——

The soldiers, far from expert hangmen, watched with interest as the rope cut into the condemned man's neck. His eyes bulged and his face turned blue. A bubbling, hissing sound came from his mouth, and his tongue stuck far out between his teeth. His legs kicked, causing his body to swing. The rope creaked under the strain. It was not a quick death.

Captain Shotzberger pocketed the coin and dusted off his hands. "Shall we go? I don't think he will escape."

He led the soldiers into the kitchen and divided the gold. "We share equally."

As they stomped out of the old house, a gaunt-faced corporal following The Ferret questioned, "What was it you called the coins, Herr Captain?"

The Ferret chuckled. "Fool's gold."

A shot exploded behind him and he fell forward through the front door onto the porch.

Secreted gold coins spilled out of his boots and onto the splintered, wooden planks. All the soldiers crowded around, grabbing up the treasure.

The corporal grinned as blood ran from The Ferret's head to pool on the worn boards. "One should not steal from the Third Reich, Herr Captain."

CHAPTER ELEVEN

FROM THE ASHES

So that others will hear and be afraid, and such evil things will not again be done in your midst.

Deuteronomy 19:20

A distant thump woke David from a sound sleep. His bedroom windowpane rattled slightly in its frame. His pulse raced. *Bombs!*

He lay still and listened. The thumping continued, growing in intensity, coming closer. "My God!" he breathed, and reached for his clothes. "Aunt Tania! Uncle Zidov! Wake up!"

David, Tania, and Zidov emerged from the house into the darkness. Sporadic flashes of bright light illuminated the buildings and yard.

Zidov held Tania's elbow as she stumbled, and he shouted to David, "Get the door to the cellar uncovered!"

The high-pitched sound of bombs spiraling down fascinated David, and he hesitated, staring at the action. The ground shook with each impact. Sharp, stunning thunderous cracks followed flashes of intense, blue-white light.

David dodged the hot shrapnel buzzing through the air.

The horse whinnied with alarm in the corral near the barn. In between the thunderclaps and percussion waves, David heard the unmistakable sound of hooves striking the side of the barn.

Zidov pulled David to him to speak into his ear, "I'm going to set the horse free. He will find safety on his own. Take Tania to the cellar."

116

Another explosion almost knocked them off their feet. Zidov steadied Tania, then lumbered toward the barn.

She screamed, "No, Zidov!"

A piece of molten metal clanged against Tania's favorite wind chimes and splintered the railing on the front porch.

"Run, David, run," Tania urged, pushing him. "Get to the potato cellar. Hurry!"

David grabbed her hand, and together they ran to the opposite side of the barn. He moved the small wagon that hid the wooden door to the potato cellar, and quickly rolled it a few yards away.

The night had fallen silent, and he hesitated again, wanting to stay outside and watch.

Tania called to Zidov.

The frantic sounds from the barn told David that Zidov was having a difficult time calming the frightened horse.

Tania touched his shoulder, bringing David's attention back to her. "Open the door, David."

Reluctantly, he did as she bid. The cool, mildew-rich air reached out of the hand-dug cellar to engulf him.

His gaze went to the sky. He wanted to see the bombers.

A flash of white light wiped away the darkness. A booming concussion wave followed quickly. It shook the earth and knocked them both to the ground.

The sturdy ladder that led down into the cellar toppled. David lay on his stomach and stared down at it.

Tania shouted, nudging him, "Get inside and put it back in place."

Explosions suddenly came in rapid succession with deafening noise.

David lowered himself into the musty cellar and struggled to adjust the ladder. His heart raced with a mix of fear and excitement.

He stood at the bottom of the slick, wooden stairs and stared up at Tania, silhouetted against the night sky.

"Zidov!" she called, looking in the direction of the barn.

A bright flash blinded David, and he instinctively put a hand to his eyes. The following concussion slammed him back against shelves of preserved beets and apples. Broken glass sliced into his back, and the earthen room collapsed around him, crushing him to the floor. An intense vacuum, caused by the explosion, sucked the air from the cellar and his lungs.

The pain and terror of suffocating cancelled out all thought. Several long minutes dragged by before he could breathe comfortably.

The weight of the cellar shelves and earthen walls pressed in on him, trapping him. Luckily, he could move his arms, and he began clawing savagely at his prison. Dirt and debris filled his mouth and eyes.

He spat and cried out, "Tania!"

Silence answered him.

He dug, pulled, and shoved at the broken wood and wet earth surrounding him. The taste of blood filled his mouth. He wept and struggled on, freeing a leg. His hand touched the debris of what had once been the ladder. He dug faster. His fingers ached.

After several fearful hours, David's hand finally broke through the dirt and rubble and reached into the cool night air. Dirt fell around him as he pulled himself out of the collapsed mouth of the cellar to lie on the buckled ground.

The scent of the hot explosion still tinged the air, the farm now only smoldering, shattered lumber.

He stared in shock at the destruction, searching for a familiar sight or sound. The night had fallen deathly silent, as if all creatures had vanished from the land.

A shoe lay a few feet away in the predawn darkness. It belonged to Tania. David reached out and pulled it to him. It felt heavy and wet. He stared at it for a moment, then screamed. The shoe had a foot in it!

He sobbed, wanting to vomit. It took a huge effort of will for him to bring himself under control.

Once thinking rationally again, he climbed unsteadily to his feet and called out for her.

No answer.

David searched desperately for Tania, knowing, if she still lived, he would need to get her to a hospital for immediate medical care. But he found no other trace of her. He sobbed and fell to his knees.

Then, numbly, he stumbled toward the barn, where Zidov had gone to free the panicked horse. After a few minutes of searching through the wreckage, he found Zidov where the corral had once stood. The disemboweled horse partially covered his guardian's body.

Vapor rose from the horse's still-warm intestines and twisted on the breeze, disappearing into the darkness.

In shock, David wandered away, crying. He had no idea where he should go, but he knew he had to escape from the horror the light of dawn would bring.

He walked aimlessly for miles, filled with despair and fear.

The night yielded to a gray, overcast dawn, and rain began to fall.

He walked on, following a dirt road, lost in grief.

Eyes downcast, David trudged toward a train crossing. Suddenly, he felt the ground trembling beneath his feet and glanced up as the hot engine of a steam locomotive flashed by in a billowing blur, missing him by inches.

David spun and fell to the gravel to keep from being drawn into the rumbling freight cars. Finally, the last flatcar filled with German military vehicles swept by, and he shakily pushed to his feet to stare after it. He had heard nothing!

He rubbed his ears with dread. Had the bomb that killed Zidov and Tania and destroyed his home rendered him deaf?

A hand touched him on the shoulder.

David jumped and pulled away.

A bearded man with a gold tooth spoke to him, but David couldn't hear what he said. A rifle hung on the man's shoulder. Three other men stood slightly behind the one who'd approached David, both armed. One looked around David's age.

David stared at the foursome, trying to understand.

One of the men pointed in the direction of the train and appeared to be shouting, though David couldn't hear his words. He looked down the tracks.

A ball of billowing fire and smoke rose into the air as the locomotive exploded. The speeding train derailed and turned into a grinding mass of twisted metal.

David gaped, then turned back to find the tattered band of partisans slapping each other on the back and pumping one another's hands. Bewildered, David watched their enthusiastic celebration, but heard none of it.

The leader said something to him and gestured toward the road. The boy offered him a rifle. David took it and slung it over a shoulder.

When the men moved away in single file, David followed. The rifle hanging at his side served to ease some of his fears.

—∘∘∘⫸◉⫷∘∘∘—

All the tragedies of the war, and the growing needs of the parishes, kept Janusz from visiting Kalman and Tova or the Gold children. It was best that way, he decided. A visit might bring suspicion, or worse. Until he felt sure of their safety, he would not endanger any of the Gold family. He kept strictly to diocese business.

When he could, Janusz officiated at the many funerals. His visits to the hospitals seemed endless. Filthy and with few resources, the facilities had filled with wounded soldiers and civilians, as well as those dying from starvation. Others died from infectious diseases because of the unavailability of antibiotics. The needs were so great, Janusz no longer knew what to pray for, so he prayed for only another day. Hell could be no worse.

Air raids by the Allied forces became relentless, destroying the German division near Krakow, but as a result, fire engulfed half the city. Many joined the homeless, destined to face a harsh, bitter winter.

During a morning mass at St. Joseph's, which Janusz held faithfully, even when the massive hall stood empty, one of the nuns handed him a sealed envelope. It had a Katowice postmark.

As soon as mass ended, he retreated to a back hallway and opened the letter. It came from an old neighbor. He recalled the friendly woman from his childhood.

The words caused Janusz to grind his teeth in despair. *Your father has died.*

Memories tormented Janusz on the ride home. The city of his youth, much like his life, lay in ruins. He felt heartsick and grief-stricken.

Who and what he was all seemed a tragic mistake. He felt as much a Jew as a Catholic, and yet could not now reduce the suffering of the Jews. Nor could he change the fact that the Church had seemingly turned the other cheek, ignoring the suffering. But he could admit what he was—the son of a Jew. Even though his father had converted to Catholicism years before, by Jewish standards, he remained a Jew—born to a Jewish mother.

Janusz walked down the old, threadbare hallway to his parents' apartment. The building smelled musty and slightly rancid. Death seemed to hang in the air as he opened the door.

He swallowed, noting the cleanliness of the cluttered living room and the vases of freshly picked wildflowers. Some of the women from the church must have come over to clean and help out.

Janusz set his coat on the arm of his father's favorite chair and called out, "Mother?"

No reply.

He sighed, guessing she'd closeted herself in the bedroom, shutting herself away from the world. The multitude of religious statues caused him to take a zigzagging route to the inner hallway. It looked just the same as when he'd been a boy.

Janusz knocked on the bedroom door. "Mother?"

No answer.

After a moment, he turned the knob and stepped inside. A thick layer of dust covered all the surfaces. Apparently, the kindly women had not felt comfortable cleaning the dismal sanctuary of his mother's private quarters.

His mother sat in a straight-backed chair, facing a filmy window, fingering a timeworn rosary, and moving her lips in silent prayer. She made no movement acknowledging Janusz's presence.

He clasped his hands and bowed his head, offering a prayer for her.

After a long five minutes, his mother set down the rosary and rose stiffly to her feet. Janusz suppressed a gasp at how much she'd aged since the last time he'd seen her. Heavy lines and wrinkles had transformed her features into those of a stranger, and her hair had turned stark white. His father had warned him that she had slowly withered within her monastic solitude, speaking only when necessary, and leaving her room only to attend church services.

She stood rigidly straight and stared at Janusz with dull eyes. "My son." No glimmer of joy pierced the blankness of her expression. "God has taken your father. Now, Stanislaw will stand in judgment for his earthly sins."

Janusz took her hand and brought the swollen, arthritic knuckles to his lips. "I will see he receives a proper burial, Mama."

She pulled away and returned to her chair, picking up the rosary again.

Janusz watched as she fingered each bead, silently praying as she faced the dirty window. He cleared his throat and murmured, "God be with you, Mama," then quietly let himself out of the apartment.

The woman down the hall, who'd sent the letter, opened her door and softly greeted Janusz. He made arrangements with her to cook and clean for his mother, now that his father could no longer shoulder the burden of Theresa's care.

Then Janusz went to the church and spoke to the priest about Stanislaw's funeral ceremony. The nuns of Janusz's church sent a humble bouquet of wildflowers.

His father would have a full, Catholic mass to please his mother. Then several of the churchwomen would take Theresa home while Janusz went on to the gravesite. He felt relieved that her ailments would keep her from the cemetery after the long mass, for he intended to respect his father's Jewish heritage as well. Knowledge of such things would certainly upset his mother, whose unreasonable hatred for Jews had escalated over the years.

After the Catholic service, Janusz presided at the head of his father's grave. He was alone; there was no one left with whom he could safely share the moment. He wished he could have had a rabbi there, but any Jews who had escaped deportation to the camps were in hiding.

He had read through the Jewish burial rites several times throughout his life, and had once attended a Jewish funeral with his father. He did his best to remember the ceremony now, stumbling his way through the *Kaddish*, the holy prayer for the dead. Traditionally, the *Hebra Kadisha*—the Society of Undertakers—would have cleansed the body, washing it in pure water and wrapping it in shrouds. Janusz had performed as much of the ritual as he could, and he knew his father would have appreciated the gesture.

At the end of the brief service, Janusz picked up the shovel and threw the first dirt on the humble casket. "I'll miss you, Father. You were a great friend."

Later, a few neighbors and relatives gathered at the Dovs' home to console the family. Janusz's mother had already retreated to her room.

Before leaving for Krakow, Janusz decided to visit Rachel.

He listened with a heavy heart to Mother Regina's account of the horrifying details of the Nazi's actions. Thank goodness Zygmunt had kept him away from the convent. Rachel would indeed have rushed to him and given herself away at the mention of her family name. Janusz wondered if even he could have shown restraint, given the circumstances.

Mother Regina told Janusz, "She has been mute since the SS came. Perhaps you can reach her."

He nodded grimly to the head nun as she promised to summon Rachel. Janusz walked, stiff-legged, to a bench in the garden. There, he bowed his head and said a silent prayer for the poor, innocent boy caught in the web of deception around the Golds' secret.

He couldn't imagine what Rachel felt, shouldering the blame for the death of the child. To witness such an atrocity could damage her for the rest of her life. He crossed himself, feeling old and empty inside. Would he ever earn God's forgiveness for his part in all the deaths attached to keeping Kalman and his family hidden?

A poised, beautiful, shapely young woman approached. He had watched Rachel blossom over the years. She stood as tall as Janusz.

He kissed her on the cheek, but she didn't react. "Rachel?"

Janusz studied her green eyes as he held her by the shoulders. He found no anger or defiance there. Seeing her rekindled the hope that had shrunk deep inside him.

He smiled gently and led her to the garden path. "Come, walk with me. The war is nearing an end. The Allied forces have invaded Europe. It should be over soon, which means it won't be long until you leave here."

Rachel stared into the distance, walking as if in a trance.

Janusz added softly, "Then you and your family will be together again."

Finally, Rachel's gaze met his. Her eyes rimmed with tears.

"The war has changed much, Rachel, but it has not changed the promise I made your father. I will come for you, and I will not rest until I reunite you with your family."

A tear spilled and ran down Rachel's smooth cheek. It disappeared beneath her chin.

"You may go now," Janusz said, and the child he had once known, who had grown into a beautiful woman, turned and walked away.

On the afternoon of May 8, 1945, as Janusz sat at his desk in Krakow, a knock sounded at the door.

"Yes?" he answered.

The door opened to reveal a nun with a lined face. "Father, the war is over."

Dazed, Janusz simply nodded. When the nun retreated, he lowered his head and wept.

The newspapers told the story:

Germany officially surrendered to the Allied forces of the United States of America, Russia, and England.

The liberated death camps of Auschwitz-Birkenau, Treblinka, Buchenwald, Dachau, and Bergen-Belsen released their surviving prisoners. The walking skeletons, emaciated and sick, totaled few in number. Six million Jews had died.

The city council of Nuremberg established a tribunal to bring to justice the Nazis who had committed the horrible war crimes. They set up transitional centers for refugees to help survivors and displaced Jews reunite with their families.

The former prisoners, orphans, and lost children who could do so listed their family members' names, places of birth, dates of birth, and the areas in which they had lived before they were sent to the camps. Some, so emotionally and mentally distraught, could not give information. Lists were compiled and posted in refugee centers for all to see. For those wishing to immigrate to other countries, the refugee centers processed papers and documents.

Janusz gathered his staff and announced his plans to leave Krakow and return only after he found his Jewish friend, Kalman Gold, and his wife, Tova. Eager, full of hope and anticipation, he left for the city of Radomsko.

Seeing Kalman again would revive his weary spirit. He needed a friend, a confidant, and who better than Kalman? Janusz hungered for one of their soul-baring talks that sometimes lasted all night. He had so much to share. So much had happened. So much lay ahead.

When he arrived at the Romanovs' house, Janusz found it occupied by dozens of tattered refugees. No one knew the whereabouts of the Romanovs or had ever heard of them—so they claimed. Janusz pleaded with them to tell what they knew, but got nothing. The paranoia brought about by the Nazis would not go away overnight.

With the help of the squatters, he pushed aside the old hutch and slowly climbed downstairs to the cellar. People whispered above him, and he guessed they'd not found the hidden room. At the bottom of the stairs, he carefully shuffled to the boarded-up window.

His hand connected with something made of straw. He pulled away a few of the half-rotted boards to let in more light.

Once he could see more clearly, he scanned the miserable room where Kalman and Tova had spent so many years of their lives. He found neither them, nor their meager belongings. He heaved a heavy sigh of relief. If the Nazis had discovered them, they would have dragged them from the cellar, leaving their worldly goods behind.

Then he looked at the straw doll lodged upon the windowsill—the same doll David had made for his parents. At his feet lay a second straw figure. Janusz bent to pick it up, and realized that both Kalman and Tova had tied strips of their own clothes to the dolls. He turned the fragile figures over in his hands and spotted a glint of gold within the straw. Both dolls held one of Kalman's gold coins—one for each child?

He carefully put the dolls in his inside coat pocket and made his way back upstairs. The people crowding around the cellar door parted for him. He read fear in their faces and knew they would not give him any information about the former occupants of this house. He decided to leave without a more thorough search. Whatever goods left by Wladislaw or Kalman most assuredly lay in the hands of the first people who'd come across the abandoned farm.

The squatters followed him out into the front yard, but not beyond the rutted driveway. Janusz stared at the old farmhouse for a long moment, then trudged down the road.

He would not return.

On the way into the city, he talked to neighbors and merchants. No one could tell him anything about Wladislaw, though all seemed nervous at his questions.

Finally, the priest in Radomsko told Janusz he had heard rumors about the Nazis hanging Wladislaw. Unfortunately, he knew nothing of hidden Jews or a man named Kalman Gold.

Janusz's disappointment sank bone deep. He felt discouraged and bewildered by the torment and anguish of life. The war had ended, but the pain had not.

After a week of searching for Kalman and Tova, frustrated and disheartened, Janusz journeyed to the Catholic convent in Katowice. He'd guessed the devoted parents had left the straw dolls for him to find, to give to Rachel and David as tokens of hope and love. Kalman and Tova must have wanted to leave some sign of their passage. If only they could have left a note explaining things more clearly.

Janusz sighed, understanding why they had not. The Nazis had searched so diligently for Kalman; the risk of revealing his identity, and even a hint of where his children hid, would have been too great. So, his friend had left two straw dolls, showing that he still thought of his children, and that he'd gone to some other place.

The coins inside the dolls also told Janusz that Kalman had trusted Wladislaw with the location of his precious strongbox, buried deep within the pit—a pit of human waste and refuse. Had Kalman and Tova needed the gold to buy their way out of the country?

Janusz could only hope they had, indeed, escaped before Wladislaw's capture and hanging.

Janusz hesitated on the steps outside the Convent of the Blessed Virgin. He had no idea what he would say to Rachel. With a prayer on his lips, he lifted the scarred brass knocker.

He asked for Rachel, and the nun who ushered him inside breathlessly said she would send for her. While he waited, another nun told him of all the changes that had taken place since his last visit. During the weeks after the war had ended, the majority of the children had left. Some, but only a few, had reunited with their families, and even fewer were adopted. Most had simply disappeared, walking away in search of their lost families. With their absence, the old convent seemed solemn and too quiet.

Janusz's arrival brought on an avalanche of demands from the staff. The nuns sounded destitute and disheartened. Food was scarce. The convent and school had fallen into decay after so many years and lack of maintenance. A raging fear of the unknown had replaced the German threat.

Janusz listened and promised help, though he had no idea how he would keep the promises. After his visit with the staff, he waited for Rachel in the office of the Mother Superior.

He prayed for wisdom. *Please, God, give me the words.*

After a soft knock on the door, Rachel finally arrived.

"Sit down, Rachel."

Rachel sat and placed her hands in her lap.

Janusz paced as he spoke. "Your parents were not where I left them, but that does not mean they will not be found. There is much confusion in the country right now. The war has changed everything. Refugee centers are being set up. Perhaps they are in one of them."

He reached into his overcoat and pulled out the two straw dolls. "Your mother and father left these for you and your brother. They hid a special gold coin in each and tied pieces of their clothes to them. Take yours, and with it, take heart. Your parents thought only of you and David every day of their hiding. They wanted nothing more than to reunite with you and your brother, and start over."

Rachel accepted the delicate token of love and hope from Janusz with trembling hands. Her fingers caressed the pitiful strips of tattered cloth, and she gently brought the doll to her breast and closed her eyes.

Janusz swallowed, feeling tears in his eyes. "I promised I would take you from here when the war ended. I have come to do that. Would you go with me to get your brother, David?"

Rachel stood and smoothed her dress, still clutching the doll against her heart. "Yes, Father, I will go with you."

So, she can now speak, Janusz thought. *Thank you, Heavenly Father.*

He waited in the courtyard for Rachel to pack her possessions. She joined him only a few minutes later, holding a small, threadbare valise. She said her goodbyes to the nuns, and then, together, they walked to the train station.

Rachel never looked back.

They made the long train journey to the small, remote farm in companionable silence.

Just before the train pulled into the station, Rachel startled Janusz by saying, "I often dreamed of coming here, after the shooting. I remember the little house where we spent the night, before you took me to the convent."

Her lovely face clouded, and she leaned her forehead against the dirty window with a sigh. "I will never forget looking over my shoulder and seeing David give our secret signal as we left him behind." She tapped three fingers over her heart and whispered, "I wonder if David is as tall as I am."

Janusz smiled. The journey for the twins had come full circle. He patted her hand and said softly, "He is taller, and broad, like my uncle Zidov. Farming has made him strong. You will see."

At her suddenly fearful expression, Janusz chuckled. "You will recognize him, and he, you. David is still your twin."

Rachel relaxed her tense posture and issued a rare trill of laughter. "When we were very young, he constantly pulled my hair, and when I tried to punish him, he would wrestle me to the floor and squeeze me until I screamed 'surrender.'"

Janusz gave a soft laugh at her childhood reminiscence. "I am sure he longs to pull your hair and hug you until you squeal."

Rachel stared out the smudged window. A faraway smile lit her face.

Janusz prayed with all of his heart that the twins would soon share many more lighthearted moments.

Then he sobered and fingered his rosary. *Please, God, let Kalman and Tova also be able to share in the blessed innocence of their children's laughter once more.*

When they arrived at the village near the farm, Janusz went to the local Catholic church to arrange for a ride.

The parish priest shook his head and said grimly, "There's nothing out there but holes in the ground, Bishop Dov."

Rachel stiffened beside Janusz. He glanced at her, feeling a mixture of confusion, shock, and concern. He managed a hoarse whisper. "The farm was destroyed?"

The old clergyman sighed and nodded. "A bombing raid by the Allies. Unfortunately, though most of the bombs hit their German targets, freeing the countryside of the Nazi threat, a few strayed into the farmlands."

He cleared his throat and continued in a softer tone of voice, "We held a service for your aunt and uncle, Bishop Dov . . . may they rest in peace." He crossed himself and turned away.

Janusz felt his world crumbling, just as he'd thought the time of pain and sorrow had come to an end. If not for Rachel clutching his arm and digging her nails into his skin, he would have collapsed. However, one look into her brilliant green eyes startled him out of his haze.

He called to the retreating, aged priest, "Father! You say that you buried my aunt and uncle, but what of my nephew, David?"

The old priest turned and frowned at them. "We found only Tania and Zidov. As far as I know, their son was never found." Then he put a hand to his head as if suddenly remembering something important. "I will ask around the town on your behalf, Bishop. Perhaps someone did take him in." He hurried along the cobbled path and went into the rectory, leaving Janusz and Rachel to stare after him.

"We will go to the farm and see what is left," Janusz told her solemnly.

She simply nodded and walked toward the parish stable, dragging her valise.

Both Rachel and Janusz kept silent on the long and bumpy ride by horse cart. When the horses finally stopped, Rachel and Janusz stared in mute horror at the sight of the craters where the farmhouse had once stood. Blackened rubble was strewn everywhere, and charred stumps replaced the trees that had surrounded the property. No one could have survived such a concentrated act of destruction.

Janusz fell to his knees, closed his eyes, and prayed.

When he finally brought his emotions under control, he joined Rachel at the remnants of the barn. A few sheep bleated in the far pastures.

He pointed to the unmarred expanse of green. "If David had been out tending the flock, he would have survived the blasts. We must keep hope alive in our hearts, Rachel."

Janusz put an arm around her shoulder, noting the dullness in her eyes, dry of tears. Had this last horror been too much for her? For a moment, words failed him.

"Rachel, I will find your brother. I swear to God I will."

"I don't trust God," Rachel whispered. She pulled out of his loose embrace and headed back to the waiting horse cart.

On the train, Rachel sat and stared silently out the window. Janusz shared her anguish. The fact that he had unwittingly given her false hope only added to his despair. He prayed for wisdom and guidance.

He took her hand in his.

Rachel looked at Janusz, then returned her attention to the window.

Finally, he gathered the courage to speak. "Rachel, I made your father a promise—a promise that after the war I would reunite your family.

I am disappointed we haven't found your mother and father, or your brother, but that doesn't mean I'll give up. I never will. I will search until I find them. Be encouraged that no one has reported their deaths. They are simply missing. Many are missing. In time, most will be found."

Rachel sniffed as a tear spilled and ran down her cheek. She squeezed Janusz's hand. "Thank you, Father."

Her eyes lifted Janusz's spirits. She had Kalman's eyes.

"Rachel, again, these are difficult times. I cannot offer you a home, unless you want to return to the convent."

She shook her head no. "I am no longer Rachel Stacowski. I am, once again, Rachel Gold."

Janusz nodded, understanding. He knew well the anguish of hiding one's Jewish heritage. "The Allied forces have set up refugee camps for the homeless and displaced. They are organizing efforts to reunite families and friends. They have resources I do not."

He hesitated, unsure of how to go on.

Rachel raised her chin. "And you want me to go there?"

"I wish I didn't have to suggest it, but the result may be finding your parents and David."

Rachel bit her lip. "I remember the camps in Lodz."

Janusz gasped, shocked that she thought he would ask her to go to such a place. He quickly shook his head. "These will be different. Those evil times are over."

Rachel held his gaze for a long, tense moment, before whispering, "Then I will go."

Janusz decided to shirk his duties, leaving the routine, day-to-day church business to his underlings. His promise to Kalman held priority over all other things. He would make every effort to find David.

He removed his priest's cassock and replaced it with simple farming clothes. He then took to the countryside, searching for David, hoping, somehow, he'd escaped the bombing. He questioned everyone with whom he came in contact, but no one had heard of a teenage boy by the name of David Gold.

Disguised as a Polish Jew, he'd found that he could assist the survivors without engendering their fear and mistrust of anything connected to the Catholic Church, which had turned a blind eye during the war. As one of their own, Janusz could gain their trust and bring them back to a semblance of civilization, giving them a chance at a new beginning.

Each Sunday, Janusz returned to Katowice, donned his cassock, and performed the Mass. He could no longer bear to hear confessions; the junior priests took his place in such things, relieving him of some of his burden.

On one of his outreach missions, Janusz guided a timid young woman, clutching an infant to her breast, into the receiving tent of the displaced persons camp, and helped her into a folding chair in front of a clerk.

Tears formed in the woman's eyes, and Janusz put a gentle hand on her shoulder, noting, with a heavy heart, her instinctive flinch. "These people will care for you, my child. Perhaps they will find the rest of your family. Do not fear them. You are safe here."

She trembled, watching him with wide, fearful eyes, but said nothing. Janusz waited a few moments, then nodded to the clerk and ducked out of the tent.

Rain fell in sheets, creating ponds of mud and making the already miserable place seem even more inhospitable. He sighed and stared at the grim mass of tents, lean-tos, and other crude structures that dotted the dull landscape. Janusz imagined thousands of poor wretches, huddling together or separately, trying to keep warm and dry—though he suspected few succeeded.

As he trudged back to Katowice from the camp, the rain felt like tears from heaven, pounding on his shoulders, his back, his head, his soul. Overwhelmed, Janusz fell to his knees at the side of the muddy road, buried his face in his hands, and sobbed.

Where is God?

The question repeated in his heart and mind, echoing Janusz's growing disillusionment. At first, he'd simply questioned the church, but now, depression made him more adamant, and he questioned the very faith that had sustained him all of his life.

It had become increasingly difficult for him to step through the doors of the various churches and convents of his diocese. So much so that, when Rome had formally offered him the promotion to archbishop, he had failed to respond.

By the time he regained control of his emotions, he'd begun to shiver. With a groan, he pushed back to his feet and staggered toward the statuesque church that loomed in the distance.

He stepped inside the back door of the rectory and stopped short, teeth chattering. The cozy warmth made him flush with guilt as he thought of the lost souls out in the storm, without heat or proper shelter or most of the basic human necessities.

A middle-aged nun bustled into the room, took one look at Janusz shivering on the threshold, clucked her tongue, and rushed to him. "Father! What were you thinking, being out in such weather? You will catch your death. Come, now, you'll need dry clothes and a bowl of soup by the hearth."

She grabbed his arm and dragged him toward his quarters, calling for one of the younger priests as she went.

Janusz hardly remembered the priest helping him out of his clothes, or starting the small fire in his sitting room, or even eating the soup the sister had brought him. He existed in a perpetual haze of depression. A cloud seemed to obscure his life and lifted only when he helped those in desperate need.

The fire popped, startling him into the present. Janusz gazed about the room, noting an envelope on his writing desk. The seal caught his attention, and he straightened in his chair. The missive had come from Rome—not just Rome, but from the Pope's personal staff.

Janusz reached for the envelope and turned it over in trembling hands. It held the papal seal. He sucked in a breath and stared at the elaborate design that represented Pope Pius XII.

"Good Lord."

He broke the seal and extracted a piece of parchment—the Pope's signature stationery. In clear, bold writing, the letter summoned Janusz to Rome for an audience with the Holy Father himself.

Janusz stared in disbelief at the neatly handwritten words, then reached back into the envelope for a packet of travel documents. The enclosed train ticket procured passage for the next day—Sunday—after Mass.

He set the letter and documents aside and stared into the flames of his small hearth.

Perhaps God had seen fit to answer some of his questions. Perhaps this trip to Rome would restore his ailing faith.

Janusz thought of Rachel, alone in the refugee camp, searching for her parents and her brother. Three months had passed since he'd left her at the Lodz camp. Had she been successful? Had she found someone to care for her?

Another wave of guilt came over Janusz. He'd promised Kalman that he'd save his friend's family, and yet he had abandoned the only survivor to a camp filled with strangers.

The urge to leave the comfort of his quarters and travel to that distant camp tortured Janusz, but the summons to Rome left him no choice. He sighed and went to bed, vowing he would seek out Rachel the moment he returned to Poland.

CHAPTER TWELVE

PASSAGE TO HOPE

Love blinds us to faults, hatred to virtues.

Moshe ibn Ezra (c. 1055 after 1135),
Shirat Yisrael

Aaron Ross completed his interview with U.S. Army Intelligence regarding his experience in the Treblinka concentration camp. He stepped out through the open gates and stared up and down the busy road. Freedom held less hope for him than some. The Nazis had taken Dina and Stefan. Kalman, his best friend and business partner, had most likely died. He remembered the Nazis transporting Kalman and Tova away from Lodz in the back of a truck.

Aaron found it difficult to believe he had survived. Ironically, the one thing that had created most of the problems in his prewar life—his penis—had saved him.

He'd not revealed to the U.S. interviewers anything about the experimental vasectomy performed on him. The Germans had sought an effective way to prevent young Aryan males from reproducing without castration, which would significantly reduce their overall performance in the variety of roles the Third Reich had found for them.

The Germans had given him a drug to induce an erection so he could copulate with an endless string of teenage Jewish girls on camera, in order for them to study the effects of the vasectomy. Aaron had not experienced a spontaneous erection since the operation.

134

He climbed up into an army truck headed for Warsaw and stared back at the place where he'd lost his soul, watching it fade in the distance. Warsaw represented the opportunity for work. Such a large city would surely need attorneys.

When Aaron arrived, the ruins of Poland's once-thriving metropolis indicated that much time would pass before the rebuilding of law practices.

He would not return to Katowice, where he'd once lived with his wife and child. It held too many painful memories. Alone and hungry, he journeyed, wandering about the countryside, lost in both body and soul.

One day, on the southern border of Warsaw, he stumbled into an American-operated refugee camp known as Number 12. Hundreds of drab-green tents with wooden floors—carefully aligned in military precision along gravel streets and walkways—provided a home for the liberated and displaced Jews.

Aaron, now older, his body weight returning and his hair grown out, registered in the camp. It smelled of canvas and freshly cut lumber, and housed 1,127 refugees.

Doctors treated the rampant malnutrition, broken bones, and diseases, while an army of administrators tried to do the impossible: reassemble broken human lives. Stories of torment, suffering, and slaughter poured out of the many disseminated Jews, while some could not speak of it at all.

After a three-day medical exam and intelligence briefing, Aaron saw the notice on a bulletin board: *Displaced person locator researcher—language, administrative & typing skills required. 50 cents per hr.*

Aaron applied for and got the position, and became one of twenty-two researchers. He welcomed the opportunity to work and quickly lost himself in it, putting in twelve to fifteen hours a day. It didn't make him forget the crying, nude girls with shaved heads who'd lain beneath him, but at the end of the work day, exhausted, he seldom dreamed.

He found it difficult to talk to Jewish women, especially the younger ones, and most particularly if they had short hair. For the most part, Aaron kept to himself.

At a late dinner in a mess tent, a young woman approached him. "Mr. Ross?"

Aaron recognized her immediately. Esther Bloom, a doe-eyed brunette who had worked in the office at the Star Coal Mining Company in Katowice—one of the few Aaron hadn't seduced, for she'd been barely a teen. She provided a welcome link to a past he longed to recapture.

They spoke of mutual friends, sharing memories of office gossip and business that brought smiles, and even a laugh. They both shared that eons had passed since they had laughed.

In the coming weeks, they met every night for dinner, and the bond between them grew.

With Esther's help, Aaron found the courage to accept the loss of his wife and son. After one of their enjoyable dinners, he held up his hand, displaying a gold band on his pinky finger. "A Jewish matron in Lodz brought me Dina's wedding band. She had slipped it off before the Nazis released the gas. Dina hadn't wanted the Germans to have it." He paused and wiped a tear. "The last I saw of Stefan, a guard was dragging him away."

Esther sighed and caught his hand. Though her quiet sympathy did not ease the pain of his grief, it did bring him a measure of peace. Her companionship reminded him that life had gone on, and gave him hope to somehow build a new future for himself.

One afternoon, Esther rushed into the locator's office and handed Aaron a camp population list. She pointed to a name halfway down the page. "Rachel Gold. Could this be Kalman Gold's daughter? Wasn't her name Rachel?"

Aaron bolted to his feet. "Yes!" His heart raced with excitement as he headed for the door.

Esther hurried after him. "It says she works in Area C."

Aaron and Esther entered the tent designated for food preparation. A young woman was wiping down the wide mess tables with her back to them.

She turned, and their eyes met.

Aaron knew Rachel at that moment. The resemblance to Kalman was unmistakable. "Rachel Gold," Aaron uttered, barely able to speak. "You may not remember me, Rachel, but I am Aaron Ross. I was your father's business partner in Katowice."

Rachel's green eyes studied Aaron carefully before she spoke. "I remember you."

Aaron took several steps and drew Rachel into his arms. He held her against his chest and stroked her hair. Tears filled his eyes. Rachel stood stiff-armed and tense at first, but then a well of emotion seemed to break, and she sobbed loudly against Aaron's shoulder.

Esther joined them, putting her arms around both, also crying.

The bond between Esther and Rachel came naturally. Only six years older than Rachel, Esther quickly became a big sister. The shared Katowice roots and link to the Star Coal Mining Company made them feel like family. Aaron became their surrogate guardian.

As they shared evening meals, Rachel described her life in hiding and told them what little she knew of her parents' and brother's whereabouts. They checked teletypes daily for new arrivals at all the refugee camps, and Aaron enlisted the aid of a U.S. Army intelligence officer he had befriended. Captain Rondino, like Aaron, had worked as an attorney in civilian life.

Two weeks after discovering Rachel, and still basking in the hope that Kalman and Tova may have also survived, Aaron was summoned by Captain Rondino to the intelligence tent.

He waved him over to a secluded corner and said grimly, "The news is not good, Aaron. A captured German corporal, taken prisoner in the area where Kalman Gold hid, reported hearing of the robbery and death of a man named Gold. He remembered the incident because it involved the theft of gold Swiss coins."

Pain stabbed at the pit of Aaron's stomach. The gold coins eliminated any doubt. Aaron had helped Kalman find the broker who sold them. He thanked his American friend and left.

Though the gunfire of the war had silenced, wounds reopened. Aaron staggered to his tent, fell onto his cot, and wept.

He arrived late that evening for the meal with the two girls. They busily talked about wedding arrangements taking place in a Section M tent. An American solider planned to marry a Jewish girl.

Esther said softly, "Things must be very different in America. This sergeant is a Swede."

Aaron made no mention of what he had learned, and vowed silently that he never would.

He slept little that night.

Even though the Allied forces brought them hope, Poland lay in ruins. The country, the life he had known . . . all gone. He'd survived, but everything he'd loved had died. Aaron longed to escape the cruel, painful hell. Esther's innocent words, spoken in the mess tent, kept echoing in his mind: "Things must be very different in America."

He would escape to America. In more ways than one, he figured.

He decided to talk to Captain Rondino the next morning. Maybe his friend could help. Rondino, a suave Italian-American, always brimmed with self-confidence and had encouraged Aaron to rebuild his shattered life.

"I'll see what I can do," Captain Rondino promised after Aaron made his plea for help. "But, if I succeed, you owe me. Someday I may need a favor."

Aaron could not imagine ever being in a position to help anyone, but he answered,

"Of course, whether you succeed or not."

Five weeks passed.

Then, once more at the dinner table, Aaron waited until they finished the meal. "I have news," he said soberly to Esther and Rachel.

The two women fell silent, exchanging quick, worried glances.

"I have received permission to immigrate to America. I leave in three days."

Esther raised a hand to her throat. She opened her mouth, but no words came.

Rachel sat frozen. Tears welled in her eyes.

Esther forced out tightly, "We . . . we're very happy for you."

Aaron grimaced at the pain he read in their eyes. "I'm glad you are. Because I have passports for both of you." He smiled. "You didn't think I'd leave without my girls, did you?"

Esther bit her lip and reached across the table to take Aaron's hand. Then she reached for Rachel's. Tears streamed down her cheeks.

Aaron squeezed both hands. "Three of us. Now and forever."

Esther stood and pulled Aaron to his feet to hug him, burying her head on his shoulder. Rachel joined the embrace.

Passports and travel orders in hand, the trio traveled by train to the port of Gdansk on the Baltic Sea, to board the refugee ship *Liberty*. Nearly eight thousand hopeful souls crowded aboard the aging ship.

Together they stood at the deck rail in a cold rain, watching the coastline fade into the mist.

Rachel whispered, as rain dripped off her chin, "Goodbye, other life."

More passengers boarded in Napoli. The converted cruise liner carried ten thousand people. Since they had to ration food and water, showering and bathing were not allowed. A large, empty swimming pool on the main deck provided extra room for human cargo on its dry, plastered bottom.

Despite all, Rachel, Esther, and Aaron acknowledged their happiness. They had something to look forward to. The departure from Europe had become a closure. They no longer looked back. Now they looked ahead. Now they had hope.

Three days into the voyage, Esther joined Aaron at the rail in the darkness on a crowded upper deck. "Can't sleep?" she asked.

The choppy sea sent up a salty spray that occasionally swept over them as the big ship lumbered through the night.

Aaron slipped an arm around Esther to protect her from the chill. "Just thinking about what's out there."

"Hope."

Aaron turned to take her by the shoulders. "That's what you've brought me." His eyes found hers. "I had nothing left, until you, Esther. You and Rachel have given me everything. I can't image life without you. I don't know what lies ahead in America, but I do know I want to share it with you."

Tears glittered in Esther's eyes.

"Esther Bloom," Aaron said soberly, "will you be my wife?"

She gasped, then smiled. "Yes, Aaron Ross. I will be your wife."

He took Esther's face in his hands and kissed her. Her arms snaked around his back. They stood holding each other for a long time, not wanting the moment to end.

Finally breaking the silence between them, Aaron said softly into Esther's hair, "Esther, there's one thing I must do. I must adopt Rachel. I promised her father that, if necessary, I would care for her as my own."

Esther looked up into his eyes. "I'm sure you'll be a good father and husband."

They learned that an Orthodox rabbi—a survivor of the Auschwitz-Birkenau death camp—had also boarded the ship.

Rabbi Berkowitz agreed to preside over the modest wedding ceremony held in a former suite on the massive ship. In addition to Rachel, two elders—as required by Jewish law—witnessed the ceremony.

Aaron fingered the gold ring his wife had pulled off her hand shortly before her death, then slipped it onto Esther's finger. He repeated the vows. "With this ring, you are consecrated to me, according to the Law of Moses and Israel."

The rabbi recited the marriage ceremony.

Esther and Aaron drank from a cup of wine and then Aaron, in true Jewish tradition, broke the glass with his foot to commemorate the destruction of the Holy Temple. The rabbi then pronounced them husband and wife.

Then the rabbi and his two elderly companions shouted, "Mazal Tov!"

The protocol of the voyage precluded a wedding night together. Aaron continued to stay in the men's quarters.

He knew their marriage would remain platonic. The virility and passion he had once enjoyed had now, like much of his life, gone forever. He would soon have to share his secret with Esther.

After three weeks on the Atlantic Ocean, the Statue of Liberty—distant and dull gray—finally emerged from a late afternoon mist. Shouts of joy came from everywhere on the ship. The refugees crowded the rails for a glimpse of America.

Rachel stared in awe at the irregular, crowded skyline. "It's so big," she said in amazement.

"Don't worry, they still have room for us," Aaron offered with a smile. "And as soon as possible, Esther and I will make your adoption legal."

Rachel's eyes teared up and she nodded. "We will be a proper family."

Her softly spoken words made Aaron swallow hard, and he couldn't answer. He simply drew her into a gentle hug and kissed the top of her head.

The processing and quarantine at Ellis Island took three days. After a spraying of lice powder, followed by a bath, doctors questioned and examined them until, finally, they faced an immigration officer who reviewed their papers.

———∘∘∘⟩◉⟨∘∘∘———

Rachel nervously glanced about the crowded auditorium. Esther and Aaron were several yards away, each occupied with their own documents and customs personnel. She swallowed and kept in her line, determined to face this step toward a new life without bothering them.

When she stepped in front of a desk, an obese, sweaty, bald officer asked Rachel, "Your name?"

When she didn't answer, he looked down at her papers. "Do you speak English, Rachel Gold?"

"Yes."

"Have you ever used any other name?"

"Yes."

"Well, what is it?"

"Rachel Stacowski."

The heavyset officer seemed annoyed. Rachel's heart raced with fright.

The man studied her. "Which is it? Are you a Pole or a Jew?"

"I am Rachel Gold," she answered in careful English. "I used the name Rachel Stacowski to hide from the Germans. But when I'm legally adopted, my name will be Ross."

"Gold, Stacowski, Ross," the officer grunted as he thumbed through the papers. "That's a lot of names for such a young woman. Plus, we've had a lot of them come through here. How about something else?"

Rachel didn't understand. "Something else?"

"Another name. We're full up on Jews and Poles." He lifted a hardbound ledger.

"See? So let's pick something simple. I've got the authority to record any name you choose."

"My name is Rachel Gold."

The man laid the book down and mumbled, "I'm beginning to understand why the Krauts had a problem with you people."

"Pardon me?"

"I'll give you four letters. You can keep that. Now pick something."

"Pick something?"

"Yeah, like Holt, Frey, Ward. Trust me, in today's world, they're all better than Gold."

"Ward?" Rachel still didn't understand.

The officer picked up his pen and pulled the ledger in front of him. "Ward it is." Scrawling the name, he said, "Welcome to America, Rachel Ward."

Trembling, Rachel answered, "Thank you, sir."

———∘∘∘⟨◈⟩∘∘∘———

The authorities deposited the trio, along with their meager baggage, onto the dock at New York City's Battery Park. The towering buildings they'd seen from Ellis Island now looked even bigger, and New York turned into a big, busy, loud place.

Rachel murmured to Esther, worried about how New Yorkers would treat them.

But New York ignored them. She stared as the noise of trucks, cars, and buses filled the waning light—exciting and overwhelming.

Esther said in Polish, at Rachel's side, "I feel lost."

Aaron dug in a coat pocket for a crumpled piece of paper. "Here we speak only English."

He unfolded the note and frowned at it. "Let's find the address Captain Rondino gave us. Twenty-seven fourteen East Essex."

Using a twenty-dollar bill Captain Rondino had loaned him, and directions from an Irish cop on horseback who told Rachel she had nice legs, Aaron bought subway tokens for the crosstown ride. They marveled at the human crush pouring in and out of the stairs to the subway, and the appearance of the women—faces bright with makeup, hair curled and styled. They smelled like flowers and had ruby-red lips.

Rachel whispered, "I feel dirty and poor. Someday, I'm going to be just like them."

` The subway train was fast, noisy, and crowded. Americans talked a lot and smiled at each other. They seemed like a happy, busy people, all rushing to get somewhere.

Aaron pushed his two women toward the door at the Essex Street Station. They walked another five blocks, tired and emotionally drained, checking each address.

The city, now bright with light, seemed to be an endless train of cars, trucks, buses, and cabs. Did Americans ever sleep?

Finally, they spotted the number on an aging, brownstone apartment building. Aaron led the way to the third floor, where he knocked on a door. A shapely Italian woman, in a robe with a plunging neckline that revealed substantial cleavage, opened the door. Music blared from a radio inside.

Aaron smiled and said, "Mr. Ray Bendici, please."

The woman nodded. "We've been expecting you." Then, over a shoulder, she called, "Ray, they're here!"

Esther took Rachel's hand in hers. They stood behind Aaron.

A round-faced, unshaven man with raven-black hair and a bulging stomach joined the woman. He wore a sleeveless tee shirt. "You Aaron Ross?"

"Yes."

"Got a letter from Sonny. He said you was coming, said to get you a place and a job."

"We would be very grateful," Aaron assured the man.

The man tried to see around Aaron, and Aaron stepped aside. "This is my wife, Esther, and Rachel."

Bendici eyed the two women and nodded. "Okay, I can use both of them in the shop—that is, if they can sew."

Esther and Rachel told him they could

"Okay then, you can use the storage room on the sixth floor. There's a toilet down the hall. One week free; after that it's five bucks a week."

Bendici's demeanor told Aaron that the favor didn't come from the heart, but rather an obligation to the captain. But, grateful for the opportunity, he wouldn't examine a gift horse too closely.

"Okay," Aaron agreed.

The man dug in a pocket for keys. "The sew room is on the second floor. We start at seven." He pulled a key off a crowded ring and nodded toward Esther and Rachel. "They speak English?"

"Yes."

"Shop's a block down on the left. Kauffman's Warehouse. Lock the door after you're in."

"Thank you."

Bendici closed the door. Aaron turned to Esther and Rachel and held up the key. "Shall we go home?"

The warehouse appeared gray and tired, with many broken windows. Time had weathered and bleached the once-red brick face.

Aaron tried the key in three doors before it finally opened a small one on the side of the building. He locked the door behind them and led the way up dimly lit, wooden stairs. The aroma of sizing and fresh-cut cloth lay thick in the air. Esther sneezed.

When they reached the sixth floor, Aaron cross the room, wiped at the dust and grime on a window, and stared out.

The window faced the street, and from the sixth floor, the view of the city at night—for Aaron, from war-torn Poland, with unavailable or forbidden light, due to air raids—created an unbelievable panorama.

"My God," he said softly. "Look." He stepped aside to allow room for Esther and Rachel. "Look out there."

Aaron whispered, "You know what that is you're looking at?"

Esther answered, "More light than in all the world."

Aaron put an arm around each woman's shoulder. "More than that . . . it's the light of freedom."

The stairs had stopped at a small storage room, piled high with bundles of twine-wrapped shirts and pants. It had only a single, dim, shade-less bulb to light the room.

Aaron piled the bundles into the center of the room, to create a divider of sorts. Although only four feet high, it provided separation and some privacy when lying down.

Rachel and Esther searched another storage room and found a wooden stool, a crate—which would serve as a table—a small broken mirror, coat hangers, a heavy bolt of wool to use as blankets, and a stack of tattered *Life* magazines. Aaron felt like they were kids at Christmas.

Aaron and Esther transformed the room into a makeshift home while Rachel flipped through the magazines, commenting on everything from shoes and clothing to automobiles and lavish furnishings. Finally, the time came to turn the light out. They undressed in the dark and covered themselves with the wool blankets from the discarded bolt. The sounds of the city reached through the walls as the newlyweds lay together for the first time.

Aaron kissed his wife's forehead and whispered sleepily, "Good night, dear."

Before dozing off, he felt Esther kissing him gently on the neck. He stirred. She kissed again in the stubble of his beard and then moved her lips to his.

Their mouths melted together. Tongues explored and teased. Warm breath raced through nostrils. Esther molded herself against him, raising a leg over his. She moved his hand to her breast, moaning in his mouth as he squeezed her nipple. Then she slid her hand down over the hair on his chest and onto the flat of his stomach. Unable to speak, Aaron tensed, knowing he would disappoint his eager wife.

She moved the hand further, but Aaron blocked her sensual assault. He started to confess his shame, but she covered his open mouth with a kiss and took his penis in her hand.

Aaron pulled away from her.

"Why . . . what?"

Aaron answered hoarsely, "Rachel will hear. Later, when we have privacy." He took her face in his hands, kissed her gently and turned over, willing sleep to come quickly and silence Esther's quiet sobs.

One thing even noisier than New York at night was New York during the day. Dawn had barely broken when Aaron, dressed in his best, walked to a nearby bakery and bought a loaf of bread and coffee. When he returned, he found the two women combing each other's hair and studying their reflections in the broken piece of mirror. Soon, they would go to work.

They talked over breakfast.

Both Esther and Rachel had the sewing jobs in the factory, and Aaron vowed he would find employment as well before the day ended. He kissed both women on their cheeks and went off to conquer New York.

"I'll bring something for dinner," he promised.

———oooﾞﾞﾞoooﾞ———

Esther and Rachel arrived at the second-floor sewing room at six-thirty. A cigar-smoking Bendici greeted them. "Let's get to work."

The sprawling, cluttered room proved to be a noisy, crowded sweatshop, jammed with an army of women bent over clattering machines and cutting tables. Bendici told Esther and Rachel they would earn twenty-five cents an hour and work at least fourteen hours a day to make their quota.

Neither woman felt discouraged. It was freedom, work, and hope.

Rachel teamed with a heavy black woman to become a cutter; Bendici assigned Esther to sewing. Rachel had never spoken to a Negro, and as she watched the skilled black hands guide shears across a cut of linen, she said in slow, deliberate English, "What language do you speak?"

The woman chuckled. "English, better than you, honey."

Aaron decided to find a way to return to the practice of law. A city like New York, a country like America, would need many attorneys, and his skills would surpass all. He walked until he found a street lined with many law offices, surprised to find their doors still locked at 7:00 a.m.

He waited, enjoying the sights and sounds of the city. At 8:00 a.m. the offices still had locked doors. After almost another hour had passed, he began to wonder if he'd happened to arrive on an American holiday. But promptly at nine, the offices opened.

Aaron looked over the posted signs and chose *Finch, Applebee, & Crowe*. A polished brass plaque adorned their door. A receptionist greeted him, briefly looked him over, and indicated a chair in the small waiting area with a disinterested murmur to take a seat. The office smelled of rich cigars . . .

Twenty-one firms later, he dejectedly tried still another. Surely someone could use his services as an attorney, an apprentice, or even a clerk. The Law Office of Samuel Sloan had no brass plaque and no receptionist.

Sloan, a gruff man in his fifties, said in a sharp, no-nonsense tone, "I'm not gonna hire you because I hardly have enough work for one. But I'm gonna give you some advice. This is New York. Even more than being an American, you gotta be a New Yorker.

"Nobody cares what you did in Warsaw. The minute you said you studied law in Warsaw, I knew you were a Jew or a Pollack. Nobody in this town is gonna hire either. You wanna practice law in this country, boy, go back to school.

"You wanna be an attorney in America, be a good one. Pick a good school, and don't give up till you get in. Sometimes nothing works better than being a pain in the ass. You're a smart man, been through law school once, got some experience. Combine that with a good law school here, and you'll hit the ground running.

"Forget about what happened in Poland. It won't buy you anything here. Anybody asks where you're from, tell them what street you live on, or change the subject. You're no longer a Jew or a Pollack. Now, you're an American. Don't just act like one, become one."

Aaron, discouraged and worried, confided the day's frustration with Esther while Rachel lost herself in the magazines. "Being a Jew in America isn't easy, either."

"Then do as the man said," Esther suggested. She took Aaron's hand in hers. "Go back to school so you can practice law. Rachel and I will provide."

"You would do this for me?"

"As you would for me," Esther answered with a smile. "If we're ever to have a home, sacrifices will have to be made."

Aaron kissed her. "I love you, Esther. I'll find a law school."

He spent the evening organizing papers he thought a law school might demand. He didn't have much. He'd lost his life before the war. He hoped his passport, visa, and papers of background authenticity from the United States Army would help.

By the time he'd finished, Esther and Rachel had fallen asleep. He turned out the light, grabbed a washcloth, and walked to the toilet down the hall. A small sink and cold water provided an opportunity to cleanse. He stripped nude and, while washing himself, the door opened and hit him in the buttocks.

Esther stood in the doorway, dressed in a cotton nightgown. She pushed the gown off her shoulders, and it slipped to the floor.

Aaron stared in mute silence, the washcloth still clutched in his hand.

Esther's breasts rose and fell with each breath. Her nipples protruded. She pulled the string on the overhead light, and the room fell black.

"Esther," Aaron protested as her hands found his hips.

"Now we have privacy."

Aaron trembled as Esther knelt in front of him. Her tongue touched the flat of his stomach. He tensed with fear, and his heart raced like that

147

of a rabbit. He had to stop her; he should have confessed his terrible, shameful secret long before.

"Esther," he said as his hands found her hair. He tried to pull away from her, but she'd backed him against the sink.

Her hands massaged his testicles, and then she drew him into her mouth. He gasped with ecstasy and fright at the spine-tingling sensation. Esther's tongue set him on fire. He arched his back in instinctive sensual submission. A mix of passion and joyous shock surged through him as he felt himself swelling in her mouth. Esther moaned and clasped his ass, then began to thrust her head up and down his slick erection.

The last of Aaron's fear surrendered to the passion. His hands traveled from the back of her head to her swaying breasts. Touching her fueled his desire.

He cupped her face and pulled his erection from her mouth. "I want you!"

Esther pushed to her feet. Aaron's hand reached between her wet and warm legs. She sighed. Aaron turned her, grabbed her, and lifted her onto the edge of the sink, pushing her legs wide. Esther breathed hard and fast. Aaron snaked his arms around her torso and moved forward as he pulled her to him. She gave a childlike whimper as his erection brushed her inner thigh and then gasped as he found her.

"Take me, Aaron!" Esther cried, arching against him.

Aaron met her passion and hunger, pounding against her soft, inviting flesh in the total darkness. The sink thumped the wall as their rhythm increased.

Esther gasped and arched her body to his, wrapping her legs around him. He thrust faster and faster. She locked into rhythm with him.

A deep, guttural groan came from Aaron's throat as his body tensed. His head went back, and he climaxed with a shudder. Collapsing atop Esther, he encircled his arms around her, their bodies damp with sweat.

He breathed deep, waiting for his heart to calm. The scent of their passion filled the small room.

Esther stroked Aaron's chest with her fingernails, then moved them down into his moist pubic hair. "I want you again, Aaron."

He felt a stirring in his groin, and his erection returned. "And I want you, Mrs. Ross." He lowered his head to draw a nipple into his mouth.

Esther sighed in the darkness.

They spent over an hour in the small bathroom. Aaron felt ecstatic. His sexual prowess had returned, his physical impairment obviously a result of psychological trauma. He would never father another child, but at least he felt like a whole man.

The next morning, as he set out in search of a law school, a definite spring buoyed his step, a smile creased his face, and a new measure of self-confidence swelled his chest.

He could do anything.

Esther had learned the first day that she disliked sewing. Her sore fingers stung with nicks and thread cuts. She had to find a way out of it.

Bendici had a windowed, cluttered office near the front door of the sewing room. Esther had seen him at a typewriter, stabbing at it slowly with his meaty index fingers. She devised a plan. She'd arrive two hours early and clean up his terribly messy office, hoping to impress him.

The next morning, Esther forced herself to get up two hours early. She dressed and went down to the sewing room on the second floor. A team of janitors ignored her arrival. She still glowed from shared passion with her husband.

God, life is good! So good, she feared it. Could it last? She prayed it would.

She turned the lights on in Bendici's cluttered office, and examined the wide desk, a paper-choked mess littered with cigar ashes, butts, coffee stains, dirty cups, and a drying, half-eaten plate of spaghetti. It would be a monumental task.

Esther worked at a frantic pace, hurriedly throwing out the trash and organizing papers. She could easily differentiate orders from shipments, vendors from customers, bills from receipts, or inventory from hardware. She sorted by category, alphabetized, and dated chronologically. Two years in the international business school in Warsaw finally paid off.

In addition, Esther washed the coffee pot and cups and brewed a fresh pot. As an added feminine, esthetic touch, she covered the cabinet with a cut of flowered cloth she'd found in the sew room, then set the coffee service on top.

Cigar smoke and grime clouded the window to the sew room. Esther cleaned it with soapy water from a janitor's bucket. When she asked them to sweep and mop the floor in the office, they didn't hesitate.

Esther had transformed the office from a disorganized, dirty mess to an attractive, functional business environment. She hoped her scheme to advance to a more comfortable position would work.

Once finished, she sat down at the typewriter at Bendici's desk. A letter stuck in the machine, waiting for completion. Beside it lay the copy he'd worked from. Esther preened her hair, straightened her dress, and started typing.

The other women from the sew room began to arrive. They looked at Esther and the office with curious and heated looks.

Rachel's mouth fell open when she entered.

"Just go to work," Esther urged. "I'll explain later."

The gruff, usually ill-tempered Bendici entered a few minutes later. Esther kept her eyes on the clattering typewriter. He walked into the office and stopped in his tracks. The cigar in his mouth fell to the floor, as his jaw dropped in shock.

"What the hell?"

Esther paused, looked to him, pretending surprise. "Good morning, Mr. Bendici." She smiled. "I hope you don't mind. I wanted to keep my typing skills up. Would you like a cup of coffee? It's fresh."

Bendici's wide eyes roamed the office before returning to Esther, who poured him a cup of coffee. She'd finished the typing.

"Get the fuck outta my office," he barked. "If I ever see you in here again, you're fired."

Esther darted out, terrified she'd overstepped with her bold plan, and worried she'd lose her job. She returned to her sewing machine on the line where she stitched sleeves, not daring a glance at the office.

Finally, after about three hours, Bendici emerged from the office. "Esther!" he bellowed over the din of sewing machine noise.

Esther hurried forward, afraid he'd fire her. Her heart pounded.

"Get in here. You're so damned ambitious, I got some typing for you."

In addition to the typing, Esther got a dollar a week raise.

She never returned to the line.

With subtle influence from the new office manager, Rachel moved from a cutter to line supervisor.

Along with the title came a raise of fifteen cents an hour.

Rachel bought a new pair of shoes and danced for Aaron and Esther in their tiny warehouse apartment.

————◦◦◦)◎(◦◦◦————

Aaron applied to six law schools, Columbia and NYU among them. The application process was time consuming and arduous, but critical for admission, and Aaron worked meticulously in the preparation. He added a carefully handwritten letter to each, declaring his love for the law and explaining why he thought it important that a new immigrant, even though an experienced attorney in prewar Poland, should return to law school to reinforce his newfound appreciation for democratic law in the United States.

After seven weeks of taking exams and interviewing, Aaron took a job making deliveries for Bendici. Along with a fellow immigrant, Aaron spent the daylight hours pulling a heavily-laden cart from one distributor to another—backbreaking work, but they needed the money.

About six months passed before the letter from Columbia University Law School arrived:

> *Dear Mr. Ross:*
> *It gives me great pleasure to inform you that you have successfully passed the Columbia Law School qualifying examination and interview. We are also pleased to inform you that your application for an immigration tuition grant has been approved.*
> *You are therefore accepted to our school of law. Please contact the admissions office for details of your enrollment.*
> *Sincerely,*
>
> *John Perot II*
> *Dean*

CHAPTER THIRTEEN

DOUBT

Remember the days of yore;
understand the years of generation after generation.
Ask your father and he will relate it to you,
and your elders and they will tell you.

Deuteronomy 32:7

Janusz peered out the dirt-smudged windows in the train's passenger car. He remembered the youthful excitement of his first journey to Rome and the Holy See. Then, everything had seemed brilliant and miraculous, but time and war had marred the landscape he'd once thought so remarkable.

Scars left over from the many battles reminded Janusz of the lost innocence, the tragedies, and the horrors wrought by man upon his fellow man. As they flew past each clump of destroyed vehicles or burned-out buildings, Janusz felt his heart contract within his chest.

He wondered, for the first time, if the war had actually reached into the Vatican itself. Perhaps the ancient, holy city also lay in ruins. Could this be the reason why the Church had not acted to stand against the Holocaust?

When he finally stepped down from the train in Rome, Janusz held his breath, but the devastation of the neighboring countries did not extend to the great city. The classical wonders of the Roman Empire still loomed in the distance. To his eternal relief, the unmistakable rooflines of the various structures comprising Vatican City met his eye as he exited the station.

Janusz inhaled deeply, feeling slightly faint. His heart could not have survived seeing St. Peter's Basilica crumbled and charred. He swallowed hard and forced his legs to work, carrying him toward the Holy See and his final destination with the Pope.

The wide-eyed wonder of his previous time in Rome did not return, even as he silently rejoiced with each new glimpse of the magnificent and unspoiled architecture that drew him forward. Rather, the disillusionment that had plagued him since the war returned in full force.

Janusz halted at the edge of St. Peter's Square and set down his traveling case. The war had not penetrated there, had left no scars upon the buildings. The Apostolic Palace gleamed across the square, facing the Basilica, seeming to exist in a different era, boasting of artistic affluence and indifference to the outside world. The beauty of the place appeared tarnished to his jaded eyes.

However, as his gaze dropped to include the people moving about him, he recognized the same suffering, depression, and emptiness that had taken over the populace of Europe. Throngs milled about in the warm sunlight or strolled toward the many wonders and museums lining the open space.

A deep sigh shook his thin frame. The wounds of the world seemed to rest on his shoulders. Janusz bent to pick up his belongings. He trudged across the square to the Apostolic Palace—the private residence of the Pope—and climbed the gleaming steps.

A member of the Pope's security force met him as he entered the building. The Pope's personal guard blocked his path. Janusz frowned at the young man adorned in the colorful military uniform, and waited on the threshold.

A team of three Swiss guards questioned him. Then they inspected his papers and the contents of his traveling case before allowing him to proceed. As he left the security point, an older woman, dressed in civilian clothes, bustled from a nearby office.

She gave a quick glance in the direction of the guards, and then turned her attention to Janusz. "Good afternoon, Father Dov. We've been expecting you."

She flashed him a tired smile and gestured toward an internal staircase. "Your quarters are on the second floor, to the right. One of the people up there will see you settled."

As Janusz nodded his thanks and turned away, she added, "Your audience will be held at two o'clock tomorrow afternoon, Father. Someone will collect you from your room and escort you to the appointed place."

Janusz opened his mouth to ask her to elaborate, but she'd already disappeared back into the hallway office. After a moment, he tiredly rolled his shoulders and followed her instructions.

The Vatican's private gardens bloomed with passionate abandon, as if to defy the debilitating pall that seemed to hang in the air. Janusz strolled along the neatly manicured paths, willing the tranquility and beauty to soothe his soul. He'd spent many an afternoon during his training surrounded by the magnificence of these same gardens.

Janusz selected a bench positioned beneath a shade tree and sat for a while, absorbing the cultivated display of nature. Instead, it reinforced the terrible suspicion that the Church had chosen to turn a blind eye to the sufferings of its worldwide flock.

Had the Church lost its way?

A cough interrupted his dark thoughts, and Janusz started. He twisted in his seat to find a middle-aged man, wearing the robes and insignias of a cardinal, staring at him with a vaguely familiar intensity.

Janusz immediately rose to his feet, but paused in his greeting to study the cardinal more closely. "Father Lopez? It is so very good to see you again!" He kissed the ring on the man's extended hand, as was proper and customary.

Cardinal Lopez grinned and enfolded Janusz in a bear hug, reminiscent of better times. He pounded Janusz on the back, and then released him. "It is good to see you also, my son. I take it as a compliment that you still recognize your old teacher after so many years."

Janusz detected only a trace of Lopez's accent, almost lost with the prolonged absence from his native Spain.

A weight lifted from his shoulders as he met Cardinal Lopez's clear, brown eyes. "You have not changed, except to wear new clothes."

Cardinal Lopez nodded and motioned toward the path. "I thought I would find you here, Janusz. You were always stealing away from your studies."

Then he sighed, and the light left his face. "That seems like a hundred years ago, I'm afraid."

Janusz walked beside the cardinal, sobered and grim. "Do you know why His Holiness has summoned me?"

His companion shrugged, and pointed the way. They strolled in silence, finally entering the Sistine Chapel—another favorite place from Janusz's youth. The chapel lay deserted, except for them.

Halfway to the front, Janusz halted and stared at the famous ceiling. He remembered sneaking in, lying on a pew, and gazing upward for hours at a time. The glorious paintings called to him, as they once had. Spectacular, stained glass windows refracted multicolored light, infusing Janusz with forgotten religious fervor.

Without conscious thought, he slid into the closet pew and craned his neck to stare at the masterpieces that had survived several centuries of human conflicts. Where the gardens had failed to penetrate Janusz's depression, the grandeur of this monument to faith succeeded.

Cardinal Lopez sat beside him and also looked upward. "Each time I visit, I feel reborn."

Janusz closed his eyes and bowed his head. *Yes, that is what I need . . . to be reborn.* "I am lost," he admitted to his former mentor.

No words of either support or condemnation, only a soft rustling of fabric, came from beside him.

Janusz kept his eyes closed and bent his head in prayer. "Show me, Lord, the way back. Your path is hidden from me."

After a moment, he raised his face and opened his eyes. The cardinal still bowed in silent prayer. Janusz experienced another lift of spirit, understanding that his teacher had accompanied him with the intention of sharing his burden. But right on the heels of his elation came a crushing sadness. "It is so beautiful here and so ugly everywhere else. This is not real."

Cardinal Lopez lifted his head and drew in a long, deep breath. "Perhaps, Janusz, what you have lost is the ability to see beyond the ugliness. There are many types of blindness. Clear your vision. Renew your faith."

Janusz stared deeply into his mentor's eyes, trying to comprehend the wisdom beneath the words.

The older man patted Janusz on the shoulder and rose. "Come, your audience with His Holiness is upon you."

Janusz followed the cardinal to the private reception area for those select few who had business with the pope. The Prelate—Chamberlain of the Vatican—Cardinal Richmond, greeted them both by name and extended a hand.

Cardinal Lopez nodded to Janusz and settled in one of the plush armchairs sprinkled about the sedate lounge. He picked up a newspaper from a nearby coffee table and began to read.

Cardinal Richmond swept a hand toward the door. Janusz exited the lounge and, together, they headed down the corridor. Walking beside the Chamberlain of the Vatican—one of the most powerful individuals within the hierarchy of the Papal Throne—made him inordinately nervous and intimidated. He managed to keep up with the Prelate's brisk pace, swallowing hard. The sound of their footsteps echoed on the paved floor.

At the end of the long hallway, Cardinal Richmond pointed to an elaborately carved door.

Janusz hesitated, recognizing the crests of the Supreme Pontiff within the intricate design.

The Prelate put a hand to the gilded knob, but paused and looked at Janusz. "You will have only ten minutes, Bishop Dov. Use the time well."

With that, he pushed open the heavy door and preceded Janusz into the audience chamber. The Chamberlain stopped a few paces inside, bowed deeply, and announced in a strong voice, "The Bishop of Katowice, Father Janusz Dov."

Janusz couldn't move for a few moments. He watched in a sort of shocked stupor as the Chamberlain backed out of the room. Just before Cardinal Richmond shut the door, he sent Janusz a meaningful nod.

A raspy, but oddly melodious voice brought Janusz out of his trance. "You may approach, Father Dov. I do not stand on formality here."

Janusz quickly recovered his senses and hurried toward the heavily robed, elderly man seated in the center of the chamber. He fell to his knees and kissed the pontiff's signet ring, then returned to his feet and whispered, "Your Holiness, how may I serve?"

The Pope's weathered features and tired eyes showed weariness, no doubt from grave responsibilities. "It is I, Father Dov, who must serve you. I have summoned you here to find out why you have not accepted your position as bishop."

Janusz swallowed. "I question my path, Your Holiness. As bishop, I am not sure I will be able to help the people of my small diocese. I feel I must go out into the countryside, give aid wherever aid is needed."

The Pope closed his eyes and bowed his head.

Janusz dragged his gaze from the Supreme Pontiff and took the opportunity to study the chamber. The plain, unadorned stucco walls had no windows. Several utilitarian torchieres illuminated the dark corners with flickering light. Only the Pope's throne reflected any type of ornamentation—minutely carved and heavily gilded, a throwback to the wealth and splendor of bygone days.

The pontiff himself wore a solid, natural-fibered fabric, skillfully made, but starkly humble. His red skull cap blazed against a crown of silvery-gray hair.

Janusz took a deep breath, mindful of his limited time. "Your Holiness, my heart—my faith—is blocked by the obstacles of this brutal life. So much suffering, so much death. My soul cries, 'Why?' but hears no answer. Has God abandoned us for our sins?"

He gulped down sobs, overcome with emotion, unable to go on.

The Pope sighed and opened his eyes. He seemed to look through Janusz. "Recall the story of Job, Father Dov. He suffered more than any man alive. He questioned God; he questioned his faith. The human mind cannot comprehend the will of our Lord."

Then he stared at Janusz with such intensity that Janusz cringed within his very soul. As the Pope paused, and appeared to sink into silence, Janusz struggled to understand the message. Anger replaced awe. Did the pontiff believe the Jews—the people of Janusz's birth heritage—would be rewarded for the atrocities rained upon their heads, as had the long-suffering Job?

Janusz stuttered, "I do not understand, Your Holiness."

"In time, God will give you enlightenment, Father."

A whisper of sound alerted him to the end of his audience. The door to the chamber swung open, and Cardinal Richmond said in a firm, final tone, "Bishop Dov."

Janusz knelt, kissed the Pope's signet ring, and slowly retreated. Just as he reached the door, the Pope's unique, raspy, singsong voice halted his steps. "Who are we to judge the Almighty? It is all of us who must face His judgment."

Janusz hesitated, but the Pope bowed his head again and remained silent. A gentle touch on his arm reminded him to complete his exit.

Before Janusz knew it, Cardinal Lopez once more guided his steps out of the Apostolic Palace. Once back outside in the sunlit afternoon, they stopped on a shade-dappled section of stairs.

Cardinal Lopez said gently, "Sit and relax, Father."

Janusz obeyed, and took a couple of minutes to redirect his focus. After a time of silence, Cardinal Lopez departed for evening prayers.

When a chill of night dampness broke his thoughts, Janusz rose awkwardly to his feet, suddenly feeling all the aches associated with holding the same position for a while.

Rather than return to his quarters, he chose the private path into the gardens—a highly restricted section. As he strolled along the darkened footways, he again thought about his next actions.

Janusz stared into a still pool of water, searching his mind for answers. He wondered how the Supreme Pontiff could so callously speak of Job's trials in the face of the millions of senseless deaths. The great evil that plagued the land, slaughtered innocents, and twisted otherwise good people into monsters could not compare to the heaven-sent sufferings of a single man.

Janusz squeezed his eyes shut, feeling as if he'd descended into purgatory. Soft whisperings of night creatures buffeted the edges of his grim thoughts. Had he lost his faith?

He stared listlessly about the lovely alcove. The dark pool drew his attention once more. Within its glassy waters, pinpricks of light appeared. Janusz lifted his gaze to the sky, noting that a few stars twinkled overhead. The trees surrounding his bench grew close enough to form a deep, green tunnel.

Janusz gasped, suddenly thrown into a far-off memory. He'd looked up at the stars through a dark tunnel once before, in his youth—desperate, lost, helpless. The old mining pit had held him captive, but had also shown him his path.

Tears flowed down his cheeks as God shone heavenly light upon him. He imagined the clear ice of his blockages shattering within his soul.

"Thank you, Lord," Janusz sobbed, falling to his knees.

A path opened before his feet in his mind's eye. The way began to clear the fog of doubt. Disillusionment turned to determination. He replayed his audience with the Pope in his head, and his heart whispered, "I understand now. I am Job."

A gentle presence joined him, and Janusz wiped his eyes to find Cardinal Lopez kneeling beside him. Tears streamed anew, but no words could express his emotions. He gazed at his old mentor, feeling humble and small.

Cardinal Lopez smiled through his own tears and nodded. "God's light shines through your eyes, my dear Janusz. You have found your answers and unblocked your soul. I rejoice with you."

Janusz raised his face to the night sky and stared at the twinkling stars overhead. He'd been saved by Kalman to enter the priesthood, to pursue his desire—his faith—to serve God. Now, he recalled his true mission: to serve; to bring hope and faith to the hopeless and lost; to save all within his power to save; to reach out and embrace; to bring light and love to a world emerging from darkness—just as he'd emerged from the pit.

His life held purpose once more.

CHAPTER FOURTEEN

THE WARRIOR

If someone comes to kill you, kill him first.

Sanhedrin 72a

February, 1946.

David Gold stood at the rail of a small fishing vessel on a bitter cold morning, keeping a sharp eye out for British surveillance ships.

The captain expertly dodged the radar, positioned atop a hill in the small town of Ako, an enclave just north of Haifa. David and several other Jewish youths had agreed to leave Poland and sneak into Israel. The defense forces of free, independent Israel, the Haganah, needed every able-bodied, experienced fighter they could find, and David had distinguished himself among the partisans in Poland after that fateful day at the railroad crossing.

Born into prosperity, but now standing penniless and alone, the Haganah had become his family and his cause. He could die; others could die. David had seen that, but the cause—the belief in something bigger and more important than life itself—would live on.

David had traveled there to join the ranks of those dedicated to forging a new country, a nation called the state of Israel—a homeland, a haven, a place for Jews, Jews who would bow to no man; Jews who had learned how to fight; Jews who were not afraid; Jews who were warriors.

Someday he would return to Poland, find his mother, father, and sister, and bring them to a new home—a place where they would never again find persecution. His own, private crusade drove him forward. He knew that anyone who came upon the old farm would believe him dead, and he regretted the added pain and grief that would cause his family, but his mission stood beyond the hurts of any one individual; the rewards were worthy of all costs.

The underground warriors had taken David to a *kibbutz*, a Jewish settlement, called Mahagan Michael—Michael's Harbor—halfway between Tel Aviv and Haifa. The people in charge of the kibbutz maintained a rigorous, daily routine. The men awoke at 4:00 a.m. to work in the fields, milk cows, and go out on fishing boats. The women worked in the nursery, kindergarten, kitchen, and cotton factory. In the afternoon, all able-bodied men below retirement age underwent training, learning how to use guns and explosives.

An aging, tattered Piper Cub performed crop-dusting for the kibbutz. The fabric-covered monoplane had a forty-horsepower engine, no brakes, few instruments, and a top speed of about seventy-five miles an hour. David, after three other men balked, volunteered to learn to fly the two-passenger aircraft, hoping to find it better than milking cows and tending the fields in the hot sun.

His teacher, Saul Trapousi, a gray-haired, Russian-Jewish immigrant, had traded six goats for the airplane, then taught himself to fly it.

David learned to fly in much the same way as one learns to swim by being tossed into a river. Saul took him into the sky, gave him the controls, and said, "Don't kill us!"

After a week of tutoring, David soloed. A few days after, Saul had him dusting the cotton fields.

The sky surrounded David with quiet solitude and turned the war-torn earth below to a place of awe and beauty. Each flight provided a new adventure, with an ever-changing sky—a sky David quickly learned to read. Moisture-filled stratocumulus clouds would produce crowds of rounded masses in the mornings, while the altostratus pushed them away in the heat of the day, to finally yield to colorful, high, lacy cirrus at twilight.

On the ground, David learned advanced battle skills. Veterans from the Haganah would visit and share their knowledge of weapons and explosives, along with the psychology of survival in combat.

As a defenseless farmer, David had once felt afraid. As a soldier, he found bravery.

A raid by Arab extremists from Baka-El-Arabia put the Israeli soldiers' training to a test. David and Saul, in the Piper Cub, directed the counterattack by circling several hundred feet above the Arabs. They pelted the terrorists with hand grenades, random pistol shots, and a dusting of insecticide, stopping them before they reached the settlement. Bullet holes riddled Saul's plane.

They had killed ten terrorists and injured two and taken them hostage. They confiscated their weapons, including a few machine guns.

The success of the kibbutz's people in defeating the terrorists served as a warning to the neighboring Arab villagers and proved a staunch deterrent from future raids until the war of Independence.

David stood among the victors on Independence Day, May 14, 1948. He wished his family could share the Jewish pride; however, he took comfort in knowing that his continued sacrifices brought him closer to providing them with a safe place to live out the rest of their lives.

But peace stayed an elusive promise for the fledgling nation of Israel. War again became reality. Egypt seized the Suez Canal from its British and French owners, cutting off all commerce to Israel.

David made the rank of captain and served as an aerial recognizance officer, despite his hearing loss. Ever since the bombing at the farm, David had failed to hear low-frequency sounds. He'd kept the disability secret.

During the Israeli invasion of Egypt on October 29, 1956, his leadership and grasp of battlefield tactics, as well as his can-do attitude under fire, did not go unnoticed. He continued to drop reports of Arab positions, even after Saul had been shot dead in the aging Cub's back seat.

Again the Israelis came out the victors, which led Great Britain and France to become their allies.

One day, months later, David received orders to report to the Division Recreational Officer—a less-than-successful cover for the military branch of the Mossad. When he reached the obscure, nondescript office, he found two men waiting. One had the look of Mossad; the other wore American shoes, exciting David's curiosity. Had the United States joined their cause?

The Mossad officer opened a thick personnel file. "Sit down, Captain Gold."

David took a seat without comment, noting his name on the folder tab.

"You have served your country well. We are prepared to offer you a great challenge, which requires considerable discretion."

David glanced at the grim, silent man who seemed to stare right through him, and answered, "I enjoy a challenge."

The man with the American shoes gave a slight nod to the Mossad man, who closed the file, stood, and extended a hand to David. "Good. Then return to your barracks. Pack all your belongings and be at hangar six at 1400 hours. Tell no one. Not even your family. You will not be returning here."

David pushed to his feet. "I have no family."

He'd kept secret all mention of his family, even from his closest friends. He felt a deep need to protect them at all costs, even though the Nazi threat had ended. Until he deemed it completely safe to reveal their existence, he would not speak of his family.

David trusted that Father Dov cared for them, as he had during the war, and he knew the kindly priest would help David find them when the time came.

Twelve other soldiers were already waiting when David arrived at the hangar. He recognized two of them, but asked no questions.

At the appointed hour, a four-engine, olive-drab military transport taxied to the hangar apron. It rolled to a halt, engines idling, waiting. Although paint-covered, its national insignias shouted, "American." He had never seen such a magnificent machine.

The Mossad officer and the mysterious man he had met with earlier emerged from the craft. The Israeli raised a clipboard and shouted names above the engine noise. David's was the fifth name called.

He followed the others onto the big plane. They sat strapped in canvas seats lining the fuselage. The noisy area felt cold and smelled of aircraft fuel.

They flew for fourteen hours. David slept—an escape he'd learned in combat; get it while you can.

Pressure in his ears woke him. They were descending. He twisted to look out a small porthole. In the outside darkness, light patterns punctured the night, revealing the still-distant ground.

Hydraulic lines hissed and electric motors whined as the aircraft's landing gear lowered. Their angle of descent increased. The plane's speed fell, and they slammed onto a runway with a yelp from the tires.

David and the others assembled on the tarmac in the cool, damp night air. The humidity took him back to the remote farm in eastern Poland, a farm he tried not to remember.

A graying, short-necked man in flight coveralls said, "Welcome to Wright-Patterson Airfield, Dayton, Ohio."

A murmur went through the ranks of the young Israelis. They were in America!

"You're going to spend the next six months here and a few other places in the States. We're going to teach you how to fly jets. Not only how to fly them, but how to fly and kill. Because, gentlemen, if you can fly and kill, you can protect your country. The country that rules the sky rules the world. That's the grim reality of it.

"We're going to put you in the cockpit of the French Mirage, the hottest delta wing fighter this side of Moscow. You're going to receive more training than most flight officers get in five years. We're building more than a new squadron, gentlemen. We're building the foundation of an air force—the Israeli Air Force."

David's heart raced with excitement. A cheer erupted from the eager young Israelis.

After two weeks of intensive practical education—twelve—to fifteen-hour days—the young warriors were flown to a remote base in Texas for flight training. Each Israeli pilot had a personal flight instructor assigned to him

A tall, thin man offered a hand to David. "Colonel Wayne Conrad. What part of Europe are you from, Captain?"

David returned the firm handshake. "I was born in Poland—Katowice. But during the war, I stayed on a farm in eastern Poland."

Conrad nodded. "I used to fly over Poland. B-17s. Felt like a lost truck driver most of the time. Vowed after the war to never fly anything with more than one engine."

"I learned to fly in an aircraft with one engine," David told the lanky colonel.

"What kind?"

"Piper Cub."

The colonel smiled and clapped David on the shoulder. "The French Mirage isn't much different. Just a little faster."

———∘∘∘)⊙(∘∘∘———

Twenty-seven hundred miles to the east, in New York City, Rachel Gold, a trusted and responsible line supervisor in the expanding Bendici sew room, was determined to escape the endless grind of the sweatshop.

Unlike most of the women in the shop, Rachel immersed herself in everything American. Using discarded *Vogue* magazines, Rachel became a fashion-conscious, highly styled, attractive young woman. She kept herself impeccably groomed and dressed in hand-sewn copies of New York's best known designers.

Rachel had fond memories of a mother in beautiful clothes, who smelled of fine talc and perfumes, who wore clean, colorful dresses, and lived in a sprawling, well-furnished house. She hungered for such a house, such a life, and felt driven to succeed, vowing never to be poor again. Once she attained her perfect lifestyle, no one would ever take it from her.

Rachel applied for a scholarship to New York's Bernard College for Women, and was accepted.

She shared the good news with Aaron and Esther at the dining room table.

The three now lived in a four-room flat on the fifth floor. Paint and the efforts of both women, combined with Aaron's sweat, had transformed the modest apartment into a comfortable home. Esther's wage as office supervisor had made possible a telephone, a small television set, and a high-fidelity record player in Rachel's room.

Aaron seemed less than enthusiastic at Rachel's announcement, wary of college education for women. Few women in Europe went to college. Those who did attended abbreviated, specialized business schools, such as Esther had. Women didn't have careers; they had husbands and children.

Although Aaron didn't say anything, Rachel read the look on his face.

"I'll go to night school," Rachel added in reassurance. "I'll keep my job."

Aaron laid aside a law book. "I'm more concerned about what kind of future a woman may have with a degree in liberal arts. From what I've seen, New York is a man's world."

Esther said quietly, "She doesn't have much of a future in the sew room."

Rachel spoke up quickly, "Dean Reynolds says times are changing. More women will become professionals." She had never challenged Aaron's authority. He had become her surrogate father in every sense, and she needed—prayed for—his approval.

Aaron gathered up his books and pushed away from the table. "I will support you in whatever you decide to do."

Rachel said boldly, "I hope to become an attorney."

Aaron paused and studied Rachel. "Don't say that to please me."

"I'm saying it to please *me*," Rachel defended firmly.

Esther's gaze moved from one to the other.

Aaron nodded thoughtfully. "Being an attractive attorney may work in America."

"Isn't that what you're trying to become?" Esther suggested with a smile.

Aaron grinned at his wife, then returned his attention to Rachel. "I am proud of you, Rachel. I'm sure you will do what is best."

Tears blurred Rachel's view of him. "Thank you. I love you for that."

Aaron turned to walk away, but not before Rachel caught a glimpse of moisture shining in his eyes.

Esther reached across the table and took Rachel's hand in hers.

In Texas, under the experienced guidance of Colonel Conrad, David quickly worked through the radial engine T-28, into the jet-powered T-33 trainer, and finally into the delta wing French Mirage fighter jet.

He discovered a dimension of the sky he never knew existed—power! Power that made him feel invincible. Power that made him ache for battle.

David excelled at air combat tactics. When not flying, he studied. The other Israelis seemed satisfied with just flying, but he wanted more than that. He aspired to be an air warrior.

Navigation and night flying made up the final phase of their training. David felt ready. He had studied hour upon hour, beyond course expectations or assignments.

The mission brief arrived in a sealed envelope the night before the flight. David eagerly tore it open: He would fly from Randolph Field, Texas, to George Air Force Base, California. Departure: 2345 hours. Colonel Conrad would fly as David's wingman—silent unless his student put himself in harm's way.

The colonel had added a handwritten note to the last page of the orders. *The area around George Air Force Base looks a lot like Israel.*

David went to work plotting the flight, eager to see California. He calculated distance and take-off weight to formulate the fuel needed. Then came the weather factors. The charts showed most of the flight, at nineteen thousand feet, would be above a solid overcast that blanketed most of the west.

He unfolded the air navigational maps and plotted an electronic course that would carry them through the night without a dependence on seeing anything, reinforced with dead reckoning notes—star navigation, as old as navigation itself. The forecast predicted a moonless night, but the familiar constellations that had guided travelers since the first man raised his face to the sky would light his way. They had saved Columbus. David Gold bet they would save him.

He finished, double-checked, and re-checked his flight plan. Five hours before takeoff, he took it to Flight Ops.

David stood ready on the flight line when Colonel Conrad arrived. He had spent a full hour pre-flighting the silver, delta wing Mirage.

The colonel smiled, pulling on his flight helmet. "Let's go to California."

The headset crackled, and the air traffic tower intoned, "Shadow-six, cleared for takeoff, runway twenty-two, right."

David strapped the oxygen mask on his face, pushed the throttle forward to afterburner, and answered, "Shadow-six, roger."

The jet leaped forward, forcing David back in his seat. Runway lights rushed at him in a growing blur.

"Power," David whispered to himself.

The aircraft lifted into the night sky and entered the base of the clouds, carrying its own thunder with it. They emerged from the dense overcast and rain at fourteen thousand feet.

David checked his magnetic and radio compasses. They flew on the correct heading. He turned and glanced to his left. The faint outline of Colonel Conrad's sleek jet followed slightly behind him. The craft's navigational lights winked out their green and red signals.

He glanced up. A canopy of stars glowed down on him. A beautiful flight lay ahead.

After two hours of slicing through the cold night air, nearly four miles above the earth, the radio came to life in David's ear. "Air Force zero-four, this is Albuquerque center."

David answered, "Air Force zero-four—go ahead, Albuquerque."

"Air Force zero-four, eastbound civilian commercial traffic reports heavy weather at fifteen to eighteen thousand. Requesting clearance to climb to your flight level—multiple aircraft. Request you descend and maintain flight level seventeen thousand current heading."

David's heart raced. The civilian aircraft wanted to switch altitudes to escape the inclement weather, for passenger comfort and safety. Though the request was both reasonable and routine, David knew it meant trouble, but he had no choice.

IFR—instrument flight rules—were straightforward. Every electronic navigational aid that mapped the sightless sky emitted a distinct, audible, low frequency sound which, when the pilot flew on course, sounded in his headset. Drifting off course meant a loss of signal and sound. Unfortunately, David could not hear the warning due to his secret disability.

Colonel Conrad would expect him to grant the request. Air Force policy, as well as the unwritten protocol of the sky, demanded they yield.

David swallowed, then pushed forward on the stick. "Albuquerque, Air Force zero-four, descending to, and maintaining, seventeen thousand, current heading." The night sky disappeared into a black boiling mass of solid overcast.

He perspired as he tuned the radio compass. It spun and drifted, refusing to hold a heading, probably due to electrical interference from the storm. The magnetic compass did the same. He looked through the windshield, but a reflection of his instrument panel replaced the starry night. Rain pelted the windscreen and streaked back over the canopy.

He strained to hear the tone of the navaid in his headset. Silence roared in his mind. He heard nothing.

David cursed fate—angry, helpless, and lost. He briefly considered breaking radio silence to tell the colonel his headset had malfunctioned, but he wasn't a liar. So, he flew on, hoping, praying, he could stay on course.

Sweat ran down his face. The powerful jet throbbed under his gloved hands, maintaining a steady speed of 375 knots.

Colonel Conrad's voice suddenly came through the headset. "Shadow-six, do you have tone?"

David answered flatly, "No tone." His dreams of returning to Israel as an air warrior were over. He'd flown off course.

"Roger, Shadow-six. Come right eight degrees. I'm taking the lead."

David felt heartsick. He had failed. He changed the compass heading and fell in on the colonel's wing, humiliated. He cursed the son-of-a-bitch who'd dropped the bomb on his uncle's farm, and slammed a fist against the instrument panel. Fate had struck him down with nothing more than a fucking rainstorm.

The long and silent last hours of the flight seemed endless as, to his embarrassment, the other jet led him to California.

At two-thirty in the morning, local time, they met in the pilot briefing room. Colonel Conrad unzipped his flight suit and barked at David, "You wanna tell me what the hell that was all about? I know you know how to fly an IFR heading."

David kicked at an open locker door. "I couldn't hear the fucking tone!"

The colonel rocked backward, eyes widened. "You couldn't hear it? What's the matter? Maybe you've got a sinus infection? A cold? I'll contact the flight surgeon."

"It's not a cold," David confessed. "I just couldn't hear it."

Colonel Conrad's shoulders slumped, and he ran a hand through his short hair. "That means you're a washout. What the hell happened to you?"

David answered with raw emotion, "I'll tell you what the hell happened to me. I was at ground zero when some asshole pilot, lost in the night, dumped a full rack of five hundred pounders on my uncle's farm. Maybe he didn't hear the tone either," he added sarcastically. "I couldn't hear anything for five months afterward.

"Have you ever been on ground zero, Colonel? It makes your ears and your ass bleed. It made sausage out of my aunt and uncle. There was nothing left of their farm but a smoldering, goddamned crater. I can still close my eyes and smell their cooked flesh.

"That's what happened to my hearing, Colonel. That's why I can't hear the fucking tone. So, thank the bastard at the controls that night, Colonel. He's the one who stole my tone. He's the son-of-a-bitch that just ended my career." Tears pricked the corners of David's eyes.

The colonel studied David for a long moment, then picked up his flight helmet and walked from the room.

CHAPTER FIFTEEN

Family Ties

Love is as strong as death.

Song of Songs 8:6

David graduated from the Air Combat Training School, along with the other Israeli pilots. He did not understand why Colonel Conrad had not washed him out of the program after his failure in IFR navigation, but he felt undying gratitude for the miracle of a second chance.

After the ceremony at Randolph Field, the colonel shook David's hand and said, "Stay out of the clouds, kid."

The special unit left the United States as quietly as they had arrived. Two days later, David returned to Israel, his secret intact.

The first of the French-built Mirage fighter aircraft arrived in cargo crates the same day.

After a week of assembly and testing, they took to the sky. David led the first combat air patrol along the Gaza strip, guns loaded. He felt almost disappointed the enemy did not rise to challenge them.

"Power," David whispered into his oxygen mask as he looked down at the endless swath of brown and gray sand, thousands of feet below.

——◦◦◦}◦◦◦——

On the other side of the Atlantic Ocean, Aaron Ross had *his* power back. The return of his sexual prowess had re-energized his life. Dread of confessing his unmanly secret had dissolved into a flare of rekindled passion and lust for sex. He had to prove his virility, time and time again, until Esther begged for relief. She complained that the physical demands of twelve—to fifteen-hour work days, combined with Aaron's desire to make love twice a day, left her exhausted and sore.

Aaron's overwhelming passion demanded direction, and he turned it to his studies. Simple success did not satisfy him, so he embarked upon a quest for personal excellence.

When Professor Feldman asked for a volunteer to prepare a dissertation on the Bill of Rights, Aaron quickly accepted the challenge.

He memorized his speech and practiced in the hallway outside the apartment for two nights, into the early morning hours. Then he tested it on Esther and Rachel. They sat spellbound through the presentation and applauded when he finished.

Then, at New York's Columbia School of Law, Aaron paced on the stage of the amphitheater-style classroom, addressing the assembled class in a mock presentation to the Supreme Court.

The professor sat in the back, listening. Beside him, in the shadows, Aaron recognized Harold Epstein, senior partner from the esteemed firm of Greenwald, Carson and Epstein.

Aaron utilized the style of an evangelist he had seen in the motion picture *Elmer Gantry*: maintain eye contact, gesture with both arms, smile, frown, lower the eyes, shift the monotone, and put fire in it. He did it all, and the silence in the shaded classroom told him his presentation choice was working.

For his conclusion, Aaron approached a student in the front row. "The Bill of Rights . . ."

He laid a hand on the man's shoulder and looked directly into his eyes, as if the student were the only one in the crowded room.

". . . describes the fundamental liberties of the people. Freedom of religion, freedom of speech . . ."

He raised an arm, gesturing to all.

". . . freedom of the press, and the right of assembly. They protect our collective and individual rights to life, liberty, and the pursuit of happiness."

Aaron moved back to the center of the stage, intensely aware of his audience as he loosened his tie and smiled. His performance rolled out with surprising ease, and he suddenly recalled his first success in court, defending Zygmunt. Confidence flowed through him, and he imagined Kalman's spirit beside him, urging him on.

"It was Thomas Jefferson and James Madison who championed the modern Bill of Rights. The concept of individual rights, historians tell us, started with the ancient Greek and Roman civilizations. I would argue they started much earlier. There is the letter of the law, and there is the spirit of the law. I would say the spirit of these basic rights is inbred in the very fiber of mankind, to the extent that they become fundamental to free government, and, as such, government cannot claim their authorship. The power was given to the government by the people. The government did not empower the people. We, therefore, become a country *of* the people, and *for* the people. A country based on law.

"Thank you." Aaron finished with a bow.

Applause filled the classroom.

Professor Feldman and Harold Epstein caught up with Aaron in the hallway.

"Aaron," the professor said. "Allow me to introduce—"

Aaron interrupted, "Harold Epstein, People verses Quinn, New York Supreme Court, 1954." He extended a hand to the attorney. "An honor to meet you, sir."

The prominent lawyer smiled and shook hands. "You knew I was in the classroom?"

"Would you address a jury without knowing who was on it?"

Epstein chuckled. "Your style is interesting, Mr. Ross. A bit flamboyant, perhaps, but effective nonetheless. We have an apprentice position open in the firm, if you are interested. You'll be graduating this year. It's not too early to be thinking about a position."

Aaron's heart raced.

The man offered a business card. "Come by and meet the other partners."

A few weeks later, Aaron reported to work as a law clerk with the firm of Greenwald, Carson and Epstein. The offices, housed in the Kent building on Wall Street, occupied the twenty-eighth and twenty-ninth floors.

"Buy a good suit," Harold Epstein ordered, giving Aaron an advance on his salary. "On second thought, buy two of them."

Aaron bought the two suits wholesale, on Seventh Avenue, at a shop with which Esther did business. With the money he saved, he took Esther and Rachel to dinner and a Broadway show.

In his third week of clerking, he met Brigitte Mason—tall, shapely, and sensual, a natural blond with pouty lips and intense blue eyes. She dressed in expensive, conservative business suits, but they did little to mask her femininity. Brigitte acted as the liaison between the firm and Marcello Industries.

Aaron had seen their voluminous file. Marcello Industries, as most knew, served as a front for the Marcello family branch of the powerful and influential New York Costa Nostra—the Mafia. Aaron's new firm had successfully defended the Marcellos against an avalanche of indictments and arrests, ranging from petty theft to bloody gangland murders. Those who had dared to face them in court ended up mysteriously missing, or dead from accidents under suspicious circumstances.

The Marcellos, he discovered, appeared to have legitimate interests in liquor distributions, night clubs, vending machines, valet and coat check operations, health clubs, and parking concessions. They were rich, powerful, and brutal.

Aaron had heard of the Mafia in Europe. Their influence had reached into Poland's prewar economy in the form of unwarranted insurance tariffs, shipping fees, and special handling. In Poland, a person either paid or prayed.

Their strong grip on America surprised Aaron. The police, especially the federal authorities, seemed to say one thing and do another. He had seen the same in Poland. The police did their job, but they worked for politicians influenced by money, and the Mafia had money to buy those politicians.

Aaron, as the law taught him, did not feel moralistic. The law rose above morality, with right or wrong seldom the issue. Lawful or unlawful always decided the case.

The Marcellos went beyond their place as clients; rather, in actuality, they had become assets. The service billing list from the firm stacked nearly as big as the file. Perhaps they had to steal to pay their attorneys, Aaron mused, as he leafed through the heavy files.

Because the Marcellos had an important relationship to the firm, Aaron deemed them important, as he intended to become the firm's next partner.

The Marcellos sought to acquire a nightclub on Forty-Second Street. Epstein ordered Aaron to research the title of the establishment. He spent three days on the assignment—most of the time at the city's Hall of Records. It quickly became obvious to Aaron that the true owners had hidden behind layer upon layer of corporations that performed the actual operations.

The trail finally led to a New Jersey company licensed to do business in New York, presently owned by Frankie Coccini. Playing a hunch, Aaron researched the name in the birth records.

Anthony Marcello, the godfather of the Marcello family, had a grandson by the name of Frankie Coccini Marcello. The Marcellos planned to buy the nightclub from themselves—a clever ploy to mask profits, launder money, and avoid capital gains. A shell game.

Aaron decided to tell no one, and kept the valuable information to himself.

The next afternoon, Harold Epstein summoned Aaron to his large corner office. "Bring the Marcello title file, would you please?"

Brigitte Mason sat on a couch, waiting, in the spacious suite. In addition to the magnetism of her presence, her scent intoxicated Aaron. She crossed her long, nylon-clad legs and offered Aaron a hand when Epstein introduced them.

Her skin felt warm and soft in his, and her smile sent heat racing to his groin. "Nice to meet you, Aaron. I look forward to working with you."

Epstein talked of deed transfers, required recordings with the city, pro-ration of taxes, and escrow costs, but Aaron heard very little. His mind undressed Brigitte. He envisioned running his tongue slowly up her naked thigh, burying his face in her pubic hair, and then, finally, plunging his erection deep into her.

Brigitte caught his look and offered a fleeting smile, then wet her lips with a dart of her tongue. Aaron shifted position to mask a growing erection. He felt boyish and embarrassed. Heat flushed his neck and ears.

Epstein said to Aaron, "I'd like you to go with Miss Mason and bring back the executed documents."

"Yes, of course," Aaron agreed, eager to go anywhere with the seductive woman.

Parked in a red zone, a chauffeured limousine waited at the curb for Brigitte. The driver, a broad-shouldered, uniformed man, got out and opened the rear door. Aaron followed Brigitte into a luxurious, well-appointed back seat that smelled of rich leather and cigars.

Brigitte smiled as they pulled from the curb into the thick evening traffic. "Tony's office is on Fifty-Second."

Aware of the driver's ears and eyes, Aaron talked with Brigitte about the weather, the afternoon traffic, and the decor in Harold Epstein's office, but their gazes said much more. The atmosphere between them fairly sizzled.

Brigitte boldly ran her eyes over Aaron. "May I see the papers?"

Their fingers touched as Aaron passed the documents to her. A jolt of excitement shot through him.

She leafed through the paperwork and handed it back to Aaron. This time her hand lingered on his. A red-varnished nail sent a shudder up his arm as it brushed his palm.

Finally, the limousine pulled to the curb. The driver said, "Would you like me to wait, Miss Mason?"

"No, thank you, John. I'll see you tomorrow."

A uniformed doorman opened the door and offered a smile. Aaron kept close on Brigette's heels. They took a private elevator to the eighteenth floor. Brigette's scent filled the car. She slanted a smile at Aaron. He hated that the intimacy would end with the introduction of others and the business of the title transfer.

A chime sounded and the elevator door opened to reveal another uniformed man, obviously posted to control access. He appeared a near carbon copy of the chauffer. His gaze went first to Aaron for a sober evaluation, then shifted to Brigitte.

With a smile, he stepped aside to let them pass. "Miss Mason."

"Hello, Harry. How're the ponies treating you?"

The man chuckled and shook his head. "Not as bad as my wife, Miss Mason." Harry tipped an imaginary hat to her, then turned back to the elevator, once more on duty.

Double doors led into a sprawling, opulent office suite. Plush red carpet padded their steps. The rich furnishings, made of polished colonial woods and woven fabrics, impressed Aaron. Tapestries and intricate oil paintings in golden frames adorned paneled walls. The whole room reeked of wealth and power.

A lock clicked as Brigitte closed the door; the only other sound was the ticking of an ornate pendulum clock.

"Nice, isn't it?" Brigitte said, kicking off a shoe.

"It's beyond nice." Aaron turned, and his elbow accidentally brushed her breast.

The touch brought an inviting smile from Brigitte. "Oh, I forgot to mention. Tony's in Las Vegas on business. Guess the titles will have to wait."

Aaron's stomach did an ungainly dance of excitement. "You knew that when we came over here?"

"Uh-huh," Brigitte purred, kicking off her other shoe. "But I just hate being alone. It's so boring. You don't like being bored, do you, Aaron? Would you help me not to be bored?" She wrapped her arms around his neck and lifted her mouth to his.

Aaron dropped the papers to the carpet. Brigette's mouth felt warm and wet and smooth, and her passion ignited his. He molded his body to hers. His hands found her firm buttocks. He lifted her dress and pushed a palm down over warm flesh.

She moaned in his mouth. They kissed until he thought her exploring tongue would drive him beyond control. He probed at her with his erection. Finally, she broke the kiss. They both breathed hard.

Brigitte opened Aaron's coat and undid his belt. She sank to her knees and unzipped him.

Aaron closed his eyes as she freed his erection. He gasped with pleasure as she drew him into her warm, wet mouth. His pants slipped to his ankles as he arched his back. His hands went into her hair and held her bobbing head.

Suddenly a male voice cut through the quiet like a knife. "Brigitte!"

Aaron's erection jerked from Brigette's mouth with an audible slurp as he turned in the direction of the intruder. A man stood in the open doorway of an adjoining library with a drink glass in his hand. He wore a tailored, pinstriped suit with a vest.

Aaron felt like an adolescent caught masturbating. He grabbed at his fallen pants, imagining he heard Kalman's warning from years before echo in his mind: *Remember you have a wife . . . all depending on you keeping your focus directed and your pants on.*

177

Brigitte pushed to her feet and wiped her mouth with the back of her hand. "You're such a son-of-a-bitch, Sonny."

"And what are you? Tony's not gone eight hours, and you're sucking some strange cock in his office!"

"You get hot watching?" Brigitte challenged. "Jealous it wasn't yours again? Want me to tell Tony about *that*?"

She gathered her shoes, straightened her dress, and walked toward an adjoining office. "No rough stuff," she warned with a final glance at the man. She stepped through the door, closing it behind her.

Aaron's heart raced as he stuffed his shirttail into his pants and zipped his fly. He no longer had an erection.

As the man walked toward him, Aaron recognized him with a shock. The carefully groomed dark hair, the angular jaw, the dark eyes.

"Captain . . . Rondino?" Aaron gasped. He offered a hand to the American benefactor he'd met at the Polish refugee camp.

Rondino's gaze held Aaron's in a sober appraisal. "It's Aaron Ross, isn't it?" He made no effort to take Aaron's hand, and Aaron sheepishly withdrew it.

Aaron flushed with embarrassment. "Yes." He had unknowingly betrayed his benefactor. "Captain, I had no idea."

"Then you're not as smart as I thought you were. You think I got you into the States so you could get a blow job? You think we pulled strings at Greenwald, Carson and Epstein so you could fuck with Tony's woman?"

A wave of nausea hit Aaron. "You got me the job?"

"Naw, big firms hire Polish Jews every day," Rondino mocked. "Of course we got you in there. You asked for help, we gave it."

Aaron felt physical pain at the cruel revelation. "I didn't know."

"You're lucky it was me in here, or your ass would be a boat anchor in New York Harbor tonight."

A sleeping anger stirred deep in Aaron's stomach. His hard work—the hours of study, the hope, the prayers—futile, false. He'd thought he'd built a path to success when, in reality, he had performed like a trained rat. The life he had pulled from the grasp of the Nazis now lay firmly in the grip of the Marcello branch of the Mafia.

Rondino sneered, "You better learn to keep your dick in your pants, Counselor."

Aaron's anger matched his words. "Who did you take your lessons from? Brigitte?"

"Don't threaten me, you Jewish fuck. I pulled your life outta the rag bag and gave it back to you."

Aaron glared at Rondino. "So I won't tell Tony that Brigitte sucked your cock. Now we're even."

"You wanna play hardball, Ross, you better make goddamned sure you got the stomach for it. We got you the fucking job and, if I pick up the telephone, you and those two Jewish princesses you call a family will be on the street tonight."

Aaron didn't flinch. "That's supposed to threaten me? I've watched women and children march into gas chambers, and then helped bury them. I've seen men eat their own shit because they were starving, and I dealt with Nazi bastards much bigger than you."

"Maybe you haven't heard, Ross. The war's over. And you lost!"

Aaron defended with a bluff. "Not yet, I haven't. I've got copies of every record Greenwald, Carson, and Epstein has on Tony Marcello. If anything happens to me or my family, it all gets delivered to the federal prosecutor. Do you understand that, Captain?" Adrenaline surged through Aaron's veins.

Rondino's tone softened some. "You're making a serious mistake, Aaron."

Aaron turned and walked toward the office door. "I made the mistake a long time ago, Captain. I trusted you." With a hand on the doorknob, he paused and gave Rondino a hard look. "I never intended to cause you problems, but if you crowd me, you'll regret it."

Aaron stepped into the hallway, where Harry considerately pushed the button to open the elevator.

Rondino called from inside the office, "Fuck you, you Jewish prick."

CHAPTER SIXTEEN

STANDING IN THE SHADOWS

You shall not commit adultery.

Seventh of the Ten Commandments;
Exodus 20:13

Aaron graduated from Columbia University Law School magna cum laude. *The Wall Street Journal* announced he had joined Greenwald, Carson and Epstein on Park Avenue, one of the most respected law firms in New York. It had branches in Paris, London, Washington, and the Far East.

Two hundred attorneys worked for Greenwald, Carson and Epstein. Aaron was older and more mature than many of the junior lawyers, and his experience in Warsaw served him well. Though he began as a junior attorney, Aaron quickly became Harold Epstein's protégé and climbed the ladder.

Six weeks after he joined the firm, a letter from Brigitte arrived. His heart raced with a mix of fear and remembered passion when he recognized the name on the envelope, postmarked Paris, France. Aaron locked his office door and tore open the envelope.

> *Dear Aaron,*
> *I hope I haven't caused you problems. Tony has sent me to his apartment, here in Paris. I hope to see you again sometime.*

Be careful with Sonny Rondino. He's a snake, as well as Tony's nephew.

Until then,
Brigitte Mason

Aaron ripped the letter into small pieces, walked to the hall bathroom, and flushed it.

His bluff with Rondino had worked. He wondered how long the lie would hold. Sony Rondino would not easily forget him or his threats.

When Aaron returned to his desk, he found a message from Harold Epstein: *See me ASAP.*

"Sit down," Harold said when Aaron reached his office. "I have a case for you, Aaron. The senior partners have all looked at the brief and, although it seems to have merit, no one thinks we can win. So I suggested we put it in your hands. You need the courtroom exposure. This is New York City, not Poland. Win this, and you're on the map. Lose it, and not to worry. It was a lost case already."

Aaron drew a quick breath. "Do you think it can be won?"

"Good question." Epstein paced back and forth. "Dewey Wallace, the head of a small engineering company in Pennsylvania, is suing the Marshal Motor Company for a violation of patent rights. Wallace alleges that Marshal Motors illegally copied his blueprint for a new diesel engine. The engine, which is more fuel efficient than anything on the market today, could revolutionize the entire industry.

"Wallace didn't have the resources to produce the engine himself, so he made a pitch to Marshal Motors. Afterward, based upon trust and a verbal agreement, he gave them his prototype, which they tested for six months. At the end of that time, the engineers returned the prototype, saying it didn't work.

"Six months after that, Marshal Motors unveiled their own, new, more powerful and fuel-efficient diesel engine. Wallace claims it's a near-exact copy of his design."

Aaron pursed his lips, liking the prospect of such a challenge. "David versus Goliath."

Epstein nodded, but held up a cautionary hand. "Yes, but there is no stone in David's sling. Everybody does research and development. Remember, Marshal Motors has been around for eighty years. Hell, everyone that owns a lawn mower, an airplane, or a diesel truck thinks the company is a part of the fabric of America, and it is."

"But you still think I should take the case?"

Epstein stopped pacing, stuck his hands in his pockets, and met Aaron's gaze full on. "I think Dewey Wallace is telling the truth."

Aaron drove to Pennsylvania. Wallace Engineering and its six employees worked in an old converted barn, crammed with equipment and smelling of oil.

Dewey Wallace, a hands-on entrepreneur, had a gentle, sincere demeanor and talked enthusiastically about the intricacies of his mechanical designs—obviously his passion. After an hour with the man, Aaron had no doubt about his honesty.

Wallace said a bit defensively, "I'm not looking for money. But my crew and I worked four years on this. What they did isn't fair."

Aaron spent the next seven hours going over the minutes of each meeting, cataloging dates, the subjects of the meetings, attendance rolls, topics, promises, inferences, test results, comparison studies of the two designs, drawings, blueprints, and correspondence. By the time he drove back to New York, darkness had set in. He had oil stains on his pants, dirt under his fingernails, and an eagerness to take on Goliath.

Esther greeted him with a worried frown when he finally arrived home. "Aaron, it's nearly one o'clock. Why are you so late? Couldn't you have called?"

Aaron pulled stacks of papers from his briefcase and sat down at the kitchen table, exhausted but exhilarated. "Epstein assigned me a big case. I've been on interviews, and I've only got a week before trial."

He grinned up at her as she set the kettle on the burner. "I can tell you this, if I succeed, you won't have to work for Bendici."

"I'm not sure I want to leave the shop now," Esther protested. "I'm the office supervisor; I'm in charge of eighty people. I earn a good wage."

Aaron chuckled as he organized his notes. "If I win this case, I'll be able take care of you and Rachel, and we'll live the life of our dreams."

The kettle whistled, and Esther poured water to make him tea. "Yes, that could be nice."

Aaron spared only a fleeting glance for her lukewarm reply. She looked tired. "Go, get some sleep, dear. I'll be at this all night."

He filed a discovery motion the next day, determined to find what Marshal Motors would present as a defense. An impressive and convincing list of eleven witnesses, including the company's top engineers, would testify that Marshal had worked on and developed the new engine for nearly a decade, and that the prototype offered by Wallace had serious carburetor problems. The Marshal engine was equipped with a turbo charger that eliminated any deficiency.

The thoroughness of their defense shook Aaron's confidence. It would take more than Dewey Wallace's sincerity to win the case. Aaron needed proof, and he didn't have it.

At Greenwald, Carson and Epstein, Aaron became a recluse. When not locked in his office pouring over records and statements, he haunted the law library researching precedent-setting cases. He found only a few.

Three days before trial, Aaron worried that he couldn't win without any hard evidence of wrongdoing. He sent out a feeler to see if the giant motor company would consider an out-of-court settlement.

He received a terse message back from the lead attorney: *See you in court.*

Aaron called Dewey Wallace. "They claim their engine is different because of the breakthrough they made in carburetors."

"Bullshit!" Wallace barked. "I gave them the new carburetor two weeks after I delivered the prototype."

"There's nothing in their records about that."

Wallace said in a mocking tone, "Oh, I'm so shocked."

Pushing through a subway gate on his way home, an idea flashed into Aaron's mind. Instead of taking the subway across town, he returned to the street above and hailed a cab. "Marshal Motors's plant in Mt. Vernon."

The cabby pulled away from the curb and said over his shoulder, "You going to work?"

Aaron settled into the back seat, his thoughts alive with possibilities. "Maybe."

He instructed the driver to park across the street from the sprawling corporate headquarters of Marshal Motors. A high fence surrounded the big complex, and it stood bathed in chalky night lighting. Aaron watched a steady stream of pedestrians and cars come and go, all through a gate manned by two security officers. He smiled, completely satisfied with his off-the-cuff reconnaissance mission.

After a few more minutes of quiet surveillance, he said to the cabby, "We can go now."

The next day, Aaron subpoenaed Marshal Motors for all corporate telephone records, meeting records, minutes, and correspondence pertaining to any and all business with Dewey Wallace Engineering, et al.

The courtroom filled to capacity on the first day of trial. Several articles had appeared in the newspapers, hinting at an underdog fighting the establishment—always a big draw. A new kid on the block, Aaron Ross, represented the plaintiff, Wallace Engineering.

King, Cardoza and Johnson from Madison Avenue represented Marshal Motors Corporation. The senior partner, Lawrence King—a seasoned trial lawyer known for his brutal cross examinations—took the lead.

He brushed past Aaron on his way into the courtroom, with a battery of six attorneys. "Stay close and maybe you'll learn something," King told his entourage.

Few recognized Aaron Ross. No one had ever seen him in court, and although he represented the prestigious firm of Greenwald, Carson and Epstein, its members were conspicuously absent.

Judge William Holt took the stand, and Aaron presented the plaintiff's opening statement. "Your Honor, we will show that Marshal Motors has conspired to deprive Dewey Wallace of rightful patent rights, royalties, and profits from a mechanical device commonly known as the Marshal Turbo Diesel Engine. A device designed, engineered, and built by the plaintiff."

King's statement exhibited an excess of arrogance and dramatic bluster. "We deny all allegations. The plans for the prototype engine were developed entirely by Marshal Motors and its skilled team of dedicated engineers. There is no proof whatsoever that any of the plans, ideas, or concepts for this revolutionary engine came from Wallace Engineering. Nor is there any evidence to suggest fraud. This lawsuit is frivolous, groundless, and malicious. There is nothing that denotes a violation of any trade, civil, criminal, or manufacturing law. The evidence will show that Dewey Wallace presented his prototype engine to the Marshal

Motors engineering team and that, after testing, it failed. It was not until a later engineering breakthrough that the Marshal Diesel Engine was introduced."

Aaron caught the defense team's smiles when he called his first witness: "Charles Cox, senior engineer for Marshal Motors."

Lawrence King whispered loudly to a colleague as the bailiff swore Cox in, "He's grasping at straws."

Aaron approached the witness, noting the man's quick glances toward the other attorney table. "Mr. Cox, you were present when Dewey Wallace pitched his engine to your development team at the Mt. Vernon plant."

"Yes, but he couldn't keep it running."

A spattering of laughter rippled across the courtroom.

Cox added with a smile, "Design flaw in the carburetor." He seemed at ease and confident, but his gaze kept shifting to King.

Aaron stepped in front of Cox, blocking the man's view of the other attorneys. "That was in November. Was this the only time you met with Dewey Wallace?"

Cox shrugged. "The engine didn't work. There was no reason to meet again."

Aaron gathered several ledgers from his desk and returned to the witness stand. "Mr. Cox, you've worked for Marshal Motors for twelve years, so you're familiar with plant security? Specifically, visitor policy that requires signing in at the gate, the issuance of visitor passes, and the inspection of incoming packages?"

Cox slanted a wary look to the defense team. "Yes . . ."

Aaron faced the judge. "Your Honor, I would like to offer Plaintiff's One—a subpoenaed copy of the Marshal Motors security gate log for December of the same year."

"So entered," the judge declared.

Aaron spread the log on the witness stand in front of Cox. "I direct your attention to line six. Would you read the name entered there for the court?"

One of the lesser attorneys stood. "Objection, Your Honor!"

"Overruled." To Cox, the judge said, "Read the name, sir."

"Dewey Wallace."

"And does it indicate who Mr. Wallace was coming to see?"

"Yes."

"And whose name is written there?"

"Mine."

"And what does it say Mr. Wallace was carrying into Marshal Motors on that day?"

"A carburetor," Cox said quietly, as if hoping no one would hear him.

Aaron leaned both hands on the witness stand and studied the nervous man. "You realize your testimony here today is under oath, don't you, Mr. Cox?"

The man looked to the judge. Sweat dotted his forehead, and color drained from his face. "They made it clear my job was on the line. I got two kids in college, a mortgage."

The crowded court exploded with excitement as reporters scrambled toward the door.

Aaron patted the polished wooden rail and nodded to the judge. "No more questions, Your Honor."

The court awarded thirty-five million dollars, plus royalties, to Wallace Engineering. Greenwald, Carson and Epstein received fourteen million dollars and promoted Aaron to full partner.

Four Marshal Motors engineers received prison terms. Cox, the engineer who'd cooperated with plea bargaining, received a six-month suspended jail sentence.

The headlines in *The New York Times*, the *Daily News,* and *The Wall Street Journal* touted similar themes: "Marshal Motors Chairman Resigns in Scandal."

From then on, Aaron received assignments for some of Greenwald, Carson and Epstein's more difficult cases. He became one of most winning trial attorneys in the history of the law firm.

With each success, Aaron's income rose dramatically, and the family moved to a luxurious apartment in an upper-class part of town. Aaron insisted that Esther quit her job at Bendici's sew shop.

Rachel prepared to transfer into the undergraduate school at Columbia University. She had decided on a liberal arts degree, with a major in English. She tenaciously pursued a scholarship, seeking acceptance to the same university where Aaron had received his law degree, but under her own steam.

Aaron basked in the limelight of the trial and his newfound fortune. He became a featured guest and speaker at a variety of private clubs, banquets, and civic organizations, many exclusively Gentile. That he was a Jew didn't seem to matter. Soon, a number of celebrity columns pushed him even higher on the A-list, and he rubbed elbows with the rich and famous.

Speculation began over the possibility of an elected office after Aaron had a private chat with a new, young President-elect. Between his busy schedule at the office, where he now primarily advised junior partners on case preparation, and his crowded social calendar, he had little time for Esther and Rachel, but he took comfort in knowing he could finally afford to give them a good life.

A cleaning lady came two times a week to the apartment, and the family of three now met only occasionally at dinner. They had time and money to travel, but never spoke of visiting Europe.

The sting and embarrassment of Aaron's confrontation with Sonny Rondino over Brigitte had faded, along with the fear of reprisal. Aaron remembered their shared passion with longing, and often daydreamed of Brigitte, wondering if she thought of him.

Work at the office consumed Aaron, and Rachel seemed to devote all her time to studying, in preparation for the entrance exams.

She passed the entrance exam to Columbia University and received a scholarship that covered half of her yearly tuition. The trio celebrated Rachel's good news with a special dinner. Rachel and Aaron had much to talk about, but Esther remained quiet. Several people in the restaurant recognized Aaron, two of them autograph seekers.

While Aaron and Rachel exchanged stories, hopes, and dreams, their lives brimmed with excitement, unfolding and growing, Esther slipped further into the shadows.

Aaron soon found work boring. Greenwald, Carson and Epstein's cases no longer satisfied his intellectual curiosity. He had achieved success in the job, but as long as he stayed with the firm, the threat of the Marcellos reaching out to pull the strings lurked over him. He had to escape. He refused to live as a prisoner ever again.

His many speaking invitations gave birth to the idea of teaching. At the different social engagements, he enjoyed being the focal point of attention. Standing in front of the groups, ranging in size from as few as twenty to over a thousand, he lectured on the Marshal case, the law, and more, loving every moment.

When Aaron approached Harold Epstein with the idea, the man gaped at him. "You're telling me you're going to quit the firm and go back to some quasi-academic career when you've become a full partner here?"

Without waiting for an answer, Epstein leaned across his desk and offered, "What if we changed the name of the firm to Greenwald, Carson, Epstein and Ross? Would that satisfy you?"

Aaron slowly shook his head. "I want to *teach* the law, not merely follow it."

A few days later, he submitted his resignation. The partners rejected the request, and instead granted Aaron an indefinite leave. He grimaced, understanding the value for them to maintain a relationship with the now-famous Aaron Ross.

However, he accepted the compromise when Epstein handed him a check from the firm—bonus compensation for the recognition and business Aaron had brought to Greenwald, Carson and Epstein. They would carry him on the company books as a paid consultant.

The week after his resignation / leave of absence, Aaron applied to Columbia University for a teaching position. They voted to accept him into their ranks with almost indecent haste.

Again, Aaron's cynicism kept him on an even keel. He knew, by adding his name to the faculty, the university would automatically draw more students—more tuition—but this didn't alter his objective of teaching.

As a newly tenured professor, Aaron threw himself into his role as an educator. His teachings soon became published books in great demand. All across the United States, attorneys read his articles in *Law Review*. His lectures became reference textbooks, and the opportunities for speaking invitations continued.

Aaron's dynamic lectures made him a popular teacher. Students, determined to absorb every word, filled his classrooms to capacity. Aaron's persuasive body language, his witticism, the tone of his voice, his penetrating eyes and, above all, his physical prowess, teetered on the verge of seduction for the female students. He hadn't forgotten the lessons learned from *Elmer Gantry*.

The faculty at Columbia University Law School presented Aaron with the prestigious "Teacher of the Year" award. The President of Columbia University, the Mayor of New York City, and a wealth of others, including Esther and Rachel, attended the ceremony.

After the presentations, Aaron made a point to introduce Rachel as an upcoming lawyer. He forgot to include Esther in the socializing, and didn't notice her until the time came to go home. Seeing his wife alone in the corner of the ballroom brought only a momentary twinge of guilt. He made a mental note to stop by a jeweler the next day to purchase something special for her.

One day during the next week, while Aaron toiled in his university office, preparing for a lecture, the intercom on his desk buzzed, annoying him. He had told Karen, his secretary, he did not want any interruptions. This particular lecture had to be dynamic, for a television news crew planned to tape it in the classroom for a network program on contemporary law.

Aaron paused from making notes and keyed the intercom. "Yes, Karen?"

"I'm sorry, Professor, but there's a lady here insisting to see you."

Aaron said curtly, "I distinctly told you, 'No interruptions.'"

The voice on the intercom answered defensively, "She won't listen to reason. Her name is Brigitte Mason."

Aaron's pulse jumped. His ego soared. She'd returned, across an ocean.

He stood behind his desk and straightened his tie. "Send her in."

Wearing an upset expression, his secretary opened the door for the unexpected guest. Aaron knew that Karen, an overweight forty-two-year-old, had feelings for him. He had knowingly fueled Karen's fantasies out of boredom, flirting out of habit, but deflecting all consequences by hiding behind his marriage.

Brigitte smiled as she swept inside. "Hello, Aaron."

"Hello, Brigitte."

Their separation disappeared into the passion of their last meeting. Electricity filled the air between them.

Karen said stiffly, "Professor, you have only five minutes before the lecture."

"Call them and delay it."

"What?"

"Call them and delay it, and hold all my calls."

"But, sir, ABC News is . . ."

"Just do it, Karen."

The door slammed shut.

Brigitte pushed the button on the lock. She smiled seductively. "Now, where were we?"

They met in the middle of the office. Her purse fell to the floor as her arms went around his neck.

Aaron's mouth found hers. Her heady, perfumed fragrance engulfed him. The pressure and warmth of her leg pressing his set him on fire. He cupped her firm hips, pulling her against him as he slid his hands up and under her skirt and felt her bare flesh.

Their kisses became more urgent. He covered Brigitte's lips, her face, her neck, as she molded her body to his. Aaron unbuttoned the silk blouse and unhooked the bra, dropping both to the floor as she unzipped his pants. Her warm hands released him.

Leaning Brigitte over his desk, Aaron hungrily devoured her breasts. His fingers probed her wetness. He couldn't hold back any longer, and drove into her again and again. Their passion became a mutual frenzy.

Framed pictures of Esther and Rachel fell off Aaron's desk and crashed to the floor. Lifting Brigitte from the desk, he laid her on the carpet as she held him between her legs.

"Now, Aaron, now!" Brigitte screamed, mindless of the thin walls between offices.

CHAPTER SEVENTEEN

BLOOD AND HONOR

Seek the welfare of the city to which I have exiled you.
Pray to the Lord on its behalf, for in its prosperity,
you shall prosper.

Jeremiah 29:7

One morning, Aaron opened up the paper. "DA dies of heart attack," shouted the headlines of the *Daily News*.

After serving the city for more than a decade, Noah Marks had been found dead on the sidewalk after a morning jog near his apartment on West Fifty-Second Street. Marks, the incumbent, had held a wide lead over his opponent, Phillip LePage, a superior court judge. His death left an ominous void, not only in the DA's office, but in the election as well.

Another article suggested Aaron, a vocal and creditable critic of crime, as a replacement.

Later that day, during a telephone conversation, a reporter from the *Times* planted the seed. "Professor, have you considered running for district attorney?"

Aaron didn't sleep the next few nights.

He tried to talk to Esther about the possibility of running for office, but she said only, "Aaron, do what makes you happy."

She had slipped into a depression he didn't understand and really didn't have time for. Pre-menopausal, he guessed. He had given her the good life—had done his part—but she had never really seemed to find her place.

Rachel would be a better sounding board. Aaron invited his brilliant adopted daughter to lunch on campus; he didn't want Esther interrupting.

He waited in the law school cafeteria. When Rachel arrived with her tray, the vivacious beauty did not go unnoticed by a fellow law professor at a nearby table.

"Hey, Aaron," the bearded young man called, "is this the fox you had howling in your office last week?"

Aaron shot the man a heated look. "This is my daughter, you idiot."

The professor grabbed his tray and made a hasty retreat.

Rachel gave Aaron a bewildered, suspicious look as she sat down. "What was he talking about?"

"I had to chew out a student. There was some shouting."

Rachel narrowed her gaze on him, but said nothing.

Aaron filled the awkward moment by telling Rachel about his pending decision. He could continue a career at Columbia University, or enter the race for New York District Attorney. Running for the public office meant resigning from the faculty, giving up a secure position, and leaving behind the life of academia.

"Will I be elected? Will I like being a politician? Will I be able to apply what I've been teaching? With my experience and knowledge of the law, I might be the best candidate. I think I could help reduce crime and improve security in the city."

Rachel smiled. Her eyes sparkled as she said enthusiastically, "You've convinced me. Now all you have to do is convince a couple million others."

Aaron took Rachel's hand and kissed it. "Thank you."

Her encouragement helped him with his decision. He could not ignore the opportunity fate had placed in his path. He registered as an Independent candidate for District Attorney of New York in the upcoming primary election.

The next day, the *Times* headline read, "Ross Adds His Name to the Ballot!"

Brigitte Mason also strongly supported Aaron's decision to run for DA. Aaron accepted her enthusiasm as a demonstration of a growing love for him.

He'd heard rumors that Tony Marcello suffered from a fatal strain of cancer. In brief moments of clarity, between their continuous, passionate assignations, he suspected that should Marcello die, Brigitte would need a new and powerful sponsor. As the district attorney, Aaron would certainly measure up in that respect. But he quickly forgot those moments amidst the scramble leading up to the primaries.

After declaring his candidacy, Aaron took a bachelor apartment not far from the Columbia campus. "I'm doing it to protect you and Rachel," he told Esther.

She didn't question the decision.

Brigitte visited Aaron at the new apartment regularly. He hoped to eventually use her inside knowledge against Marcello and Rondino, but that could wait until after the election. Even during the election, he rationalized, if the press discovered the affair, they could use her connection to organized crime against him.

Four weeks prior to Election Day, a television station set up a debate between Aaron and his opponent, Judge LePage, to take place at Studio Six, Rockefeller Center. The audience, split equally between the two candidates, was by invitation only.

Aaron sent invitations and a personal note to both Rachel and Esther. He hadn't seen either in two weeks and didn't really think they would attend.

Brigitte Mason arrived twenty minutes before the scheduled start time, sporting a scarf and a pair of dark sunglasses.

Aaron, nervous and pacing, welcomed her arrival.

Brigitte guided him to a seat at the mirrored dressing table and massaged his tense shoulders. "You'll do fine."

She ran her hands inside his shirt and down his bare chest, purring, "I know what will help you relax."

"Brigitte, there's not much time."

She sank to her knees in front of him and unzipped his pants. "Won't take me long."

Aaron's head fell back, and his eyes closed as he sat slumped in the chair. He played with the long, blond hair on the head that bobbed in his crotch. A knock came at the door, but Aaron couldn't form the words to answer.

Just as Aaron climaxed, a woman's high-pitched scream jolted him out of his sexual stupor. His head snapped back, and he stared at the two young women frozen on the threshold of his private dressing room.

Rachel and another girl her age stared at him with expressions of horror and revulsion. The girl who'd accompanied Rachel pivoted and ran from sight.

Aaron froze, his mind still hazy with sex. He tried to swallow, but his throat wouldn't work properly.

Rachel's wide-eyed gaze riveted on the blond.

Brigitte stared back.

Finally, looking pale and ill, Rachel turned and ran down the corridor.

Aaron's voice escaped from its paralysis of shock, and he called after her, "Rachel, wait!"

The debate started fifteen minutes later.

Aaron came out the decisive winner.

Reporters commented in television newsbreaks throughout the evening that Aaron Ross had given a flawless performance.

"This guy really seems at ease under pressure," one such report suggested.

Aaron's ratings in the polls went up six points.

The victory celebration lasted hours.

Brigitte teased, "You won by a head."

Aaron was not amused.

Just past midnight, Aaron collapsed in a chair in the darkness of his empty apartment. The umbilical cord from his tragic past in Poland—Esther and Rachel—had abruptly ruptured. The life he had built with Esther had vanished, leaving only excruciating emotional pain.

Aaron's calls to Esther and Rachel went unanswered.

After several weeks of silence, he wrote a note to Rachel, asking to have lunch.

She met with him at a small sidewalk café near Central Park.

Once seated and alone, Aaron asked Rachel to forgive him and to convey his apology to Esther. "Please, Rachel. Talk to her for me. I need to see her."

Rachel's voice broke as she said, "Why? Obviously you don't love her anymore."

"I do love Esther. Things have happened in my life. Things you would never understand."

"I understand what I saw."

"Do you? Do you understand what it means to lose everything? Even your pride? Your ability to be a man?"

"I may not be a man, but I know what it is to lose everything," Rachel shot back at him. "I lost my father, my mother, my brother, and even my name. Now, I've lost you."

"You can never lose me, Rachel. It doesn't matter if you love me. It kills me that you may not, but my love for you is unconditional. I will love you no matter what."

"Isn't that what you promised Esther when you married her?"

"And I do love her. What you saw wasn't about love."

"Exactly my point. This is one case even I could win in court, Counselor."

"You are young and innocent, Rachel. You will learn a man has needs—"

"And so do women. So do I! So does Esther. You have betrayed us. I loved you, Aaron!"

Others at nearby tables stared at them, but Aaron ignored everyone for Rachel. He took her hands in his. She moved to pull them away but he tightened his grip, and she stilled.

Moisture flooded Aaron's eyes. "Listen to me, Rachel. You will never know how much I love you. You will never know the troubled thoughts that have teased my mind. I need your forgiveness. Please, grant this."

Rachel stood. "I don't want to hear any more. I don't know what to think or feel." She turned and marched away.

A tear ran unchecked down Aaron's cheek as he watched Rachel leave.

Later, alone in the small apartment he'd rented for his trysts with Brigitte, Aaron realized, in order to survive, he had to pull himself together. Rachel had said she had loved him, and that gave him hope. He prayed time would bring her understanding.

Unwittingly, Brigitte Mason's dressing room indiscretion had given Aaron what he needed most to win the election—resolve. He would pick up the pieces of his life and prevail.

Esther and Rachel had abandoned him. Instead of what he had once dreamed of—family, a challenging career in law, punctured with Rachel's marriage, births, graduations, the fabric of happiness—his life had turned into a horrific nightmare.

He'd once blamed the Nazis for the chaos in his life. Now, he had only himself to blame. He'd spun out of control, like a leaf caught in a torrent of water.

Election as district attorney could offer a new beginning, a salvation, a chance to right all wrongs, a reason to be. Alone and approaching midlife, Aaron Ross needed a reason. He needed a victory. He needed salvation. He needed to change. Perhaps the mask of district attorney would provide the answer to his personal dilemma.

Along with the resolve to win the campaign, Aaron knew his relationship with Brigitte Mason could not continue. He had to protect his image, both public and private.

At first, Brigitte seemed devastated, but then she smiled serenely and said, as a parting shot, "I'll see you after the election."

Aaron campaigned from predawn in produce markets to late night on radio talk shows, determined to have his voice heard by all of New York. In the final days before the election, he gained support in Manhattan. Many remembered Aaron as the brilliant young lawyer from his time with Greenwald, Carson and Epstein, while others knew him as the dynamic Columbia University law professor who'd championed new anti-crime programs.

The Teamsters and the United Auto Workers backed Aaron's opponent, Judge LePage. They constantly challenged Aaron's lack of experience in public service.

"He's a one-case civil attorney," LePage hammered through the various forms of media. "That's not enough."

Aaron referred to the judge as a career politician who was "part of the problem." He published articles in *The New York Daily* depicting the judge as soft on crime. "Read his record," became Aaron's battle cry.

On election eve, Aaron held a midday, open-air rally in Washington Square, themed "United We Stand." Thousands crowded the streets where Aaron took the platform.

Aaron's amplified voice echoed over the throng. "I come here today asking for your help. I can't do the job without you. This isn't your city. It isn't my city. It's *our* city. UNITED WE STAND!"

A roar of approval came from the crush.

Aaron paced on the platform, again in his evangelistic style, gesturing to the crowd. "Criminal wolves prey on the weak and the defenseless. Alone, we become their victims. Together, we can stand and face them—not only face, but drive them away. UNITED WE STAND!"

Again, the crowd roared.

Election Day dawned gray and wet in New York City. Aaron told his small army of veterans and volunteers—most from the staff and student body at Columbia—that with the exception of an early-morning visit to a polling place, he would be spending the day in quiet seclusion with his wife and daughter. He promised to return to election headquarters late in the evening.

In reality, Aaron spent the day in his small apartment, alone, pacing as he listened to the radio and television. The election news sounded less than encouraging for him.

"Too close to call," a field reporter from WNBC television stated after the polls closed. "This one's going down to the wire."

Rain pelted the city throughout the gray day, but voter turnout remained high. When the polls closed at 8:00 p.m., the electronic count between the two candidates made the contest too tight to call. An army of clerks began a manual tabulation.

Two hours later, Aaron Ross had generated a twenty-two-thousand-vote lead. Thirty minutes more, and his lead had increased to nearly thirty thousand votes.

Near midnight, Judge Charles LePage stepped in front of a cluster of microphones and conceded defeat.

Aaron watched the concession speech on television from his apartment, while eating a peanut butter sandwich. He was the new District Attorney of New York City. However, the anticipated feeling of triumph didn't come.

He wanted to phone Esther and Rachel, but because of the late hour, he felt uncertain about their accepting his call. So, Aaron gathered his jacket, checked his appearance in a mirror, and headed for the door.

He had a job to do.

CHAPTER EIGHTEEN

Rise to Power

The law of the state is the law.

Babylonian Talmud,
Baba Kamma 113a

Atop the twenty-seventh floor of City Hall, Aaron Ross assumed the position of district attorney. He had the office redecorated to his personal taste, with leather chairs, a massive, cherry wood desk, and brass lamps.

In his new role, Aaron would control an army of people responsible for law and order in the massive city. The courts in the New York City boroughs—including Manhattan, Queens, the Bronx, Brooklyn, and Staten Island—all fell under his jurisdiction. A plethora of judges, prosecutors, senior attorneys, clerks, and assistants would all report to him.

Aaron assembled his personal staff from the young lions of the campaign—all bright, aggressive, idealistic, and eager to serve. Most hailed from Columbia University, but Aaron also recruited from within, choosing his Senior Criminal Advisor from the ranks of the former DA's office.

He also had a special choice for one position. He had two plainclothes investigators summon Attorney Samuel Sloan from his cluttered office. Sloan blustered down a long hallway on the twenty-third floor, meeting Aaron in front of a solid, wooden door.

"Counselor Sloan, you once turned me down for a job, but gave me invaluable advice, which I have never forgotten. You will be the best Director of Immigrant Affairs this city has ever seen."

He stepped aside with a smile and indicated the brass plaque that bore Sloan's name beside the door—something the aging attorney had not owned when Aaron had come seeking employment.

The old man grinned from ear to ear.

After six weeks in office, Aaron called a staff meeting. All but Aaron sat around a massive conference table. He, instead, paced as he spoke, touching shoulders, making eye contact, and gesturing. "Getting here may have been the easy part. Now, we have to prove correct the people who voted for me. Now we have to deliver.

"I don't want more of what has been done. I want innovation and originality. I want programs, recommendations, and solutions.

"Law and order in this city, as in all America, must be restored. No one kills in this city and escapes justice. Whether homeless or wealthy, life is sacred, and we will defend it with all the might of this office.

"We do not have hours in this office; we have jobs. When the job is finished, we go home. Criminals don't work nine to five, nor do we. As district attorney, I no longer want to see a *reaction* from this office after a criminal event. I want *pro*-action. From now on, things are going to change. The amount of crime is this city should be an embarrassment to each and every one of us. I hold us all responsible to not just prosecute criminals, but head them off before they hurt other innocent victims. The tail no longer wags the dog."

In Aaron's first media speech after the elections, he vowed, "As promised, I will do my best to end crime on the streets. The goal isn't low tolerance; it's intolerance. You have placed your security in my hands. I pledge to do what I must to make this a safe city. A lower crime rate will attract new businesses. More factories will provide income for our families. Parks and playgrounds will once again be places of pleasure, not fear. If you're a criminal in New York, you'd better look for a new career."

The *Times* headline read, "DA Ross Targets Street Crime." Every New York paper, and most radio and television news stations, quoted Aaron.

Telegrams and letters of congratulations poured into the office. A staffer answered most, but Aaron reviewed and initialed all, scrawling instructions and notes on some.

Late one evening, Aaron, dog tired and laboring through the mail, recognized a name on a handwritten note.

Dear Aaron,
    Congratulations on your election as district attorney.
    Next stop, the White House!
    I'll be here when you need me. Call.

        Love,
        Brigitte

He paused and studied the short message, then brought the pastel-colored paper to his nose and sniffed. Brigitte's unmistakable scent wafted up from the stationery. Her heady perfume stirred in him a mix of apprehension and passion.

With an effort of willpower, Aaron crumpled the note and dropped it into a trash can, then turned in his high-backed swivel chair to look out over the panorama of New York at night. His reflection on the window, mixed with the lights beyond, made him appear as one with the city. He felt old; more than old, he felt lonely.

The note from Brigitte had reminded him he was a man with passions and hungers, fallible and weak. Even as head of one of the most powerful government organizations in the city—the city's chief law enforcement officer—he'd been powerless in combating the gnawing guilt in his stomach over the loss of Esther and Rachel.

He had won it all, only to lose everything.

Aaron deposited money into an account in Esther's name every week. She had suffered because of him, and he didn't want her to compromise her lifestyle. She was still the wife of the district attorney, and although the inner circle knew the truth about the relationship, few—if any—in the public sector did.

He sighed, remembering nights that now seemed so long ago, when Esther would climb into bed with him on the floor of their tiny apartment above Bendici's sew room. Life had been good and simple and warm. He closed his eyes, imagining the scent of Esther's wet hair after she had washed it in the sink down the hall.

Aaron also kept tabs on Rachel's progress. He missed her. The ache felt as real as the pain he'd suffered when he'd lost his son, Stefan. His son he could blame on the Nazis, but Esther and Rachel . . . he had no one to blame but himself.

He prayed that time would bring change, and had no choice but to wait. While he waited, he worked.

———∘∘∘▶◀∘∘∘———

After leaving Aaron, Rachel and Esther leased a third-floor apartment in Upper Manhattan, close to Columbia University, where Rachel continued to work on her law studies.

Esther buried herself in volunteer duties and socials. Her conversations with Rachel always focused on their early years in America. She referred to life with Aaron before Rachel had told her of the affair, and spoke of events—years old—as if they had happened yesterday. She spoke of Aaron, still in a fantasy world, and Rachel's anger towards Aaron smoldered.

As Rachel entered her senior year, job offers poured in from headhunters sent to recruit young, talented, and promising attorneys. Rachel, connected to the powerful District Attorney of New York City, would be a prime catch. Aaron Ross cast a long shadow.

Rachel received the prestigious Dwight Eisenhower Award for a thesis, *Human Rights and Immigration to America.* The legal periodical *Law Review* published her work. The Dean of Columbia University and the Chairman of the Board of Trustees announced they would recognize Rachel's achievement at a formal ceremony.

She agonized over sending an invitation to Aaron. The school knew nothing of the estrangement between them. When the award chairman informed her that he'd reserved two seats for the district attorney and his wife, and that formal invitations had already been sent, the problem solved itself.

Rachel, although not completely ready to accept a new beginning to their relationship, did feel eager to see Aaron once more.

As her anger had faded, Rachel had finally admitted to herself that her rage had resulted, in part, from jealousy. Aaron Ross was the only man, other than her father, that Rachel had ever loved. Thus, his infidelity had shattered the fantasy love she'd harbored for him. Rachel had never thought of it as a sexual love—that is, not until she had seen him with the woman in the dressing room.

Now, with time, reason, and heart, Rachel finally understood. The love she felt for Aaron had matured, and with that maturity had come acceptance. She loved him as a father. Anything more, and she would become the woman from the dressing room.

Rachel had no idea how she would react upon seeing Aaron, but the public place dictated decorum. Nothing adverse would occur, and she would be protected from any possibility of an awkward scene.

When Rachel explained to Esther that Aaron would likely attend, and that they may be sitting beside each other, Esther simply smiled and said, "That's nice."

Aaron had just gathered his coat, set to leave the office to attend Rachel's presentation, when his private line rang. He hesitated at the door, then turned back to his desk and picked up the phone.

"Aaron Ross."

Brigitte's husky voice purred in his ear, "Hello, Aaron. Thought I'd call and see what you were . . . *up* to."

Aaron's pulse raced, but he quickly stepped down hard on his automatic, physical reaction. Disgust at his weakness for her made him angry. "How did you get this number?"

She laughed softly. "Aaron, you know I've always had your number."

He swallowed, enjoying the tingle of awareness caused by her breathy laugh. His tone lost its initial sharpness. "I was just leaving for a presentation for Rachel at Columbia."

"Isn't she the little number who walked in on us?"

The reminder served to cancel out all desire for his one-time lover. "Brigitte, I really don't have time."

"Isn't it sort of tit for tat? A friend of mine walked in on us, and then a friend of yours walked in on us."

"Rachel's much more than a friend, Brigitte; she's my ward."

"Pretty sexy little ward, if you ask me."

Aaron said, his voice icy, "I would never stoop that low. Goodbye, Brigitte."

"Wait," she said. "I need you. Rondino is pressuring me . . ."

He slammed down the phone.

Rachel took her seat, just to the right of the podium, and looked up in time to watch Esther walk into the university auditorium, her head held high.

Esther wore her favorite "American patriotic" suit to the award ceremony. Gloves had become an intricate part of Esther's wardrobe. Others thought they made her look sophisticated, but in reality the mid-length gloves hid an identification number just above her right wrist, tattooed by the Nazis.

Rachel stiffened when Aaron entered the auditorium. Blood pounded in her ears. An usher walked him down the center isle to the front row and the empty seat beside Esther. A murmur drifted over the audience. Heads turned, eyes followed.

He wore a tailored, gray, pin-striped suit and vest. The close-cropped hair at his temples had begun to turn gray, but he still moved with an athletic grace—handsome, and the epitome of success.

A lump of pride rose in Rachel's throat. She fought the urge to run down the steps and throw her arms around his neck.

Aaron took the seat beside Esther. He patted Esther's hand as Rachel had seen him do a thousand times before. Esther offered him a smile of acknowledgment. It seemed as if they had been apart only since morning coffee.

When Aaron turned his attention to the stage, Rachel's gaze found his. He smiled, and the distance between them melted.

Tears welled in Rachel's eyes. She tremulously returned his smile.

The ceremony started, but Rachel heard little of the speeches. Her heart raced with excitement. That afternoon, she would receive more than the Eisenhower Award. She would get her family back.

The dean finally introduced Rachel, and she somehow made it through her prepared remarks, but the upcoming reunion at end of the ceremony filled her thoughts. Applause erupted in the hall as Rachel sat down.

She looked out at the audience, her eyes only for the couple in the front row. Aaron and Esther stared back at her with obvious approval and pride.

Out of the corner of her eye, Rachel spotted two men in dark suits entering the auditorium just as the dean began his closing remarks. They conversed with a campus official, who then escorted them down the aisle to the front. One of the men bent close and spoke to Aaron. Aaron nodded several times, stone-faced.

The two men stepped back, but did not retreat. Rachel held her breath.

After a moment, Aaron leaned toward Esther and said something in her ear. She showed no reaction.

Then he stood and looked to Rachel. His eyes seemed to beg for understanding, frightening her with the intensity of his gaze. She bit her lip as he turned and hurried out with the two men.

Rachel tried valiantly to suppress her disappointment at Aaron's untimely departure. His position as district attorney required sacrifice. If he had to leave, it must have been urgent. And damned important. Hopefully, he would call later. Maybe he would even visit.

The dean completed his speech, "Thank you all for coming."

Rachel absently acknowledged congratulations as she worked her way through the crush of students and faculty to Esther. Esther still sat in her chair, staring blankly, looking detached. Rachel knelt in front of her. "What happened? Where did Aaron go?"

Esther seemed to give the question serious thought, then murmured, "He said something happened—a shooting." Her right eye twitched, and she rubbed it with her index finger. "He had to be there. It was someone important."

Rachel nodded. Her assumptions had been correct. Aaron would not have left for any other reason, not after such a long separation, not after sharing such complaisant glances. "What else did he say?"

Esther frowned and suddenly looked around as if surprised to see all the people in the auditorium. She seemed confused. "I'm not sure."

Rachel studied Esther's sunken cheeks and deep-set eyes. "Have you eaten anything today?"

When Esther just stared, Rachel took an elbow and gently helped her to her feet. "Come on. Let's get you something to eat."

They took a cab to Wing's Chinese Restaurant in midtown, a favorite of Esther's. On the way, Esther said nothing. Perhaps she, too, thought about Aaron and the missed opportunity to bring their family back together.

Rachel stroked Esther's arm, and then held her cold hand. Maybe she could get Esther to talk at the restaurant.

An obsequious maître d' escorted Esther and Rachel to a private table in a corner section, at Rachel's request.

Rachel told a waiter, "We'll start with some egg flower soup."

She turned to Esther as soon as the man left them. "So, what did Aaron have to say?"

Esther again rubbed her right eye. "I think I may . . ." Her voice trailed off, and she just stared at the flower arrangement on the table.

Rachel said tentatively, "It was nice seeing him, wasn't it?"

Esther picked up a napkin and wiped her mouth. "Yes."

Rachel understood Esther's reticence. She also struggled with her emotions. Neither of them had ever spoken of their deeper feelings. "It was nice seeing the two of you together," she added, hoping Esther would take her cue and open up.

The waiter returned with two bowls of soup, bowed, and withdrew.

Esther fumbled with the soup spoon. She dipped it into the bowl and raised it to her lips, but rather than her usual graceful habits, Esther tipped the spoonful sloppily into her mouth. Soup ran down her chin and plopped onto her silk blouse. Her eyes looked blank.

Rachel grabbed a napkin and reached across the table. "Esther, what's wrong?"

Esther's eyes rolled back into her head. Her tongue pushed from her mouth, and her body went into a stiff, trembling seizure. She twisted in her chair and then crashed to the floor, dragging the tablecloth and dishes with her.

Rachel's scream filled the quiet restaurant.

---∞∘⊰❁⊱∘∞---

Aaron and the two DA investigators stepped off the elevator into the hallway on the eighteenth floor of the apartment building, crowded with police. A cluster of officers moved out of the way as the trio headed for a set of wide double doors.

Aaron remembered the ornate penthouse entry. He'd walked through it before.

Inside, a small army of detectives and technicians took measurements, photographs, and fingerprints. One looked up as they entered the posh rooms. "They're in here." He straightened from where he'd crouched over some obscure piece of evidence, then led the way to an adjoining library.

Once inside, he gestured to a bloody hulk on the plush carpeting. "Meet Anthony Marcello, late head of the Marcello family. Biggest bunch of assholes in New York. You can bet they ain't gonna take this lightly. Someone's gonna bleed."

Marcello lay on his back, pajamas open, pudgy hands atop gray folds of intestines that spilled from a wide gash across his bulging stomach. The ropelike organ had ruptured, or been cut, spilling a mix of pasty liquid and something that looked a lot like pasta noodles. Lifeless eyes stared at the ceiling, beginning to glaze.

"And this," the detective continued, "is Brigitte Mason, Tony's main squeeze. What a waste of a great set of tits."

Brigitte lay on her side, not far from Marcello, her knees drawn up in a fetal position. She wore only an open pajama top, exposing her perfect breasts. Her matted blonde hair, thankfully hiding her face, lay in a wide pool of coagulating blood, where her throat had been slit ear to ear.

Aaron felt nauseous. A torrent of memories and emotions flowed through him like molten rock—her touch, her voice, her scent . . . her telephone call.

Had it been a plea for help? Had his refusal to see her cost her the ultimate price? Had he sealed her fate the day he'd walked into this room with her?

The DA mask slipped. Aaron's path to salvation suddenly came into doubt. He had lost his wife and son to a Nazi death camp, Rachel and Esther to his immorality, and his lover to a madman's knife. Death had been his constant companion—sparing Aaron only to torment him by killing those who had touched his life.

His chest felt as if it were in a vice. His mind swept him back to the horrors of the concentration camps, where death lurked, an ever-present threat—a threat that numbed the senses and stung the brain.

The detective said, unwrapping a piece of gum, "I'd say these two were playing kissy-huggy when someone surprised them. They're not dressed for entertaining company. No evidence of forced entry, so whoever came in had a key. No ransack, so it wasn't robbery."

Aaron turned away. He could hardly breathe. "Got anything at all?"

The detective followed him back into the main salon. "Yeah, for once, fate was kind. Cleaning woman saw a guy come off the elevator in the lobby. He stuffed something in a trash can and went out the door. She was pissed because she had just emptied the can. Went and took a look. Bingo, we got us a bloody knife."

Aaron forced himself back to business. "Can she identify the man?"

"She's down at the Twenty-Second going through mug books. We started with Tony's inner circle. This is a crime of passion, not a hit. Maybe we'll get prints off the knife."

Aaron slumped on the passenger seat in the car, watching the lights sweep by, while an aide drove. A fine rain fell in the dark, enough to blur images on the other side of the glass.

Brigette's last words kept echoing in his mind: "Rondino is pressuring me."

Doing nothing wasn't an option. Aaron may have acted discretely, but he was an honorable man. He would tell the police what he knew, and that would probably end his short career as DA.

Aaron silently damned fate for the web of circumstance that had trapped him. He had much to do and felt eager to do it, confident he *could* do it, but now his chance drifted away, torn from him by his own weakness.

"Son of a bitch," he muttered.

The driver glanced at Aaron. "What was that, sir?"

Aaron sighed. "Nothing."

A filtered male voice came from a radio mounted on the floor between the two. "King base to King ten."

The driver picked up a microphone. "This is King ten. Go ahead."

"King ten, imperative Staff-One land line base, code two."

"King ten, roger."

The office wanted Aaron to call without delay. He knew why. The police had somehow discovered a link between Brigitte and him.

He thought of the phrase the cops used: You play, you pay. It was pay time.

Aaron pushed up straight in the seat. He would take what came, and make damned sure Rondino did, too. "Find me a phone."

Rain pelted the glass of the telephone booth. "Parsons in operations," Aaron told the operator.

A male voice answered, "DA, Operations, Parsons."

"Tom, it's Aaron. What do you need?"

"Sir, I'm sorry, but your daughter Rachel called. She's at Mt. Sinai Hospital. Your wife was taken there by ambulance."

Aaron didn't wait for details. He bolted for the idling car, leaving the telephone receiver swinging at the end of its cord.

———∘∘∘❂∘∘∘———

The ride in the ambulance had been horrific. Siren blaring, it weaved through traffic while an attendant gave Esther oxygen and started an IV line.

Unable to find a pulse, the man had looked to the driver and shouted, "Get on it. She's not responsive!"

At the hospital, Rachel nervously waited in a hallway alcove, not far from the emergency room reception counter, rigid with fear. Egg flower soup stained her blouse, and dried tears had created stiff trails down her cheeks. She sat on the edge of a cushioned bench, staring at the double doors to the emergency room.

Several doctors had hurried inside while she'd kept her strained vigil, but none had come out. Nearly forty minutes had passed—not a good sign.

She'd gone to the nurse's station a half dozen times. "As soon as I hear anything," was the refrain.

Her hands balled into fists in her lap. Rachel prayed, but didn't really expect an answer, perhaps because she knew the answer. Esther had died.

She couldn't imagine life without Esther. The thought brought panic to Rachel, a panic that stole her breath and logic—a panic that told her to run. She shivered with a bone-deep chill that made her flesh crawl, aching for the comfort of her dear friend's loving arms. Esther had always been there for Rachel. Now, Rachel felt helpless and powerless. She owed Esther so much, and she could do nothing. Nothing but wait, wait for them to come and tell her what she already knew.

She lowered her head to her knees and wept. Her body shook with soul-deep sobs.

Memories of past horrors returned. At her family's door, the Germans once again ordered them from their home and onto a truck. An obese woman shaved her mother's head with sheep shears. Her mother wept when Father Dov took her away. And then came the agonizing nights at the convent.

Rachel felt God's presence with her there, in the hospital—not to save Esther, but to punish Rachel. She'd left Poland, abandoning her blood family, and had never looked back, even changing her name in the process. Anyone searching for Rachel Gold would never find her. She had become Rachel Ward upon arrival in the United States, and soon after that, Rachel Ross—pseudo-daughter of Aaron.

Father Dov, her father's best friend, had promised to keep looking for David and her parents, but Rachel had boarded a ship and started a new life. He had kept all of his promises, had risked everything to protect Rachel and her family, and she had repaid his sacrifices by disappearing without a trace.

She flinched and instinctively drew away when a hand touched her shoulder.

Rachel looked up to find Aaron standing over her. She stood and threw her arms around his neck, burying her face between his throat and shoulder. He drew Rachel into his arms and held her in a strong embrace.

After a long, silent, emotional sharing, Aaron set Rachel back on her feet and stared into her eyes. "How is Esther?"

Rachel shook her head and shrugged, unable to speak.

Aaron gasped, then turned and barked at the head nurse, "You don't know what's going on? Well, find out, goddammit!"

Soon the senior resident from the emergency room and a hospital administrator joined them. Rachel and Aaron stood hand in hand, facing the two medical men. Rachel drew courage from Aaron's presence.

The physician cleared his throat and said, "We are profoundly sorry. Your wife came in with no blood pressure—in respiratory arrest. She was unresponsive to stimuli, and her pupils were dilated. There was little we could do."

Aaron whispered hoarsely, "But why?"

The doctor blew out a deep breath. "We really don't know, in the absence of any complaints of health. With what the ambulance attendant reported, I would say a stroke. Intra-cranial hemorrhage." He lowered his voice. "I noticed the tattoo. We may be dealing with head trauma inflicted some time ago."

Aaron squeezed Rachel's hand as they sat on the bench in the alcove after the two men had left. The scene suddenly reminded Rachel of similar times, in the convent, when Father Janusz Dov had given her his silent love and support. Pain rendered her almost catatonic.

Aaron's aide kept others away. Soon, more of his staff arrived, but stayed well back. Several quickly removed two reporters who'd appeared with cameras.

After a long while, Aaron spoke. "Today, when I sat down beside her on campus, I said, 'Hello, Esther, how are you?' I wish I had said, 'Hello, Esther, I love you.'"

His choked words brought Rachel out of her shocked stupor. "She knew."

Aaron nodded, blinking hard, his expression bleak. "I'll make the necessary arrangements. Let me drive you home."

Rachel swallowed, watching him struggle against tears. "I want to tell her goodbye."

Aaron pushed to his feet and helped her up. A solemn nurse led them into a dim corner of the emergency room.

A child cried somewhere close by, and a woman's voice murmured words of comfort.

The nurse pulled a green curtain aside for Aaron and Rachel to enter. Esther lay in a curtained cubicle. A sheet blanketed her body. The curtain scraped back into place, giving them a small measure of privacy.

Aaron stepped up to the bed and lifted an edge of the thin cover to reveal Esther's face. Her eyes were closed, lips slightly parted, hair mussed.

He murmured, "She looks asleep." Tears glistened in his eyes.

Rachel raised Esther's hand to her lips and tenderly kissed it. "Here we are again," she whispered. "The three of us, meeting in a tent." She sniffed, holding back a sob. "I will miss you, Esther."

Rachel leaned over and kissed Esther on the forehead. A tear fell from her face to Esther's. Rachel gingerly wiped it away, then turned and walked out of the emergency room.

———ooo❧❦❧ooo———

Aaron watched Rachel's stiff-backed retreat, feeling strikes of pain with each step she took away from him. Then he looked down at the woman he'd vowed to love and honor in a simple wedding ceremony aboard the miserable, crowded ship headed toward freedom. Anguish strangled him.

He struggled to force the words to come, battling the heavy grief and the torment of his soul. "You may not be the first woman I loved, Esther, but you are the last. You gave me back my life. I thank you. I will regret hurting you for all eternity, and I will live what remains of my life to make you proud."

He leaned over and kissed her on the mouth. "Goodbye, my love."

Then he replaced the sheet over her face and turned away.

CHAPTER NINETEEN

ECHOES FROM THE PAST

*The most difficult of all commandments is
"Honor thy father and thy mother."*

Tanhuma, Ekev, 2

After driving Rachel to the apartment she'd shared with Esther, Aaron sat with her until well after midnight, when she finally fell asleep. He wrote a note saying he would be back in the morning, and drove to the Twenty-Second Precinct. He had no thought of sleep.

Rain was pounding down on the city when Aaron reached the police station. He sprinted to the door, pulling his coat flaps over his head to avoid most of the deluge. Inside, a mix of reporters and members of the Marcello family crowded the lobby.

When Aaron uncovered his head, several flashbulbs went off. "Any comment on Tony Marcello's murder, Mr. District Attorney? Is it true your wife died?"

Aaron ignored them all and headed for the detective bureau on the second floor. A grim-faced Detective Lasski poured him a cup of coffee while Aaron wiped the rain from his face and took off his coat.

The detective said gruffly, "My condolences on Mrs. Ross. This could have waited until later, sir."

Aaron accepted a steaming mug with a sharp nod. He couldn't think about Esther, couldn't face the pain. "Have you made any progress with Marcello?"

Lasski's mouth twisted into a brief smile. "The janitor from the lobby picked out a mug shot of Sonny Rondino. Got a team bringing him in. He's not positive, but it's enough to do a lineup in the morning." He shoved his hands deep into his pockets and gave Aaron a worried look. "The guy's already nervous. He may suffer a sudden case of amnesia."

"I want to talk to Rondino when he gets here. In private."

Lasski stared at Aaron with raised eyebrows. "You know this bag of dog shit?"

"Yes, I know him."

Aaron waited in the detective commander's office until Lasski escorted Rondino in. If the confrontation had shaken the man, it didn't show. Rondino wore his usual air of confidence and aura of power.

He grinned when he saw Aaron. "Picking up a few extra bucks working overtime?"

"Sit down," Aaron ordered.

Lasski stepped away and closed the door.

Rondino took the chair facing Aaron. "Better make this quick. I got a call in to Greenwald, Carson and Epstein. You remember the firm, don't you, Counselor? Oh, but that's right, you can't talk about anything you saw there, can you? Be a violation of privileged communication between attorney and client, wouldn't it, Mr. District Attorney?"

Aaron's pain and grief at Esther's and Brigette's deaths turned to cold, controlled anger. "You think you've got all the answers, don't you, Sonny?"

"I think I got the answer this time. You don't let me walk outta here, I may have to tell the fine citizens of New York about seeing their noble DA with his pants around his ankles."

Aaron folded his hands in his lap, feeling ice steal through his body. "And you think that will save you?"

"No, I just wanted you to know what it was going to cost you." Rondino shook a cigarette from a pack and lit it. "Nobody gives a fuck about Tony Marcello and his whore. He was an old man worried more about hair loss than business, and she was a high-school dropout with a great set of tits. You gonna give up a career for that?"

"You're right, Sonny, I can't reveal anything I saw in those confidential files, but you're still not going to get away with this. You were betting you would be arrested and found innocent because you could extort me.

But you're wrong about what I'm going to do. I'm not going to arrest you. You entered this building, walking right past Tony Marcello's family. You're going out the same way. That is, after Lasski tells them you're the prime suspect. He'll be sure to remind them that you slashed Tony Marcello and Brigitte Mason to death when he shares his frustration about the DA balking at an arrest based on the testimony of one shaky witness. Isn't that what you wanted, Sonny?"

The color drained from Rondino's face. "Wait a minute, goddammit!"

Aaron pushed to his feet, wanting to end the unpleasantness. "As you once told me, Sonny, the war's over, and you lost."

Rondino smiled nervously. "Come on, Aaron." His facade of confidence slipped. "We can make a deal. I have a lot of information that could make you look good. We go way back. Let's talk this over."

Aaron rapped on the door to notify Lasski that the interview had ended. "Tony trusted you, Sonny. I'm not going to make the same mistake. You wanted out, now get out."

Lasski opened the door behind Rondino. "Come on, Hot Shot, lemme show you to the front door. Some people downstairs are looking forward to seeing you."

Rondino growled, "You won't get away with this!"

Lasski grabbed him by the lapels and shoved him out of the office. A couple of officers rushed to lend him a hand.

They buried Esther three days later in the Brooklyn Jewish Cemetery. Aaron stood with his arm around Rachel at the graveside. Ray Bendici and several of the women from the sewing room attended, along with a few of Esther's friends from the many charities she'd helped.

"God has a plan for every life," the rabbi intoned. "Some we understand, some we accept, some bring us pain, and some bring sorrow. Nevertheless, they remain God's plan. We thank God for making us a part of Esther's life—of Esther's plan. And we pray for understanding and guidance in where the path may now lead."

In the limousine, after the service, Aaron took Rachel's hand in his. "I'd like you to move in with me."

"Thank you, but I graduate at the end of next semester. If I'm old enough to practice law, I think I'm old enough to live alone. I don't want to be the one who gets the job because her father is the district attorney."

"Where you live doesn't change who you are."

"I've given this a lot of thought."

Aaron sighed. "All right, I understand. Esther's estate will provide for your needs."

Tears stilted Rachel's speech. "She's still taking care of me, isn't she?"

"Yes."

A message waited on his desk when Aaron returned to his office: *Call Detective Lasski.*

He loosened his tie and dialed the police station. When the detective answered, he said, "Lasski, it's Aaron Ross."

"Yeah, Mr. DA, thought you would want to know. The super found Sonny Rondino dead in his apartment this morning. Someone tied him up, cut his dick off and stuck it in his mouth. He bled to death. Gruesome, huh?" Then he gave a crooked smile. "We're all taking it real hard."

Aaron sucked in a quick breath at the reality of his premeditated actions. He'd as good as murdered the man. He cleared his throat. "Yes, that's terrible."

Rondino had lived and died by the sword. He had killed, so he was killed. That was just. Not legal, but just.

Aaron pushed away his misgivings. "Any make on the prints from the knife recovered after Marcello's murder?"

"Little finger, right hand. Twelve point match . . . Sonny Rondino."

Aaron collapsed in a chair and stared at the wall. "Thank you, Detective."

"Hey, thank *you*, sir. Anytime you wanna work a case, come on down to the Twenty-Second. You got our vote."

"Thanks." Aaron hung up.

He'd initially felt angry and hungry for revenge, but right then, he felt only a deep sense of loss. Esther, Brigitte and Rondino—three lives that had touched his . . . not only touched, but profoundly influenced—gone. Each loss had extracted a heavy toll.

Aaron had hoped for a sense of satisfaction. Reconciling justice and the law troubled his conscience. He had lived in a lawless, brutal society in the death camps. He hated the absence of law. He believed in the law. He lived the law.

Now he felt like a dark hypocrite. He had abandoned his faith in the law to ensure justice. Or had he circumvented the law to protect his career?

Neither choice changed Rondino's guilt, but had one of them changed District Attorney Aaron Ross?

Rachel lost herself in her studies. Graduation from law school did not mean completion. Instead, it meant preparation for the bar exam. Nearing the former, Rachel now prepared for the latter.

A recruiter from the firm of Davis and Collins, on Park Avenue in Manhattan, offered Rachel a position as an associate attorney. Davis and Collins was an established law firm, and highly regarded in New York for its expertise in corporate, civil, and international law. Their list of nearly one hundred and seventy attorneys included graduates from Harvard, Stanford, and Columbia Universities. Rachel felt flattered to be chosen.

She graduated from Columbia, passed the bar examination, and went to work for the firm. Her future looked bright.

Rachel, with her slight accent and perceived European sophistication, drew many clients, and her skills quickly transitioned her into a lead attorney representing foreign dignitaries in the United States. She handled legal affairs, real estate, and businesses for prominent personalities from Monaco, Greece and Wales.

Of the vast stable of lawyers the firm controlled, Rachel fast became a front-runner. After a few years, the partners promoted her to the rank of vice president.

Rachel personally represented Kevin Davis III, the Senior Partner and CEO of the firm, at a variety of social functions. On several occasions, she saw "the district attorney," as she now referred to Aaron.

They'd never recaptured the opportunity to begin again as a family. Their relationship had become cordial and professional, but nothing more. That fateful day at Rachel's award ceremony had been a crossroads in the life they'd once shared. Rachel had gone one way, Aaron the other.

Aaron certainly didn't need her, and she had found success on her own, which pacified any guilt Rachel carried. Maybe at some point in her life, she would need him, but in Rachel's mind, that time seemed very far off.

Weeks had passed since they'd last spoken, months since they had seen one another. Rachel saw more of him on television than in person.

———∘∘∘▬◉▬∘∘∘———

The telephone woke Aaron. The District Attorney of New York seldom got much sleep. He glanced at the illuminated bedside clock as he reached for the receiver. 4:40 a.m. *Never good news at this hour.*

"This is Ross."

The voice of Jack Mills, one of his senior field investigators, sounded choked. "Sorry to bother you, sir. The Twenty-Second just had an officer killed in a liquor store heist."

"Who is it?"

"Detective by the name of Lasski."

Aaron grimaced as the news pulled his stomach into a painful knot.

"He stopped to pick up a pack of cigarettes—walked into a robbery in progress. There were three of them. They shot him twice with a shotgun. You know, he has a wife and three kids."

Aaron struggled to breathe through the emotionally gripping pain.

"Are you there, sir?"

Finally, Aaron gritted out, "Yeah, I'm here. Do we have the shooters?"

"Yeah, trio of three-time losers. All on parole. All addicts. They drove their stolen car into a trash truck two blocks from the store. One's in the hospital, the other two in jail."

"Have the reports put on my desk, Jack. I'll be there in an hour."

"Yes, sir."

At 9:00 a.m., Aaron called a press conference on the steps of City Hall.

Speaking into an array of microphones and cameras, he said angrily, "This morning, while most of us still slept in the comfort of our beds, one of the city's finest, Detective Sergeant John Lasski, walked into a liquor store on Second Avenue. The store was being robbed by three armed parolees. First they shot Detective Lasski in the shoulder as he drew his gun. He may have survived that wound, but when Detective Lasski dropped his gun and fell to the floor, one of the parolees, with the other two urging him on, shot Lasski twice in the face."

Aaron paused for a moment, glaring at each stunned reporter. "I want to say this as the District Attorney of New York: You kill one of our cops, you're going to get the death penalty!"

Then he blew out a long, dramatic breath and lowered his voice. "I knew Detective Lasski. He was a friend. I will personally try this case and see those three animals all get the death sentence."

The afternoon papers and news broadcasts all carried the headlines about the incident: "Angry DA vows revenge; DA promises death sentence for cop killers."

The next day, Aaron appeared in court for the arraignment of the three suspects. After he addressed the court, the judge ruled to hold the trio without bail.

Aaron pointed a finger at the men after they all sneered at him. "I'll see you in court. And I'll see you executed."

The judge cautioned Aaron, "One more word and you're in contempt."

Aaron shot back, "I'm already in contempt of animals like this, Your Honor."

His fiery remark filled the headlines and evening newscasts.

———oo₀∘}◉{∘o₀o———

Late that same afternoon, Rachel's senior partner, Kevin Davis, invited her into his office. After offering a cup of coffee, he sat in a chair across from her. "Rachel, I have someone I want you to meet. His name is Stefan. Stefan is in charge of the international division in our firm, assigned to our London office. He's flying in tomorrow for a deposition."

"I know him by reputation, Mr. Davis. I read his brief on the oil rights dispute with the Saudis."

"And you know he's my son?"

"Yes, sir."

The old man pushed out of his chair, adjusting his suspenders as he limped on an arthritic knee to a window. He stared outside and continued, "Stefan has been invited to the Rathburn Estate tomorrow night. They own sixty percent of Proto-Chem Oil."

"Whom we represent," Rachel added.

Davis turned and faced her, raising an index finger with a little shake, as if lecturing a jury. "Precisely. And the Rathburns have a twenty-two-year-old daughter, fresh out of Princeton, with a degree in planning to marry well. Every time Stefan's in the same time zone, they try to force-feed her to him. I've met the girl and . . . it's not that she's not a nice girl with nice parents, it's just, well, she's just dull, and dumb as a stump."

Rachel arched an eyebrow, curious. "And how do I fit into this?"

Davis limped back to the plush leather chair and leaned on it, meeting Rachel's gaze. "I would be pleased if you would accompany Stefan, and save us from an awkward situation."

Rachel narrowed her eyes on the brilliant and formidable old man. "And if I say no?"

He folded his arms behind his back and smiled. "I'll understand, and your reassignment to small real estate would have nothing to do with my request." He chuckled.

Rachel stood. "As we say down at my level, Mr. Davis, you'll owe me one."

She turned and walked toward the door.

"Thank you, Rachel. I'll give Stefan your number."

Rachel spent the evening going through her wardrobe. At first, the idea of pretending to date the senior partner's son seemed the subject for another bad joke about attorneys, but she found herself feeling like a teenager getting ready for a night out. No social recluse, Rachel regularly attended a variety of business and social functions, but she hadn't wanted any "real" relationships. After mourning the loss of Esther, she had learned how to live alone and enjoy it.

She'd dated in college, but tongues in the mouth and hands on her breasts and up her skirt hadn't unlocked the passion she'd dreamed about. After several uncomfortable situations, she'd decided: better to wait, rather than experience further disappointment. Dating would eventually have its place in her life.

A sleeveless, green, ankle-length, formfitting dress became the choice. Rachel hoped it wouldn't betray the fact that, despite her sophisticated position in life, she was timid in the feminine wiles and still a virgin.

She rationalized the appointment with Stefan Davis as business, and not a date. Her assistant had described him as a handsome, broad-shouldered hunk, a former soccer player, and an Oxford graduate.

By three o'clock the next day, when Stefan had not confirmed their arrangement, Rachel grumbled about the Oxford graduates' obvious lack of education in common courtesy. She'd expected a note, a call—something—from this chosen son of the senior partner, and began to feel like an unappreciated commodity.

Her assistant's voice on the intercom interrupted her thoughts.

"Rachel," the voice said, "Stefan Davis on line six."

Rachel straightened her shoulders, wet her lips, and picked up the telephone. "This is Rachel Ward."

"Hello, Rachel. This is Stefan Davis."

She kept her tone cool. "Hello, Stefan."

"I apologize for calling so late. My flight from London was delayed, and I've been stuck in this deposition in midtown all afternoon. I wanted to come by and introduce myself before tonight. I'm very sorry."

He sounded sincere, and his voice held a decidedly attractive quality. A breeze of relief calmed Rachel's irritation. He might not be a jerk after all. "I understand how that could happen."

"I'm looking forward to meeting you. Several associates, as well as my father, speak very highly of you."

"Well, I appreciate having a decent track record for a relatively new lawyer."

"Oh, no one said you were an attorney!"

"*What*?"

Stefan laughed, then said quickly, "I'm just kidding, Rachel. I know who you are. Columbia law graduate. Studying for your doctorate at NYU, daughter of the DA, five-foot-nine, green eyes, dark hair. You drink your coffee black, and you love French fries."

After a slight pause, he added softly, "My father arranged for a car. I'll pick you up at seven?"

Rachel frowned at the telephone. "Does your father make all your arrangements?"

"In this case, yes. That way, if you don't like me, it's his fault, not mine. See you at seven."

Rachel bathed and shaved her legs. After toweling dry, she dusted herself with powder and dressed. She worked at her hairdo. She didn't want her hair to turn out just good; she wanted it perfect, and decided to wear it up. The doorbell rang, and Rachel checked her makeup in the mirror, rubbed some of the red from her cheeks, and went to answer.

At the door, she took in a deep breath of reassurance. "Hello, Stefan." His brown eyes seemed to look deep into her being, unnerving her.

He offered a hand. "My father was right. You *are* beautiful. I'm pleased to meet you, Rachel." He squeezed gently, and she felt his warm, firm touch throughout her entire body.

"Would you like . . ." His heated look stirred something deep inside Rachel. The feeling stole her thoughts, and although she opened her mouth, she couldn't think of what to say.

Rachel finally managed, ". . . to come in?"

Stefan nodded and brushed by her. His scent intoxicated her. Stefan Davis didn't just enter her living room; he took it over. He had a presence—a masculine prowess—that could not be ignored. He had the thick neck of an athlete and a full head of sandy blond hair.

Stefan glanced about. "Very nice. Do you live here alone?"

Rachel pushed aside the rush of schoolgirl giddiness and deliberately drew on the protective facade of an attorney. She closed the door and strolled into the living room to join him. "Yes, I like living downtown. It's convenient."

"I like New York. London gets a little stuffy."

"Couldn't your dad have you transferred?"

"No way. I don't use his influence if I can help it. But, I must say, his meddling, in your case, is turning out great."

Rachel grinned. "I suppose sometimes it's not easy being the senior partner's son."

Stefan nodded. "And I would bet it's not always easy being the DA's kid. So, we've already found something we have in common."

They rode to Long Island in the back of a chauffeured limousine. Stefan asked Rachel if she'd met the Rathburns.

"No, I haven't," she replied.

221

"They don't invite guests to dinner, they invite crowds. It's as if being surrounded by people convinces them they're not lonely."

Rachel shrugged and leaned into the comfortable seat. "Wealth creates isolation. You can't amass a fortune and maintain contact with people."

A long silence ensued.

Stefan glanced out the window. "I sometimes dream about having a farm in the country."

Rachel followed his gaze, watching the lights sweep by in the darkness beyond him. He seemed to have woven a spell about her.

He continued as if speaking to himself, "A small practice in a nearby town, a wife in the PTA, and a couple kids."

Rachel affected a hillbilly accent and teased, "How ya gonna keep 'em down on the farm after they been to Oxford?"

Stefan chuckled. Then, in a serious tone, he said, "What's your dream, Rachel Ward? Where is *your* heart?"

The question took Rachel by surprise. She didn't have an answer. She loved the law—had spent nearly a third of her life preparing to practice as an attorney. Now, not only had she realized her dream, she'd also become very successful. The achievement provided a real sense of accomplishment and pride, yet she knew something was missing, something that, until now, she hadn't recognized—something pointed out by this soccer player from London.

The handsome young man with twinkling brown eyes had unknowingly touched her soul. She didn't feel lonely, but in reality, she was alone—an unfinished painting, a sky without clouds, an ocean without waves, a woman without dreams of a farm, or anything else.

"I don't know," Rachel answered candidly.

Stefan gave her a knowing smile. "If you don't come up with something, let me know. Maybe I can get you a job on my farm."

The arrival of Stefan Davis and Rachel Ward did not go unnoticed. People stared, whispered. One woman suggested in a loud aside, "New York's Ken and Barbie."

Stefan slipped an arm around Rachel's bare shoulder and drew her close. "Stay with me. Remember, your duty is to protect me from Candy Rathburn."

Rachel relaxed in Stefan's firm but comfortable grasp. "Candy?"

He whispered in her ear, "Not the kind you would want to unwrap."

The Rathburn banquet proved noisy, crowded, and artificial. Politics—see and be seen. Everyone toasted the celebration of Proto-Chem's thirty-fifth anniversary in the international oil market, but the number of robed Arabs present suggested to Rachel that the company might be posturing for another acquisition.

They had cocktails, made the rounds of recognized faces, introduced one another to associates, friends, and business acquaintances, and enjoyed the comments their pairing generated.

The hand around Rachel's shoulder yielded to her hand, laced in his. She didn't object. It felt natural, comfortable.

When Rachel recognized Aaron's familiar figure across the room, she tensed.

Stefan looked at her with a slight frown. "What is it?"

"Aaron."

He looked thinner. His hair had grayed beyond the temple, but he still cut a charismatic figure. Seeing Aaron, as always, quickened Rachel's pulse.

He spoke with a man she recognized as an appellate judge. Others hovered nearby, awaiting their turn to talk with the popular district attorney.

She'd heard growing speculation that Aaron Ross would soon announce his candidacy for senator. The party, as well as the current senator, had already laid the groundwork.

Most, Rachel among them, believed that Aaron Ross's political ambition would not stop at the senator's office. Beyond stood the challenge of the governor's office, and more. He would do it—she knew he would. He had always achieved everything he'd desired.

Stefan excused himself, saying, "I'll get us something to drink. Be right back."

Aaron soon spotted Rachel, smiled, left the others behind and crossed over to her.

He kissed her on the cheek. "Hello, Rachel. You look beautiful." He beamed at her with obvious pride.

Rachel felt a tingle of pleasure.

Aaron gave her a determined smile. "When are we going to find time for dinner, young lady? I noticed that my competition for your time is increasing."

Rachel swallowed, then decided she'd like them to meet—but later, with some privacy. "Yes, he's my boss's son. We're having dinner in Manhattan tomorrow night. Perhaps you would like to join us?" She would make sure Stefan would not refuse.

Aaron forced a smile as a photographer's flash went off beside them. "I'd like that very much."

"La Fayette's on Fifty-Second at eight."

"I look forward to it." Aaron kissed Rachel's cheek again. "Now, you'll have to excuse me. I'm doing some back-channel lobbying with Judge Hodges."

Rachel glanced at Stefan as he handed her a glass of champagne. "You're joining Aaron and me for dinner tomorrow night."

He raised an eyebrow, then shrugged with a debonair smile. "Tonight was for my father. Tomorrow night is for Aaron."

"And what happens on the third night?"

Stefan grinned. "Third time's a charm, they say."

Rachel slipped a heel off and rested her nylon-clad foot on the rungs of the chair through the long dinner, which was filled with mundane speeches and seemingly endless toasts to Proto-Chem Oil.

She and Stefan hurried to their car as soon as they could.

Stefan loosened his tie and relaxed in the back seat. "So, tell me, what it was like growing up with the district attorney?"

Rachel pushed off her shoes and slumped beside him. "Between you, me, and the back seat?"

Stefan took her hand in his. "Privileged communication."

"Aaron Ross isn't my biological father. He's my adopted father."

Stefan fell quiet for a moment. "Kevin Davis isn't my biological father. He's my adopted father. How's that for coincidence?"

"You're kidding!"

"I was born in Poland. My parents died during the war."

Rachel's heart raced. "Jewish?"

"Is that a problem?"

"No."

"Family name was Ross. Just like Aaron's," Stefan continued. "I can't remember much about my parents. They lived in Katowice. I think my father was an attorney. A Catholic adoption agency brought me to the States when I was fourteen. Everything before that is a blank. My dad,

Kevin, picked me because I looked like the son he'd lost in a drowning. Who knows, maybe he looks like the father I lost."

Rachel's heart pounded in her ears so loudly, she could barely hear Stefan's words. Could fate do this? *Would fate do this?* She hyperventilated as panic swelled in her.

Stefan straightened in the seat beside her. "Rachel, what's wrong?"

"Hold me," Rachel answered softly.

Stefan drew her into his arms.

Stefan sent the limousine away and, with his arm around Rachel's shoulder, helped her to her second-floor apartment.

They sat on a couch, not speaking for a long time.

Finally, Stephan took her hands. "Rachel, if it's something I said . . ."

Rachel shook her head. Tears filled her eyes. She took in a breath and steadied herself. "It's not what you said. It's who you are."

"Who I am?"

Rachel sniffed. "Is Stefan your birth name?"

"Yes, why?"

"I may know your father."

"My father! That can't be. He's dead."

Rachel squeezed his hands. "Listen to me, Stefan. Aaron Ross was an attorney in Katowice, Poland, before the war."

Stefan stiffened.

"He had a son named Stefan. His wife's name was Dina. They were separated in a concentration camp. Aaron thought his son was killed. He searched for months after the war. He was my father's business partner. When he found me in the refugee camp, I became his ward." Rachel felt close to breaking, her voice thick with emotion. "My name isn't Rachel Ward."

"I didn't think it was," Stefan answered. "I assumed you changed it so you wouldn't have to stand in your father's shadow."

"Nothing nearly as noble," Rachel said, wiping tears from her face. "I'm an immigrant just like you. When we landed at Ellis Island, the immigration officer chose Ward because he had too many people with Jewish names. My real name is Rachel Gold; my father was Kalman Gold."

"My God!"

Rachel fell against his chest, sobbing.

Stefan held her and murmured, "I remember a picnic, and laughing children and fishing poles, and a little girl named Rachel, and her brother—twin brother. What was his name? It was a common name. The boy's mother had called him when he'd taken off his shoes to wade in the water. David. The boy's name was David. Rachel," Stefan whispered into her hair as she sobbed against his chest, "do you have a brother?"

"He's dead."

"What was his name?"

Rachel raised her face and met his gaze. "David."

Stefan grimaced. Tears traced down his cheeks as he lowered his head to hers.

They just held each other, both in their own haze of shock.

Stefan said in a rough whisper, "What impact will this have on Mr. Ross and my father? Who should we tell first? How should they be told? How could it be proven?"

Rachel sighed. "So many questions."

Stefan stood and paced—so like Aaron, so like his father. "Listen, we have a dinner set with Aaron tonight. It's the logical time to bring up family. He was an adult during the war. We were children. He will remember much more than we do. As a father, he will know his son."

"Well, Stefan Davis, or whoever you are," Rachel said, forcing a feeble smile, "dating you certainly hasn't been dull."

"And *I* was concerned about my father setting this up! Now I've got fathers on both sides."

They laughed, hugged, and then kissed—a hungry, emotional kiss. They molded themselves together as breath rushed through nostrils and tongues touched. Their hands explored and fueled the passion.

Finally, Rachel broke it off with a gasp as she felt Stefan's eagerness growing against her. He moved his kiss to her neck, but her hands cupped his face, stopping him. "Enough, Stefan. We have to be careful. You may be my brother."

Stefan raised his eyes to hers. "You're kidding, aren't you?"

Rachel studied his brown eyes soberly before smiling. "Yes."

They kissed again, at the door. Stefan hungered for more, but Rachel again broke it off.

He whispered hoarsely, "I'll pick you up at seven."

"I'll call you ten times before that," she promised.

"Make it six o'clock," Stefan added.

"Will you sleep?"
"Will you?"
"Not unless you leave."
He kissed Rachel on the nose and left.

Sleep didn't come easily for Rachel. A mix of excitement, guilt, and worry filled her. Nearly twenty years had passed, but a searing flash of truth had stripped away the secret separating father and son.

What was it she'd learned in the convent? Jesus had told his disciples, "The truth shall set you free." He'd failed to say at what price, though.

Would the revelation be a good thing? Weren't some secrets better if never revealed?

She padded barefoot to her jewelry chest and gently extracted a special box. Her hands shook as she opened the lid. A beautiful gold coin rested on a velvet puff, and beside it—tattered and shredded—lay an awkward braid of threadbare material. Rachel gingerly stroked the precious strips of cloth, torn from her parents' clothing.

∘∘✦∘∘

Even on a Saturday, Aaron Ross spent the day in his City Hall office. This particular afternoon, he prepared for the trial of the three men who'd killed Detective Lasski. The first motions would be heard on Monday, and Aaron felt encouraged by the progress of the case, confident he would win.

Not only was winning important for his friend Lasski, but the highly publicized trial would herald in Aaron's candidacy for senator in a big, dramatic way. Deferring the announcement until after the trial would be perceived as noble.

Anticipation for joining Rachel and Stefan at dinner made the day's labor speed by. Rachel's obvious glow the night before had eased his worry about her. The two young people had made a handsome couple.

The irony of Rachel dating a good-looking, blond-haired attorney by the name of Stefan had not gone unnoticed by Aaron. When Stefan Davis had introduced himself, hearing the name of his dead son had brought a lump of emotion to Aaron's throat. He knew fate would never return his son, but perhaps beloved Rachel might give him a son-in-law named Stefan. The prospect acted as a balm for a wound never healed.

Maybe God had forgiven what Aaron had done to Esther and his first wife, Dina. He hoped so.

Aaron glanced at his watch. Seven-twenty—time to clear his desk.

He washed and shaved in the executive bathroom and put on a fresh shirt. After locking his office, he headed for the elevator, intending to hail a cab.

The cool air of early evening greeted Aaron when he pushed through the double doors and moved down the steps to the sidewalk. A line of cabs sat waiting at the curb. He headed toward one at the front of the line, and glanced at his watch again. Rachel and Stefan may already have arrived at the restaurant.

Several steps from the cab, someone grabbed him by the shoulder. Aaron turned with a growl, ready to berate an overzealous reporter. He refused to be late for his dinner with Rachel. Seeing her again, glowing with happiness, had brought back all of Aaron's desperation for them to once more be a family. He missed her so much; the ache of loneliness never left him.

A black man with red and angry eyes, somewhere in his fifties, still clutched Aaron's shoulder. The gray stubble of a beard covered a deeply lined face. "You're the sonofabitch that said you was gonna execute my son." The man's breath reeked of alcohol.

Aaron forcibly brushed off the restraining hand. "I'll forget this, but you'd better find somewhere to sober up."

The man raised a gun. "I'll show you sober, motherfucker!"

The first blast propelled Aaron backward a few paces. He rocked on his feet, unable to do anything more than stare at the gun as the man pulled the trigger again. The deranged father fired again and again, following Aaron as he fell against the door of the cab.

After five shots, the gun clicked empty.

Aaron slumped to the sidewalk, sliding down the car door, clutching his chest. He left a swath of crimson on the door of the yellow cab. He sat awkwardly, the breath wheezing in and out of his lungs, ears roaring.

His assailant pocketed the gun and walked away. The cab driver shouted for someone to stop the man, then called for help.

Aaron crumpled over to lie in a pool of his own blood. His vision blackened, and he gasped, "Rachel," then slipped into darkness.

CHAPTER TWENTY

ALL THE KING'S HORSES . . .

When a father gives to his son, both laugh.
When a son gives to a father, both cry.

Yiddish Proverb

Rachel and Stefan sat in a secluded booth in the restaurant, waiting for Aaron to arrive.

Seeing Stefan, being near him, quickened her pulse and heated her cheeks. Everything about him seemed to call to her. He slid closer to her in the semicircular leather seat, bringing warmth and also an odd sensation of peace. He put his arm around her shoulders.

Rachel's anxieties eased once Stefan held her again. He confessed, "I got no sleep last night. Then I spent the entire day composing a speech to Aaron Ross. It was not unlike preparing a jury summary—proposing the idea, and then presenting the supporting evidence."

Rachel smiled, charmed by his honesty and awkward nervousness.

He took a sip of water and, after a hard swallow, slanted her a wry glance. "I threw it all away." He shrugged. "This has to come from the heart. No speeches, no bull, just the truth."

The minutes ticked by, past the appointed time for Aaron to appear. They made small talk about the firm, their mutual passion for the law and, eventually, the weather.

Stefan finally broached the subject. "Okay, you should know. Is he a punctual man?"

Rachel flipped a wave of hair over her shoulder and gave him a crooked grin. "Give me a break. He's the DA."

"Then you think he'll be here?"

"Yes, I think he'll be here. He always has a full plate. If he's late, it's for a good reason. Trust me," Rachel assured. "He won't let anything stop him. We've been trying to get together for weeks."

A man entered the restaurant and headed toward their corner booth.

"Miss Ward," the man said somberly, "I'm Jack Mills from the DA's office. We found the name of the restaurant on your father's desk calendar."

"Yes, he's meeting us here."

Stefan leaned forward. "Is there a problem?"

"I'm afraid so. I have a car waiting. Perhaps I could explain on the way to the hospital."

"Hospital! What happened?" Rachel demanded.

"The DA has been shot."

Rachel felt all the blood drain from her face, and she swayed into Stefan. Her mind seemed to blink on and off in tandem with the flashing lights. In a haze, she realized she rode in the back seat with Stefan, and had no recollection of leaving the restaurant or how she'd entered a car equipped with a red light and siren—both on.

They sped across Manhattan, weaving in and out of traffic.

Jack Mills twisted from where he sat in the front passenger seat to talk to them as another man drove. Rachel heard his words from a great distance, as if detached, a spectator instead of a participant. She felt numb with shock, beyond tears.

Mills spoke of witnesses to the shooting that had taken place on the street in front of City Hall. "The shooter, a father of one of Lasski's slayers, is in custody after being arrested by transit police on a subway. The district attorney is still alive, but in critical condition."

Rachel wanted to pray, but couldn't. She remembered being on her knees in the convent, begging God to bring back her family—her real family—mother, father, and twin brother. God hadn't listened then. Why would he listen now?

Stefan held her hand in a tight grip as the siren wailed, but Rachel felt abandoned and alone—adrift.

A tangle of vehicles, parked at hard angles to one another, blocked the street entrance to the hospital. Police cars with flashing lights and blaring radios, news vans, and an assembly of unmarked cars crowded the parking lot.

When the sedan carrying Rachel and Stefan braked to a stiff halt near the tangle, an army of waiting reporters swarmed them. Flash cameras wiped away the darkness. Microphones and questions bombarded them. "Miss Ward, any comment on the DA? When did you last see him? Had he been threatened?"

Mills ordered, "Get the hell outta the way," and, with his partner's help, he pushed through the crush toward the emergency entrance.

Stefan dragged Rachel by the hand, running close behind Mills and the driver. A group of uniformed officers arrived and helped to hold back the throng.

Police officers jammed the hallway inside.

Mills barked above the din, "Let the lady through."

They squeezed past the crowd and pushed through the double doors of the emergency room entrance.

In the glassed-in surgical unit, three blood-stained doctors in green gowns and masks worked over a man on a table under glaring lights. Bits and pieces of cut-away, blood-soaked clothing, along with an assortment of bloody bandages and gauze, littered the floor. An attentive trio of nurses offered support, responding to demanding calls for instruments and medications.

Rachel recognized Aaron's shoes, and denial surrendered to reality. Stefan slipped an arm around her shoulders.

A nearby plainclothesman, with his badge displayed on his belt, gave Rachel and Stefan a hard look.

"She's related," Jack Mills said, thwarting any protest.

An oscilloscope above Aaron recorded an irregular heart rate. A ventilator made a hissing sound, and a thick, clear plastic tube disappeared into an incision in the rib cage.

Aaron's hairy chest had turned into a backdrop for a patchwork of bloody gauze and taped bandages.

A portable x-ray machine stood next to a treatment tray filled with a collection of red-stained instruments and syringes.

Rachel concentrated on an IV line and its slow, steady drip. She didn't know where else to look.

Finally, the activity around Aaron subsided, and the doctors huddled in muted conversation, with an occasional glance at Rachel. When they parted, one of them pulled off his gloves and mask.

His face reflected strain. "We're trying to stabilize him before surgery."

Rachel tightened her grasp on Stefan's hand.

"He's lost a lot of blood. That usually causes shock. One of the bullets collapsed a lung; another is embedded in the heart. We've done what we can . . . I'm not optimistic."

Stefan cleared his throat, then said softly, "We would like to talk with him."

"He's not conscious."

Stefan's tone turned measured and firm. "You said you've done all that you can?"

"Yes, that's correct."

"Then there's no harm in talking to him."

The doctor spread his hands. "You don't understand."

Stefan insisted, "I understand perfectly. Now, we'd like to talk to him, and we would like it to be private."

The doctor hesitated, but Jack Mills, who stood at Stefan's shoulder, took over. "All right, everybody out. Right now!"

The emergency room staff looked to the doctor standing with Rachel and Stefan. He studied Rachel's anguished expression for a long moment, and then nodded to the others. They moved for the doors.

They strode toward the outer hallway. The doors swung shut, leaving Rachel and Stefan alone with the still form on the operating table.

Tugging on Rachel's hand, Stefan led her into the triage room and to Aaron's side. Only the sounds of the soft electronic beep of the heart monitor and the hiss of the ventilator broke the heavy silence.

Rachel forced herself to look at her adopted father. His face appeared ashen and swollen. She bit her lip as emotion overwhelmed her.

Stefan released Rachel's hand and picked up Aaron's, holding it between both of his. Then he gently lifted Aaron's hand and kissed the fingers. Tears glittered in his eyes.

Rachel watched in silence.

"Father," Stefan said, leaning near Aaron's placid face, his voice choked. "It's Stefan, your son. I'm not dead, Father. I'm here. Here with

Rachel. It took twenty years, but I found you. Do you hear me? Can you squeeze my hand?"

Rachel trembled as tears traced down her face, her attention riveted on the fingers held in Stefan's hands.

"Come on, Dad," Stefan begged quietly. "You can do it."

The fingers sandwiched in Stefan's hands trembled and curled around his.

"Oh!" Rachel cried, bringing her hands to her mouth. Aaron had heard.

Stefan spoke quickly, urgently. "Rachel and I talked last night, Dad. My given name is Stefan Ross. I am from Katowice, Poland. I remember Rachel and David, and the Golds. I remember the picnics—you cooking my fish—and I remember I am your son. I love you, Dad."

The fingers in Stefan's hand relaxed, and the rhythmic beat of the electronic pulse from the oscilloscope became a constant tone. The green line tracking the pulse went flat.

Stephan, still clasping Aaron's hand, lowered his head and wept.

Rachel, numb with shock, sobbed quietly.

CHAPTER TWENTY-ONE

THE PILGRIMAGE

You shall live by them,
but you shall not die because of them.

Babylonian Talmud, Yoma 85b

Father Janusz Dov felt old and worn. *The heart of Poland has lost its innocence.*

Before the war, Poles had looked ahead. Now, more than twenty years later, they remembered the past horrors instead of dreaming of what the future could hold. Many believed the lucky ones had died in the war.

The German bombs had destroyed more than cities, towns, and villages. They had destroyed the Polish spirit. Where once the Poles had believed in God, the church, and themselves, they now looked to their Communist leaders who offered only promises—many promises. As man could not live on bread alone, neither could a society live on hollow promises. The consequence: a relentless succession of convulsive riots, uprisings, strikes, and reforms.

Initially, the government—in an attempt to elude blame —incorporated a campaign of anti-religion and imprisoned Cardinal Wyszynski—the head of the Roman Catholic Church in Poland. More riots had followed.

Janusz had seen men with little promise, particularly men who built a government alienating God, but he walked a different path. With no political agenda, Janusz ministered to the needy, spreading the word of God, peace, and love.

The Communist government, trying to re-invent itself after failing to root religion from the country, embraced the disciplines of the church schools to provide scholars for Poland's new frontier. The churches welcomed the influx of money and the newfound acceptance.

In Janusz's mind, the church once again rode the tiger, but he did realize the future lay in the young hearts and minds of the nation's students. Possessing an inherent love of teaching, Janusz agreed to accompany an archeological class from Warsaw on a field trip to Syria, to study the country's many ancient ruins.

While in Rome, as part of the required curriculum for the priesthood, Janusz had made a pilgrimage to the Holy Land. The newest Polish government had cited Janusz's international experience as the reason for his selection, though he suspected the low odds of an aging priest defecting fell closer to the truth of their decision.

The thirty-day trip would focus on the ruins at Palmyra—a two-thousand-year-old city in central Syria that had once thrived as the caravan crossroads of the world. Most of the twenty handpicked students were in their late teens—eight boys and twelve girls—brilliant, agnostic, and avowed Communists.

Undiscouraged, Janusz firmly believed God had chosen him for the educational journey, although he had no idea what God had in mind as an outcome.

Janusz quickly fell in love with the challenge of the sharp, hungry young minds in his charge. They questioned everything and anything.

His favorite New Testament scriptures included the words spoken by Christ: "You shall know the truth, and the truth shall set you free."

Walter Koslovich, a broad-shouldered, six-foot-tall nineteen-year-old, fingered the cross Janusz wore around his neck. "I do not believe what I cannot see."

"Oh," Janusz responded after a moment's thought. "Do you believe the earth is round?"

"Of course," the youth replied.

"And the Atlantic Ocean? Do you believe it exists?"

Walter grimaced, then smiled. "I may not have seen those things, but I have read accounts of those who have. And, if I go there, I am sure I will see an ocean."

Janusz nodded. "So it is with God."

The Polish government highly publicized the student delegation's departure from Warsaw's International Airport. A bevy of rotund Communists crowded the tarmac in the shadow of the Soviet-built TU-154 turboprop scheduled to carry Janusz and his students to Damascus. The self-promoting, propaganda-filled, amplified speeches droned on for nearly an hour while everyone stood in a cold rain.

Finally, the goodbyes were said, and the already weary travelers filed up the steep steps into the aircraft. They squeezed through the narrow cabin, ripe with the smell of kerosene.

In addition to the students, a mix of swarthy Arabs in robes and head wraps, crated cargo strapped in passenger seats, and a group of grim Soviet military officers with rows of colorful medals on their chests crowded the airplane.

Janusz and his charges sat near the front of the cabin on folding chairs and thick, hard-back manuals. They huddled, exchanged notes, and cast suspicious looks at those who passed. No native Pole trusted the Russians. They'd come to Poland promising liberation, but after driving the Germans out, they forgot to leave, quickly becoming Poland's new taskmasters. They installed a puppet government, took over the country's economy, and closed the Iron Curtain around its borders.

The powerful engines started, deafening Janusz with their roar. Then came the vibration, compounding the noise. Everything shook, including his teeth.

Janusz had never flown before and felt far from convinced it would bring him closer to God, but, knowing that many of his young charges suffered the same anxieties, he swallowed his fear and went about the cabin counting heads and making sure to calm any fearful students.

When the aircraft reached the end of the runway and swung into position for takeoff, it rocked and braked to a halt. Janusz dared a glance out his porthole-sized window. A gray rain masked everything beyond the wing tip. Sheets of water cascaded off the wide wing.

Then the roar of the engines increased dramatically. The cabin shook and the plane lunged forward.

Janusz felt himself pushed back into the seat cushion. He crossed himself and muttered a prayer, gripping the armrests, as the tires thumped over the rough runway. The noise, speed, and vibration reached a crescendo that disappeared once the craft lifted into the air.

The porthole window displayed a solid gray sky, as clouds engulfed them. Janusz felt as if they now floated.

He began to relax, almost enjoying the powerful hum of the engines and the muted gray light reflecting from the clouds. Then, suddenly, they burst into bright, dazzling sunlight. Janusz squinted and peered out, awestruck.

The boiling, lumpy cloud deck, falling away below them, stretched to the distant horizon. Above it, the sky had turned a deep, clear, azure blue.

Janusz whispered, "Hello, God."

Over the Black Sea, at nearly twenty thousand feet, the cloud layer yielded to a vast panorama of water and land. Janusz and the students crowded the windows to take in the view. Below, the earth looked tranquil and at peace. Janusz prayed it would stay that way at ground level. Turmoil and deadly conflicts plagued Syria, keeping it constantly in the news.

After nearly five hours in the air, the engine sound changed, the cabin pitched forward, and the craft slowed. They had begun the descent for landing.

During his field trip sponsored by the Vatican so many years before, Janusz had walked the rock-strewn hills and tree-choked valleys of the Holy Land. He'd visited the heart of the fabled Fertile Crescent, as well as the parched wastelands surrounding it. It was one thing to walk it, and quite another to see it from the air.

As the turboprop closed on Damascus, the sprawling city came into view. It looked like a smudge on the landscape, rubbed in a sea of desert sand—an unlikely oasis. The only evidence of green appeared in uneven patches dotting the perimeter of the city. Its outer limits consisted of a hodgepodge of scattered shacks, tents, and ghettos. Lines of highways and rail beds reached out from the smear of civilization, looking like long veins tracing into the surrounding desert.

Near the heart of Damascus, contemporary architecture clashed with ancient, as the glass faces of high-rises stood in the shadow of towering spires and rounded domes. Janusz thought the city looked troubled, locked in a battle between what had once been and the modern, inelegant reality of technology.

As the aircraft banked for its final landing approach, he looked at a wide street, busy with a mix of horse-drawn carts, trucks, and bicycles—more evidence of the endless struggle between past and present, which would eventually conquer all, old and new.

Janusz braced himself as the craft thumped onto the runway. A swirl of sand spewed over the wing. The outside heat had already reached into the cabin as the turboprop slowed and they swung onto a taxiway.

The students crammed the windows for their first ground-level view of Damascus International Airport. An atmosphere of uncertainty, anxiety, and excitement spread among the young faces. Janusz felt much the same.

Once the craft halted and the engines spun to a stop, the temperature in the cabin soared. When the door opened, Janusz welcomed the warm, dry air that greeted them.

He counted his flock as they filed by him and headed down the stairs.

A tall, thin, gaunt-faced Arab smiled when Janusz reached the tarmac. "Father Janusz."

He offered both hands—bronze-colored, with long nails. A gray, full-faced, untrimmed beard contrasted the man's dark and deep-set eyes. He wore a *keffiyeh*, the traditional Arab head wrap, and an ankle-length robe.

"My name is Assad. I am from the Department of the Interior. I will be your host. Welcome to Syria. I have arranged for transportation."

Janusz and the teenagers took the baggage from the airplane and loaded it onto an aging, dilapidated open-bed truck while their host watched. The boys quickly shed heavy shirts and jackets in favor of loose-fitting shirts and tee shirts, but the girls found little relief, for they remained confined within proper dress, as per the Muslim rule for the modesty of women.

"Today we will travel to Sab Biar," Assad told Janusz as they climbed into the cab of the truck. "It is about a hundred kilometers. We will be there by nightfall. We will camp. Tomorrow we will visit the ancient Well of the Damned. Many slave caravans stopped there. My government will allow you to dig for artifacts there. The next day, we will travel to Palmyra."

Janusz held up a hand as their guide shifted the truck into gear. "We were on the airplane for over four hours. Some need to use the toilet."

Assad smiled. "Of course. I will pull to the side of the road as soon as we are out of the city."

Their stop came nearly two hours later. During the hot and bumpy ride, several of the students mumbled about rethinking careers as archeologists. Most, after hours of unchanging desert landscape, slept on the piles of luggage on the truck bed's floor.

By the time the truck finally turned off the main road, the sun hung low on the western horizon. They followed little more than a path for another mile, then braked to a dusty stop beside a dry riverbed and a clump of trees.

As Assad stepped down from the cab, he announced, "Welcome to Camp Sab Biar."

The camp looked little different than hundreds of other spots in the desert. Were it not for the presence of the truck, they could have been travelers from a thousand years ago.

Assad erected two canvas tents while the boys scrounged the surrounding desert and gathered scrap to build a fire.

A taxi cab arrived as they watched the waning color of the sunset. The old yellow car sported only one headlamp, and it had a broken windshield. Arabic writing covered the doors, hood, and trunk, with the exception of one English word on the driver's side door: TAXI.

The driver unloaded his passengers—two young goats—and the students laughed. They quickly sobered when Janusz told them dinner had arrived.

While the students made themselves useful in other areas of the camp, deliberately keeping their backs to the older men, Assad and the taxi driver slit the throats of the two animals, bled them out, and prepared the carcasses for cooking. Goat's meat, pita bread, and a minty herbal tea comprised the meal.

The Arabs thanked Allah.

Janusz said the blessing while the agnostic students sat mute.

The goat—roasted over an open fire—proved to be tender and tasty.

After the meal, Assad and the taxi driver lounged and smoked American cigarettes. The girls sang popular Polish songs from school, and the boys romanticized about the historical days of Lawrence of Arabia.

Janusz declared curfew and made a head count of both tents. Once he confirmed his charges' presence, he hiked up a nearby knoll. At the top, he raised his face and gazed at the moonless desert night sky. Velvety darkness accentuated the vast array of stars and bright constellations.

As he stared, time fell away and, in his mind, Janusz returned to the bottom of a slimy, water-filled pit outside of Katowice. He'd felt certain he would die, and remembered looking up and seeing nothing but stars. Tears welled in his eyes as he thought of Kalman Gold and all they'd shared.

Janusz woke his students at first light. They struggled with the desert's paradox; the sizzling heat from the day before had yielded to a bitter, bone-chilling cold. All huddled around a small fire, drinking weak tea and eating sticky, dried dates.

Assad pointed to a well-worn path that disappeared into the desert. "The Well of the Damned is about a two-hour walk. Three palms mark its location. You will have no problems, but do not drink the water. I will remain here with the truck. Bedouin bandits sometimes roam these hills."

Janusz remembered the lessons of desert survival, learned as a student himself many years before, and ordered the teenagers to dress light, and in layers. They fashioned head covers out of shirts and scarves. He assigned them into teams of two. Three team leaders would carry canteens. They would eat and drink only on the command of Janusz. They would walk in single file. Janusz would set the pace.

He expected to reach the ancient well by noon. After four or five hours of digging and searching for artifacts, they would return to camp before darkness.

Spirits high, filled with a sense of adventure, the long column set off.

Assad shouted after them, "Keep the sun to your left!" Then he climbed into the shaded cab of the truck.

They arrived at the ancient site an hour beyond Assad's estimate. Exhausted, overheated, and parched, Janusz gave thanks for the three palm trees as the students clustered in the shade.

The well—little more than a rock-strewn depression near the trees—appeared as a lumpy, green pool of stagnant water. Several insect-infested piles of camel dung gave evidence of other recent visitors.

Janusz announced, "Everyone is to have a drink. Then we will plot our search for artifacts."

After their break, the students outlined a grid on the dirt and began their archaeological excavations. Janusz sat in the shade, prepared to field questions or give motivational support.

CHAPTER TWENTY-TWO

HAUNTED MEMORIES, SOARING REALITY

As for the heavens, the heavens are God's;
but the earth He has given to mankind.

Psalms 115:16

David enjoyed working in the small garden behind the house. His wife, Toby—a Stanford-trained pediatrician—had left to drop Kalman, their four-year-old son, at the kibbutz nursery before going on to the hospital.

As a rebellious teen, he'd resented the backbreaking, dawn-to-dusk chores his foster parents, Tania and Zidov, had forced upon him. David had balked at so many things during those years of hiding on the farm. Even though the separation from his family had probably saved his life, during the time of his exile, he'd never once expressed appreciation for their bravery, their generosity, and their unconditional love.

Guilt twinged David, creating a deep ache of remorse. That ache never went away, and each time he held his wife, laughed with his son, or worked in the small garden, he sent up a mental prayer of thanks.

Now, as an adult, fond memories of tending a garden with his mother and sister always brought him a feeling of deep peace.

In the garden, David didn't worry about enemy aircraft, fuel levels, or fighting the pull of gravity in gut-wrenching maneuvers that pushed him toward unconsciousness. In the garden, he reigned as master of tomatoes, cabbages, and beets. He pulled weeds, watered, loosened the soil, and dreamed of a day he could become a farmer instead of a fighter.

As he tossed the last of the weeds into an old refuse bucket, he smiled in acknowledgment of the irony of his life. While on the farm in Poland, he'd dreamed about joining the military, fighting in heroic battles, and operating powerful war machines. Now, as an adult, he'd achieved those once-romantic daydreams, and he wished for nothing more than the simple life of a farmer. But the harsh reality of a different war, in a different country, stood in the way.

For now, Kalman wasn't yet old enough to take care of the garden, and Toby didn't have the time. Pulling the weeds from the small plot of land in the backyard remained David's job. He looked forward to retiring from the military and spending time with his son on a small farm—living in peace.

The only comfort in David's life—the only hope for his family—came in his strength and his ability to outwit his many enemies. Heavily armed allied nations surrounded Israel, each vowing to wipe the Jews from the face of the earth.

The searing, frightening hatred he had witnessed as a child and had tried to escape as a teen still haunted him, as it did all displaced Jews.

While most of the world went to bed every night with the hope that tomorrow would bring a new beginning, David slept with the ever-present fear of enemy attack. He'd even given his wife an M-14 assault rifle to keep in her nightstand.

David felt old—weary of the fight. The endless strain and tension of waiting for, preparing for, and recovering from attacks had taken its toll—not only on him, but on the collective spirit of the country as well. Others could lose battles and survive. Israel could not. The grim reality was win or die—a difficult climate in which to find love, bear children, and have a life.

As a veteran wing commander, he routinely read intelligence bulletins and sat through classified briefings on enemy activities. The latest reports indicated that the Syrians planned something in the Golan Heights. Increased radio traffic, troop movements, and continuous probing with reconnaissance aircraft subtly relayed the growing threat. Day after day, Syrian aircraft violated the fringes of Israeli airspace—quick in, quick out.

David wondered if they hoped the Israelis would eventually choose not to rise to challenge them. If unchallenged, would they shatter the kibbutz with a five-hundred-pound bomb?

Some days the constant vigil and battles frightened him. Not so much for himself, but for his wife and son. He imagined his father had experienced such thoughts during the early days of the war in Poland.

This concern for his family brought David closer to his own parents. He finally understood their courageous but terrible decision to split up the family. The desperate move had afforded Rachel and him a better chance of surviving.

As a father himself, David not only understood, but had considered the same action for the safety of his own family. He had tried to encourage Toby to take little Kalman and move back to her native New Jersey. No one fired rockets at nurseries in New Jersey. No one blew up school buses there. No one wanted to kill a person simply because he happened to be a Jew.

Toby had staunchly refused. "Giving in to the demands of hate doesn't cure the hate."

One day, a few weeks later, as he listened to a briefing in the air base ready room, David heard the piercing sound of the alert klaxon. His pulse jumped, and he grabbed his flight helmet and ran for the standby aircraft waiting on the runway apron.

His thoughts immediately focused on air temperature, takeoff weight, and radio frequencies.

David's wingman, Ben Wizan, caught up with him, huffing and puffing, and shouted a greeting.

Beside the craft, the auxiliary power unit purred, already running. David and Ben scrambled into their cockpits. David slammed the throttle to the start position. The jet engine came to life with a whump beneath him. Needles and dials danced on the instrument panel.

A ground crew member helped him strap in. With a slap on the helmet, the man dropped away, and David hastily flipped the "close canopy" switch.

Taxiing toward the runway, his thoughts drifted back to his garden, threatened by weeds and unwanted intruders. Also true in the sky—he would help rid Israel's garden of the weeds.

He swung the jet onto the runway and shoved the throttle to afterburner. The aircraft roared and lunged forward as the hydraulics in the aircraft throbbed.

A voice in David's headset advised, "Gideon-Six, bandit, Angel's nine, zero-six-zero, six hundred and forty knots. Intercept and identify."

The landing gear came up and the air speed surged.

"Roger." David pulled the jet into a gut-wrenching, climbing turn.

"Gideon-Six, come left three degrees. Bandit now zero-eight-zero, Angel's seven and descending. Twenty-nine miles and closing."

David glanced to his left. His wingman had tucked in close. Ben, a gentle, soft-spoken man, carved birds out of wood in his off time. David smiled. A bird carver and a gardener defended the skies over Israel.

He peered ahead into clear sky, then glanced at his control panel. It indicated an approach of four hundred miles an hour. His plane closed in on the other, yet-unseen aircraft at a combined speed of nearly one thousand miles an hour. They wouldn't have to wait long to see what the Syrian had in mind.

David tripped a switch to arm his guns and air-to-air missiles. "Gideon-Six is hot," he said for Ben's benefit.

"Gideon-Seven hot," came the immediate reply.

David glanced at the earth rushing beneath him. His four-year-old son, Kalman, sat somewhere down there in a kibbutz, with many other sons and daughters.

He pushed forward on the stick and felt himself rise in the seat as the jet plummeted. "Gideon-Six, Bandit now zero-nine zero, Angel's six-five, descending. Eight miles and closing."

Again David searched the sky ahead, then nudged the rudder pedal to correct the compass a degree. While David found, intercepted, and killed the weed creeping into the garden, Ben would protect his ass.

Then he saw a glint of silver-swept wings, a few thousand feet below and three to five miles ahead.

The enemy aircraft turned away, descending, running.

David's heart jumped. His grip tightened on the control stick. "Bandit, three o'clock low." He pushed the throttle forward and steered into a dive.

This close, David could visually identify the craft. "MiG-17," he said into his oxygen mask.

"Roger," the bird carver answered in a calm voice.

The Israeli air controller said, "Gideon-Six, thirty-five seconds to threshold ice." The code warned that they fast approached the Syrian border.

Crossing into Syria lay at David's discretion. Pursuit of an aircraft violating Israeli airspace provided "just cause" under international law, but more important were the Israeli eyes, several thousand feet below, looking to the sky, wondering if bombs would fall.

He and Ben would not allow that to happen.

Descending on the turning Syrian craft gave David an advantage. His American-made A-4 Skyhawk, although older and slower than the Syrian's Russian-built MiG-17, swept into a turn and cost the intruder power and airspeed. David dove on the enemy aircraft.

The last Syrian pilot he'd centered in his gun sights had ejected without a shot fired.

The controller announced, "Threshold ice," as the two Israeli Skyhawks plummeted earthward in pursuit of the distant, swept-wing aircraft.

As they continued to close on the fleeing craft, David transmitted to Ben, "Let's see if our Arab friend is wearing his jock strap."

David pulled out of the dive, grimacing under the g-force, to slide squarely onto the tail of the enemy. He targeted the MiG with an air-to-air missile. The Syrians would think twice about sending another intruder to Israeli airspace.

Ben shouted in David's headset, "Tone! Break off."

A chill flowed through David. The tone his wingman had heard probably warned of radar tracking. If so, that could mean only one thing; the enemy targeted them from a hidden position on the desert floor, and had led them into an ambush.

Ben's A-4 banked sharply left and disappeared from David's peripheral vision.

David kept his attention focused on the aircraft framed in his sights. He played a deadly game of Russian roulette, determined to dispense of the MiG before the ground troops locked on to his position. He'd gambled and won before; he would do so again.

A powerful explosion rocked David's aircraft at the same moment he applied thumb pressure to the missile launch button. The shock slammed him up against the canopy. A ball of yellow flame and black smoke swallowed the sky.

The instrument panel sprang to life with flashing red alarms and warning buzzers. An electrical fire filled David's oxygen mask with an acidic scent. The control stick wobbled in his hand, and the craft tumbled.

David's head slammed against the instrument panel. He tasted blood from biting his tongue. Bracing a hand against the canopy, he pushed himself down in the seat.

Ben's voice pierced the roaring in David's ears. "Get out! Eject! Eject!"

David looked up to see the desert spinning overhead as the earth rushed up to meet him. The uncontrolled vertical dive slammed his body from one side of the cockpit to the other.

Gasping for breath, David neutralized the controls and pulled back on the stick with all his might. Smoke swirled in the cockpit, obscuring his view.

He coughed and spit blood into his oxygen mask, then jerked it off his head. Tears filled his eyes as smoke stung them.

The needle on the altimeter spun wildly as the craft continued to fall.

David reached for the yellow ejection-seat yoke between his legs, but hesitated when he felt the g-force begin to build on his head and shoulders. The A-4 was responding.

He pulled back harder on the stick as the ground rushed toward him. The Skyhawk slowly pulled out of the vertical dive a few hundred feet above the sandy earth, and began an arduous climb.

David glanced at the instruments: tail pipe temperature, fuel pressure, oil pressure, RPMs—the engine still functioned. Fuel content: *Almost gone.* An array of hydraulic pressure warning lights blinked at him. He would soon lose control of the craft.

Out the window to his left, he saw that he'd lost a large piece of the wing, and vapors spewed away into the slipstream from a dozen punctures in the fuselage. He could only guess at other damage. He wouldn't last in the sky much longer.

Airspeed had slowed to 310 knots and continued to decrease.

Smoke still filled the cockpit, evidence of an electrical fire. *How long before an explosion?*

The compass read north, north-east. *Goddamn!* Away from base, deeper into Syria.

David eased a foot on the left rudder, but nothing happened. No longer a pilot, and unable to steer, he'd turned into a passenger riding in a doomed plane. Luckily, though, the craft maintained a level flight pattern.

The radio noise in his headset had fallen quiet. That didn't surprise him. Ben would use another frequency, broadcasting the emergency, giving coordinates for the air rescue attempt that was certain to follow.

The Israelis did not take the loss of a pilot lightly. They would do everything possible to keep a downed pilot from capture. The thought brought little comfort, for the enemy most assuredly had planes searching for him.

Israeli pilots were trophies, worth a fortune to the Arab who delivered one alive. Captured pilots provided the enemy with a pool of military tactics, policies, and practices. A combination of drugs and torture would follow. Capture meant certain, agonizing death.

David looked down at the vast, sprawling wasteland beneath him, and felt very alone. Miles slipped by, carrying him deeper and deeper into Syria. He decided to wait until the airspeed fell below two hundred knots and then eject.

Suddenly, a powerful explosion sent a flash fire into the cockpit. The plane bucked, then spun into a steep nosedive.

In desperation, David grabbed for the ejection yoke and pulled. Another explosion shot him out of the doomed A-4.

As the rocky landscape sped toward him, he pressed his knees together and bent his legs. He'd ejected too low to the ground for the parachute to completely soften his landing, but the closer to the earth he bailed out, the less chance an enemy outpost had to pinpoint his position. The risk—if he survived the impact—could give him enough time to escape capture, at least for a while.

He hit the ground hard and rolled. The billowing canopy of his parachute collapsed around him.

Pushing to his feet, David quickly balled up the parachute. He didn't want it spotted from the air. The Syrians would soon search for him, if they hadn't started already.

His face stung from burns sustained from the flash fire in the cockpit, but he suffered no other injuries.

Sweat gathered on his forehead from the still dangerously high daytime temperatures. He'd had to eject without his survival kit. He glanced at his watch—early afternoon, the heat of the day. He needed to find shelter. With no water, he had to take care to conserve energy.

David stood a moment longer, surveying the monotonous desert. *Where the hell am I?* The sun sat high in the sky, and he couldn't tell in which direction to go.

He'd bailed out somewhere over central Syria. The good news: few people occupied central Syria—little more than a vast, barren, desert wasteland. The bad news: he'd landed in a vast, barren, desert wasteland.

More to the point, he'd landed beyond the reach of Israeli ground forces and beyond the range of rescue helicopters. Even if Israeli Command knew his exact position, they could do little to help, and any attempt would point the Syrians to him.

Since his people couldn't get to him. David would have to rescue himself. He'd done the same thing long ago, as a teenager—shell-shocked, battered, and temporarily deaf. He could certainly do it again.

His mother had once read him the story of Jonah in the belly of the whale. At that moment, he felt much like Jonah.

He gathered the parachute under one arm and headed for the shadow of a rocky outcropping. The afternoon sun would indicate the way to safety . . . and home.

CHAPTER TWENTY-THREE

NO COUNTRY FOR AN OLD MAN

*Leadership is practiced not so much in words as in
attitude and in actions.*

Harold Geneen

Earlier that day, Janusz and the students had felt disappointed. The expedition had not found much at the Well of the Damned—the search had revealed a Coke bottle and a Canadian penny—and all looked forward to moving on.

In the midst of their explorations, a blond nineteen-year-old girl shouted, "Look!"

Janusz and the others stopped digging and raised their faces to the sky.

A large ball of yellow and blue flame erupted in the clear desert air, high above them, and a tumbling mass appeared out of the flame. An indistinguishable object arced toward earth, trailing a plume of smoke behind it. It whistled and howled as if in pain.

Janusz had once seen an American bomber, hit by German ground fire, fall from the sky in a cascade of flame. Now another aircraft hurtled to earth and, although years had passed, the sight still shook him.

They stared, transfixed at the spectacle, until the aircraft disappeared from sight beyond the horizon. A moment later, they heard a distant boom.

Janusz felt his mouth go dry with a near-forgotten fear. He murmured a quick prayer for the safe deliverance of the pilot.

One of the students whispered in a choked voice, "What was that?" Another replied, "It was an airplane, wasn't it?"

Conspiring against the German occupation during the war had taught Janusz the value of caution. Dodging threats of violence had become almost second nature, due largely to Zygmunt's hard, on-the-spot lessons. The Middle East was a volatile powder keg, filled with much of the same bigotry and hatred that had fueled the war in Poland. Janusz knew what he had to do.

He ordered calmly, "Gather your things. We are leaving."

Fighting the searing heat of the day, Janusz led his students across the desert floor. He allowed them a swallow of water every hour. They made him proud, with very little complaining and no straggling.

Two hours into their hike back to camp, a helicopter appeared in the distance. The craft skirted along the horizon and then disappeared.

Looking for the downed craft, Janusz concluded.

He didn't think it likely the helicopter crew had seen the group of students moving along the dry ravine, and offered up a prayer for the protection of his small teenaged flock. If the crashed plane belonged to another country, the Syrian military would soon swarm the area, perhaps detaining Janusz and his charges.

The situation could become uncomfortable, at the very least.

Perhaps Assad would have some idea of what had taken place. Janusz hoped so.

He worried for the students, sweaty and strung out in single file behind him. However, he felt purely selfish relief when he spotted the final, rock-strewn rise before the roadway where Assad and the truck waited. He would soon rest his arthritic hip.

When Janusz reached the top of the hill, a bolt of fear shot through him. Where the two tents should have been, scattered clothing and the contents of all the suitcases littered the ground. The tent poles lay broken. The truck's doors stood open, and the tires were flat. Assad was nowhere in sight.

Janusz stared in shock. The students gathered around him, and he snapped into action. "Get back, get back," he ordered, pushing them down behind the slight rise.

They retreated to the cover of the hill and huddled together on the ground.

"What happened?"

"Where's Assad?"

"Who did that?"

"I want to go home."

Janusz ignored their rush of questions and looked to Vladic and Walter, two of the biggest boys. "I want you to stay here. Keep everyone quiet and still."

As Janusz rose to leave, Vladic grabbed his sleeve. "Where are you going?"

Janusz patted the boy's trembling hand. "To have a look. If I don't return, you are not to come down. At darkness, follow the road back the way we came."

"To where?"

"Just do as you're told."

Three students started to cry. Janusz offered a comforting look, said a prayer, and hiked up to the top of the hill.

He heard the insects—swarms of them—before he reached the truck, and he grimaced when he realized what had attracted them. Assad lay across the front seat, nude, his wrists bound in front of him, his throat cut from ear to ear, and his mouth and eyes wide open—filled with buzzing flies.

"My God! My God!" Janusz spun around and covered his eyes. It took a few moments for him to gather enough courage to turn and look again.

Janusz swatted a fly off his face and turned away, feeling chilled, even in the heat of the desert afternoon. The bloody scene reminded him of other horrors he'd witnessed in his own country. The memories never faded.

As he had so many times before, he wondered why God had placed such things in his path.

Then he pulled himself together and checked the supplies Assad had stored in the back of the truck. The water jugs and food stuffs . . . gone.

He shuffled to where the tents had stood, feeling the pain in his bones as if he'd suddenly aged a hundred years. Everything of value, also gone. What remained had been torn and strewn over the dirt.

As Janusz lifted his gaze to search the rest of the camp, he spied a fresh pile of camel dung. His pulse pounded with fear. He had seen the same at the Well of the Damned. Bandits, marauding bands—mainly nomadic Bedouins, notoriously violent—roamed the Syrian Desert.

"God help us."

Assad was dead, the truck disabled, and the food and water gone. Would the villains return? They had to know there were others. The tents and luggage would have given more than ample evidence.

Was the road still safe?

Since the bandits had killed a fellow Arab, Janusz shuddered to think what might befall the teenaged girls in his charge. He suddenly feared the passage of time. The murderers might have reached the Well of the Damned, where they'd perhaps missed Janusz's group earlier in the day, and would soon return to the camp to finish their terrible job of violence and destruction.

He took one more look around, saw nothing he could use to help their cause, and hurried back over the hill.

Janusz briefed the youngsters on the situation, trying not to panic them, though they needed to understand the urgency and gravity of their situation. Hope lay in evasion, and evasion meant flight. They would walk through the night, find shelter during the heat of day, and then walk again. Their trek would parallel the dirt road, to which eventually Janusz planned to return.

He felt tired, and knew the students must feel the same. They had already walked three to four hours.

Janusz forged ahead, encouraging them. He led them by following what he thought was the North Star. As the grueling hours passed, the sky moved above them, and they walked further and further into the wilderness.

He ignored the pain in his hip and pressed on, praying that God would give him strength. His badly blistered and terribly sore feet stung with each step. He had deliberately chosen the most strenuous, rocky course, with the hope of making it difficult for anyone to follow their tracks, and he'd fallen several times, bloodying both hands on the unforgiving rock. The others had also taken tumbles, but had uttered no complaints.

Janusz smiled up at the guiding star, imagining the three wise men raising their eyes to a similar beacon. The thought brought him a bit of comfort in the midst of the horror.

Finally, his throat dry, lungs gasping for breath, feet on fire, he signaled a stop. The column of youths halted and dropped to the ground like broken dolls.

Janusz had not taken a drink since he discovered the water jugs missing from the truck.

He whispered hoarsely, "Everyone is to take one sip." He twisted the cap off a canteen and handed it to a dark-haired girl, who'd been walking directly behind him.

After all of the students had taken their ration of water, Janusz allowed himself a gulp. He had hoped the stop would restore his waning strength, but it had not. His throbbing feet swelled in his shoes.

Worried that if he sat longer, he wouldn't be able to get up, Janusz struggled to stand. The others followed his lead.

Janusz held up a hand and whispered, "Not yet."

The students relaxed and flopped back down on the ground.

He hobbled off into the darkness to relieve himself. Each step brought a new stab of pain.

CHAPTER TWENTY-FOUR

CROSSING PATHS

Every parting is a form of death,
as every reunion is a type of heaven.

Tyron Edwards

Two hours after the crash, from the shaded cover of a rocky outcrop, David watched a Syrian helicopter land near the smoldering wreckage of his jet. Shaken by the thought of enemy troops, he took the automatic pistol from his belt and cocked it.

They would discover the ejection seat and start looking for the pilot. He guessed he'd moved along about five or six miles, but was still too close for comfort.

After another half hour or so, the helicopter rose into the sky and disappeared over the horizon. David felt relieved, but more secure with his weapon in hand. They would come back, probably in force.

He had little doubt the Arab bastards would find him—his footsteps in the desert were easily discerned—but some would pay a high price for their diligence. He checked his ammunition clip—full. The only problem with killing an Arab, in David's mind, lay in their belief that they would find glory in death.

Rather than panic and rush out into the deep heat of the late afternoon, he decided to wait for total darkness before setting out again.

As night began to fall, David's thoughts took him to his kibbutz near Haifa. Toby would have picked up Kalman from the nursery and arrived home.

He often had to work late, so his wife would feel no concern until a knock came at the door. The news would come from the wing commander and, maybe, also Ben Wizan.

David could almost recite what they would tell her. He had done it for others. They would minimize the danger. The radio beacon in the ejection seat would give them all hope that David had gotten out of the plane before the crash. Forces worked on his rescue.

After the grim visitors left, Toby would cuddle Kalman and hold onto the slight hope that David's commander and Ben had given her. Later, their rabbi and neighbors would come to join in on the long, tense vigil.

He prayed for God to spare him. He still had much to share with his son. He was not yet ready to die.

Exhaustion finally overtook him as he lay under the cover of the rocks. The stress and tension of the interception, the terror of blasting into the sky, and the tension of knowing he lay behind enemy lines all combined to push his mind into a numb, dreamless sleep.

Hours later, David opened his eyes to the sound of voices in the darkness. He lay frozen and gripped the automatic pistol to his chest. The voices came closer—so close he could hear their footfalls, and then their words.

Shock confounded his fear. He distinguished young, female voices... speaking Polish. He hadn't heard his native language in years. He held his breath and listened. A passing voice spoke softly of being lost.

David didn't understand all of what they said, but he managed to catch some words and phrases. It bewildered him. Nothing could explain the voice of a young Polish female in the middle of the Syrian Desert.

He bit his lip to assure himself that he wasn't hallucinating. The pain reinforced his sanity.

David listened carefully, trying to count their numbers, detect the movement of military gear, the squeak of a rifle sling, the clink of a canteen, the scent of a cigarette. He heard none of the telltale sounds of soldiers.

A group—more women than men, and all young—stumbled past his position. None made any attempt to mask their presence, nor did they march in cadence or in any type of uniformed order.

They were not soldiers.

When the last of the footfalls and voices faded into the night, David rolled from his hiding place. He allowed his eyes to adjust in the dark, moonless night, pushed the pistol into his waistband, and set out after the unusual group.

They had something he needed—water. Without it, he could not survive.

David watched the silhouette of a man from where he crouched in the darkness. He had followed the column for nearly an hour. They obviously had no idea where they were going. At one point they had nearly walked in a circle. David, a skilled navigator, had grumbled about the ineptitude of the leader, biding his time.

The leader of the group seemed older than the rest. He walked slightly stooped, shoulders rounded, and with slow and uneven movements.

David had initially suspected that a Syrian guide led the way, until the man spoke to the others in flawless Polish.

When the leader moved away from the group of youngsters, David followed.

The man stumbled through the darkness some distance from the others. David shadowed his every step, only a few yards away when the older man stopped.

David crept closer.

The man urinated, and hefted a deep sigh.

Before the old man could start back to the others, David lunged and grabbed him around the neck, clamped a hand over his mouth, and jammed the pistol hard into his neck.

In halting Polish, David whispered, "Make a sound, and you are a dead man."

—∘∘○❋○∘∘—

Janusz went rigid with fear. His heart pounded in his chest. He slowly raised his arms and held up his hands.

The words had been spoken in his ear, thick with accent—the accent of a Jew. Syria did not welcome Jews. The man was probably on the run, perhaps desperate, dangerous.

But Janusz could not show sympathy toward this man—could not give comfort to another of his heritage. The students were more important than his conscience.

So he said simply, "I am a priest."

The man snarled, "And I'm Santa Claus." He pushed the gun harder into Janusz's neck. "Now, try again before I scatter your brains."

Janusz gritted out through clenched teeth, "I am from Warsaw, Poland. I have twenty students with me. We are fleeing Bedouins who killed our guide."

The man continued to hold Janusz tight against him. "Are you armed?"

"Only with the Word of God."

Suddenly, the man released Janusz and stepped back. Janusz massaged his neck and turned to face his captor.

About twenty years separated their ages. The younger man wore a flight suit. A military belt around his torso held a gun holster and a survival knife. His uniform had no national emblems or insignias.

Janusz guessed he was the pilot. "We saw your plane crash."

"You saw *a* plane crash. You don't know it was mine."

Janusz understood the pilot's denial. An Israeli in Syria—enemy territory—had to be extremely cautious. "It is a long walk to Israel."

The man countered, "It's a longer walk to Warsaw, especially when you're walking toward Iraq."

Janusz gasped. "I thought I was going west." He pointed toward the bright pinpoint of light in the night sky that he'd used as a navigational guide. "Isn't that the North Star?"

The pilot grunted and shook his head. "You thought wrong. That is Jupiter, a planet. Do you have water?"

"Some. Come, we'll give you a drink."

Janusz started off toward where he had left the students.

"Father."

Janusz paused and looked back. "Yes?"

The man pointed in the opposite direction. "You came from over there." He pushed the gun in its holster and led the way.

An embarrassed flush filled Janusz's cheeks. "Thank you."

The pilot's appearance brought a flurry of excitement from the students. They crowded around him as he drank from a canteen.

"Take more," Janusz urged.

"Thank you." He took another mouthful, appearing to savor it, then swallowed.

Vladic sidled forward. "He is the pilot."

Walter added, "An Israeli, an enemy of Syria."

They spoke in Polish, but the newcomer seemed to follow the conversation.

Janusz said sharply in English, "He is like us, lost in the desert. We have water. He knows the way to safety. We can help one another."

The young man drew his pistol again, causing some of the students to cry out and shrink from him. "I will give you my gun for water. It will keep the Bedouins at bay."

Janusz quickly waved him off. "A gun cannot show us the way. You can."

The pilot frowned, holding the gun toward Janusz in an unthreatening gesture. "I didn't bring you here. I am not your savior."

Janusz smiled. "God may think otherwise. He brought us all here."

The pilot sighed and re-holstered his pistol. "You are a demanding man, for a priest."

Several of the students elbowed each other and snickered.

Janusz chuckled, enjoying the stealthy humor of the teenagers. "I work for a demanding God." Then he sobered and said softly, "I don't think it's His will that children be left in the desert. Do you have children?"

The pilot cleared his throat, then glanced at his luminous watch. "Sit down," he ordered, with a fierce look at the young faces gathered around him.

They all obeyed, including Janusz.

The Israeli paced before them like a general addressing his troops. "We have five hours before sunrise, and much to do, so listen carefully. Your lives depend on it.

"Who I am and who you are is of no importance. As the priest said, what is important is where we are, and what we can do for one another.

"You have been going in the wrong direction. If you had survived the journey, then most of you would have ended up in a prison cell in Iraq. The Iraqis do not welcome border intruders.

"West of here is the Trans-Syrian Railroad—a two-hour walk. A single train runs from Abu Kamal, in eastern Syria, across the desert to Tyre in south Lebanon. It travels at night to escape the heat, carrying raw sheep wool and sugar beets. Poor men pack the train. Poor men are not good workers. There is much wasted space. It is also an old train. It goes slowly up the Jabal Ar Range—slow enough for a man on the run to jump aboard.

"Two hundred kilometers later, near midday, the train stops in Damascus. You will find safety there. You have given me water. I will take you to the train."

"But there are twenty-two of us," Janusz said apprehensively. "We must all run and jump onto a passing train in the darkness?"

The pilot tapped his fingers against his thigh as if in annoyance.

Janusz felt his heart stutter for a moment. Kalman had tapped his thigh in a similar fashion when he concentrated on figuring out a difficult problem. The sudden shock of remembrance so stunned Janusz that he almost missed the young military man's words.

"Those who don't want to can wait for the Bedouins or the Syrian Army. One or the other will find you. There is a chance they will not kill you."

Janusz exchanged a look with the students. Then he pushed a hand to the ground and struggled to his feet. "Those who would go, stand with us."

The students, without hesitation, all got to their feet.

The pilot looked at Janusz and smiled. Then he turned to the teenagers encircling him. "There is one more thing I must ask. You will find refuge in Damascus. It is not so for me. After we board the train, you must forget me. Any mention of me before you leave Syria will cause you great harm. You do not know my name. You have not seen my face. When daylight comes, I will be gone. I wish you a long and prosperous life. I will not forget you gave me water."

Vladic answered in broken, accented English, "We will not forget your taking us to the train."

The man nodded. "We must go now." He set a pace faster than Janusz had.

No one complained. Missing the train was not an option.

Janusz struggled to keep up. Vladic and Walter offered help whenever he fell behind.

As they walked through the night, the pilot summoned the eight boys in the group, two at a time, to his side. He spoke to them as a father, encouraging, instilling confidence, fueling their spirit of adventure, briefing them on his strategy.

Janusz listened to the brilliant plan, nodding at the pilot's eye for detail. They would have four teams of boys, two in each team. The military man designated the teams: Alpha, Bravo, Charlie, and David. Each would be responsible for assisting three girls, and then each other, onto the moving train, leaving no one behind.

A boxcar carrying wool would be the target. As the others ran alongside, the pilot would unlock it, first help Janusz inside, and then assist the others, in order. He would board last.

When he finished the briefing, the column reorganized into the teams. A sense of excitement rose among them.

Walter said to Vladic, "I am going to become a fighter pilot."

Janusz smiled at the two and glanced at his watch. *Only three more hours until dawn.*

They walked over two hours with no rail bed in sight. Several students fell among the rocks and cried out. The team leaders helped them up and kept them moving.

A girl called out, as they picked their way along a rocky hillside, "Sir, may we have a drink?"

The pilot raised a hand, and they stopped. He said softly, "Everyone take one sip."

Word quickly passed back through the column. Janusz studied the shadowy forms of the students as they sat down to rest.

The distant sound of an air horn electrified the exhausted group.

One of girls shrieked, "The train!"

The Israeli shouted, "Come on!"

Janusz spotted the rail bed a few hundred yards away in the darkness—a welcome sight. The pilot ran ahead and dropped to the ground beside a metal rail, carefully placing an ear to it. Breathless, Janusz and the students gathered round him. They stood silent.

Finally, the Israeli man rose back to his feet. "Soon."

Working quickly, the pilot strung the teams of students—in their assigned order—out along one side of the tracks. He positioned them far enough away to avoid being seen from the train.

At the head of the line, Janusz waited with the Israeli. He searched the darkness for sight of the train, but saw nothing.

"Father, I have one thing more to ask."

Exhausted, Janusz looked up at the younger man. The night had lightened just enough to make out his features. In that instant, Janusz saw Kalman, and heard the voice of his old friend asking him to keep his precious children safe from harm. Janusz's legs wobbled, and he instinctively clutched his crucifix.

The pilot grabbed his elbow, steadying him.

One of the girls whispered urgently, "Father Dov? Are you unwell?"

The moment passed, and Janusz cleared his throat, slightly embarrassed by his behavior. The heat, the stress, and the lack of water must have conspired against his mind.

He gave the girl a reassuring smile and nodded. "No, my child, I am fine. Do not worry about me."

Then he straightened his shoulders and turned back to the pilot. "Forgive me, young man. You wished a favor of me? Do you require sanctuary?"

The man laid a hand on Janusz's shoulder, and Janusz felt the strong fingers tremble. The Israeli drew in a deep breath and seemed to gather his thoughts, worrying Janusz with his strange hesitation.

"It's not that, Father. When you have reached safety in Damascus, please call the Omar Hotel. Tell Ali Said, the desk man, the package is on its way to the port in Tyre. It will arrive tomorrow night."

Janusz nodded, understanding the gravity of the pilot's request. He asked Janusz to risk exposure by passing on a message to the Israeli underground. Again, Janusz felt his mind begin to slip back in time, to another place—another request for secrecy against an enemy of the Jews.

He met the younger man's sharp gaze and repeated, "Ali Said at the Omar Hotel. The package will be at the port in Tyre tomorrow night."

The Israeli closed his eyes for a moment, then visibly swallowed. "Right."

When he opened his eyes again, Janusz smiled and said softly, "May God grant you safe passage, my son."

An excited student interrupted, "Here it comes!"

Janusz tore his attention from the young warrior's stealthy demeanor and stared down the rails. A pinpoint of light punctured the darkness far down the track.

The pilot called out, "Lie down! Everyone keep quiet."

Janusz glanced from student to student. They lay silent on the desert floor, shivering, surely not only with the bitter cold, but with fright and anticipation. An ancient, time-weary diesel throbbed and hissed as it labored slowly up the long grade toward them. Its dim headlamp vibrated in the darkness.

Janusz, his heart racing, silently thanked God as the engine chugged by, filling the clear, cool air with the stench of exhaust and fuel oil. He smiled with relief. The train moved much slower than he'd dared to hope.

The pilot waited until only three cars had passed before lunging to his feet. "Now!"

Suddenly they all jumped up and ran. Slow train or not, the task of getting everyone safely aboard would be formidable. The students at the end of the line would have to run for as long as it took all the others in front to jump and climb aboard.

Janusz and the Israeli ran alongside a weathered boxcar. The wheels clicked loudly as they thumped over joints in the track. The pilot grabbed a latch on the door and jerked. It slid open. Janusz, close on his heels, gasped for breath as he struggled to keep up.

"Now, Father!"

Janusz gritted his teeth and ran harder, then dove for the open door. The pilot pushed from behind, and Janusz landed face first in a heap of gritty, musty-smelling beets.

He scrambled aside when one of the girls landed squarely on his back. Another quickly followed, knocking them over. Beets tumbled out the door into the night.

Janusz and the two girls helped pull others in. Students appeared in rapid, orderly succession.

Janusz prayed aloud. He felt exhilarated. The plan was working. The boxcar filled with student after student. Shouts of relief and laughter accompanied each as they tumbled inside.

"Come on, Sarah!"

"Pull, Mishelle!"

"Run, Sasha, run!"

More beets spilled away as the teenagers waded in the gritty mound of vegetables. Then Vladic, the last student, jumped aboard. A cheer mixed with the clatter of the track.

Only the Israeli ran alongside the open boxcar door. His face glistened with sweat. A dozen hands reached out to him as the students and Janusz crowded the doorway.

His intense gaze riveted Janusz. They stared at each other for a long moment.

Janusz suddenly recognized the eyes—Tova's beauty shone through them—within Kalman's handsome features. He grasped the doorframe. *David!*

The Israeli stopped, his eyes large in his face. As the train passed him by, he called, "Travel safely, friends." Then the darkness quickly swallowed him.

A collective howl came from the boxcar, "NOOOooo!"

Janusz closed his eyes. There could be no mistaking the Israeli pilot's identity.

Thank you, dear Lord, for bringing me here, and placing Kalman's son in my path.

David stood panting in the darkness.

The train shrieked past, reminding David of his precarious position within enemy territory. He resumed his run and managed to keep pace with a boxcar a few up from the rear of the train.

The cries from the priest and the students, urging him to join them, still echoed in his ears. But better this way; what they didn't know, they couldn't tell. His hesitation may have added a secondary buffer of safety for them.

He quickly reached for the latch on the door, jerked, and slid it open. He ran harder and then jumped, only to collide with a wall of lumpy burlap sacks stuffed with prickly, unprocessed cotton.

David slid off the rough threshold, catching himself before he fell. His fingers grappled for a hold, and he managed to grab the slatted doorframe as his feet and knees dragged in the rail bed. He grimaced and pulled himself up into the car, pushed several sacks out of the way to gain space, and pulled the door closed.

He crawled up and over the crush of spongy sacks, and wormed his way down into their midst—out of sight, and warm. He relaxed with the rhythmic clatter of the track and allowed his thoughts to meander.

He remembered the start of the Second World War, when a priest named Father Janusz Dov had rescued his family from a Nazi prison camp. The priest, his father's boyhood friend, had risked his life for theirs.

The students had called their leader "Father Dov." David had seen recognition spark in the priest's eyes as the boxcar pulled away. Obviously, the old man was the same Father Dov who had taken him to the farm in eastern Poland. It seemed an impossible, miraculous coincidence.

In his mind's eye, David again watched his sister walk away down the rough dirt road, hand-in-hand with Father Dov, the last time he'd seen her.

Once he had settled into a stable life in his new country, he'd made inquiries at the administrative office of Yad ve' Shem for Holocaust survivors. Among the seven hundred thousand survivors listed, David had found over three thousand with the name of Gold. When he read the names of Kalman and Tova Gold, his father and mother, among the list of victims, he'd stopped searching. He didn't want to find Rachel's name.

As long as he had no confirmation of her death, as long as he didn't see her name, he held on to the chance of her having survived. He'd hoped for years that a knock at the door, a telephone call, a letter, would bring news of her, but when the years turned to a decade, his hope had turned to bittersweet memories.

The rickety boxcar bumped and groaned, bringing David's thoughts back to the present. The priest had told him that Bedouins had murdered their Syrian guide, which had caused the old man and the students to strike out on their own.

Those same Bedouins would've also seen David's jet go down—its plume of smoke was visible for miles. The nomads, like the Syrians, would receive a handsome reward for delivering an Israeli pilot.

He thanked God the train had arrived late, something he'd counted on from intelligence briefings. Eventually, dogs or skilled trackers would lead the Syrians to the rail bed. They would torture for information whoever they discovered there.

David listened closely to the sounds of the old locomotive. Sometimes the train didn't run at all, due to breakdowns, but with any luck, and no mechanical failures, they would reach Tyre before the trackers reached the end of the trail at the train tracks. The odds of success weren't high, but the priest's presence gave David an almost euphoric sense of hope.

Then he shook his head at his uncharacteristic mood. Perhaps Toby's faith had finally rubbed off on him. She still believed in miracles.

The train seemed to pick up speed. David looked up at the slatted top of the boxcar. The dark of the desert sky had begun to yield to the light of dawn.

CHAPTER TWENTY-FIVE

FROM THE VALLEY OF DEATH TO THE SEA OF FREEDOM

After the game, the king and the pawn go into the same box.

Italian Proverb

The ancient train bumped to a jerky stop in Damascus's central rail yard.

Walter and Vladic pushed the sliding door open, and Janusz eagerly alighted into the early-afternoon heat. After long hours in the vibrating, rattling boxcar, he felt like a sailor stepping onto the shore after months at sea.

The students dropped down and huddled around him, awaiting his lead. Janusz glanced about, expecting to be accosted by someone from the railroad authority.

A group of Syrians labored nearby, replacing a section of rail on an adjoining track. They lifted bronzed faces to stare at the priest and teenagers, but their interest proved fleeting, and they resumed their work as if Europeans climbing out of a boxcar filled with beets were seen every day.

Janusz, momentarily shocked by the display of apathy, said just loud enough to be heard over the noise of the rail yard, "Let's stay together."

He spotted several tall buildings in the distance, and started off across a maze of rusty tracks. The students followed, automatically forming into the teams the Israeli pilot had assigned.

Janusz paused at the edge of the train depot and looked back at the battered locomotive and boxcars that had brought them to safety. As he watched, rail yard workers connected three open flat cars onto the end. Each carried green military trucks. A few minutes later, a succession of bumps reverberated through the train, and it began to inch slowly forward.

He heaved a deep sigh, wishing he'd had more time to speak with the young man he knew as David Gold.

Janusz bowed his head and said a silent prayer for Kalman's courageous son. *Protect him and carry him to safety, Lord. Kalman, my old friend, if you are watching, witness that David has kept his promise. He has done you proud.*

As the train left the yard, Janusz raised a hand, extending three fingers, and slowly tapped them over his heart.

He sighed again, then turned and herded the students toward the center of the city, saying, "I have heard that the Omar Hotel is not too frightening. Let us try to find it and see if they have rooms available."

Janusz had one last mission to perform for Kalman's family.

David watched the priest led his weary students over the rails, with a sense of heartache. If only things had been different. If only they had met in another time, another place. If only he'd had the opportunity to further question the clergyman.

He kept to the shadows in his sweltering hiding place as the train began to move again, but he shifted his position to allow him to maintain a view of the retreating group of Polish vagabonds, strangely unwilling to let them out of his sight.

Suddenly, David caught his breath as the priest turned and seemed to stare directly at him. He saw the old man lift a hand and give the signal he and Rachel had devised to incorporate Father Dov into their secret refugee family—the old man tapped his chest with three fingers.

Time seemed to stop for David. He could only stare wordlessly, helplessly, as the priest turned his back to the train and led the teenagers into the city.

———∘∘∘⟩◉⟨∘∘∘———

That evening, Janusz stood at the open window of his third-floor hotel room. The lights of Damascus spread into the distance. The city had fallen quiet with the coming of night, creating an almost foreboding atmosphere. The only movement came from the headlamps of an occasional passing bus or taxi.

Once they'd left the rail yard, Janusz had succeeded in flagging down a police car. The police, unable to find an interpreter, had turned the group over to the military.

The military had many questions. Had they seen a plane crash? How had they found the train? Did any of them have relatives in Israel? The interrogations had lasted nearly five hours, but the students had not betrayed the Israeli pilot. Janusz felt immensely proud of them.

In the late afternoon, the government agents assigned to them took them to the Omar Hotel at Janusz's request. However, the hotel had no rooms available.

While the harried official in charge of their group haggled with the manager, Janusz had located the deskman and drawn him aside. Ali Said had acted as if he didn't understand when Janusz tried to deliver the pilot's message. After a rather shocking outburst in Arabic, the smaller man had hurried out a side entrance and disappeared.

Disheartened, Janusz had watched him go. He hoped the deskman's loud display had been for show, and that the undercover agent had truly understood Janusz's message. He'd slumped his shoulders in defeat, realizing that he'd done all he could for David. God would take care of the rest.

The frustrated official had rounded them all up and taken them to the less-elegant Yarmuk Hotel. There, after another argument with another manager, he'd procured four rooms and announced that Janusz and his students were guests of the Syrian government.

What a huge relief to finally rest his weary bones, although Janusz knew more questions would come the next day. However, the official had assured him about the arrangement process for a flight to Warsaw.

Janusz sipped a bitter cup of coffee as he studied the night, waiting for a telephone call. After a dozen attempts at a long-distance call to the Minister of Education in Warsaw, he had given up, and walked down to the lobby to ask for help.

The desk clerk had apologized, promising to place the call and then ring Janusz, who'd waited nearly two hours.

The students had crowded into the three other rooms, but hadn't seemed to mind. After spending a night in the Syrian Desert, the spartan Yarmuk Hotel drew few complaints.

Janusz sighed and set down his coffee. The appearance of David had re-awakened an aging, yet still smarting, deeply buried guilt, but through the process, a growing sense of self had emerged.

He shared a common bond with the man who had fallen from the sky. Both were Jews—one an Israeli fighter pilot, the other a Roman Catholic priest—but Jews, nonetheless. Even though Janusz had served as a priest for over twenty years, in his heart, he had always felt like a Jew.

Once upon a time, living as a Jew in Poland held no unnatural tendencies. Anti-Semitism had to be learned and taught, and it had been—to an unfathomable, murderous degree. Being a Jew in post-war Europe still exacted a high price.

He looked to the sky and prayed his Jewish friend had found his way to safety.

∘∘∘·❧·∘∘∘

Late in the afternoon, just an hour or so before sunset, the train rumbled to a stop in Tyre, only a few blocks from the port docks—David's destination.

He dropped down from the boxcar and immediately hunched over, camouflaging his true height. He'd garbed his tall frame in an ankle length, loose-fitting robe fashioned from burlap sacks.

He no longer looked like a fighter pilot. Grease and grime from the boxcar's door hinges covered his face and hands, turning his light-tan skin dark, with an added, filthy shine. He'd wrapped his head in a traditional Arab headdress—the product of a torn Israeli flight suit.

Limping to promote the appearance of a street beggar, David headed off toward the scent of the sea and the towering cranes of ocean freighters that rose above a line of warehouses. A street vendor pedaled by on a three-wheeled bicycle. A cab and a truck also passed. No one gave him a second look.

David entered the port in the growing darkness, searching for a friendly flag. Row after row of freighters crowded the piers and docks: Iraqi, Turkish, Egyptian, Russian, and Cuban, but nothing he considered neutral, or a friend of Israel. Israel had few friends.

He happened upon a flattened orange among a pile of debris in the littered street, wiped it on his sleeve, and ate. Its tangy moisture helped ease his parched throat.

The commercial docks and ships in Tyre's main harbor yielded to a poorer, smaller collection of fishing boats. Nets and floats cluttered their decks, ripe with the strong odor of fish. There, the boats and ships glowed with lights. Once in a while, David caught a whiff of the heady aroma of cooking, and his stomach growled.

He passed by unseen, keeping the fading light of day on his left shoulder, walking south, toward Israel. A small, wooden rowboat, weathered and worn, rested on the water, tied to a massive post where a sea gull sat preening itself.

David's pulse quickened when he spotted the old craft. It looked seaworthy and sturdy, despite its battered appearance.

The bird took to the air as David approached. He paused and glanced around. Seeing no one, he then climbed down a ladder nailed to the post and stepped into the boat. It rocked under his weight as he untied the rope. His heart raced as he tossed the line onto the dock and pushed off from the post.

Gingerly lowering himself to the splintered seat, David fed the wooden oars into their locks and rowed away. He worked casually, almost lazily, not wanting to draw attention, fighting the urge to apply all his might to the task.

After an hour, he'd rowed well south of the harbor and about a quarter of a mile from the glimmer of shore. Once certain he'd gone beyond sight, he pulled off his makeshift turban and leaned into the oars.

He could only hope that Father Dov had made contact with Ali Said, the Israeli operative who worked under the guise of a hotel's deskman. Even if the priest hadn't succeeded in passing on the message, David considered the open sea a better choice than having electrodes wrapped around his testicles in a Syrian dungeon.

The thought of other, more horrific tortures made him row harder. Sweat covered his body, and his arm muscles cried for relief, but David toiled on.

After nightfall, David no longer felt alone. Raising his face to the sky, he found his friends—Cassiopeia, Hercules, Orion—all there, familiar, reassuring.

The light of countless stars punctured the dark canopy, welcoming him. A fighter-pilot-turned-sailor could use them to navigate the sea. He sought and found the North Star. Turning the boat so the star hung above his left shoulder, David rowed west.

If Father Dov had managed to convey the message, Israeli patrol boats would now be searching for their downed pilot. Escape and evasion training called for loitering at the twelve-mile limit—the point where a country's territorial waters end and the open sea begins. In the darkness, the lights of Tyre made the task simple. Once positioned, his loitering would facilitate a search by radar.

David stopped rowing. He had done all he could.

The old, wooden boat rode low in the water. Thankfully, the sea felt relatively calm. Saltwater filled the bottom of David's small craft and sloshed back and forth with the gentle roll of the swells, chilling his feet.

The quiet unnerved him.

The sea, he'd discovered, was not so unlike the desert—a vast plain of nothingness, a watery wilderness as deadly as the sand.

For hours he searched the blanket of darkness surrounding him, until his eyes ached. Finally, David lowered his head to his knees, closed his eyes, and tried to sleep. He dreamed of gardening. His son, Kalman, knelt at his side as they dug up a plump radish.

Bright, hot, white light wiped away the pleasant dream. David grimaced, opened his eyes, and stared into a wide beam of light—a patrol boat.

His heart leaped with excitement, and he bolted to his feet, waving his arms wildly. "Here, here!" he shouted in Hebrew, squinting, trying to see. He heard the throb of an engine.

The craft pulled closer. On the mast above the powerful spotlight, fluttering in the night breeze, flew the red, white, and black bars of the Syrian flag.

A sinking feeling of defeat knotted David's stomach. He lowered his arms. A flood of harsh warnings came from behind the light. The voices spoke Arabic.

"Son-of-a-bitch," David muttered.

The gunship bumped his stolen rowboat, rocking it. Two soldiers jumped aboard, aiming rifles at him.

David looked to the man closest to him and said in English, "I have no weapons."

The second man struck him hard from behind, against the base of his skull, tearing his flesh. Lights danced in front of David's eyes. His knees buckled, and he fell.

The first man kicked him in the face with a heavy boot. Blood spattered from David's nose. His head splashed into the cold saltwater in the bottom of the boat. Pain, searing and hot, shot through him, and he fought to remain conscious.

They lifted him, jerked his wrists behind his back, and bound them tight with thin twine that cut into his flesh. David cried out, and they kicked him again, this time in the chest. Something cracked. He gagged and spit blood.

The Syrians laughed and dragged him onto the larger boat, talking fast, celebrating.

David forced himself to take slow, deep breaths, struggling to calm himself, to fight the pain. He lowered his chin to his chest, hoping they would think he'd lost consciousness.

When they relaxed, and he knew they would, he would bolt and jump overboard. He'd rather drown than have to endure torture by those Arab bastards. He decided to dive headfirst and kick as deep as he could. Then he'd open his mouth and suck in the seawater.

Amidst the rush of Syrian chatter, David heard the clink of a cigarette lighter, followed by the scent of burning tobacco. They were relaxing, congratulating one another. The moment had come.

David closed his eyes and silently said goodbye to his wife and son. He started drawing in air, oxygenating his lungs. If he could kick far enough, deep enough, the currents would take his body out to sea, away from any chance of discovery. He did not want his wife and child to see him hung from his heels like a fish. The Arabs relished displaying dead Israelis, especially fighter pilots.

Just as he'd gathered his feet beneath him and poised himself to dive overboard, an explosion of gunfire jolted David upright, stiffly alert. Flashes of red-hot light danced in front of his eyes. The noise deafened him. Bits and pieces of wood, metal, flesh, bone, and blood erupted around him.

One of the Syrians slumped over and fell onto him. Blood pulsed from a hole in the man's head. David grimaced and kicked the body overboard.

The spotlight mounted on the mast exploded and went out. Glass rained down onto the deck. Flashes continued to fill the night, washing away the darkness with loud bolts of manmade lightning, as bullets and shells ripped into the Syrian gunship. Screams and shouts mixed with the hellish cacophony, and as quickly as it had begun, it ended.

In the tense silence that followed, David heard only the gentle slap of seawater against the sides of the listing Syrian gunship. He sat frozen, waiting.

Then an engine growled to life. Lights winked on, illuminating the silhouette of an Israeli patrol boat. It idled toward the sinking vessel.

David gasped with relief and joy. Tears filled his eyes. "Here!" he screamed in a voice that sounded distant and faint.

His shout made his ears ring and filled him with nauseating pain.

The spotlight found him, and the patrol boat bumped alongside the disabled enemy ship. A half-dozen heavily-armed Israeli soldiers, in black face paint and dark jumpsuits, scrambled aboard. More gunshots rang out, accompanied by a few weak screams, and then silence.

A man knelt beside David and cut his wrists free. His rescuer spoke Hebrew in a strong, proud voice. "Welcome to the Israeli Navy, Major."

CHAPTER TWENTY-SIX

PICKING UP THE PIECES

Then God blessed them and said:
Be fruitful and multiply and fill the earth.

Genesis 1:28

Stefan took Rachel home from the hospital and tenderly guided her to the sofa. She'd withdrawn into herself, and had allowed him to handle the press and the police, too stunned to deal with the repercussions of Aaron's passing.

He sat beside her and held her hands, staring deeply into her eyes. "If I announce that Aaron was my natural father, it would detract from his death and turn a tragedy into a circus. It would be a grievous disservice to him, and to you. I care about both of you too much to do that. Fate was kind. I met him in life. I was with him at death. He knew we were together. No one else need know. I would like it to remain our secret."

Rachel nodded, warmed by his thoughtfulness and generosity of spirit. No stranger to the task, she could keep a secret.

The mayor declared an official day of mourning for the funeral. The city government's functions literally stopped.

Aaron's friends and associates from Columbia University, the District Attorney's office, and New York's see-and-be-seen crowd all attended. A mix of the rich and famous, the elected, and the want-to-be elected mourned. Both the police and the press estimated the crowd in

275

excess of ten thousand. Instead of a dignified farewell to a father and public servant, the funeral became a tug of war between officials vying for the chance to fill Aaron's shoes, and jeering protesters lining the streets for the procession.

After the funeral, Rachel felt listless and adrift. For the second time in her life, she had lost both parents. Recriminations over the way she'd treated Aaron haunted her.

Esther had accepted Aaron's affair. Only Rachel's indignation had forced Esther to leave him—the beginning of the end of Esther's life. And if Rachel hadn't allowed Stefan to include Aaron in their dinner plans, he would not have died. Aaron had reached out to Rachel, trying to recover from a matter that had been none of her business in the first place, and it had cost him his life.

In Rachel's mind, Aaron hadn't been killed by an irate black man. His love for her had caused his death.

As the weeks went by, guilt and depression smothered and debilitated Rachel, forcing her to take a sabbatical from the firm.

Stefan became her rock—always there, even at times when she rejected his help. He understood Rachel's anguish, and even shared some of it. He listened, consoled, encouraged, and loved.

When she told Stefan how guilty she felt, he responded gently, "No good came from the Holocaust. But psychologists did gain an understanding of the survival syndrome. Those who survived—especially those who lost family members or loved ones—experienced acute guilt. Guilt because they lived; guilt because they failed to prevent the loss or harm; guilt that somehow, something they did, or failed to do, had caused it all. I understand your guilt, Rachel, for I share it. But what's important is that I know Aaron would not want it. If you search your heart, you will realize this is true. Aaron would not blame us. And he would hate to have us suffer because of him."

Time seemed the only balm for Rachel's psychological wounds and, as it passed, Stefan continued to demonstrate his love with patience and understanding. Slowly, Rachel began to emerge from her depression. She set up a scholarship program in Aaron's name at the Columbia School of Law.

Stefan assumed a leadership role at Davis and Collins.

Seven months after the funeral, Rachel married Stefan. At his insistence, they immediately bought a sprawling estate in Forest Hills, hoping the move would become therapeutic for Rachel. It did. She quickly lost herself in decorating the house.

With only three weeks remaining in her leave, Rachel looked forward to a return to work. The anticipation, the hope, blossomed in Rachel, a near-forgotten experience. It warmed her spirit. Both she and Stefan loved the law, a common bond shared with Aaron.

Rachel remembered sitting in one of Aaron's lectures at Columbia, "An Introduction to Law." He had scrawled on a blackboard, "The law: a rule of conduct, established by custom, agreement, or authority."

"The abstract definition," Aaron had explained, "is the glue that holds all society together. The rule of law governs the affairs of man. The absence of it means tyranny. I've seen it up close," Aaron had told the collection of law students. "I don't want to see it again."

As an attorney, Rachel felt like a part of Aaron's vision—a part of something bigger, something important, something vital. She worked as a servant, becoming a part of the glue—feeling needed and, perhaps most importantly, ready to resume her life.

One fall, after Stefan left for a conference in London, Rachel made plans for a weekend drive north into the mountains. *The fall foliage has turned beautifully.*

After a night at their favorite bed and breakfast, she would tell him that she looked forward to returning to work. He would be pleased.

But while shopping at a local market, she became faint. She retreated to a restroom and threw up.

At first Rachel attributed the illness to a fish dinner shared with Stefan the night before, although Stefan had not become sick. However, when nausea returned with the morning paper and coffee, she grew worried. She felt lousy and, for the next two hours, made several trips to the bathroom.

She had vague memories of her mother's agony over an aunt and grandmother in Poland who had both died slow, painful deaths from stomach and intestinal problems.

Did she now suffer some genetic curse from her mother's bloodline? She decided to call the doctor.

During her appointment, the doctor listened to Rachel's complaints and suspicions, and then gave her a complete physical.

When he finished, he left Rachel to get the test results. She nervously sat on the examination table, staring at an anatomy chart. The longer the wait, the more she began to panic.

She decided to leave, and just as she reached for her purse, the doctor returned.

He pushed his glasses up onto his forehead and, with twinkling eyes, said, "You're pregnant, Mrs. Davis."

"Pregnant! A baby?"

"Yes, indeed."

Rachel's joy knew no bounds.

———∘∘∘ ⦅◉⦆ ∘∘∘———

While flying from New York to London two days earlier, Stefan had watched the latest news and sporting events on a private video screen. He tried to tune everything out in order to reread the volume of paperwork detailing the situation awaiting him in England. One of his father's established clients, a Saudi prince, wanted to buy the building where he lived in Kensingston Gardens. The prince occupied the top three floors, and wanted to build a helicopter pad on the rooftop, but the management company representing the Germans who owned the building had refused the prince's proposal.

The Brits living in the building had also protested, but said they didn't really care about helicopters; their argument focused on the rich Arab himself.

The savvy prince had told Stefan that he knew about the tenants' personal belligerence, which made him even more determined to buy the building and throw them all out.

Stefan walked into in the Saudi's twenty-second-floor conference room to find the thirty-three-year-old billionaire prince sitting with three men in Arab garb and six Caucasians in Armani suits. All sat watching the news on a big-screen television. A terrorist's bomb had exploded in downtown Jerusalem, killing three people.

The prince quipped, "Nobody killed but Jews." Then he turned off the set. "Let's get down to business."

Stefan found himself sitting with ten people whose nationality and heritage, in all probability, made them anti-Semites. Being a Jew wasn't a new realization to Stefan Davis. His adoptive father had never made it a secret.

He resented being placed in such a situation, where good business dictated that he remain silent and squash the impulse to lash out at the slurs against his race. With a tight rein on his emotions, Stefan guided the conversation back onto a more professional footing.

They negotiated for almost four hours, arguing at times, but they ended with agreement. The prince got his building, and the Germans got their price.

Stefan maintained a cool, calm composure through it all, but he felt inordinately tense when he finally closed his briefcase.

The prince laid a hand on Stefan's shoulder. "Stefan, we're flying to Monte Carlo this evening for a little roulette. Please join us. I will gladly be your sponsor."

"No, thank you. My wife waits in New York."

The Arab royal inclined his head. "I appreciate your service, Stefan."

"Remember that when you get our bill."

Stefan left the conference room and went directly to a washroom to scrub his hands. Studying his image in the mirror, he found himself looking at a man driven to earn; his only motivation was self-serving.

Until the revelation that his biological father was not only alive, but Aaron Ross, the District Attorney of New York City, Stefan had not questioned his path in life. Ironically, both his adoptive father and biological father had become successful attorneys. The distinct difference between the two lay in the arenas in which they worked.

Kevin Davis, born into a rich, successful family practice, had dedicated his life to perpetuate it. Aaron Ross, although a successful attorney, had abandoned a lucrative partnership in a major firm to return to Columbia to teach. Success as an educator had paved the way into the political arena, and his subsequent election as District Attorney. More than that, Aaron had found success on two continents, in three distinct cultures, as an attorney, teacher, and elected official. He'd been driven by a desire to serve, rather than a desire to earn.

The observation had settled deep into Stefan's being.

His meeting with the Saudi prince and the Germans had graphically illustrated the decadence of easy money. Money, Stefan had learned, often had power as much as or more than the law.

As one of the senior partners in a prestigious international law firm, his earnings had soared. He had a beautiful wife and a fourteen-room estate in Forest Hills. In the eyes of the world, Stefan Davis had it all—the epitome of success.

He had coat-tailed on Kevin Davis's success, and suddenly found himself empty; the reward of simply working to compound wealth had become meaningless. He hungered for more.

He thought about following Aaron Ross's footsteps into public service, but quickly realized it would mirror his following Kevin Davis—following, not pioneering.

Stefan knew he had to go his own way. He had no idea what to do or how, but accepting the fact calmed the storm brewing in his soul. The answer would come. He settled in his seat, savoring the thought.

Rachel will understand. She may even have suggestions. He looked forward to getting home.

———∞o∘)|◉|(∘o∞———

Outside the doctor's office, Rachel confronted a stranger in the hallway and beamed at the startled man. "I'm pregnant."

Dr. Hanson had given her the number of an OB/GYN, but Rachel wanted answers *now*. She stopped at a bookstore and bought eight books on pregnancy and child rearing, determined to have the healthiest and brightest child in the Western Hemisphere.

She made a second stop at a health-food store to buy vitamins, grinning broadly at the clerk. "I'm pregnant."

Arriving home, Rachel went directly to the telephone and called the OB/GYN. He would confirm a due date.

A receptionist told her the first available appointment required a five-day wait.

Rachel declared, "You do understand I'm pregnant, don't you?"

The receptionist said, with a smile in her voice, "And I expect you will be, five days from now."

Rachel curbed her impatience and marked her calendar. Once she hung up, she strolled into the master bedroom suite and headed for the massive bathroom.

Stripping nude, Rachel studied herself in a full-length mirror. Her stomach looked normal. Disappointed, she strained, making it pooch out some. She massaged her stomach carefully, marveling at the fact that a life grew inside her. A life born from the love she carried for her husband. A child of love.

With a sigh of contentment, she stepped into the shower and turned on the taps. Comforting, warm water cascaded over her. She cradled her still-flat abdomen and closed her eyes. Rachel could not remember ever feeling a greater sense of joy and satisfaction.

Maybe this child was God's gift.

She and Stefan had been robbed of so much, but now they would share a child—a child born of the bloodline of Aaron Ross and Kalman Gold. Rachel and Stefan no longer had their fathers, but they would soon have a part of each man, in their child.

Tears welled in her eyes. Rachel now understood why she had survived—not to become an attorney, nor to win important cases, but to be a mother.

The big, blue British Airways 747 taxied toward runway two at New York's Kennedy International Airport.

Stefan had spoken with Rachel by telephone two hours earlier from the airplane to see if she planned to meet him at the airport. "You don't have to come," Stefan assured. "It's Friday night. Traffic's going to be heavy. I can catch a cab."

"I don't care," Rachel said a little breathlessly. "I have exciting news."

"You found a dog?" They had talked about buying one.

"You'll just have to wait. See you at the gate."

"Wait, wait! You didn't buy the little whiny one, did you?"

"I said you'll have to wait."

"I love you, Rachel."

"And I love you, Stefan."

Rachel waited with a crush of others at a rail near the mouth of the arrival jetway. She shivered with anticipation as the plane braked to a halt. Her heart raced as the noise of the engines subsided.

She glanced at an older couple beside her. "He doesn't know I'm pregnant."

Soon passengers emerged into the terminal. Rachel searched for Stefan, excitedly scanning the flow of arriving passengers, and then she spotted him.

"Stefan!"

He looked up and met her eyes. His face broke into a smile as he moved toward her.

Rachel couldn't contain her feelings. "Stefan," she screamed, "I'm pregnant!"

"What?"

"I'm pregnant! We're going to have a baby!"

Movement in the crowded terminal stopped as all eyes turned to Rachel.

Stefan pulled her over the rail. He held her face and looked into her eyes. "Are you certain?"

"Yes! I went to the doctor today. We're going to have a baby!"

Stefan kissed her.

A cheer of approval came from the crowd.

Rachel squelched the thought of going back to work, and decided to dedicate herself to staying healthy and fit throughout the pregnancy. She extended her leave of absence.

Busy or not, waiting was waiting, and although excitement carried them through the next four months, the final four dragged by for Rachel, as she grew larger and more uncomfortable each day. Rachel and Stefan busied themselves with decorating a nursery, picking names, and shopping.

Stefan curtailed foreign travel and spent time with Rachel in exercise classes and Lamaze classes, and Rachel's friends and associates from the firm held a baby shower.

"I'm not having a baby," she cried, looking at her reflection in the mirror. "I'm having an elephant. I can't see my feet."

After what felt like her ten-thousandth visit to the doctor, Rachel went away disappointed.

"At least another two weeks," the doctor had told her.

The next morning, ten minutes after Stefan left for the office, Rachel's water broke.

———∘∘○⟊◉⟊○∘∘———

Stefan reached the firm's corporate office twenty minutes late for a staff meeting.

"I'm sorry," he apologized, joining the others already gathered in the conference room. "There was an accident on the expressway."

The senior Davis smiled. "It's all right. I'll preside today. You better go to the hospital."

"The hospital?"

"Rachel arrived there forty minutes ago. Your son arrived twenty minutes later."

Stefan burst into the hospital maternity ward, and a nurse led him to Rachel's room.

Mother and son were fine and, several hours after his birth, the birth certificate read, "Kevin Aaron Davis."

"He's named after your boss / my adopted father, and your adopted father / my biological father," Stefan quipped as he cradled the infant in his arms at Rachel's bedside.

Rachel smiled. "All right, but when he asks, *you* explain it to him."

Stefan and Rachel scheduled baby Kevin's circumcision for eight days hence, according to Jewish custom.

Rachel arranged to hold the ceremony at Temple Emanuel on Fifth Avenue and 65th Street in New York City.

The mohel performing the circumcision held the infant as Rachel and Stefan stood witness.

He spoke softly, "Blessed are you, Lord our God, King of the Universe, who has sanctified us with Your commandments and commanded us concerning circumcision."

The mohel paused to make the circumcision cut.

"Our God and God of our fathers, preserve this child for his father and mother, and his name in Israel shall be called Kevin Aaron, the son of Rachel and Stefan.

"May his father rejoice in his offspring and his mother be glad with the fruit of her womb, as it is written. May your father and mother rejoice, and she who bore you be glad."

He concluded with, "L'chaim."

Kevin Aaron, not unlike most children, became the joy of the Davis family. He brought a breath of new life to Stefan's aging, adoptive parents, and Rachel and Stefan found the child adding to the bond between them as they grew even closer.

Stefan presided over a merger of the firm with a Chicago group, creating a nationwide web of law firms under one umbrella, with offices from coast to coast. The business of law changed dramatically, using advertisements of services and franchising. Stefan's election to president/CEO and chairman of the board came as no surprise.

Although Rachel remained on leave to devote her time and energies to their child, Stefan kept her informed and relied heavily on her council. This considerate sharing made Rachel feel like an active partner in the firm, and also served to take the sting out of his time away from home. She became accustomed to his frequent trips between New York, Washington, Chicago, and L.A.

The strain of constant travel softened when Rachel and Kevin Aaron joined Stefan on the road. The firm bought a private corporate jet, fitted with a playpen, a crib, and a variety of toys. Associates tagged the aircraft "Diaper One." Kevin Aaron, now a curious, playful toddler, quickly became a veteran air traveler.

"Another six months or a year, max, and I'll turn this road show over to someone else," Stefan told Rachel.

The year gave way to two, and then three, as the demands for Stefan's hands-on management of the growing firm continued.

After years of hardship, disappointments, and soul-searching, Rachel and Stefan finally found peace and tranquility. Parenthood brought a sense of fulfillment, personally and professionally.

They lived the good life. Such a life, Rachel had once thought, belonged only to others. She felt content, but a deep, intuitive fear warned her not to trust it.

As Kevin Aaron grew, he suffered through the normal array of childhood mishaps and sniffles, along with an occasional bloody nose. But, although an active child, he also seemed overly susceptible to infections and odd maladies. Frequently, Rachel discovered him tangled in his bed sheets, drenched from recurring night sweats. On a few occasions, when Rachel helped him brush his teeth, his gums bled.

However, the pediatrician assured Rachel that she had nothing to worry about, and she soon eased back on the first-time-parent appointments.

Little Kevin adored wrestling with Stefan, but her boy bruised so easily, Rachel had to put a stop to the rougher play times. Even the common cold held more severe complications for the toddler—swollen lymph nodes and fungal infections, sometimes turning his tongue a horrible shade of white—symptoms other children didn't have.

As time went by, the nosebleeds became more frequent, and Rachel began to worry about the possibility of something more serious. Kevin complained of headaches and joint aches, which Stefan had attributed to growing pains.

Shortly after Kevin Aaron's fourth birthday, his energy level dropped and he began taking longer naps. Dark circles formed under his eyes, making his face appear unusually pale. Sometimes he ran fevers for no apparent reason, but then they'd disappear as mysteriously as they'd come. He became a finicky eater—so different from his prior voracious appetite—and he lost weight, making him look almost fragile, waif-like.

On a return flight from Chicago, a few months before Kevin Aaron's fifth birthday, he experienced another nosebleed. He fussed as Rachel held a tissue to his nose and instructed him to hold still.

She looked over at Stefan, feeling slightly apprehensive. "As soon as we get home, I'll call the doctor. This shouldn't be happening. He hasn't fallen or bumped his nose."

"Altitude," Stefan assured her as he moved to the cockpit to order the pilot to a lower flight path.

The bleeding stopped, and Kevin Aaron struggled out of Rachel's arms to dart toward his father. Stefan raised a newspaper in front of his face, teasing his son. Both adored the game.

Her mischievous child pushed a file folder full of documents onto the floor, then giggled and raced away. Stefan chuckled and arched an eyebrow at Rachel as if to say, "You see, he's fine; stop worrying." Then he laughingly gave chase to his shrieking son.

Halfway to New York, Kevin Aaron threw up. Rachel comforted him and stroked his cheek. "He's burning up, Stefan!"

Before Stefan could respond, another nosebleed started. Rachel gasped and held a washcloth to his face. Kevin Aaron didn't struggle, but went slightly limp in her arms. His eyes took on a glassy appearance, and Rachel cried out for Stefan.

Stefan knelt beside her. The bleeding, rather than trickling off, remained constant. No matter what Rachel tried, she could not stop the flow. She began to sob as Kevin Aaron's eyes flickered closed.

After a moment of trying to wake the boy and failing, Stefan rose, his face almost as pale as his son's, and strode toward the cockpit.

He soon returned. "An ambulance will meet us at the airport. The doctor has arranged for Kevin's admittance and immediate blood tests. He thinks Kevin has become acutely anemic."

Rachel stared up at Stefan, unable to form words. Tears dripped onto her cheeks. She clutched the sleeping child to her breast.

She gazed down upon her son's dear face and prayed that nothing more sinister had caused his illness. God would not be that cruel.

Rachel closed her eyes, and a memory forced its way through her tortured mind. She re-lived the terrible scene when the Germans came looking for her, and she had kept silent. She vividly saw the little boy, about ten years old, standing in front of the gathered children at the convent, and then the Nazi officer raising his pistol and shooting the boy in the head. She'd looked into the lifeless eyes of an innocent child and knew that he'd died to keep her secret safe.

Now, she jerked upright, opening her eyes in a panic. Her heart raced wildly in her chest, and she breathed so quickly she felt faint.

Kevin Aaron slept fitfully in her arms. His nosebleed had lessened.

Stefan sat next to her and covered her hand with his. "It will be all right, Rachel. Kevin Aaron has the strength of our fathers in his veins."

CHAPTER TWENTY-SEVEN

In the Eye of the Storm

A time to weep, and a time to laugh . . .

Ecclesiastes 3:4

By the time the plane touched down, patches of blood stained Rachel's silk blouse. Kevin Aaron had not awakened, and his nose still bled. A fever burned throughout his little body, and no amount of cool washcloths had brought it down.

The jet taxied toward the smaller runway that led to the private terminal. In the gloom, Rachel spotted the flashing lights of a waiting ambulance.

The moment the plane came to a complete stop, Stefan took Kevin from Rachel's arms and raced for the exit. She followed in a daze of shock and fear.

She climbed into the cramped operating section of the emergency vehicle. Stefan helped her into a seat and held her hand.

A medical technician started an IV, and the driver slammed the back doors shut. The vehicle started to move after only a moment's wait. Sirens blared above and around them as the ambulance left the airport and turned onto the heavily traveled streets. Rachel and Stefan sped through the night, watching silently as the attendant continuously took the child's vitals and checked the intravenous drip.

The ambulance screeched to a halt at Mount Sinai Hospital. An emergency-room doctor and two nurses took charge of the gurney and wheeled Kevin Aaron inside. The driver helped Rachel out, wished her good luck, and then took off.

Stefan dragged Rachel as he ran to catch up to the gurney. The doctor shouted unintelligible orders to the waiting staff, and people bustled in all directions. One of the nurses checked the IV. The other took the child's blood pressure and heart rate as the doctor bent to lift one of his eyelids and flash a tiny light at the pupil.

A nun stepped in front of Stefan and Rachel, blocking their path to Kevin Aaron's bedside. "You'll need to come with me, Mr. and Mrs. Davis. The doctor will conduct a thorough examination of your son and take some blood to send to the lab. In the meantime, you can fill out the necessary paperwork."

After what seemed like dozens of forms, the nurse finally deemed the registration and admittance process complete. Rachel stumbled beside Stefan as they hurried back to the pediatric intensive care unit and their son's curtained-off cubicle. They took turns holding Kevin Aaron's hands and pacing at the foot of the narrow bed. The various machines chirped and beeped, unnerving Rachel.

Finally, after another hour of mindless waiting, a different doctor pulled aside the curtain and stepped inside the crowed, private area. The tall, forty-ish man had unruly hair and a face dark with the stubble of an unshaven beard. "I'm Dr. Marshal."

He held a clipboard with several printouts, and frowned at something he read.

Rachel swallowed hard and held her breath, watching his grim expression with a sense of heavy dread.

Stefan cleared his throat and said hoarsely, "What is wrong with our son, Doctor?"

The doctor flipped through the papers again, then looked up and pushed his glasses to his forehead. "I'll start him on a blood transfusion, then speak with you in my private office." Before either Rachel or Stefan could respond, he called, "Nurse!"

Two nurses rushed to him. One coaxed Rachel and Stefan along, herding them from the ICU. The other remained with the doctor.

Rachel followed the nurse, feeling disoriented and numb. She glanced at Stefan, who looked as if he walked in a daze.

The nurse ushered them into a homey-style office, indicated a coffee service, then left them on their own.

Stefan poured two cups of black coffee, brought them to a sofa, and set them on a scarred and cluttered coffee table. Rachel and he stared at each other in silence. Neither drank.

Another half hour crawled by before the doctor came in. He blew out a deep breath and sat in the armchair facing them, looking from Rachel to Stefan, then coughed and studied his clasped hands for a moment.

When he spoke, his voice sounded unnaturally calm, measured. "There's no easy way to tell you this. The early diagnosis is not good. Your son has acute lymphoblastic leukemia. A.L.L."

Stefan tightened his grip on Rachel. "What the hell's that?"

"Cancer of the blood."

Rachel raised a hand to her mouth. "My God!"

All of the air seemed to be sucked from the room. Rachel swayed in her seat. Stefan put his arm around her. She felt him shudder beside her.

Stefan exploded to his feet and paced. "Cancer! Are you certain?"

Dr. Marshal nodded. "All of the tests indicate that diagnosis."

The doctor watched them for a moment, then sighed and continued, "A.L.L. attacks the blood system comprehensively. Luckily, with a blood transfusion, we can perk him up. You'll notice that he'll be more active, alert, and have almost-normal coloring once the transfusion is complete."

He paused again, waiting, perhaps, for them to say something.

Rachel drew in a shaky breath, fighting to understand what he'd told them. Her mind wanted to shut down, and her heart refused to believe what the doctor said.

Stefan held one of her cold hands in both of his. "So, you're saying, Doctor, that Kevin Aaron will be cured of this—this A.L.L.? He won't bleed any more than a normal boy would bleed?"

Dr. Marshal cleared his throat. "No . . . the transfusion is only a temporary fix. It will boost your son's blood count, giving him a new batch of red and white blood cells, along with the platelets that make blood clot. However, the cancer will again destroy the blood, and Kevin Aaron will need another transfusion."

The doctor stood and went to pour himself a cup of coffee. He took several sips, then carefully placed the Styrofoam cup on the table between them.

Stefan ran a hand through his hair. "Son-of-a-bitch! What can we do? How can this be cured?"

"After we give him blood, he'll also need a platelet transfusion, and I'd like to get him started with chemotherapy treatment."

Stefan lurched to his feet and paced again.

Rachel reached out to him. "Stefan, please."

Stefan ignored her and crossed to confront the doctor. He sobbed, mumbling, "We don't want him treated, Doctor. We want him cured."

Doctor Marshal put his hands on Stefan's shoulders and said in a firm tone, "Cures in cases like Kevin's require an exact blood-type match for a bone marrow transplant. We could start with immediate family members. He's AB negative. That's going to limit potential donors. I'll need to test both of you to see if one will be right for the donation."

Stefan said softly, "And if neither of us can be a donor?"

"We'll have to have him back here once a week until we can find a match for a bone marrow transplant. What about aunts, uncles?"

Rachel found her voice and croaked, "There's only the two of us."

The doctor returned to his chair and stared at them for a long moment. "We will test all relations. Parents and siblings have the best chance for a match. We must find someone with an exact match, or we risk what's called a "graft versus host reaction." The host—Kevin Aaron—will die if the transplanted bone marrow is rejected and attacks his own body."

Rachel gasped, clutching Stefan's hand so hard that her knuckles cracked. "But there is no one else! We are both adopted. Our families were lost in the Holocaust. We have no extended families, no siblings, and Kevin Aaron is our only child."

Stefan turned to her. "Rachel, what about your twin brother? He was never confirmed dead."

The doctor lifted his eyebrows and stared at Rachel. "A twin blood sibling of the birth mother in an instance of AB negative would be an excellent candidate."

Rachel closed her eyes and said dully, "My brother is dead."

The doctor frowned and his expression turned grim. "There is the possibility that a match will be found in the national donor bank. However, let's not panic just yet. Let's first test you two."

Stefan's voice still sounded weak. "You—you mentioned cancer. Will the marrow transplant cure everything and not be a temporary fix, like the blood transfusions?"

The doctor cleared his throat and nodded. "Once we get to that point, and all precautions have been met, yes, the transplant is a one-hundred-percent cure."

Stefan said, with a tremor in his voice, ever the prosecuting attorney, "Describe in full detail the precautionary process, Doctor."

The doctor took another sip of coffee, then ticked off on his fingers: "First, the blood transfusion to bring him back to a healthier, stronger existence. Second, we begin chemotherapy, to stop the progression of the cancer. Third, once we're ready for the marrow transplant, we will put Kevin Aaron on a course of radiation to knock off any cancer cells, in order to provide the best host for the clean marrow."

Rachel finally found her voice, "And then?"

After a moment of tense silence, the doctor continued, "Without the chemotherapy and the marrow transplant, the blood and platelet transfusions can keep your son alive for only a few more months—maybe as long as a year. With the chemo, and supportive therapy, we can buy him a few years, and he has a fifty-percent chance for a cure. However, our best bet is a bone marrow transplant, which would guarantee a cure—a one-hundred-percent guarantee."

Rachel's heart pounded. She found it difficult to breathe. Her body stiffened and froze in place. The doctor had just given her precious son a time limit on life.

Stefan lunged to his feet and stood rigidly straight. "Then let's not waste any further time talking. Test our blood, Doctor."

He reached down to Rachel and pulled her up beside him. She stood, supported by his arm about her waist.

The doctor said something, but Rachel's malfunctioning brain couldn't process his words. He led the way down the corridor to a nurse's station, and left them to the care of a kindly-looking nun.

Stefan dragged Rachel after the sister, whispering things in her ear. She found herself seated in an uncomfortable, one-armed chair with a rubber tourniquet around her upper arm. Her shocked mind took blurry snapshots of a lab worker drawing several vials of blood from her.

Stefan sat across the narrow room with another lab tech. Their eyes met, and Rachel read the same shock, horror, and grief in her husband's gaze.

A rational part of her, floating somewhere in the numbness, took hope, for she knew that Stefan would not give up on their son. He would do whatever it took, sacrifice anything, to save their child, just as both of their fathers had done in Poland.

The same nun swooped in the moment the lab workers finished and led them back toward the ICU. Her pleasant, business-like voice pierced Rachel's mental fog. "Your son has just completed his transfusion, and should be awake by now. Go sit with him for a while. His next treatment will be in about an hour."

Kevin and Irene Davis rushed into the special lobby connected to the ICU. The nun took the worried grandparents to a waiting room, calling over her shoulder, "You two spend a little time with your son."

As Rachel rounded the curtain barrier, she saw her son sitting up in bed, laughing at something the nurse did with a hand puppet. She took what felt like her first full breath in hours, and rushed to Kevin Aaron.

The smiling nurse left the room, and Stefan stood on the other side of the bed.

Rachel grasped Kevin Aaron's hand and brought it to her lips. Tears formed in her eyes as she noted the healthy glow in his cheeks, and his beautiful, light brown eyes, sharply focused.

"Mama! Daddy!"

Stefan sighed, cupped the boy's chin, and said with only a hint of strain, "The nurses are flirting with you."

Kevin Aaron giggled and snapped his teeth at his father's hand, a common game with them. "What's fir-firting, Daddy?"

He gently poked the fragile body. "They think you're adorable, because you are."

Stefan chuckled and pulled his hand away just before the little teeth could get him. He pretend-punched the tot under the chin, then looked up at Rachel and gestured with his head toward the boy, silently urging her to join in.

Rachel forced back tears and plastered on a smile. "One of these days, Daddy, he's going to bite your hand right off. Then how will you eat?"

Kevin Aaron erupted into gay laughter, his eyes sparkling with life. Stefan nodded and reached across the bed to hold Rachel's hand, giving her the strength to continue the charade.

Too soon, a nurse came in to usher them out to the waiting area. "It's time to start the platelet transfusion. We'll bring you back in when he's done."

Kevin Aaron paled, and his eyes grew wide with fear. "Don't leave me, Mama!"

Rachel choked back a sob and leaned over his bed, gathering him in her arms. His little body felt so delicate, so breakable. "Daddy and I will be right outside, talking to Grandma and Grandpa. The nurse told them they had to wait until later to see you." Her throat closed up, and she couldn't go on.

Stefan gently pulled her away and patted Kevin Aaron's shoulder. "We'd better get out there before Grandpa spanks someone and ends up in jail."

Kevin Aaron giggled, and his expression cleared. He shifted his attention back to the nurse, who'd brought along another hand puppet.

Kevin and Irene rushed them the moment they stepped into the waiting room. Irene's eyes looked red and swollen. The senior Kevin Davis looked old beyond his years, and haggard. Apparently, they'd gotten the bad news.

Stefan guided Rachel to a small sofa. Her legs gave out, and she collapsed onto the cushions. He steadied her, then moved away to speak to his parents.

Hours passed. Stefan paced. Rachel sat staring.

The waiting took her back to a dark night at a convent school near Katowice. There she had sat and waited for Father Dov to return. He'd promised to take her to her parents as soon as the war ended. She'd waited all night, bladder aching for relief, fighting sleep, filled with panic. As long as she waited, she held onto hope. Leaving meant giving up, and the thought proved so ghastly it made her want to die.

One of the nuns, Sister Rosa, had found her in the alcove of a long, dim hallway, weeping in the half-gray light of dawn. She ordered Rachel to her room, but Rachel would not go.

"He must come back," she cried.

"Who must come back?"

The sister had taken her by the arm, but Rachel jerked free. "Leave me alone!"

Sister Rosa called for help. Two other nuns arrived and overpowered Rachel. They had dragged her away and locked her in a small room. She had refused to eat for days, wanting to die, but a doctor sedated her.

Now, the fear had returned. She once again waited, with building anxiety.

Her son—the fruit of her womb, the rabbi had declared—now hung onto his life, struggling to survive. Voices spoke around her, speculating, consoling, but she existed alone, in a black void.

Dr. Marshal approached, and all conversation ceased. Rachel pulled herself together enough to see and hear. Her in-laws took the facing sofa, while Stefan joined her.

The doctor looked at each in turn.

"I'm sorry; neither of you were a match." He glanced at the older couple. "Of course, if either one of you is AB negative, we will test you as well, but since you do not share the same bloodlines, there is little hope that either of you will provide a match."

Irene slumped against her husband and sobbed.

Stefan turned Rachel toward him and stared into her eyes. "Rachel, you survived. I survived. David may have survived. I'll go to the Holocaust Center in Jerusalem. They could help me check."

Rachel pulled from his grasp and pushed to her feet. She turned away and walked to the window. "He's dead. I know he's dead."

Stefan followed her. "But you don't know for certain." He put a hand on her shoulder.

Rachel spun from Stefan's touch to face him. "David is dead!" she cried. Tears streamed down her face. "I know he's dead. I saw the farm. No one could have survived." The words poured out fast, raw.

Stefan and the doctor stared at her in silence.

She clamped her hands to her face and sank to the floor, sobbing uncontrollably.

Stefan knelt beside Rachel and drew her into his arms.

She screeched, "Take me, God, not my baby!"

A nurse rushed to Rachel's side. The doctor crossed the room, picked up a telephone, and ordered a sedative.

CHAPTER TWENTY-EIGHT

THE QUEST

*Let a man always strive to be one of the persecuted
rather than one of the persecutors.*

Babylonian Talmud,
Baba Kamma 93a

Rachel awoke hours later in a private hospital room. Stefan sat at her bedside, holding her hand. She blinked, struggling to bring her thoughts into focus. What had happened?

Her first instinct centered on their son. "Kevin Aaron?"

"I saw him just a few minutes ago. He's sleeping."

Memory flooded back—Her helplessness, the horror of knowing her baby stood at death's door . . . the panic attack. "Stefan, I'm sorry . . . so sorry."

Stefan raised her hand to his lips and kissed it. "For better or worse, in sickness and in health."

"I love you, too."

"Rachel, I have to at least try to learn what happened to David. If he *is* alive, he may be Kevin's only hope. A search for another donor could take months. Dr. Marshal says time is critical."

Rachel squeezed his hand. "Nothing is more important. I would give my life for our child." Tears welled in her eyes.

"Do you have any idea where we should start?"

Rachel shook her head as she considered the question. "He was taken to a farm in east Poland. After the war, a childhood friend of my father's—a priest, Father Dov—took me there. All we found was a bombed-out ruin. Locals told the priest there were no survivors.

"Father Dov said he would continue to look for David and my parents, but I knew he would never find them. After he took me to a refugee camp, I never saw him again."

"You once said someone died because of you. Did you mean the priest?"

"No."

"Who?"

Rachel's grip on her husband's hand tightened.

Stefan closed his eyes for a moment, and then met her gaze. "You don't have to tell me, Rachel. There's much I don't want to remember, either."

Rachel drew in a deep breath to gather herself. Her voice broke. "I kept the secret. When the Nazis came to the orphanage, looking for me, I kept the secret."

She paused to wipe a tear from her face.

"When no one came forward about the Jew hiding among the children, the soldiers threatened us. A boy was found with a circumcised penis. They shot him in the head, right in front of all of us. He . . . he fell beside me. I stared into his eyes . . . his dead eyes. But I still kept the secret." She bit her lip and closed her eyes.

Stefan leaned over the bed rail and drew Rachel against his chest. He held her and stroked her hair. "You didn't kill anyone, Rachel. I would have done the same thing. You didn't do anything wrong."

Rachel snaked her arms around her husband and wept. Stefan held her for a long time. The emotional storm raging in Rachel rose and fell, then eventually began to subside. Her husband's arms brought comfort and security—a long-sought refuge.

"Rachel," Stefan said, finally breaking the silence, "I'm praying there's a chance David may be alive."

Rachel raised her face and wiped her eyes. "But wouldn't he have found me?"

"Maybe he tried. Rachel Gold became Rachel Ward, then Rachel Ross, and now Rachel Davis. And it's not easy to trace someone through the ashes of a war where millions were incinerated in furnaces."

Rachel released Stefan and stared into his loving eyes. No judgment or accusation marred their depths.

He softly said, "Think back. When the priest questioned the locals, what exactly did they tell him?"

She swallowed and forced her mind to go back to the horror of her last days in Poland, before the refugee camp.

She whispered, "We got off the train and walked through the little village. Many shops and houses were damaged and burned. Before we took the long road to the farm, Father Dov stopped by the church. He told me that during the war he always checked in there first, giving a valid reason for his visits. Otherwise, he said, the Nazis would have become suspicious of his movements."

Rachel shuddered and sucked in another deep breath, feeling the crushing return of forgotten terror.

Stefan pushed down the bed rail and reclined beside her, gathering her in his all-encompassing embrace. "You can do it, my love. I am here. No one will hurt you."

She panted, focusing on his nearness, his strength. "The local parish priest met us with grave news. The farmer and his wife, David's adoptive parents, had been killed in a bombing raid. Father Dov was so sad. I think they were his true family—an aunt and uncle. I remember just standing there, numb. Then Father Dov asked the priest about the son. I had no hope for David, and I'm sure Father Dov didn't either, but he asked, just the same."

Rachel paused again, fighting off the feelings of helplessness and horror that had once been a large part of her life. Stefan stroked her arm, holding her tight.

She cleared her throat, feeling as if she'd begun to choke, forcing the words to come. "The local priest stared at us as if he'd suddenly awakened from a deep sleep. He became very excited, and then very horrified. He told us that they'd not found anyone else, that they'd forgotten about the boy in all the chaos. Father Dov grabbed my hand and pulled me down the old dirt lane. I remember my heart beating so loudly that I couldn't hear anything he said. It took a long time to get to the farm. The road was muddy and full of holes."

Rachel covered her eyes, picturing the terrible scene that had greeted them. "The buildings were beyond recognition, charred and, in some places, melted. A massive crater lay between the farmhouse and the barn. Nothing could have survived. But Father Dov did not give up hope. He pointed to the sheep in the far pastures and told me that if David had been tending to the herd, he would have survived, just as the livestock had."

She blew out a choppy breath and uncovered her eyes, as though she still saw the devastation of that long-ago farm.

Stefan said softly, "Is that all, Rachel?"

She shook her head. "Father Dov took me to the refugee camp. He hoped that David had made his way there. He wanted me to search through the paperwork as he searched the countryside. But I . . . I didn't believe that David had survived, and I . . . I gave up. I met Aaron as he searched for you and, together, we found his wife's name—your mother's—on the list of the dead. After that, we couldn't look any more. It hurt too much."

When Aaron had procured tickets to go to America, Rachel had not looked back. The opportunity to leave Europe, and all the reminders of her loss, had been an answer to her prayers. She'd begun a new life, with a new identity and a new family.

Now, she suddenly realized, given the way she'd left and the undocumented name change she'd accepted in New York, no one could have found her. Not until that moment had she ever regretted not taking the time to find the kindly priest and let him know her intentions.

Rachel clutched Stefan's arm. "You're right. David or Father Dov could have tried to contact me, but they wouldn't have been able to follow my trail after I boarded that awful ship."

Stefan hugged her and then gently rolled off the hospital bed and paced. Energy seemed to spark off him. "David may be alive, still wondering about you."

He came back to her bedside and grasped her hand. His voice took on a breathless quality. "I must go to the Holocaust Center, Rachel. I must find your brother."

Rachel raised a hand to her husband's face to run a finger along his unshaven jaw line. "Then go, Stefan. I'll stay with Kevin."

"You'll be all right?"

Rachel nodded. "As long as I know you're coming back."

Stefan leaned into her, and they kissed.

Together, Rachel and Stefan took an elevator to the pediatric critical care unit on the hospital's third floor. They found Stefan's parents with Kevin Aaron. The grandparents embraced Rachel and Stefan, then left without comment.

The sight of her ailing son brought Rachel's fears back with a rush. She willed herself to be strong, and pressed a shoulder to her husband. Stefan slipped an arm around her as they stepped to the side of the bed.

Stefan whispered, "Hello, little buddy."

Rachel reached out and touched the boy's face.

Kevin Aaron lay on his back. A series of pasted-on monitors dotted his upper torso. Thin leads traced to electronic monitors above the railed bed, where green LCD screens displayed his vital signs. An IV line was taped to the back of a hand, a clear tube disappeared into a nostril, and an oxygen line was taped beneath his nose.

Kevin's small, bare chest rose and fell with an irregular pace that added to Rachel's fear. "He seems to be resting well," she said in an attempt to deny her worries.

Stefan released Rachel and leaned over the rail to kiss his son on the forehead. "You wait here with your mother, little guy. I'll be back soon."

Rachel hugged Stefan. He took her face in his hands to look directly into her eyes. "We're in this together. You, me, and Kevin."

"Call me. I'll be here."

"I promise." Stefan kissed her and moved for the door.

Rachel watched her husband disappear and then returned her attention to her son.

Stefan took a cab to the family home in Forest Hills, asking the driver to wait while he packed. Twenty minutes later, he jumped back in the taxi and headed for Kennedy International.

He stood in line for thirty minutes at El Al Air in the international terminal before finally reaching a clerk at the ticket counter.

The woman smiled. "Your ticket and passport, please."

Stefan dug out his wallet. "I'd like to buy a ticket to Israel."

"I'm sorry, sir. The flight is sold out."

"First class, coach. I'll take whatever you have."

"I'm sorry, sir. We're fully booked. There are no seats available. I could get you on a flight tomorrow."

Stefan left the counter frustrated and angry. He spotted a young, college-aged boy with shoulder-length hair, dark sunglasses, and tattered jeans—the last person in the check-in line. The youth closed his book and slung a small travel bag over a shoulder.

Stefan quickly walked up to the young man before he could leave the area. "Excuse me, are you going to Israel?"

The youth looked at Stefan over the top of his sunglasses. "No, man, I just figured this was a quiet place to read."

Stefan grimaced at the sarcastic retort and pulled out his wallet. "If you have a ticket, I'll pay you twice what it cost you."

The young man raised his eyebrows and studied Stefan with sharp interest. "You want on this flight, huh?"

"Yeah, desperately."

The youth adjusted his sunglasses and said curtly, "Desperately will cost you three times, man!"

Stefan nodded and opened his wallet.

He had to pay another hundred dollars at the counter to transfer the ticket to his own name. The agent continually stole glances at his face as she did the paperwork. Stefan, too wound up to think deeply about her scrutiny, just shrugged it off as idle curiosity. His mind raced with the details of Rachel's story. Hope surged through him.

Not until a supervisor joined the ticket clerk behind the counter did Stefan pause to consider the ramifications of his impulsive and rather desperate actions. He forced himself to calm down and maintain his patience. He could not afford to have them suspect that he planned some type of subversive action against Israel, and deny him passage. After answering many questions, the supervisor scrutinized Stefan's passport and identification one last time, then finally confirmed him in a coach seat and checked his baggage.

Stefan headed for a public telephone to call Phil Krupp, a senior member of the firm. "Phil, I want you to reach out to every blood bank in the country. They may be able to lead us to an AB negative donor. Talk to our doctor. Rachel will get you in touch with him. He'll give you specifics on what Kevin Aaron needs. I also want you to hire Taylor, Parker and Trepp. They're the best PR firm in New York. Get them started on Kevin's plight. Cost isn't a factor, Phil. Make sure they understand that. I want results, and I want them fast. I'll call you when I get to Israel."

Accustomed to private jets and the comfort of first class, Stefan found the coach seat a miserable lesson in humility. He sat between a grandmother from Canton, Ohio, and an auto parts franchiser from Newark.

The man talked nonstop, outlining a get-rich plan to open a string of auto parts stores in Israel. "Peace or no peace, they still need spark plugs and radiator belts," the man stated several times, as if he needed to drive the point home.

Stefan willed the El Al DC-10 to fly faster.

Self-doubt consumed him. While his wife stayed with their stricken son, he flew off into the sunset. As each agonizing moment took him farther and farther away, Rachel would be struggling to reconcile the horrors of her life while standing beside the bed of their dying child.

Had he started on a wild goose chase? Wasn't it likely he would find hundreds of David Golds? Wasn't looking for David Gold in Israel like hunting for John Smith in America?

Stefan passed on an unappetizing dinner of salmon and rice. The sight of others eating angered him. How could they be hungry? How could they plan on opening auto parts stores or visiting relatives while his son lay dying? Why didn't the world stop? What could possibly be more important than saving Kevin Aaron?

His silent raging took him back to thoughts of his father's agony. Stefan could only imagine the pain and anguish Aaron Ross must have suffered when the Nazis had forcibly separated him from his wife and son. But at least Aaron could see the enemy. He could hate them. Plot against them. Stefan could only damn fate for choosing his Kevin Aaron. Why an innocent, defenseless boy? How could Stefan fight the cancer? How could he defend his son from an unseen killer brewing deep inside the boy's bones?

The rush of thoughts only fueled Stefan's misery, but he was powerless to halt them. He closed his eyes and tried to will himself to relax. His stomach felt knotted up, but he laid his head on a small pillow and closed his eyes.

A decrease in air speed roused Stefan from a coma-like sleep. They were finally descending. He didn't remember falling asleep, and now, awake, he found that the rest had brought him no comfort.

The auto parts salesman picked up where he'd left off. Stefan tightened his seat belt and glanced at his watch—nearly ten o'clock at night, local time. A search of official files and sources would have to await a new day. *Damn!* Everything took too much time.

Since Stefan had sat in the rear of the big craft, he waited among the last to deplane. The delay added to his dissatisfaction. He presented his passport at customs, where workers examined it with an infrared lamp for authenticity.

The customs officer looked him over. "Your business in Israel, sir?"

"Trying to locate a family member," Stefan answered.

"I hope you are successful." The officer returned the passport. "Have a nice visit."

Stefan claimed his bag and walked to a rental car counter. The night air felt warm and humid compared to New York. He rented a Ford Taurus for three days, asked for a road map and directions to Jerusalem, and headed toward the parking lot.

An unusually friendly, attractive young woman drove the tram that took Stefan to his rental car. "Your shoes and raincoat say American." She smiled, navigating the rows of parked cars. "New York? I studied at NYU last summer."

Stefan nodded. He wasn't in the mood for small talk.

"You here on business or pleasure?"

"Neither, really. I'm looking for family."

"In that case, you'll want the government buildings. They open at seven." The girl spoke matter-of-factly, braking to a halt in front of a Ford Taurus. "Drive safely."

Stefan gathered his bag and stepped off the tram. Rather than drive straight off, the young woman remained parked beside his car and watched as he unlocked the door and sat behind the wheel. He frowned at her over his shoulder, for the tram blocked his way. She appeared slightly embarrassed, and quickly drove away with a wave.

He grunted, not amused by her long regard. Rachel would have teased him about his good looks, and they would have laughed together. Her absence underscored his loneliness and the urgency of Kevin Aaron's condition.

As Stefan left the airport and drove along the highway, he spotted a public phone and stopped. He disregarded the early morning hour in

New York and dialed the hospital, needing reassurance of the status quo from Rachel.

The Mount Sinai receptionist transferred him to the pediatric critical care unit.

"Pediatrics, this is Cathy Parker," the nurse's brisk voice echoed from nearly five thousand miles away.

"Cathy, my name is Stefan Davis. My son is a patient in the critical care unit. Can you tell me his condition?"

"He's resting, Mr. Davis. I checked his vitals about five minutes ago. We moved a bed into the room for your wife. Would you like me to transfer the call there?"

"Is she asleep?"

"Yes."

"No, just let her rest. When she wakes, please tell her I called. I'll call back a little later."

"I'll see she gets the message."

Stefan leaned his forehead against the top of the phone kiosk. "Thank you." He hung up, aching for Rachel's sweet voice, but grateful that she'd been able to get some much-needed sleep. With a hard swallow, he straightened up and jogged back to the rental car.

Stefan drove fast through light traffic on the wide Ayalon Freeway. He paid little attention to the few cars that occasionally passed him.

Ninety minutes later, the lights of Jerusalem came into view. Sitting atop a distant hill, the ancient sprawling city cast a glow into the sky. Stefan marveled at the sight of the Knesset, the Israel parliament building, standing on a low hill in West Jerusalem, all lit up with yellow flood lamps. A glut of parked cars and an endless string of stores, markets, and shops lined the streets.

Stefan, emotionally drained and weary with jet lag, spotted the familiar red neon of a Hilton Hotel sign with relief. He wheeled the car into the entrance, surrendered it to a valet attendant, and headed for the registration desk, eager for a hot shower and a few hours of sleep before dawn.

After several hours of sleep, Stefan felt less disoriented. The grip the jet lag held on him had faded. *Good.* He had a busy day ahead of him. He intended to start at the Holocaust Survivors Administrative Offices. If

David Gold *had* survived, they would have a record of it. He planned on being there when they opened their doors at 7:00 a.m.

As Stefan sat on the bed in his hotel room, pulling on his socks, the light of dawn spread across the city beyond his window. The streets, quiet when he'd arrived, now teemed with traffic.

A knock sounded at the door. Room service, Stefan concluded. He had ordered coffee. The knock sounded again.

"Coming," he said, pushing on a shoe.

Stefan crossed to the door and opened it. A trio of two men and a woman stood outside. They wore casual, opened-collared shirts, windbreakers and jeans.

He recognized the girl from the tram, but said nothing.

The older of the two men stepped forward. "Stefan Davis?"

"Yes."

The man showed Stefan a government identification card, indicating they were agents. He said in clear English, "We're employees of the Israeli government, Mr. Davis. May we come in?"

As the first man spoke, the other two peered into Stefan's room.

He stepped back, opening the door wider. "Of course, come in."

When they stepped into the room, Stefan closed the door and asked: "What branch of the government do you represent?"

The lead agent said quietly, "We would prefer this remain informal."

Stefan frowned. *Israeli secret service.* "I'm a long way from home. I'm careful who I talk to."

"And so are we," the older man countered. "What is it you say in America? Let's cut to the chase. When you bought a ticket from another passenger in New York, you seemed to have been in a hurry. So, we did some checking. You claim you're here looking for family members, but you keep your Jewish heritage private. In business, you associate with some who openly claim to be enemies of Israel. In Israel we have a saying: 'Caution is like life. You cannot have one without the other.'"

Stefan studied their blank expressions, thinking that only high-ranking operatives could have access to such minute details of his background. Then he sighed, realizing how suspicious his actions must have appeared. "I appreciate your caution." He glanced at the woman. "But as I told her last night, I'm here looking for family. I am not a terrorist. My four-year-old son is dying of cancer. His only hope is a bone marrow transplant. That requires an exact blood match. My wife is also Jewish, and family members are the best candidates, for obvious reasons—bloodlines."

The older man nodded sharply. "We know who your wife is. I'll give you a choice. We can either take you to a holding facility and conduct a full interrogation, which could take days, or we can check your things here and have you on your way in no time . . . as long as we find nothing of a dangerous nature."

Stefan stepped back, allowing them access to the hotel suite. He could not afford the time it would take for a messy government investigation. "Go ahead and search. I have nothing to hide. I'm not a terrorist."

The man who'd shown the government ID stayed next to Stefan, but his attention seemed to focus on the other two as they rummaged through Stefan's bag and the empty drawers provided by the hotel.

Stefan watched the efficient search for a moment, and then said in a calm, level tone of voice, "My wife had a twin brother. David Gold. They were separated in Poland during the war. She thinks he was killed, but she has no proof."

The agent took out a small notebook from his inside jacket pocket and clicked open his pen. "If he were in Poland, why are you looking in Israel?"

Stefan narrowed his eyes on the man as he jotted something down. They were testing him. He had to keep his patience, earn their trust. These people could help him speed along the search process. They had access to documents he couldn't hope to see. "Don't you have computerized records of Holocaust survivors?"

The man nodded, looking up from his journal. "Yes. Who is your father?"

Stefan covered his emotional reactions with a businesslike demeanor. They had put him on trial, and he must give the most important testimony of his career. His son's life depended upon his success. "I am the adopted son of Kevin Davis, an American, but my natural father was Aaron Ross, a Polish immigrant . . . and a Jew."

The agent spoke to the other man. "Reach out to Levi in records. See if we have anything on David Gold."

Stefan felt almost lightheaded with relief. There were going to help him!

The other agent picked up the hotel telephone. "Get us details. Otherwise it's a needle in a haystack."

The man next to Stefan said, "Tell me what you can about David Gold. We will try to help, but as you may know, Gold is a common name."

"What little I know I learned from my wife. Her birth name is Rachel Gold. She and her twin brother, David, were born in Katowice, Poland. He would be thirty-four years old. Their father's name was Kalman and their mother, Tova. They were held as prisoners in the Lodz concentration camp."

The man busily jotted notes on the small tablet and then glanced up at Stefan again. "His parents died in the camp?"

"No, they escaped with the help of a priest disguised as a Nazi officer. He rescued my wife, David, and both their parents. Father Dov took Rachel to a convent school, and David to a farm in east Poland. She doesn't know where her parents went."

The other man had listened intently to the exchange, and spoke into the telephone.

The lead agent pocketed his notebook and pen. "And you, Stefan Davis, were you also a prisoner?"

"Yes," Stefan answered, without explanation.

"Wait," the younger man said. "We have a match!"

Stefan's heart raced in his chest. Could it really be this easy? He put a hand out to brace himself against the hotel's well-worn armoire.

Then he chilled as the man on the telephone raised a hand and said, in a shocked tone of voice, "Where? Restricted! Why?"

CHAPTER TWENTY-NINE

BLOODLINES

What is in your heart about your fellow man
is most likely in his heart about you.

Sifre Deuteronomy, Piska 24

Ironically, being blown out of the sky had saved David's wings. After the Syrian missile had downed his jet, the Israeli Air Force had immediately changed tactics. They needed his experience, for few pilots had lived through such circumstances. That, and the fact that his own air-to-air missile—launched as his craft exploded—had brought down the Syrian MiG had guaranteed David's return to the cockpit. The only requisites to his flight status: no combat, daylight only, and no flight closer than twenty miles to Israeli borders.

The higher-ups reassigned him to a counter-aggression unit just as the American, twin-engine, supersonic Phantom F-4s—the fastest, meanest fighters in the sky—came on line, which softened the sting of his loss of combat status. David Gold—a man in love with his airplane—felt confident that when war came, need would override his handicap and he would fly in battle once more. At thirty-four, though, he no longer craved warfare. As a lifelong warrior, he'd given the Syrians a few scars of their own.

After leading his two wingmen fifty miles out over the Mediterranean Sea, David used a hand signal to maintain radio silence and ordered a dive from eighteen thousand feet to sea level. They skimmed the water surface so low that they had to pull up to clear several Russian tankers headed for ports in Egypt.

The three Israeli Phantom F-4 fighter jets swung in a circle and roared over the rugged face of the Sinai Desert, traveling in excess of four hundred knots, less than five hundred feet above the ground—a dangerous tactic. Lack of concentration, or simple human error, could quickly reduce the sophisticated aircraft to a mushroom of flame and twisted metal fragments scattered over a mile of rock and sand.

Their training target, an Israeli early-warning radar station near Beersheba, expected the mock attack, but the ground forces didn't know the hour or the day of the surprise exercise. The theory behind the mission: if David's fighters could sweep in beneath the eyes of radar, so could the Egyptians.

However, heavy risk accompanied the exercise, for the Israeli ground forces had only seconds to discern between a training battle and an actual enemy attack. The burden of decision lay with the man who pushed the button. A unit of deadly surface-to-air missiles, poised near Beersheba, didn't care what aircraft they brought down.

The supersonic noise, although deafening, trailed well behind the jets, while the cockpit of David's F-4 remained relatively quiet. At four hundred knots plus, the big machine hummed. His subtle changes in altitude to clear ridgelines or hug valley floors created surges of hydraulic sounds as movements of the stick and rudder pedal brought pumps and valves to life.

The oxygen mask strapped over David's face chaffed the fresh scar across the bridge of his nose—a gift from a hard-soled Russian boot worn by one of the Syrians who'd boarded his rowboat. *But*, David thought smugly, *that bastard paid for his assault on an Israeli pilot.*

A sun-bleached, rusty Egyptian tank, lying on its side, partially swallowed by sand, flashed by, looking like a whale in a desert sea.

David checked his readouts on the control panel. *Less than twenty miles to the radar site.* They would arrive there in seconds. He pushed the throttle to afterburner. A burst of acceleration pushed him back into his seat, and the desert rushed by his windscreen in a blur.

His pulse quickened as the faint outline of a cluster of low, camouflaged buildings came into view. He aimed his craft at them.

A calmly measured voice in his headset shocked him: "Wolf-eight, code two, ops ten." The base commander sounded low-key, but the surprise order to return to base without delay worried David.

He pulled back on the stick, and the aircraft shot skyward with the speed of a bullet. David grunted as he fought the resultant g-force.

Rolling into level flight at twelve thousand feet, already sixty miles from the radar site, he keyed his radio: "Wolf-eight, roger."

The three Phantoms flashed over the radar station at a mere three hundred feet. A second later, a sonic boom rocked the site with an earth-shaking clap of thunder. It most likely sent coffee cups spilling, windows rattling, and men diving for cover.

David nudged the craft to a north-northwest heading. Without the roundabout stealth approach they'd utilized in anticipation of the mock attack, they would reach the air base in a matter of minutes.

He taxied in the F-4 and braked to a halt near a hardened shelter. The ground crew chief signaled for engine shutdown, and another crewman pushed chocks under the wheels.

Once the craft sat at secured rest, David pulled off his flight helmet and unbuckled both shoulder harnesses. He glanced at a waiting Jeep, parked just in front of his jet. In it sat the squadron commander and the wing intelligence officer.

David blew out a sharp breath. What had recalled his small squadron and brought the top brass out onto the tarmac to greet him?

He unlatched the canopy and pushed out of the seat. The fresh air and physical activity felt good after two and a half hours cooped up in the cramped cockpit. David stretched and strode toward the waiting vehicle.

When David climbed into the Jeep, the squadron commander said, "We'll debrief the mission later. First, we have to talk about something else."

David's chest constricted. "My wife and son are all right?"

The commander held up a hand and smiled. "They are fine."

David relaxed. Nothing else mattered.

They went to the intelligence office where a third man waited—one of the national security officers. They gathered around an oval table, poured coffee, and lit cigarettes.

The base commander said tersely, "Major Gold, this is Martin Rabin from the Armed Forces Security Council."

David offered the man a nod and set down the bitter coffee with a grimace.

Rabin did not acknowledge or return the greeting. He fingered a small file of papers and stared intently at David. "Major, we've had an inquiry from someone regarding your whereabouts. The individual in question claims to be your brother-in-law."

Completely caught off guard, David frowned. "Brother-in-law? Impossible. My wife's sister is only fifteen."

"It's not your wife's sister, Major. It's yours."

David gaped at Rabin, then managed a strained whisper. "*My* sister?"

The government man flipped open the file, but continued to stare at David. "According to our records, you have a fraternal twin, a sister by the name of Rachel."

David straightened in his chair, hardly daring to hope. "*Have?* I thought she died in Poland, during the war." An image flashed to mind; the old priest in the train yard had given David the sign from his childhood—the sign of three conspirators hiding from the Nazis.

Agent Rabin nodded. "She may be alive, Major."

"Alive?" David felt a flush of awe tremble through his body, though he held himself rigid and outwardly calm.

"Yes, and her husband . . ." Rabin paused to look at something in the file, ". . . an American by the name of Stefan Davis, is in Israel trying to locate you."

David rolled his shoulders, squashing the budding warmth of hope, denying the possibility of such a miracle. He'd accepted the loss of his family years before. Nothing good could come of reopening old wounds. A familiar, bitter feeling of grief and loss crept into his heart.

He swallowed and shook his head. "This must be a mistake."

"They had knowledge of your birth in Poland, your parents' names, the detention and rescue from the Lodz concentration camp, and you being hidden on a farm in East Poland. All of which is reinforced by what appears to be the legitimate bloodline of this Rachel Gold."

David felt stunned. Despite his resolve to leave the anguish of the past behind, fate seemed to want to play with his emotions. Just the thought of his beloved twin sister surviving brought a shaft of relief through his entire being. "I . . . I don't know what to say."

"Major, as a member of the Israeli Armed Forces, you are shielded from inquiry under the interest of national security. You are not obligated to respond to this matter. And, if you do, any subsequent exposure may compromise your future service."

David pushed out of his chair, enraged by the subtle ultimatum. "So it's a sister I haven't seen in over twenty years, or flying? I can't have both?" He wanted to rush out, catch the first plane, and hold Rachel in his arms. He could barely think of anything else.

The stoic man closed the file and folded his hands on the table. "That's a call we can't make at this time, Major."

The squadron commander barked, "Goddamnit, Rabin, quit bullshitting him. Tell him what the hell you know."

Rabin glared at the commander, then shrugged. "All right. Major Gold, your sister is the adopted daughter of the late District Attorney of New York. She's married to a well-known international attorney. Their child is suffering from a type of cancer that requires a bone morrow transplant. Blood relatives are often the best donors. That's what led them to search for you."

The wing intelligence officer cautioned, "The problem, Major, is that this is the kind of thing the American press loves. If you come forward, they're going to want you to do interviews, talk shows, books, movies."

David waved a hand, disgusted by their superficial concerns. "I'm not interested in any of that shit! You said Rachel's child is dying."

Rabin leaned into the table. "Let me be blunt, Major Gold. You step forward to do this, you're going to be exposed in the press. Theirs, ours, somebody's. Anyone suffering such exposure becomes a candidate for terrorist kidnapping, blackmail, and extortion. In short, we cannot take such a risk. You would be asked to submit your resignation, for national security interests. You understand, of course."

David reached to his chest and ripped the wings off his flight suit. After so many years and so much loss, nothing would keep him from Rachel's side. He held the emblem in the palm of his hand for a moment, and then tossed it onto the table. "Where is this man who says he is my brother-in-law?"

David flew by helicopter from the air base to the Hadassah-Hebrew University in Jerusalem, still dressed in his flight overalls.

Three security officers flanked a tired-looking man in an expensive business suit, who waited on the helicopter landing pad. As David drew closer, the man straightened and seemed to study David. He extended a hand and said, "Thank you for coming. I see Rachel in you, David. I am her husband, your brother-in-law. All of these years, she thought you'd died on that old farm."

David shook hands, feeling slightly shell-shocked. He swallowed hard. "I also believed the worst of my sister's fate." He stared into Stefan's bloodshot eyes. "I pray that I can give what you need."

Before David could ask about Rachel and his nephew, an orderly rushed up to David and led him inside to get a blood sample.

When the technician finished, the two men retreated to a hallway to wait.

Stefan said softly, "I remember meeting you years ago, at a family picnic. My father was partners with yours. Would you like to see your sister and our son?" He showed David pictures of Rachel and Kevin Aaron.

David studied the wallet-sized photo with a lump in his throat. After a moment, he handed the picture back and said in his best English, "Rachel is beautiful, so like our mother. Your son is good looking. He takes after you. I, too, have a wife and son. I hope I'll be able to see Rachel soon. She'll like Toby."

A doctor approached and both men stood.

The doctor extended a hand to David. "Major Gold."

They shook hands, and David introduced Stefan. "This is Stefan Davis. My brother-in-law."

The doctor took Stefan's hand. "I'm Dr. Telushkin, and I'm in charge of the blood bank here at the medical center. I just finished a conversation with Dr. Marshal at Mt. Sinai in New York. I'm afraid it's not good news."

Stefan grimaced and covered his eyes. "Sonofabitch!"

David laid a hand on his shoulder, unable to think of anything appropriate to say.

After a long moment, the doctor spoke in a gentle tone of voice. "I share your disappointment. We looked at your HLA—that's human lymphocytic antigen. In comparing your results to the proposed recipient's, we find there simply is no match."

David watched his newfound brother-in-law turn away with slumped shoulders, feeling sick at heart. Profound silence fell upon the wide, polished corridor.

Then Stefan drew up straight and faced the doctor. "Please tell Dr. Marshal in New York to allow me the opportunity to tell my wife this news when I return."

Dr. Telushkin nodded and said gravely, "Of course. I am sorry."

———∘∘∘▸◉◂∘∘∘———

Rachel continued her bedside vigil with Kevin Aaron, who'd been too weakened by his prolonged illness to go right home, as they'd originally hoped. Stefan had departed nearly thirty-six hours before, but for Rachel, time no longer mattered. She didn't know, or care about, the hour or the day. Only the survival of her son held any significance. Rachel's focus, her silent, incessant prayer, centered on Kevin Aaron.

Doctors and nurses came and went. Rachel received words of encouragement, talk of medical procedures, and visits by neighbors, associates from the firm, and Kevin's grandparents. The room had slowly filled with flowers and balloons, but she heard and saw little of it. Only the steady rise and fall of her son's chest drew her undivided attention.

After another transfusion, Kevin Aaron lay sleeping, sedated. The boy looked pale but comfortable.

Rachel had begged God to take her instead of her child, but God had answered with silence.

She fought the urge to rip off the maze of IVs and monitors, gather her son into her arms, and will the cancer from his frail body.

Then she rested her forehead on the bed rail, damning herself for bringing Kevin Aaron to the hospital. If only the nosebleed had stopped. If they had just gone home. Then everything would have stayed all right. Then they wouldn't know.

"Rachel." The familiar voice of her husband cut through the insulation of the emotional wall Rachel had built around herself.

She lifted her head.

Stefan stood in the open doorway. The blue shadow of an unshaved beard covered the lower portions of his handsome face. His clothing was wrinkled, and he looked unspeakably tired. He offered a compassionate smile that brought tears to Rachel's eyes.

A grown-up David stood at Stefan's shoulder. A purple, jagged scar ran across his cheek and nose, but didn't detract from his stunning good looks.

Rachel rushed to him, knocking over her chair in the process. "David!"

He met her in the middle of the room, arms wide. Rachel threw herself into his embrace, and he held her as she buried her face against his neck.

David whispered into her hair, his voice thick with emotion, "Rachel, Rachel."

———oo◦❧◦oo———

Stefan turned and walked away, giving them a private moment. He bought a cup of coffee from a vending machine, and paused to chat with Dr. Marshal before going back to the room. He hesitated just outside the doorway, struck by the poignant scene inside.

Rachel and David sat facing one another in the bedside chairs. Between them, dangling from Rachel's hand, hung the gold coin and locket Stefan had commissioned a jeweler to make into a necklace for a first anniversary present. Stefan swallowed. His vision blurred.

Inside the locket lay fibers of old clothes—clothes Rachel's parents had worn while in hiding. The threadbare material that Kalman and Tova Gold had left for their children.

David fingered the diamond-crusted bezel surrounding the beautiful Swiss Helvetia, then gingerly turned it over and opened the locket. Stefan shuddered at the sobbing gasp his brother-in-law released, and withdrew to lean against the hallway wall, overcome with shared emotion.

Rachel and David's parents had given their lives to save their children. Stefan would do the same for his son, as would Rachel.

He closed his eyes and thought about his own blood parents. His mother had died in a death camp. He remembered the torturous moment when he was given to a Polish woman while waiting in the line for the gas chamber that swept Dina Ross from his life forever. His mother had begged the woman to save her son and find him a good home, away from war and horrors.

Then, years later, fate had brought him to his biological father, whose unselfish and noble legacy would live on in Stefan. Aaron had bequeathed his only son a deep love of the law, and had unknowingly guided Stefan's steps through both past and present. His father had given his life for his greatest passion and left a shining example for Stefan to follow—the pursuit of truth and justice.

Stefan blew out a breath and straightened away from the wall. Now his son needed saving, and he would do whatever it took to see that Kevin Aaron live a long and safe life. He could do no less than what his father and Rachel's father had done before him.

When Stefan entered the small, private room, Rachel stood to kiss him. "Thank you for bringing my brother."

Stefan smiled at her teary expression and moved to the bedside to gaze down at his sleeping son. "How's Kevin?"

Rachel joined him, caught his hand, and brought it to her lips. "He slept nearly all the time you were gone."

David stood on the other side of the narrow hospital bed and laid a tentative hand on Kevin Aaron's shoulder.

Stefan leaned over the rail and kissed his son on the forehead. He whispered, "Hello, little guy. I missed you."

Rachel reached for her brother's hand, still holding onto Stefan. "Did Stefan ask if you would have your blood tested?"

Stefan cleared his throat from the crush of emotion at seeing his son so helpless and vulnerable. He put an arm around Rachel's shoulder and drew her back to the chairs, standing behind her as she took a seat. "We had David's blood analyzed in Israel."

Rachel glanced from David to Stefan. "And?"

Stefan squeezed her shoulders and nodded to David.

David leaned forward and captured her hands. "I'm sorry, Rachel. My blood didn't match."

Rachel gasped and covered her mouth with trembling hands. The color drained from her face.

David said quickly, "But my son's did!"

Rachel shuddered under Stefan's massaging caress, then jerked upright and stuttered, "Wh-what?"

David continued in his lightly accented English, "His name is Kalman, after our father. He's with your doctor and my wife, Toby. She's a pediatrician. As a matter of fact, it was her idea to test our son."

Rachel slipped sideways, and Stefan lunged to catch her. She clutched his supporting hands and whispered, "Your son? *Kalman*! He's here?"

Stefan extricated himself from her death grip and crouched down beside her chair. He cupped her face in his hands and stared into her eyes. "And he's a perfect match!"

Rachel sobbed and fell into his arms, then reached for David as well. "I want to see him, David!"

David hugged her tightly. "He's downstairs prepping for the transfusion; my wife is with him. You'll meet them both soon."

At Stefan's urging, the senior Kevin Davis made a call to an old friend in the U.S. State Department in an effort to help reinstate David's sacrificed career. Before day's end, the records of David Gold's entry into and departure from the United States were purged. Another call to an airline executive deleted the computer-recorded purchase of the airline tickets for him and his family.

Dr. Marshal spoke with a friend at Mt. Sinai, who erased the name of minor Kalman Gold from all hospital records.

That same week, an official at the U.S. State Department called the Israeli Ambassador to his Washington office. "We think it's tragic that Major Gold's compassionate act to save his nephew's life resulted in his forced resignation from the Israeli Air Force."

Eight days after David and his family left New York, the commander gave David the good news. Once again, David patrolled his realm, the sky.

After three weeks, Kevin Aaron's bone marrow began producing normal white blood cells. His body had absorbed and retained the donor's bone marrow without rejection.

Dr. Marshal announced to Rachel and Stefan, "We'll continue to monitor his progress, but the transplant seems a success. It's time for him to go home."

The moment Rachel stepped inside their house, she led her son to the phone and placed a call to Tirat Karmel, in northern Israel.

"David," Rachel said when her brother answered, "I have someone here who would like to say hello to his cousin, Kalman."

———∘∘∘ɬ⊚ʆ∘∘∘———

Later that year, Janusz sat in his cozy study, composing a missive to Rome. He dropped the pen on the letter he'd been writing and sighed. His gnarly fingers had swelled into uncooperative claws, making it difficult to write. Krakow's first snow and his arthritic bones conspired against him. Nevertheless, he'd managed to complete his request for retirement.

After nearly forty years as a priest and archbishop, he felt ready to step down. He wasn't running from the commitment; it had outrun him. At sixty-four, his body reflected the harsh conditions of his life. He'd aged beyond his years. The unexpectedly physical trip to Syria had aggravated his inflamed joints, leaving him slightly lame.

Many of those in his service showed intelligence and capability. In the note, he'd told Rome he would mentor them, but he could no longer lead them.

Janusz pushed his reading glasses up onto the bridge of his nose and stared at the hand-carved, wooden box on the edge of his desk. In it resided the gold coin and strips of cloth Kalman and Tova Gold had left for their son, David. Janusz closed his eyes and leaned his forehead against his clasped hands.

Ever since the chance meeting with David in the desert, Kalman's spirit had haunted Janusz. He didn't know what had driven him to give the secret hand signal to the departing train, but he'd come to understand that his path had not yet ended.

Yes. He opened his eyes and stared at the box again. When he retired, he would make one last journey on behalf of his old friend.

Two weeks later, a note came back from Rome, warning Janusz to expect a visit from an emissary of the Pope.

Janusz smiled. He would be invited to Rome—what the old corps of priests called "the farm"—to teach. He remembered the palm trees in Rome with nostalgia. There, he'd experience a gentler winter, better for his aching bones.

His gaze slid to the timeworn box on his desk. Free now, he would finally complete an old promise.

A knock sounded at the door of his study. *The emissary?*

"Coming."

Janusz closed his Bible and lifted himself out of his chair with effort, remembering what Peter had said to Christ: "The spirit is willing, but the flesh is weak." He moved slowly to the door, favoring his arthritic hip, and pulled it open.

The pilot—David—stood across the threshold with a beautiful young woman. She clasped a gold and diamond pendant.

A bolt of lightning struck Janusz as he glimpsed a singularly beautiful gold coin between her fingers. On it, in high-polished relief, posed the famous Swiss Miss—one of the coins from Kalman's treasure. *Rachel!*

Janusz glanced at her again, filled with awe. Finally, he whispered hoarsely, "My child." He felt Kalman's warm presence in the room with them, and took a few unsteady breaths.

Then he looked at David as tears began to fog his glasses. "I recognized you before we parted. And I meant to retire and continue my search for you in Israel. But God has taken pity upon my old bones and brought the final leg of our journey to me."

He gazed at Rachel for a long moment, drowning in her beauty. "I could not follow your trail after you boarded the ship to America. There was no record of you ever getting off. I hoped—I prayed—that you had survived to find a new life." His throat closed with a spasm of emotion, and he could not go on.

Rachel's eyes filled with tears, and she said in a choked voice, "The immigration officer changed my name. They had too many Golds."

Janusz bowed his head for a moment to collect himself, and then pointed a gnarled finger at the box on his desk. "I have something for you, David."

David leaned forward and, with shaking hands, opened the box Janusz had kept safe for so long.

Rachel gave a soft cry as her brother lifted out an identical gold coin and several strips of cloth. She rushed to his side and hugged his broad shoulders as he shook with silent tears.

Janusz murmured a prayer of thanks. His mind traveled back to a flooded mine pit, where he'd seen the light of God's star and pledged himself to the service of the church. Then he had leaned on Kalman for support, wet, exhausted, and snatched from certain death. Janusz had vowed to return the favor of his life.

A hand on his shoulder brought him out of his reverie. He looked up to find Kalman's tall, handsome son smiling down at him, tears still wet on his scarred face.

"Father, we owe you so much. You saved our lives. We have come to thank you."

Rachel released David's arm and stepped forward to kiss Janusz on the cheek. "And in saving my brother's life, you also saved the life of my son."

Janusz covered his eyes and wept. He'd kept his promise.

THE END

"L' chaim"—to life

17178670R00193

Made in the USA
Lexington, KY
28 August 2012